RUINED HOPES

A RIXON HIGH NOVEL

L A COTTON

Published by Delesty Books

RUINED HOPES
Copyright © L. A. Cotton 2021
All rights reserved.

This book is a work of fiction. Names, characters, places, and events are the product of the author's imagination or used in a fictitious manner. Any resemblance to actual persons or events is purely coincidental.

No part of this book may be reproduced or used in any manner without the written permission of the publisher, except by a reviewer who may quote brief passages for review purposes only.

Edited by Andrea M. Long
Cover Designed by Lianne Cotton
Proofreading by Sisters Get Lit.erary Author Services

Love is an anchor through every storm.
 Unknown

PROLOGUE

PAIN.

That's all I could feel.

Excruciating, blistering pain.

"H-help..." I forced the word from my lips in an agonizing breath. My lungs felt tight, burning me from the inside out.

Something was wrong.

Very wrong.

I tried to shift against the crushing weight, but pain lashed up and down my spine, exploding inside me.

A whimper tore from my throat.

"A-Ashleigh," a voice called out to me from the darkness. "Fuck."

Something crackled. Heat licking up my skin. I tried to strain against the darkness again, but it was futile.

I couldn't see.

I was powerless. Alone.

Except, I wasn't alone... *was I?*

"H-help," I choked out again, blindly trying to reach out and find something—*anything*—to help me.

Think, dammit. Think, Ashleigh.

But it hurt too much.

Everything hurt.

My limbs, my muscles, my head. At least I could feel everything. My arms and legs, fingers and toes. Everything felt whole.

That was a good sign, wasn't it?

Wasn't it?

"Ashleigh," a voice cried out from the darkness. "Hold on, you have to hold on."

"W-what..." the word died in my throat, the pain too much to bear as I hovered in and out of consciousness.

"I'm sorry." The voice sounded further away now. A whisper on a distant wind. "I'm so fucking sorry."

CHAPTER ONE

Ashleigh

MY EYES FLUTTERED OPEN, the sunlight streaming into the room. I blinked, then blinked again, scanning the unfamiliar room.

Where the hell was—

The rhythmic beeping caught my attention and that was when I spotted the wires connecting me to a monitor.

A hospital monitor.

I was in the hospital.

But... how?

I racked my brain searching for an explanation but came up against a thick fog. As if the memories were there but just out of reach, enveloped in an impenetrable haze.

"H-hello?" It was a weak croak against my dry, sore throat.

Panic began to snake through me. Something had happened, something bad. You didn't wake up in a hospital bed, hooked up to machines with no memory of how you got there, for a simple case of strep throat or mono.

Clutching the wires between my achy, stiff fingers, I

found the call button and pressed it. I needed answers. I needed someone to tell me what the hell was happening.

The door burst open a second later, and a nurse appeared, looking at me with kind eyes and a warm smile. "Hello, sleepyhead. It's good to see you awake," she said, her soft voice instantly putting me at ease.

"W-what happened? Where am I?" I asked, a trace of fear in my voice.

"You're at Rixon General, sweetie. You were in an accident."

"I was? I... I don't remember." The fear snaking through me turned to blind panic, making my blood run cold.

"Try to relax." She looked over at me. "Take a deep breath for me, okay?"

I nodded, forcing myself to inhale through my nose and exhale out of my mouth. My heart galloped in my chest like a band of wild horses, but the deep breathing helped, slowing my pulse.

At least enough not to send me into an all-out panic attack.

"Are my family—"

"Ashleigh, thank God."

"Mom, Dad." Tears sprung from my eyes as they rushed to my bedside. Mom took my hand gently in hers, brushing the flyaway hairs from my eyes.

"Gosh, baby, we were so worried."

"The nurse said I was in an accident, but I don't remember... I..."

Dad glanced at the nurse, something passing between them, but then he was smiling at me, leaning down to kiss my forehead. "We're just glad you're okay."

"I'll give the three of you some privacy." The nurse made

some notes on my chart and dropped it back in its holder. "The doctor will want to see you soon."

"Thank you," Dad said.

The second she left the room, I turned to my parents. "I'm okay, right?"

"Of course, sweetheart." Another smile, but it didn't reach his eyes.

"Dad?" My voice cracked, reminiscent of the little girl I used to be. Unsure and afraid of the world, always looking to her father, her hero, for support and guidance.

Daddy's little girl.

He swallowed back the emotion written all over his face and said, "You were in a coma, Ashleigh."

It was a good thing I was lying down because that revelation tipped my world upside down.

A coma?

"F-for how long?"

"Almost a month."

A month? No, it wasn't possible.

"But... I don't understand."

Dad and Mom both pulled up chairs and sat down, Mom taking my hand in hers again.

"There was a car accident, sweetheart. You and Ezra—"

"Ezra?" I lurched forward, pain slamming into me. "Is he okay?"

"Ezra's fine, sweetheart." Dad shifted as Mom encouraged me to lie back down. "You came off worse. You had a nasty bump on the head, so the doctors put you into a coma to give the swelling on your brain a chance to go down."

Thank God, Ezra was okay. He was... well, it was hard to put into words what I felt for Ezra Jackson. He wasn't my boyfriend or even my friend really, but he was important to me. If anything had happened to him... it didn't bear thinking about.

"I... I don't know what to say." It's only then I realized my right leg felt clunky. Lifting up the sheets, I frowned. "I'm guessing I also broke my leg."

"Your ankle, and two ribs."

"Wow." I sucked in a sharp breath and my rib cage smarted.

"Okay, baby?" Mom asked, concern pinching her brows.

"Just a little sore." A beat passed as they watched me, and I couldn't shake the feeling they weren't telling me everything.

But things were hazy still, a giant black hole where the memory of the accident was supposed to be.

"Everyone's worried sick," Mom said, eventually breaking the heavy silence. "Avery spent the first three nights camped downstairs in the family room. He point blank refused to leave."

"H-he did?" My brother was supposed to be in Indiana, so it touched my heart knowing he'd rushed back to be at my side.

"I don't want him jeopardizing his junior year," I said. Avery played football for Notre Dame and had a real shot at going pro. "Once he's seen I'm okay, he needs to go back. I won't be the reason he messes up his—"

They shared a strange look.

"What?" I asked.

"Nothing, sweetheart." Mom squeezed my hand.

Just then, the doctor came into the room. At least, I assumed he was the doctor given his appearance. "Ah, Ashleigh, it's so good to see you're awake." He greeted my parents before his attention came back to me. "I need to examine you, Ashleigh, if that's okay?"

"Yes, of course."

"It shouldn't take long. Did your parents fill you in on what happened?"

"I was in an accident."

"You were. You suffered what we call a traumatic brain injury." He approached the bed. "Are you okay with your parents staying in the room during my examination?"

"Yes, it's fine."

He nodded and gently eased back the sheet, taking my hand in his. "Flex your fingers please."

I did and he smiled. "Good. Now if you could follow my light." He produced a small flashlight and shined it in my eye, left then right. Then he held up a finger at different angles and made me focus on it as he moved it slowly toward me.

"What's your name?"

"Ashleigh Karen Chase."

"Good, good. And where do you go to school, Ashleigh?"

"Rixon High. I just started senior year."

Mom sucked in a sharp breath and my eyes immediately went to hers. "What is it?" I asked, another flash of dread snaking through me.

"When's your birthday, Ashleigh?" The doctor asked, sympathy shining in his cerulean eyes.

"September twenty-second. I'll be turning eighteen."

"How is this possible?" Dad asked, clearing his throat.

"What is going on?" I demanded, hating that they seemed to be having a conversation about me, without me.

"Sometimes, when the brain suffers trauma, it causes memory loss."

Memory loss? That made sense.

"That's why I can't remember the accident?"

"Yes, and..." He glanced at my parents again, and they both nodded.

"Ashleigh, I suspect you have something called retrograde amnesia."

"Amnesia." The word rattled around my head.

"The part of the brain responsible for memory was damaged in the accident. It's not uncommon for some patients to experience memory loss, particularly of those memories stored in the immediate days and months leading up to the accident."

"Do they ever return?" There was a tremble to Mom's voice that made the knot in my stomach tighten.

"They... can. Over time. Some people get all of their memories back. Others find some return, but some remain inaccessible."

"Guys." I let out a strangled laugh. "This is silly. It's just a few weeks. I'm not sure I want to remember the accident anyway."

Mom and Dad both gave me a tight smile.

"Ashleigh, this will be hard to hear." The doctor settled his kind gaze on me. "But you're not seventeen."

"Of course I am. I turn eighteen in a couple of weeks. I'm a senior at Rixon High School. My best friends are Lily Ford and Peyton Myers. I have a brother named Avery, who has a girlfriend named Miley. My parents are Hailee and Cameron Chase. My uncle is Xander. He's helping coach the football team this year with my other uncle. Uncle Jason." Panic swelled inside of me like a storm.

"Sweetheart, take a breath." Dad stood, running a hand down his face.

"I-I don't understand..." I silently pleaded with him to fix this. To reassure me that everything was going to be okay. But then he said eight little words that changed everything.

Everything.

"It's almost July, sweetheart. High school is over."

RUINED HOPES

TEN MONTHS OF MY LIFE... gone.

Just like that.

The doctor called it retrograde amnesia, said that sometimes after a TBI a person lost the days or weeks or months leading up to the accident.

I'd lost my entire senior year save for the first few weeks.

I didn't know how to process that. How to accept that such a crucial part of my life was just... gone.

At least Ezra was okay.

I'm not sure I could have survived it if anything had happened to him too.

My parents had informed me that Mr. and Mrs. Bennet—his foster parents—had finally adopted him. So he was no longer Ezra Jackson, but Ezra Bennet.

They said he was fine, but I wanted to talk to him, to look him in the eye and know that he was okay. Maybe seeing him, talking to, would fill in the missing pieces of that night.

According to Dad, there had been a graduation party at Bryan Hughes's house. He was on the football team with my cousin Aaron. Ezra was giving me a ride home when we got run off the road.

It still didn't feel real. That they were talking about something that happened to me, when the last thing I could remember was everyone talking about the upcoming pep rally at the beginning of senior year.

Frustration welled inside me again as I tried not to get worked up over the lost memories. But memories made you who you were. They shaped you, influenced the road you walked on. Without them, was I even me anymore?

I mean, it wasn't like I was missing a day or two; I was missing some of the most significant moments of my life.

College applications.
Homecoming.
My eighteenth birthday.
Finals.
Prom.
Graduation.

My entire high school experience had been blown wide open, leaving a gaping hole right at the heart of what should have been the best year of my life.

Mom and Dad had tried to talk to me about it, about college and all the important things I'd missed, but I couldn't do it. I couldn't lie there and be a bystander to almost a year of my life.

So I'd faked a headache and asked them to let me rest. But sleep didn't come, and I'd been lying here for too long, trying to will the memories back into existence.

The door opened and my brother peeked inside.

"Avery," I breathed.

"Hey, Leigh Leigh. Mom and Dad said you were sleeping but I had a feeling you—oh shit, Sis, don't cry."

But the floodgates had torn open, big fat ugly sobs spilling out of me like a torrent.

"Hey, it's okay." He rushed to my side and took my hand in his. "It's okay."

"Is it?" I choked out. "I can't remember, Ave. I can't remember any of it."

"Fuck," he hissed. "I... I don't know what to say."

"There's nothing to say."

Senior year was gone.

Lost.

And worst of all, I might never get it back.

"You want me to get Mom and Dad?"

"No," I rushed out. "They'll only worry, and this isn't something they can fix."

It wasn't something anyone could fix.

"The doctor said there's a chance your memories could return, right?"

I nodded. "But they also might not."

And then what?

Was I supposed to repeat my entire senior year when everyone else's lives had moved on?

My friends were all set to start college in a few weeks. I was supposed to be heading to the University of Pennsylvania.

Now everything was ruined.

I was ruined.

"Feel better now it's all out?" Avery asked, dropping into the chair beside my bed.

"A little, I guess. It just feels so surreal, you know? I can remember the week before the pep rally as if it was only yesterday..."

"I'm so fucking sorry, Leigh."

"I appreciate you coming home," I said. "How's Miley? You guys are still together, right?"

The last I could remember, they'd been blissfully in love.

"Yeah." A slow grin tugged at his mouth. "We're engaged."

"Engaged?" I gasped. "How? When? Tell me everything..."

"I... uh, you were there..."

"I was?" The constant knot in my stomach tightened.

"Well, not at the proposal," he chuckled, "but yeah, we came home last September, pep rally weekend, to tell you all."

"I hope you got her a big diamond." I smiled, but it felt all wrong.

Nothing about this situation was worth smiling over. I'd forgotten my own brother's engagement.

What else had I forgotten?

Part of me was too scared to ask. And Mom and Dad's attempts at filling in some of the blanks made it very clear I wasn't ready to go there yet.

My eyes shuttered as I inhaled a deep breath. Things were messed up. I was messed up. But it could have been worse.

So much worse.

I had to hang onto that.

Because right now, it felt like all I had.

CHAPTER TWO

Ashleigh

THE NEXT COUPLE of days were a never-ending cycle of trying, and failing, to remember the last ten months. My parents insisted on keeping me company, even when I didn't want to talk, and my Aunt Felicity and Uncle Jason stopped by. But aside from Avery, none of my cousins or friends stopped by.

I was starting to think they didn't want to see me because of how awkward it would be...

Until I heard my parents talking.

"What if it's too soon?" Mom said quietly as they stood over by the window.

I was supposed to be asleep, but I'd woken up a few minutes ago to the sound of their voices.

"She'll get suspicious if we keep them away any longer."

"I just worry... you saw how she got when we tried to piece together the year for her."

"It's early days, Hailee. The doctor said we can't rush it. We have to go at her pace."

"Her whole senior year, Cam. Gone. How do we help her come to terms with that?"

Emotion rose inside me as I swallowed back the tears threatening to fall. Of course, this wasn't only hard on me.

Fisting the sheets, I screwed my eyes shut tight and tried to will the memories back into existence. They were there somewhere, buried deep inside my psyche. But no matter how much I tried to find them, I couldn't. As if the tether between me and them had just vanished.

"Ashleigh?" Mom said and I cracked an eye open to find her looming over me.

I hadn't even realized they had moved closer, too focused on the impossible task of triggering a memory. Something to give me hope that it wasn't all lost for good.

"Hey, Mom."

"Are you okay, sweetheart?" The concern in her eyes almost gutted me.

"I... yeah."

She took my hand and squeezed gently. "You were sleeping. We didn't want to wake you."

"I heard you," I said.

"You did?" The worry on her face deepened.

"It's okay, Mom. I get it. You want to protect me. But this is my life now."

I couldn't avoid people forever. And for as much as I didn't know how to feel about seeing my best friends again, I also *needed* to see them.

I needed to know that not everything had changed.

"Lily is desperate to see you," Dad said, dropping his arm over Mom's shoulder. "She hasn't stopped calling."

"Lily can come by." Of course she could, she was my best friend. Family. And if anyone would understand, it would be her.

"That's great, sweetheart. I'll tell her you're ready for visitors."

"Jeez, Dad. Don't make it sound so weird."

He smiled but it slipped. "You'll get through this, Ashleigh. I know you will."

I nodded, not trusting myself to speak. Because there was no guarantee. Even if my memory returned, the doctor said I might have permanent gaps.

Parts of my life... vanished.

Forever.

It was a lot to wrap my head around.

But what choice did I have?

———

"ASHLEIGH?" My cousin peeked around the door, and I smiled.

"You're here."

"I am." She came over, pulling a stuffed toy from behind her back. "For you."

"Thank you." I took the bear from her, running my hands over its soft fur.

"How are you feeling?" Lily sat down in one of the chairs beside my bed.

"I feel okay. The whole memory loss thing is weird but I'm dealing."

"I'm so sorry." Tears glittered in her eyes. "I can't even imagine—"

"Please, don't. I just want to talk. Mom said you and Kaiden are getting ready to move to Penn State. I can't believe you're going to college... with a boy."

"If you'd have told me this time last year I'd be here, I wouldn't have believed it either."

"I'm happy for you. Even if I want to tell you not to jump so quickly into anything with him."

I had memories of Lily and Kaiden's early relationship, when everything was new and shiny, and they were both trying hard to fight the inevitable.

Ten months had passed since then.

God, I'd missed so much.

"What's wrong?" Lily asked.

"Nothing." My smile was strained. "Did I miss anything exciting at prom?"

"Nothing worth mentioning. Although Bryan and Carrie-Anne finally got together."

"Bryan Hughes and Carrie-Anne. Wow, I did not see that coming. In my mind, he's still hung up on Peyton."

This was so weird.

"That ship has long sailed." Lily shook her head. "You know Xander and Peyton are like a thing now, right?"

"What?" My eyes almost bugged out of my head. "Peyton and... *Uncle Xander*?"

"Crap, your parents didn't tell you?" Guilt flashed in her eyes.

"No. No they did not. When? How?"

Holy crap. I had so many questions.

"Last year over the holidays. It went sour for a while, but they figured it out."

"What did my dad say? And Uncle Jase?"

She grimaced. "Things got bad for a while. Xander moved to Halston, and we didn't see him for like two months. But everyone is cool about it now they've had time to adjust. Peyton lives with him. She graduated early and got a job."

"Wow... that's just... wow."

Peyton was our age, and Uncle Xander was ten years our

senior. Part of me was surprised he was still breathing knowing how protective my dad and Uncle Jason could be.

"I feel like I've missed so much."

"You didn't really." Lily gave me a sad smile. "You were right there with us, Leigh. You just..."

"Can't remember, yeah." A heavy sigh slipped from my lips. It didn't feel like much of a consolation.

In fact, it felt like a double blow.

To know you experienced something and not be able to remember a single second of it.

"Poppy and Sofia didn't fall in love and run away with their boyfriends or anything, did they?" I asked, referring to Lily's younger sister and her best friend.

"No." Lily chuckled. "Although Poppy is ready to take senior year by storm. She has big plans, apparently."

"The boys of Rixon High better watch out."

"Indeed. Dad is already dreading it."

"Poppy is definitely going to give him a run for his money."

"I'm almost upset I won't be around to see it." Lily grinned but it immediately dropped when the reality of her words hit.

She wouldn't be here because she would be off at college, living her life and chasing her dreams.

And me... I'd be stuck here, trying to recover the last year of my life.

"I'm sorry." Guilt washed over her. "I didn't think."

"It's okay. I've got to get used to the fact that everyone's lives are moving on." Even if mine was stuck ten months in the past.

Then a thought struck me.

"Me and Ezra, did we...?"

For the first time since waking up, I felt a seed of hope.

I'd been focusing so much on what I couldn't remember that I hadn't stopped to think about all the good things that might have happened to me.

Like say for example, the boy I'd wanted since eighth grade finally noticing me.

Something flashed in Lily's eyes that made my stomach drop. But it was gone so quickly I wondered if I'd imagined it.

Strangled laughter bubbled in my chest. "Of course we didn't."

"Leigh, I'm sor—"

"It's okay, really." I inhaled a deep breath and asked the question on the tip of my tongue. "Has he... asked about me?"

Ezra Jackson wasn't like his adopted siblings, Sofía and Aaron Bennet. He was a lone wolf, preferring to hang out in the shadows than do all the normal teenage stuff most kids did.

I'd tried so hard to pull him into our group, but the more I'd pulled, the more he'd pushed back.

"You know Ezra," Lily said. "He doesn't exactly talk to the rest of us."

I did. But it didn't stop the slight sting when she didn't give me the answer I hoped for.

"He's a Bennet now though."

"I know, my mom and dad told me." I could barely contain my smile. We all knew Asher and Mya had wanted to adopt Ezra for some time.

"Yeah, they were so happy about it."

This was hard. I wanted to see Ezra, to make him tell me everything. But he didn't handle change well. And everything was different now.

Not to mention the fact he'd walked away from the accident unscathed, and I hadn't.

"I'm so pleased for them all. Ezra needs family," I said. "He needs to know he belongs."

But Lily wasn't smiling. In fact, she looked downright miserable.

"What is it? What's wrong?" I asked.

"There's something else, something about Ezra..."

Oh God.

My heart ratcheted in my chest.

Had he finally met someone? A girl he wanted to open his heart to?

I'd always held out hope that one day I would burrow through his walls and find a way inside. But that dream would wither and die if he'd found someone else.

"Did he... did he meet someone?" My stomach twisted, anticipating the pain that would follow if she confirmed my worst fear.

"What? No. No, it's nothing like that."

"It isn't?" Sweet relief slammed into me.

There wasn't someone else.

Which meant there was still hope.

Until Lily said, "Ezra failed senior year, Leigh. He didn't graduate."

"I WANT TO SEE EZRA," I said the next morning when Mom and Dad arrived. It seemed that they had cherry picked what information to tell me during our many chats.

They shared an awkward look, and Dad cleared his throat. "I'm not sure that's a good idea, sweetheart. Being around him... it might trigger you."

"Trigger me?" I gawked, disbelief coating my words. "You can't be serious, Dad. If anything, it might help. Ezra was there, he knows what happened. Maybe if I talk to him, it will unlock something."

Really, I just wanted to talk to him about school—about the fact he flunked out.

I could remember him being indifferent at the beginning of senior year. But everyone expected him to pull his head out of the sand and at least graduate.

"You know how Ezra is, sweetheart." Mom intervened. "And Asher is riding him hard about failing school. He's not in a good place. I think it would be better to wait."

"Is there something you're not telling me?"

"What? No, no, baby. We just don't want you to have any extra stress than you already have. The doctor said—"

"Yeah, Mom." I knew what the doctor said. I'd been right there when he'd tried to talk to me about how to avoid pushing myself too much too soon.

But I needed to see Ezra. I needed to look him in the eye and know we were okay. That he was okay.

"Did you guys pick me up a new cell phone yet?" I changed the subject.

They shared a look of guilt and Dad said, "Once you're home and settled, we'll sort it out."

My old one had been a casualty of the accident.

"Dad!"

"No, Ashleigh. The doctor said you need to give yourself time. You're still healing. Screen time isn't—"

"Screen time?" I scoffed. "It's a cell phone and I'm sev—eighteen." That would take some getting used to. "I think I can manage my screen time appropriately."

He leaned in and kissed my head. "A few more days won't hurt."

"Fine." An indignant huff left my lips. It wasn't like I could go buy one from the hospital gift store.

"There is something we need to talk about though." They both sat down, and Mom took my hand in hers.

Oh God, what now?

Nervous energy vibrated through me, making me feel a little nauseous.

"We spoke to Mya and Principal Kiln." Mya was the guidance counsellor at Rixon High. "They've been talking to UPenn, and they all agree that given the circumstances you should defer."

"Defer." The word echoed through me like a gunshot. Deep down, I knew college wouldn't be an option this year, not with my entire senior year's classes missing. But knowing it and hearing it were two very different things.

I felt like I'd been punched in the stomach. Breathless. Hollow and raw.

"Mya thinks, and the doctor agreed, that it would be a good idea for you to repeat your senior year. Be in familiar surroundings with your friends."

Right. Because Poppy and Sofia would be seniors. Aaron too.

And so would Ezra.

CHAPTER THREE

Ezra

"WHOA, HOLD UP," Asher said, looking up from his position at the breakfast counter. "You're going out?" His brow rose.

"Yeah, I mean... I am allowed to leave the house, right?"

"E, come on, Son. You're not a prisoner. But I am your father. I just want to know you're okay."

Father.

Fuck. That would take some getting used to.

"I'm fine," I muttered. "Can I go now?"

I didn't wait for his answer, slipping out of the kitchen.

"You can't shut me out forever, Ezra," he called after me. "I'm a patient man. I'll be here waiting when you're ready."

A muted groan slipped from my lips as I yanked up my hood and left the house.

It sucked that I didn't have a car anymore, but it had been totaled in the accident, so my options were walking on foot or taking Aaron's bicycle.

The familiar rumble of his car stopped me in my tracks. Fuck. I was hoping to sneak away before he got home.

Shoving my hands in my pockets, I kept my head down.

"E, wait up." His car door slammed, and Aaron jogged over to me. "You're going out?"

"Just going for a walk."

"A walk, right. Well, I'm free. So I'll tag along."

"Did your dad put you up to this?" I narrowed my eyes.

"E, he's *our* dad." Aaron gave me a pleading glance. I knew what he wanted—he wanted things to be okay between all of us. But it was easy for him. He was Asher and Mya's biological son. He was a part of them.

I was... different.

I appreciated everything they'd done for me over the years, appreciated that they'd cared enough to want to keep me and make it official by adopting me.

But I wasn't like them.

The Bennets were a close-knit family. Aaron, his twin sister Sofia, and their parents Asher and Mya. They had a tight group of friends and family. A whole network of people in Rixon who had their backs.

I'd been a part of their lives for seven years, but the truth was, I'd always been on the outside looking in. The piece of the puzzle that didn't quite fit.

And now I was the bitter disappointment.

But that was my M.O., and no matter how hard I tried to break the cycle, I ended up back at square one. Sabotaging everything good in my life.

"I keep thinking about Leigh, about what it must be like, waking up with ten months of your life just gone. Some trip, huh?"

"Yeah." I grimaced, trying to school my expression. Even

though my heart careened against my chest at the mention of her name.

"Shit, sorry, man." Aaron cast me a sympathetic glance. "I know it can't be easy for you."

"I'm just glad she's okay," I said over the giant fucking lump in my throat.

Waking up that day to discover she was in a coma, was one of the worst moments of my life. But realizing it was all my fault... that was something else.

"Hey." He clapped me on the back, and I winced. "It wasn't your fault, E."

Had I said that out loud?

"I was driving." The words were like acid on my tongue. Because I'd been doing more than just driving that night.

It should have been me lying in that hospital bed with no memories of senior year. Fuck only knew it would have been an improvement. Then I wouldn't have to endure the constant stares of disappointment, and the cold shoulders from Ashleigh's parents.

Not that I blamed them.

Their daughter had been in a coma... because of me.

I'd done some shitty things in my life, but what happened that night... the truth behind the accident... I would never forgive myself.

"Ezra, man. You gotta let that shit go. It was an accident." Aaron gripped my shoulder. "I know it sucks that Ashleigh got hurt, but she's okay. She's going to be okay."

Such bullshit.

But I didn't argue. What was the point?

"Yeah," I murmured.

"You should go see her," he added. "You know she'd want you to."

And if that wasn't the whole fucking problem.

AARON INSISTED on sticking with me as I headed for The Junction. It was a rundown diner on the edge of town, but I preferred it over the more popular places downtown. Maybe it was the fact kids from school didn't hang out there. Or the fact that Manny, the owner, let me stick around for as long as I wanted without asking questions.

The house special burger didn't suck either.

"What is this place?" he asked as I shouldered the door open.

"The Junction."

"I can see that." He flicked his eyes to the faded signage. "But why have I never been here before?"

I shrugged, making a beeline for my regular booth.

"Usual, Ezra?" Manny called across the counter and I nodded. "Better make it two."

"Coming right up."

"You come here a lot?" Aaron gawked at me.

We were brothers by definition, sure. But I didn't spend a lot of time with him, or his sister, or their friends. They liked partying and football and high school drama, and I... didn't.

I kept to myself. It was easier that way.

When I'd first arrived at the Bennets', they had all tried to encourage me to hang out with Aaron, Sofia, and their friends. But everything was different in Rixon. And the Bennets... they had money. They had a big house and nice things, and I had the clothes on my back, a boatload of bad memories, and a closet full of skeletons.

It wasn't easy trying to fit in, knowing I never really would, and as time went on, it just became easier to stop trying.

"Now and again."

"You know, E, we've been brothers a long time now." Aaron drummed his fingers against the Formica table. "Yet, sometimes, it's like I don't even know you. But since we're going to be seniors together—"

My spine snapped straight. So he knew. Aaron knew what his father had demanded of me.

I wasn't surprised, not really. Asher had probably railroaded Aaron into taking me under his wing once the start of the semester rolled around. But I was still hoping to get out of it. High school was over. Done. It wasn't like I had plans to go to college.

Asher and Mya had wanted it for me, but they hadn't pushed. Not too hard. Not until it was apparent I wasn't going to graduate.

I hadn't witnessed Asher lose his shit much over the years. But when Mya came home at the beginning of senior year and handed him my transcripts... his anger had been a living, breathing thing.

They'd expected me to turn it around, and I hadn't.

I hadn't even tried.

"It would be cool to hang out occasionally." Aaron yanked me back to the present. "Dad's hoping you'll join the team. Coach Ford said—"

"I'm not joining the team," I said, flatly.

"But I've seen your throwing arm and you're fast, E. Really fucking fast. You'd be an asset to the Raiders, and with Kaiden, Gav, and Bryan all moving on, we could use fresh blood."

I couldn't think of anything worse than training with the Rixon Raiders under Coach Ford's leadership. Ashleigh was his niece for fuck's sake. It was a disaster waiting to happen.

One I wanted no part of.

"Here you go," one of the regular servers, a sweet girl

called Penny, said as she delivered our drinks. She flashed me a warm smile. "Your food will be out in a minute."

"Thanks, Pen," I drawled.

"Any time, E." Her cheeks flushed as she hurried away.

"Friend of yours?" Aaron craned his neck to get a better look at her retreating form. "She's cute."

"Sure, if you like that kind of thing."

He snorted. "And you're telling me, you don't?"

"Pen is... cool."

"Cool, yeah. The way she was looking at you, bro, so cool." He smirked, glancing back over to where Penny was wiping down the counter. She glanced over and flashed us a bright smile.

"I don't recognize her from school."

"She's at college, asshole."

"Nice. Where does she go?"

"Rixon Community College."

"You should ask her out."

"What?" I ran a hand over my hair and down the back of my neck, gawking at him.

Aaron shrugged. "She's hot and older and has a job. What's not to like?"

"Does Asher know you're such a dog?" I tsked. "Besides, I thought you had your sights set on Poppy."

"Ew gross, Poppy is..." He hesitated, his eyes flickering with something. "Poppy's like a sister to me. It would be totally weird."

"Two house specials." Penny reappeared with our burgers.

"Wow, this looks great, thanks." Aaron shot her a wide grin.

"Can I get you anything else, Ezra?"

"I'm all good, thanks." I gave her a small nod. She lingered for a second, her eyelashes fluttering.

"You know where I am if you need me." She hurried away.

"She wants a piece of you, man." Aaron's eyes twinkled as he tore into his burger.

"Yeah, well, I'm not interested.

There was only one girl who had ever caught my eye in Rixon...

And I didn't fucking deserve her.

―――

WE STAYED at The Junction until the sun disappeared into the horizon. Aaron didn't tease me about Penny anymore, and she was too busy dealing with other tables to hover at ours.

"I don't know whether to be pissed you kept this place to yourself," Aaron said as we settled the check, splitting it. "Or whether to high-five you. That burger was fucking awesome."

"Yeah, Manny's burgers are the best."

"Damn straight," the man in question hollered across the diner, winking at me.

We'd almost made our way to the door when Penny intervened. "You're leaving?"

"I'll be outside," Aaron said, flashing me a knowing grin.

"So, I was wondering..."

"Listen, Pen, I'm not—"

"Oh God, this is embarrassing." She pushed her dark bangs out of her eyes. "I thought... okay, let's just pretend this didn't happen."

"Sorry," I said, feeling like a giant asshole.

"Yeah, no, it's fine. I'm fine. Totally fine." She smiled but it didn't reach her eyes. "Well, I should go."

"See you around."

"Bye." Penny took off toward the counter, not sparing me a backward glance.

Fuck, that was awkward. But I liked it here too much to get tangled up with the staff.

It was one of the few places I could come and avoid people: the kids from school; Asher and Mya, their friends; my brother, sister, and their friends.

"Got yourself a hot date?" Aaron teased as I joined him on the sidewalk.

Rolling my eyes, I jammed my hands in my hoodie pocket and took off down the street.

"Come on, E, it was a joke. I'm joking." He nudged my shoulder with his, falling into step beside me.

"I know," I murmured, putting some space between us. Shaking off the discomfort I felt at his close proximity.

Silence lingered as we kept walking back toward the house. The place I'd called home for the last seven years.

Even if after all this time, it still didn't feel like it.

It was my problem though, not theirs. I knew that. Asher, Mya, Aaron, and Sofia had done everything to welcome me into their family, to make me one of them.

But something inside of me was broken. Jagged and cracked.

And I didn't know how to fix it.

CHAPTER FOUR

Ashleigh

"READY, SWEETHEART?" Dad asked me for the third time.

He was nervous; they all were.

Mom, Dad, and Avery.

Because after two weeks and three days of going stir crazy in the hospital, I was finally being discharged.

"As I'll ever be." I gave a small sigh, my body still weary from its recovering injuries.

Mom helped me sit up, helped drag my legs over the edge of the bed, and handed me my crutches.

I'd worked all week with the physical therapist, practicing supporting my body weight with the walking aids. It was tiring work, muscles straining and working overtime to compensate for the lack of movement in my right foot.

"Okay?" Dad asked, gently holding my elbow while I stood. He let me get my balance then slowly backed away. "You seem much sturdier on these now."

"I slipped once, Dad."

"Twice." He grinned. "Just be careful, okay? You've given us enough near heart attacks these last few weeks."

Six weeks and two days to be exact.

It was strange. It felt longer, and yet, it felt like no time at all. I guess that was just one of the many strange side effects of my amnesia. Like time had been folded in on itself.

I'd spent all week with Lily and Poppy and Sofia, letting them slowly feed me pieces of the last ten months. They were patient but I saw the pity in their eyes every time I stared vacantly at them.

And I hated it.

But I had two choices. I could choose to succumb to the gnawing devastation and grief I felt every time I let myself go there, or I could face this thing head on.

As Mom and Dad walked me out of the hospital, giving me time to go at my own pace, I was somewhere in the middle. I didn't want to let my new reality overshadow my future. But I also wasn't ready to embrace the possibility that my memories—the last ten months of my life—were lost.

"Ashleigh?" Mom touched my arm and I blinked up at her. "The car..." She motioned to where Dad's SUV pulled up in front of us.

At least some things were the same.

A small smile played on my lips as I climbed into the back seat.

"It'll be good to get you home," Mom said, glancing back at me as she buckled up. "The doctor said being in familiar surroundings might help."

"Hailee," Dad said, quietly.

"It's okay, Dad. You guys don't need to do that." Whisper and confer as if they were plotting behind my back. I understood my diagnosis, the likelihood of my lost memories never fully returning.

I got it.

I was the one living it, after all.

"Sorry, sweetheart. We just don't want you to—"

"Mom," I snapped. "I'm fine."

Even if my mind insisted it was the beginning of senior year instead of the middle of summer.

She gave me a tentative smile, and I could see the concern swirling in her eyes. She was worried. They both were. But she didn't push, and we rode the short distance back to our house in comfortable silence.

"Avery's still here," I said, noticing his car in the driveway.

He was supposed to be returning to Notre Dame for football camp.

"He wanted to see you before he left."

I smiled at that. The truth was, I wanted to see him too. He was my big brother, my protector, the one guy who didn't try and sugarcoat things for me.

As if I'd summoned him, Avery appeared at the door. He wasted no time, bounding over to me and yanking the door open. "Welcome home, Leigh Leigh." He grinned, offering me his hand. I let him pull me from the car.

"How are you feeling?"

"Good." I nodded. "Better now that I'm out of that place."

"Come on." He slung his arm around my shoulder. "Let's go find you something to eat."

"Because eating solves everything."

"It does when it's cupcakes from Sprinkles."

"Tell me you got the red velvet ones, oh and the chocolate fudge ones."

"You know it." Avery smiled down at me as we walked into the house.

Everything was so familiar. It was like coming home after a day at school. Except, I couldn't help but pick out everything that was different. Like the new family portrait on the sideboard or the lingering scent of vanilla.

"That's new," I said, sniffing the air.

Mom was typically a jasmine and freesia kind of woman.

Avery gave me space, letting me acquaint myself with everything. I ran my fingers over the photographs lining the wall. Candids of our life. Me and Avery as children. Mom and Dad as doting parents. Avery and Miley the night of their prom....

Me the night of senior prom.

I sucked in a sharp breath, staring at the photograph through the eyes of a stranger.

"Leigh—" Avery came up beside me, his hand resting on my shoulder. "Does it... spark anything?"

"Nothing." Not a damn thing. My voice quivered as I stared at the girl smiling back at me.

Me. Dressed in a black fit-and-flare dress, my hair curled and pinned up in some intricate coronet.

It was me; I knew that.

Yet it didn't feel like me.

I sucked in another sharp breath, trying to keep my tears at bay.

"It's going to be strange," Avery said, gently trying to guide me away from the photographs. "But you've got this, Leigh Leigh."

Funny, because I didn't feel like I had it. In fact, I felt like I was wading through dark muddy waters.

"Is everything okay?" Dad called from the front door as he and Mom came inside.

"Everything's fine," Avery replied for me, keeping his arm tight around my shoulder as we headed for the kitchen.

Tears welled in my eyes when I spotted the balloon and tower of cupcakes and the small 'welcome home' banner.

"It was Mom's idea." Avery squeezed my shoulder before releasing me. Giving me a second, I figured.

"People aren't about to jump out from behind the furniture, are they?" My brow arched and he chuckled.

"No, there's no one hiding around the corner. We just wanted to do... something."

"It's sweet," I said, losing the fight against the emotion clogging my throat.

"We're just so happy to have you home," Mom said, wrapping her arm around me and kissing my cheek.

"Thanks, Mom. Dad." I caught his eye over her shoulder.

"It's going to be okay, Ashleigh." He smiled.

Those words.

Words that I wanted so badly to believe.

But I couldn't.

Not yet.

———

"ASHLEIGH," Mom called, and I pulled out my earbuds.

"Yeah?"

"The girls are here."

Laughter filtered down the hall outside my bedroom and the knot in my stomach tightened. Lily had texted earlier asking if her and Peyton could come visit. Of course, I'd said yes. But it felt different now.

In the hospital, there had been a buffer. I could hide behind my injuries and the constant check-ups by the nurse and doctor. If I didn't want to talk, I could feign being exhausted.

I couldn't hide now.

People would expect me to get back to some kind of normal.

"Hey." Lily's face appeared around the door. "Aunt Hailee sent us up."

"Come in." I smiled, hoping they couldn't see the strain there.

"We brought supplies." Peyton smiled, holding up a grocery bag.

"You didn't have to."

"We wanted to." She dropped down in my desk chair. "How are you feeling?"

"Okay."

"It must be nice to be home," Lily said.

"It's... nice, yeah." I ran my hands over my bedcover.

"Sorry, I didn't—"

"No, it's fine. I just... I saw the photos from prom in the hall and it was like looking at someone else."

"It didn't help?" Peyton asked.

Worrying my bottom lip, I shook my head.

Did they expect it would be that simple? That I'd look at a few photos and everything would come rushing back?

The doctor said it would take time—if it happened at all.

"It's going to take time," Lily said with a warm smile. She sat on the edge of my bed, her soulful blue eyes seeing too much.

"How's work?" I asked Peyton, changing the subject.

"It's work." She shrugged. "I like it and the people are nice but..." She trailed off, not meeting my eyes.

"But what?" I frowned.

Peyton looked to Lily and she nodded. "She'd want to know."

"Know what? Will somebody just tell me what's going on?"

"I've been thinking about applying to college."

"That's great, isn't it?" I glanced between them.

"It is, but I just thought…"

"She was worried it was a sore subject."

"Oh." Because I wouldn't be going off to college this year. I'd be stuck at high school, repeating the year. Without my best friends.

"I haven't decided anything yet."

"What does Uncle Xander think about it?" I asked.

It was still so weird to imagine them together. They'd avoided coming to the hospital together and I wondered if it was another attempt at easing me into things. But everyone seemed okay with it. Even Uncle Jason and Aunt Felicity who had practically raised Peyton for the last year of her life.

"He's supportive, although I don't think he likes the idea of me around a bunch of horndog college guys. His words, not mine." A faint smile played on her lips.

"What about you and Kaiden?" I asked Lily. "Are you excited about moving to college?"

"I am so excited." Her expression didn't exactly look excited. "But I'll miss you both. I'll miss Rixon."

"Well, I'll be right here, waiting for you to visit."

It was supposed to be a joke, but it came out in a rush of strained breath.

"Leigh…"

Pity and sympathy. That was the only emotion etched into my best friends' expressions as they watched me.

So much pity…

As if they knew the cost of my injury. But even if they knew, they couldn't understand.

No one could.

I'd survived the accident. I could remember their faces, our history, the bonds connecting us. I could remember a whole childhood. Almost eighteen years of memories and experiences, highs and lows.

But I couldn't remember senior year. And that hole, that gaping hollow hole, was like a black void sucking everything else dry.

You're lucky, Ashleigh. It could have been worse.

Much worse.

I knew that; I did. But it didn't change anything.

"Has anyone heard from Ezra?" The words were out before I could stop them. "He didn't visit me."

"He's... not in a good place, Leigh." Lily pressed her lips together. "I heard Sofia and Poppy talking about it. She thinks he blames himself."

"Because of the accident?" My brows knitted, an icky sensation clanging through me.

"Because he walked away with a couple of scratches, I guess... and you didn't."

"Have you texted him?" Peyton asked.

"No, my parents still haven't gotten me a new cell phone."

"Yeah, what's up with that?"

"I think they're just worried that I'll log onto all my social media, and it'll mess with my head or something."

"They have a point," Peyton said. "Sometimes social media sucks my soul dry. Everyone's so fake. You're better off without it."

I didn't care about social media. I cared about Ezra, about him blaming himself. He already carried so much darkness, I didn't want to be responsible for adding to that.

"He hung out with Aaron, took him to some diner. The Junction or something. I think it's that place on the edge of town with the red and white canopy," Lily said.

"The Junction?" I didn't recognize the name.

"Yeah, Aaron told Poppy that Ezra knew the owner and waitress."

Waitress.

My stomach sank.

"Oh no, Leigh." Lily backtracked. "I don't think it's anything like that. But it's weird that Ezra has a place none of us ever go to, isn't it?"

"He's never hung out with us," Peyton added.

"No, but Aaron said he was comfortable there. As if he hangs out there all the time. It's like... I don't know, he chose somewhere he knew none of us would ever find him."

My heart cinched at her assessment. But more than that, it hurt at the fact Ezra had somewhere he'd kept a secret, even from me.

Or maybe he hadn't and I just couldn't remember.

"At least you'll have each other next semester." Peyton smiled, but I didn't feel like smiling.

I'd crushed on Ezra ever since he'd arrived in Rixon seven years ago. Lost and alone and wary of everyone around him, something in him had called to me. And the protective feeling I felt toward him had only developed over time.

I wanted to know him. To unravel the quiet boy with the weight of the world on his shoulders. But he'd always kept me at arm's length, pushing me away the second I got too close.

And now... now I'd lost ten months of memories.

And the distance between me and Ezra felt bigger than ever.

CHAPTER FIVE

Ashleigh

"ARE YOU SURE ABOUT THIS?" Mom asked for the third time that morning.

"It's just the store, Mom."

"I know, sweetheart." She gave me 'the look.' The one she cast my way every time I didn't react the way she expected, as if she was waiting for the other shoe to drop. Waiting for me to break down.

But the truth was, I was going stir crazy.

I'd been home three days and hadn't seen outside the four walls of our house. Besides, it was a trip to the store with my mom.

It seemed like a safe option.

"Okay." She breathed. "Okay."

"Mom." I let out a weak chuckle. "It's the store. I'm sure it'll be fine."

"You're just... you're so calm about all of this."

Oh, I wasn't. But I couldn't let those feelings consume me. Because every time I gave them even an ounce of space, fear put me in a chokehold. And I didn't have the luxury of sitting around, waiting to see if my memories returned. Not with the summer break passing me by and senior year 2.0 fast approaching.

"It's hard," I said, barely able to meet her stare. "But I'm trying."

"You're such a good girl, Ashleigh." She leaned in, cupping my cheek and pressing a kiss there. "And I'm so proud of how you're handling everything."

"Thanks, Mom."

I followed her out of the house. Avery had gone back to Indiana yesterday. I'd miss him, but part of me was relieved I wouldn't have to endure his quiet, assessing gaze any longer.

It was one less person I had to pretend with.

We rode to the store in comfortable silence, humming to the familiar songs on the radio.

So strange, that I could remember lyrics to songs almost ten years old, but I couldn't remember graduating high school only weeks ago. I could remember the square root of Pi but couldn't remember ten months' worth of conversations with my friends.

And the list went on... and on.

"I thought I'd make mac and cheese tonight. It's your favorite."

"I know, Mom."

"Sorry, sweetheart, I didn't mean—"

"Oh look, Mya is here." I spotted her car almost immediately.

"So she is." Mom murmured as she shouldered the door open and climbed out.

She came around to help me onto my crutches. "Okay?"

I nodded, testing my balance. At least I could bear weight now because I really wasn't getting the hang of these things.

Mom grabbed a shopping cart and together we entered the store, running straight into Mya and...

"Ezra."

Relief slammed into me. He was here, and he was in one piece.

Thank goodness.

But before I could get another word out, Mya blurted, "Hailee, Ashleigh, what a surprise." She smiled, but it didn't reach her eyes. "How's... everything?"

"It's Ashleigh's first trip out since... well, you know."

Mya said something, but I was too busy staring at Ezra, silently willing him to say something. He looked sick, standing there, watching me through those haunted amber eyes of his.

"How are you?" I said, hating how awkward things felt between us.

To me, it had been mere days since I'd last seen him. Since I'd refused to leave when I'd followed him down to the lake behind the Bennets' property.

We'd been hanging out in Aaron's man cave—the shed his father let him turn into a hangout—when I'd spotted Ezra heading toward the lake. He'd made no effort to join us, he never did. But I couldn't stand the thought of him being alone, so I went after him.

I always went after him.

"Ezra," Mya's voice yanked me out of the thoughts. "Why don't you go on ahead and start loading the groceries in the trunk?" She handed him her keys, and I watched with disbelief as he grabbed their cart and walked off without so much as a word.

Anger flared inside me as I gripped my crutches.

"I'll be right back, Mom," I said, maneuvering around to follow him.

"Actually, Ashleigh, we're in a bit of a hurry. See you both again soon."

Something passed between my mom and Mya.

"But, Mom—"

"I'll call you," she said to Mya's retreating form.

"That was... weird." I glanced back, watching Mya and Ezra exchange terse words near her car. Dread snaked through me.

Something had changed, I felt it just now. The way he'd looked at me. Was it guilt I'd detected in his amber gaze, or was it something else?

"You know how Ezra gets," Mom said a little too defensively, even maybe a little flippantly.

I frowned.

"He has to know it isn't his fault, Mom."

She cast me a weak smile. "He'll come around."

There was a tightness in her words that made me wonder if she believed he wasn't to blame. He'd been driving, sure. But it was an accident. It wasn't fair to hold him responsible or resent him because he'd walked away with a couple of scratches.

Scratches that had since healed if his face was anything to go by.

If he'd just stuck around to talk to me, I could have told him not to feel guilty on my behalf. He had to know I would never blame him.

Surely.

"Don't worry about Ezra, sweetheart." Mom made a beeline for one of the aisles as I hobbled behind her.

Don't worry about Ezra.

Such a simple statement.

Such an impossible, unimaginable request.

But she didn't know that I harbored a special place in my

heart for her best friend's son. That, for years, I'd desperately tried to break down his walls and burrow my way into his heart.

She didn't know.

Few people did.

Ezra knew though. He knew and yet, he'd just walked away from me as if there was nothing between us.

As if I was nothing.

WHEN MY DAD turned up at home later that day with a brand-new cell phone for me, I thought I'd feel a kernel of excitement.

I didn't.

It was a connection, a tether to all that I'd lost. If I logged into my social media accounts, I would be able to relive those memories, but they wouldn't be mine. Not anymore.

It left a deep ache inside my chest as I clutched the shiny new phone in my hand.

"We thought it would make you happy," Dad said, his brows pinched.

"It has... I mean, it does. I'm just not sure I'm ready to... You know what, it's fine." *I'm fine.* "Thanks, Dad." I hobbled over to him using the furniture to steady myself. "I'm going to head upstairs."

"You don't want to hang out with us?" Mom asked. "I got your favorite ice cream."

"Maybe later. I'm kind of beat."

Shopping—and running into Ezra and Mya—had sucked it out of me. The doctors said I could expect to feel exhausted in the days and weeks to come. Any traumatic brain injury left its mark, and this was one of them.

"Okay, baby. Holler if you need anything."

"Thanks, Mom," I said, gripping the handrail. Getting up and down the stairs was no easy feat but I refused to have Dad carry me, like he'd offered yesterday.

When everything felt so out of my control, I needed to be able to stand on my own two feet. Literally.

They watched me struggle, breathing through gritted teeth as I made the slow, painful ascent. The second I turned the corner, out of their sight, I rested back against the wall, trying to keep the tears at bay.

How had everything gone so wrong?

I should have been enjoying the summer, spending the last few weeks with my friends before we all went our separate ways and headed to college.

And now... now, I would be returning to Rixon High to repeat my senior year. A decision made so easily by my doctor and parents that it made me wonder if they knew the truth—if they knew the chances of my memories returning anytime soon were slim.

I dragged myself into my room and closed the door, shuffling over to my bed and flopping down. Part of me wished the summer was already over. At least then I wouldn't have to suffer seeing my friends, hearing about their exciting lives and preparations for college.

Ugh.

I lay down and stared up at the ceiling, unable to fight the tears burning the backs of my eyes. Silently, they rolled down my cheeks, dripping onto my t-shirt, the covers. Evaporating into nothing as easily as the memories I'd lost.

Crying made me feel weak when I knew how lucky I was. I was still here, still breathing and in one piece.

But I wasn't in one piece, not really.

A part of me was missing now. Lost to the accident.

My cell phone pinged, and I dug it out of my pocket, smiling at Lily's name. Dad must have loaded all my old contacts for me and given her my new number.

Lily: So I was thinking… Girls' night tonight?

Me: Don't you and Kaiden have plans?

Lily: I think he can manage one night without me. Besides, you need me more right now.

GOD, I loved her. My best friend. My cousin. A girl who knew me better than I knew myself sometimes.

A girl who in less than a month would be leaving.

I tried, and failed, to keep the tears at bay as I texted her back.

Me: I'd like that.

Lily: I'll bring snacks.

Me: See you later.

I CLOSED MY EYES, hugging my cell phone to my chest. Lily got it. She knew what it was like to be lost. Drifting through life, uncertain and afraid. I'd stood by her side for years as she'd battled her own demons. But I'd never been that girl before.

Until now.

"I THINK I'm in a sugar coma," I announced, groaning as I tried to eat the rest of my Twizzler.

Lily had turned up earlier armed with enough snacks to feed the entire street. She also brought her photo album... just in case I wanted to look.

I hadn't, not at first. But a packet of Swedish Fish and Reese's later, I'd given in to the urge to peek.

"It's so surreal," I said, flipping through the pages. Photo after photo of us, our friends and families. I paused on the page filled with photos of our eighteenth birthdays. They were only three days apart, so we always celebrated together.

A couple pages on, my breath caught at a rare photo of Poppy with Aaron and Sofia... and Ezra. Tracing my finger over his face, I smiled softly. He was just as I remembered. Same strong features and full lips. Same amber eyes that looked right into your soul. Same silver hoop through his nose and a diamond stud glinting in his ear. Same dusting of hair over his upper lip and jaw, and same dark hair styled into twists.

Physically, he'd been the same when I'd seen him at the store... but I'd felt something different about him.

"I don't think I've ever seen a photo of him before."

"You know what E is like."

"I saw him today," the words fell out in a rush of breath.

"You did?" Her brows furrowed.

"Yeah, at the store with Mya."

"Did he... say anything?" There was something in the way she hesitated.

"He barely looked at me." Dejection gnawed my insides. Ezra had never been open, not even with me. But he'd never ignored me so vehemently before.

"It's been a stressful time for everyone," Lily said. "But now you're okay, things will calm down." She reached for my hand and squeezed. "You'll see."

I smiled weakly...

Wishing I could believe her.

CHAPTER SIX

Ezra

SWEAT ROLLED down my back as I cut through the dense trees down by the river. My feet pounded against the overgrowth, leaves and branches crunching as I pushed harder. Faster. Trying to outrun the image of Ashleigh earlier at the store.

Seeing her there had completely thrown me for a loop. I rarely went with Mya or Asher on trips to the mall or grocery store, but she'd asked, guilted me into it really. I'd never imagined Ashleigh would be there, not so soon after being discharged from the hospital.

Mya hadn't expected it either if the shocked look on her face was anything to go by.

Ashleigh had just stared... and stared. Silently willing me to say something, anything. And I'd just fucking stood there, speechless. But what the hell was I supposed to say?

I'm sorry you almost died.
I'm sorry you lost the last ten months of your life.
I'm sorry it's all my fault.

The words had almost choked me and before I could get out a single syllable, Mya sent me packing.

And I was relieved, I was fucking relieved to have a reason to get the hell out of there. Away from Hailee's wrath, from Ashleigh's pleading expression. From the tension stifling the air around us.

Fuck.

I ground to a halt, dropping my hands to my thighs and sucking in a deep breath. My muscles burned, popping and zinging with exertion, but it was better than sitting around the house, with Mya's constant disapproving looks and Asher's attempts at bonding with me.

So I ran.

I ran and ran and ran until I couldn't run anymore.

Staggering down to the river's edge, I dropped down onto the grassy bank and lay back, staring up at the stars. Life wasn't supposed to turn out like this. I wasn't supposed to be here, in a place like Rixon, trying every single day to fit in, when deep down, I knew I never would.

I didn't want to feel like... like this. But I couldn't get out of my head. I couldn't stop thinking about Alyson Jackson.

My birth mother.

The woman who had abandoned me when I was just a kid, condemning me to a life bouncing from one foster family to another.

She hadn't wanted me.

Those families hadn't wanted me—not enough to keep me.

Until the Bennets.

But the damage was already done. And even now, I couldn't trust that this was real. That it was forever. Even with the signed papers declaring me one of them.

Ezra Bennet.

Because I'd been Alyson's once. I'd been her son, carried her name… and she'd left me as if I was nothing more than a discarded toy she no longer had a use for.

I couldn't wrap my head around that. Around willingly giving up your own flesh and blood. Something so innocent and helpless.

A child.

A fucking toddler.

The blare of my cell phone pierced the silence and I dug it out of my shorts pocket.

"Ezra?" Asher breathed a sigh of relief, and I hated the pang of guilt I felt.

"Yeah?"

"I was worried."

"I told you I was going for a run."

"It's been almost three hours."

It had?

Fuck.

I sat up and ran a hand down the back of my neck.

I hadn't planned on running for so long, but it made everything quiet.

And I liked the quiet.

When you grew up in loud, usually overcrowded houses, where you had to fight to be heard, fight to eat and wash and sometimes to sleep, you learned to appreciate the silence.

"I'll be home soon," I said, preempting his lecture.

"Don't let me down, Son," he murmured, hanging up.

His parting words were like a shot to the fucking chest. As if I hadn't already majorly disappointed him. Everything I did —or didn't do as the case was—was a disappointment. But I just couldn't find it in myself to do better.

To be better.

WHEN I GOT BACK to the house, I hoped everyone was asleep. But the second I opened the door and heard the television, I knew Asher had stayed up to wait for me.

I headed straight for the kitchen, grabbing a bottle of water from the refrigerator. When I closed the door, he was standing in the doorway, watching me.

"Good run?"

I nodded, twisting the cap and downing the whole bottle.

"You're pushing too hard," he said, stepping into the room.

"I'm fine. I need to shower though." I went to move around him, but he threw out his arm.

"Mya said you saw Ashleigh and Hailee today at the store."

"So?" I held his stare, tension rippling through me.

"You need to give her space," he said, eyes narrowed to thin, assessing slits.

"I know. You don't have to worry."

I wanted nothing to do with her.

"Senior year starts soon. You're both going to—"

"I said you don't have to worry."

He gave me a curt nod, but I saw the concern glittering in his eyes. He didn't trust me.

I didn't blame him.

But he could trust me with this. I had no intentions of going after Ashleigh, of getting close enough to cause any problems. She needed to heal, to adjust to her... situation. And I needed to keep my head down and stay out of trouble.

It was the only way we were going to survive repeating senior year.

"Can I go now?"

Asher studied me, his gaze like a hundred spiders under

my skin. He did this sometimes, looked at me as if he was trying to see past my bravado and cool façade.

It unnerved the shit out of me.

But this time, he stepped aside, letting me off the hook. "Get out of here," he said. "I'll see you in the morning."

I mumbled some reply before heading straight to my room, hoping to avoid Sofia and Aaron. Neither of them appeared, and I breathed a little easier as I slipped into my bedroom at the back of the house.

It was so different to any of the rooms I'd had in foster care. Big and spacious with two windows that overlooked the yard, and the lake beyond that. It was still decorated in gray and blue tones from when I'd first arrived. Mya had begged me to let her redecorate last year, to change it to something more to my taste. But I hadn't wanted it. She'd given up asking eventually.

Sometimes, I wondered why they bothered trying with me. I definitely wondered why they went to so much trouble to adopt me. Part of me thought it was because once I'd turned eighteen, they were worried I'd leave. That I'd just walk out of here and never look back.

I was an asshole, but I wasn't a total douchebag. So I'd given them that. I'd let them make me theirs.

Their son.

If I was expecting it to change things, that once the papers were signed some thread inside me would snap into place and bind me to these people, this family who had done nothing but care for me and try to be there, I was wrong.

Nothing changed.

Nothing felt different.

I didn't suddenly feel like one of them.

A Bennet.

And then the accident had happened, and everything went to shit, and now I wondered if they regretted it.

If they realized what all the other families before that realized—that I wasn't worth it.

THE NEXT MORNING, I ventured downstairs, only to wish I hadn't.

"Morning, Son," Asher said. "Coach Ford stopped by to talk to you."

Shit. That didn't sound good.

My eyes darted to the door I'd just walked through, planning my escape. But Asher was already one step ahead of me.

"Take a seat, Ezra," he said, firmly.

Well, okay then.

Sliding onto one of the stools at the breakfast counter, I glanced between them.

Jason Ford was one of Asher's best friends. He was also the football coach at Rixon High. An NFL legend and local celebrity.

And he was glaring at me like I was the devil incarnate.

"Ezra," he said, coolly. Too fucking coolly. My blood ran cold.

"Hey, what's up?"

"A little birdie tells me you've got a ton of energy you need to burn."

My eyes shot to Asher, and he shrugged. "You're running yourself ragged."

"I am—" I clenched my fist against my thigh, trapping the words behind my gritted teeth.

Just breathe.

"Running helps take my mind off things," I said.

"Me and Ash have been talking and we want you to join the team this year."

"No." I stood up, ready to bolt.

Ready to run.

"It's not a request, Son." Asher pinned me with a hard look. One that said you will fucking do this or suffer the consequences.

"I'll do the year again. I'll keep my head down and study hard." Hard enough to get my diploma at least. "But I'm not cut out for team sports. I'm not—"

"Which is exactly why we want you to become a Raider. You're lost, Son." Asher's expression guttered. "What happened—"

"Don't." I gritted out, unable to stand the invisible weight bearing down on me.

"This will be good for you," he said, giving Coach Ford a strange look. The two of them seemed to have a silent conversation.

I didn't need to decipher it to know what Jason was thinking. Ashleigh was his niece. His family. And it was all my fault she was suffering.

"And if I say no?" I met Jason's heavy stare.

"It's not a choice, Ezra. Training camp is in a few weeks, I expect to see you there."

"But—"

"No buts, Son." Asher let out a heavy sigh. "You will do this."

"Fine. Are we done?" It took everything inside me not to lash out, but it was pointless. They knew I wouldn't argue.

I couldn't.

"Ezra, please—"

"I'm going for a run."

"Don't you think you've been doing enough of that?"

"Let him go," Jason said. "He's going to need all the stamina he can get for practice."

"Whatever." I skulked out of there, grabbing my sneakers off the rack and shoving my feet into them. Maybe I was pushing too hard, but it was better than the constant noise in my head. The images of blinding lights, the sound of Ashleigh's screams.

I'd take physical pain over that any day.

Taking out my cell phone, I opened the music app and jammed my earbuds in, letting the music flow through me.

And then I hit the ground running.

WHEN I GOT BACK to the house, I found Aaron and Sofia hanging out with their friends by the pool. He spotted me before I could make a dash to my room.

"E, come join us," he beckoned me over.

I ignored him, grabbing a drink from the refrigerator and turning to get the hell out of there. But Lily appeared in the doorway, frowning at me.

"Hey," I said, her gaze laser focused on me.

"She's worried about you."

Four little words I didn't want to hear.

Four little words I didn't *deserve* to hear.

She let out a frustrated huff when I didn't reply. "Seriously, Ezra, what the hell is wrong with you? I tell you Ashleigh is worried about you, after everything she's going through and you're just standing there, gawking at me."

"She shouldn't be," I gritted out, every word like glass in my throat.

"Shouldn't be what?" She pursed her lips, judgment swirling in her steely gaze.

"She shouldn't be worried about me." I barged past her, but Lily grabbed my wrist. My eyes dropped to where she was touching me and then flicked upwards. Lily scowled, instantly dropping my arm.

"You know, sometimes I wonder what she sees in you."

As I walked away from her, only one thought ran through my head.

You're not the only one.

CHAPTER SEVEN

Ashleigh

"ASHLEIGH, LILY'S HERE," Dad boomed up the stairs.

I checked my reflection again, nervous energy zipping around my stomach. After too many days cooped up in the house, Lily had suggested we go out somewhere. Just a trip to Riverside. There were food trucks, entertainment, and an arcade. We'd been a hundred times before. It was familiar. Safe.

Except for all those trips I couldn't remember.

"Ash—"

"Yeah, Dad," I yelled back. "I'm coming."

Inhaling a shaky breath, I grabbed my purse and slung it over my body. I hadn't bothered making too much effort, sticking to casual jean shorts and a rainbow motif t-shirt. My long, dark-blonde hair hung in a loose braid over my shoulder, and I'd swiped a layer of gloss onto my lips.

Part of me didn't want to go. I wanted to stay here where it was safe, where I didn't have to deal with my new reality.

But Lily was only in Rixon for another few weeks, and I knew I would regret not spending time with her while I had the chance.

Besides, I was going stir crazy. Some fresh air and a change of scenery would do me good.

I gritted my teeth as I tried to walk the short distance to the staircase unaided. My ankle was still healing, but the cast had finally come off this week. They'd said to take it easy for a while, but every day, I pushed myself a little harder because it gave me some semblance of control.

And I needed that right now.

I needed to feel like I had control over something.

"Hey," I said as soon as Lily came into view.

"Do you need some help?" She went to take a step toward me, but I held up my hand.

"I've got it."

"Ashleigh, we talked about this. You don't need to push—" My dad said.

"And I already told you, Dad, I'm fine." I forced a smile, pain shooting in my leg as I hit the floor a little too hastily.

"Sweetheart?" Concern coated his words, but I made myself smile again, despite the whimper crawling up my throat.

"I'm okay."

"Please take your crutches."

"Dad..."

"You need to give yourself time to heal. The doctor said—"

"Fine, Dad. I'll take them." But whether I would use them was another thing.

"The guys are waiting in the car."

"Guys?" Dad frowned.

"Yeah, Kaiden and Gav."

Relief washed over him. "Oh, that's okay then."

"Come on, let's go," I said. "Before he changes his mind and locks me away in my bedroom."

"Ashleigh, that isn't fair."

"Joke, Dad." I leaned up to kiss his cheek. "I'm joking."

"Be safe, okay. And if you need me..."

"I'll call, I promise."

He gave me a reassuring nod, but I saw the reluctance to let me go in his eyes.

I was his daughter, his little girl. I couldn't even imagine what he and Mom had been through in the days and weeks following the accident.

Before the flood of emotion got the better of me, I grabbed my crutches and followed Lily out to her car.

"I still can't believe you got your driver's permit."

The last I could remember, she still hadn't been ready to take driver's ed.

"I still don't really like driving." She shrugged. "But it's kind of a necessity."

"Well, I'm proud of you, Lil. You're kicking ass."

"I am, aren't I?" She chuckled, going around to the driver's side. Gav, one of Kaiden's best friends, climbed out of the back seat and grinned.

"Remember me?"

"Ha ha, funny." I poked my tongue out at him. But part of me was relieved he wasn't handling me with kiddy gloves. Even if I had limited memories of us ever being friends.

Of course, Lily had filled me in enough to know that me and Gav were friends. We'd even gone to prom together. Platonically, she'd reassured me.

I'd always had this fantasy of prom. Of Ezra finally

realizing he felt the same way about me and asking me to go with him. Him all dressed up, dancing with me in front of our entire class. Holding me, kissing me like he couldn't get enough.

But obviously that didn't happen, not if I went with Gav and our friends.

That pesky pit in my stomach churned a little wider.

"What can I say, Leigh Leigh, I'm a funny guy."

I jerked back at that nickname.

Leigh Leigh.

Lily had said we were friends... she hadn't said he felt comfortable enough around me to call me by the nickname reserved for those closest to me.

"Shit, Leigh, I'm sorry... I didn't—fuck."

"What's the matter?" Lily twisted around to look at us.

"Nothing." I smiled. Strained. All wrong. "Everything's fine. Shall we?" I met Kaiden's stare in the rearview mirror and he nodded.

"It's good to have you back, Ashleigh."

"Thanks."

But as Lily backed out of my driveway, I couldn't shake the feeling that this was a really bad idea.

———

RIVERSIDE WAS CROWDED. Kaiden and Gav kept close to me and Lily as we navigated the streams of people wandering along the promenade.

"What shall we do first?" Lily asked.

"I could eat. They have a taco stand." Kaiden dropped a kiss on her head.

He was sweet with her. Always touching some part of her,

holding open the car door, and guiding her around the place with a hand to the small of her back.

Kaiden was one of the good guys.

And I was so happy she'd found him. Lily was a different girl to the girl I remembered. In some ways, our roles had reversed. I had become the shy, uncertain girl afraid of her own shadow. Except it wasn't my shadow I feared; it was ten months of lost memories and the knowledge that I might never get them back.

"Ashleigh?" he asked.

"Sounds good."

We managed to find a table and the guys joined the line.

"You good?" Lily asked me.

"Yeah, it's weird being here. In the middle of summer." I glanced around, spotting a group of kids from school. Quickly, I ducked my head.

"What's wrong?"

"I... I don't know." I lifted my eyes to meet Lily's concerned gaze. "It's just... I'm guessing everyone knows; about the accident, I mean?"

"Well, yeah, word got around. But people won't know about the amnesia." She reached across the table and laid her hand on mine. "You get to decide who you tell what to, Leigh."

I wasn't sure that was a good thing.

I didn't want to be the local freak, but I also didn't want to have to explain to everyone why I didn't remember anything from the last ten months.

"Hey." Lily must have noticed the sheer panic on my face. "It'll be okay, I promise."

She couldn't promise that though. No one could.

"Oh my God, Ashleigh." Candice Willis, a girl from our class, approached our table with her younger sister in tow.

"You're okay. I mean, I heard about the accident. We all did." She and her sister shared a nod. "You're okay then?"

"I... yeah, I'm fine." My lips pursed.

"I heard Ezra Jackson was driving."

"It's Bennet now," I snapped. "Ezra Bennet. His parents adopted him."

Candice cast me a strange look. "Oh, okay. Well, I just wanted to say hi. Zara and I are enjoying some quality sister time before I leave for college."

"That's... great."

What was happening?

Candice wasn't my friend, there was no way that had happened in the last ten months. She was a vapid mean girl, who basked in the misery of others. We'd avoided her like the plague at school. So the fact she was standing at our table, pretending to care, was utter bullshit.

Thankfully, Kaiden and Gav returned before things got any weirder.

"Move, I'm sitting there." Gav practically barged Candice out of the way and I could have kissed him.

Candice let out an indignant huff before muttering something to her sister and storming off.

"What the fuck did she want?"

"To give me a headache?" I shrugged.

"We got a bit of everything." Kaiden started dishing out the food containers and Gav handed us extra plates and wooden sporks.

"Did you ask her yet?" Kaiden grinned.

"Ask me what?"

"Bryan's parents are away on the weekend."

"When are they not?" Gav mumbled.

Kaiden shot him an irritated look and continued. "Since

he and Carrie-Anne are leaving for college early, we talked him into one last party."

"Oh, I'm not sure—"

"You have to come," Lily said. "It's the last time we'll all be together until who only knows when."

God, those words hurt far more than they were supposed to.

"We're keeping it low key. Us, Aaron and Cole, Sofia, Poppy, a few guys from the team and their girlfriends."

"I don't know..."

"Come on, Leigh. You have to come." Gav pouted. "If for nothing else, then to save me from a night of playing fifth wheel."

"He's right." Lily flashed me her best puppy dog eyes. "You have to come. Gav needs you." Her soft laughter filled the air.

"Okay, Ford. I'm not that desperate."

"I don't know, man. You are pretty desperate."

"Oh, it's like that now?" Gav balled up his napkin and threw it at Kaiden.

I smiled and laughed because that's what you did when your friends were goofing around. But my smile was a little too tight and my laughter was a little too strained.

"At least that's settled," Gav said, flicking his eyes in my direction. "Leigh will come to the party and be my wing-woman."

"I'm sorry. Your what now?"

"Wing-woman. You know, my sidekick."

"He means, you can help him with the ladies."

"I... I'm not sure I want that job."

"Ouch." Gav winced.

"Relax," Kaiden said. "Gav is going through a dry spell; you have nothing to worry about."

"Dude, what happened to the bro code? I know you and Lily are practically joined at the hip now, but you don't have to tell her everything we talk about."

"I'm sure we can find you a nice girl to hook up with." Lily smirked.

"I can get my own pussy, thanks."

"Seriously?" Kaiden's brow lifted.

"What?"

"You're an asshole sometimes."

"The girls aren't offended by the word 'pussy,' am I right?"

"I..." Lily's cheeks burned, but I just shrugged.

"Doesn't offend me."

"See, Leigh isn't offended. She's—"

A woman tripped into our table, spilling her soda everywhere. "Oh my God," she shrieked. "I'm such a klutz."

"Here, let us help." Lily grabbed a wad of napkins, and we began mopping up the mess.

"Thank you. I didn't see the table until it was too late. I'm practically sleepwalking."

We finished cleaning up and the woman hovered. "I'm Penelope by the way."

We all shared a strange look, but Lily smiled at her. "I'm Lily. This is my boyfriend, Kaiden, and my friends Ashleigh and Gav."

"It's nice to meet you. I appreciate the help." A blush worked its way up her neck and into her cheeks. "Well, I guess I should get going. I'm meeting a friend."

"Have fun," Lily replied.

"Bye." Penelope lifted her hand in a small wave and walked off, one soda lighter.

"Well, that wasn't weird at all." Gav snickered.

"Don't be mean," Lily said. "She seemed nice."

"Nicer than Candice," I mumbled.

"At least you won't have to put up with her next semester." Gav stuffed half a taco in his mouth.

"He has a point," Kaiden said. "Candice Willis is a bitch."

"She is," Lily agreed. "But I heard her sister Zara is ten times worse. Poppy and Sofia hate her."

"Great," I grumbled. "Something to look forward to."

CHAPTER EIGHT

Ashleigh

THE PARTY WAS loud and crowded. More crowded than Lily and Kaiden had said it would be.

"I'm so sorry," she said, lacing her arm through mine. "It was supposed to be low key."

"I guess someone let the cat out of the bag."

"Yeah." Bryan strolled up to us. "And when I find out who, heads will roll. Hey, Ashleigh." He smiled. "It's good to see you."

"Hey. Nice party."

"It would have been if half our class hadn't showed up." A loud crash pierced the air and Bryan tensed. "That's my cue. Ladies." He strolled away, bellowing, "I swear to God, I will fuck you up if you've broken anything."

"Oh dear." Carrie-Anne appeared. "This is... not what I expected."

"You're dating Bryan Hughes," Lily said with a smile, as if the two of them were old friends. I guess they were now. "It kind of comes with the territory."

I rubbed my chest, trying to force my racing heart to calm down.

There had been a time I'd lived for a good party. But this: the noise and the people and the constant stares, it was too much. Still, I didn't want to give them anything else to whisper about, so I plastered on a fake smile, clutched my drink like a life raft and kept my mouth shut.

"He isn't like that, not really."

"Yeah, I know." Lily smiled again. "How are you? Are you excited about college?"

"Yes, I can't wait. What about you, Ashleigh?" Carrie-Anne gave me a sympathetic glance. "How are you feeling?"

"Honestly? A little out of my comfort zone."

"Well, I'm glad you came. And Bryan gave me the key to his movie room, so we could go hang out in there... if you want to."

"Actually, that sounds pretty perfect."

"You two go," Lily said. "I'll tell Kaiden and the guys where we're going."

"Come on." Carrie-Anne held out her hand, an offer of friendship, and I took it.

People stopped and stared as we passed them. But I realized they weren't only staring at me. They were staring at Carrie-Anne too.

"Here we go." She pulled out a thin rope necklace from inside her blouse and unhooked the key. "No one will bother us in here."

It was an impressive room. A gray sectional and smaller couch faced a huge movie screen. The lights emitted a blue glow, giving the illusion of an actual movie theater, and there was even a bar area complete with popcorn maker and snack bowl. It was completely over-the-top but I loved it.

"Have I... been here before?"

"You don't remember?"

"I... Lily didn't tell you?"

"Tell me what?" She frowned.

"The accident... something happened." We got situated on one of the couches, the party raging on beyond the door.

"You don't have to tell me," she said.

"I know. I want to. It's just... you're the first person I've actually explained it to." I inhaled a shuddering breath, trying to find the courage to explain it to her. "I have something called retrograde amnesia."

"You lost your memory."

I nodded. "Ten months."

She gasped. "Senior year?"

Another nod. "I woke up and thought it was still September."

"Oh my God, Ashleigh. I had no idea."

"It's not something I'm advertising but I guess people will find out eventually." My shoulders lifted in a small shrug.

"So you can't remember anything?"

"Nothing."

Not a damn thing, and it was becoming increasingly frustrating as the days went on.

"Lily and Peyton filled me in on some stuff, and my parents tried to piece things together. But the memories are gone. Finals... prom... graduation..."

"That must be so hard, I'm sorry."

"Thanks." A strained smile tugged at my mouth. "So, you and Bryan, huh? I gotta admit, I never saw that coming. I mean, obviously, I did, but..."

Carrie-Anne laughed. "He's... my best friend. That sounds so corny, doesn't it? But being with Bryan is... it's everything I never knew I needed."

"You deserve to be happy."

Lily appeared at the door. "Hey, mind if we join you?" She pulled Poppy and Sofia inside, and the three of them joined us on the sectional.

"God, Bryan has the best house."

"He really, really does." Carrie-Anne grinned. "But it makes me so mad that he's here so much alone."

"He won't have that problem soon when you're both away at college."

Gav had grumbled something about Bryan's parents always being away, but I didn't want to ask about the specifics. People would grow tired quickly of having to keep getting me up to speed about things. So I sat quietly and listened.

"Yeah. God, I can hardly wait. Five more days."

My chest constricted.

They were leaving. Then it would be Lily and Kaiden. And Gav.

And I'd be stuck here.

"Senior year will be fun though," Poppy said as if she heard my thoughts. "I know it isn't what you wanted." She gave me a sympathetic smile. "But at least you'll have me and Sofia."

"Yeah." I wondered if my expression looked as forced as I sounded.

Carrie-Anne jumped up and went over to the bar. "I thought we could celebrate." She pulled out two bottles of champagne. "Since this is the last time we'll all probably be together."

Lily glanced at me and frowned. "Carrie-Anne, it's not—"

"Lil, it's okay," I said. "She's right. Who knows when this might happen again?"

Besides, a glass or two of alcohol might settle the tumultuous storm raging inside me.

Carrie-Anne let out a shriek of approval, handing around

pink plastic champagne flutes. "I've been waiting for a reason to use these. Bryan's parents bought the champagne for my mom, but she didn't want it. It was all very awkward, so I stashed it here."

"Fill me up." Poppy grinned, holding her flute up.

"Two glasses," Lily said with a pointed look.

"Relax, *Mom*. I promise not to get wasted and do anything too questionable."

"Oh my God, Poppy, you're so bad."

"I know." She grinned. "It's fun, isn't it?"

"Maybe it'll give you enough courage to put the moves on Aaron." Sofia threw her a knowing look.

"He's not... I mean... we're friends."

"But you could be friends with benefits."

"Seriously, Sofe, that's your brother you're talking about."

"So? I know he's not a saint! Besides, if he's hooking up with you, at least I won't have to deal with any psycho-girlfriends." She scrunched her nose as if the idea repulsed her.

Carrie-Anne finally reached me and filled my glass. I brought it to my lips and slowly sipped at the bubbles. It was nicer than I expected. Fizzy with a fruity aftertaste. Without overthinking it, I knocked the glass back and downed it in one.

"Another won't hurt," I said, noticing the four of them watching me.

Carrie-Anne shrugged, giving me a refill.

"Thanks."

"Senior year could be interesting, you know," she said. "Poppy is hung up on Aaron, you're hung up on Ezra, and Sofia likes—"

"No one. Sofia likes no one."

"So, I didn't see you and Cole Kandon making moon eyes

at each other the other day when we were all over at your house?"

"He's my brother's best friend."

"And?" Lily said.

"And there's a rule for that kind of thing. Even if there was something between us, and there's not, he would never act on it."

"You know my mom and dad got together despite dad being Uncle Jase's best friend," I said to no one in particular, staring at the bubbles in my drink. The way they drifted toward the top and then popped into oblivion.

"Guys like to think they have a bro code, but when it comes down to it, they only think with their dicks."

"Poppy!" Lily gasped.

"What? It's true." She slurped her drink and I realized she was probably already a little drunk. "Guys have a one-track mind."

"You mean, most guys."

She shrugged. "I guess Kaiden is different."

"Kaiden *and* Bryan." Carrie-Anne cleared her throat.

But I was barely paying them any attention, too stuck on the part where Poppy had said guys had a one-track mind.

It wasn't all guys, I knew that, but she had a point. Most teenage guys thought about sex—a lot. Heck, most of them were doing it a lot. They usually wanted no-string hookups.

Ezra had never once tried anything with me.

Not once.

All the times I'd been there, forced myself into his space and refused to budge, he'd never once taken what I would have gladly offered.

My stomach sank. Ezra was gorgeous. Mysterious and brooding. Girls noticed him, got all dreamy-eyed and breathless whenever he was around. And yet, I'd never seen him with a single girl.

How was that possible?

Surely, he had needs. Urges and fantasies.

Even if he didn't want a relationship, he would have zero issues finding someone willing to fool around. Maybe he already had.

Someone except me.

Irritation flashed inside me. I hadn't been this self-conscious before the accident. Sure, I'd been knocked back by him a couple of times, but I never let it dent my persistence. Because there were moments, small glimpses where Ezra did let me in. They were rare and precious, but real, nonetheless. And I treasured them. Clung onto them and held them tight, letting them grow into something bigger.

But never once did I feel so... so uncertain about who I was and what I wanted.

Oh God, what if I'd been fooling myself all this time.

"I need some fresh air," I said, downing my second drink.

"Do you want me to come—"

"No, stay." I locked eyes with Lily, silently telling her everything I couldn't say. "I'll be back."

Before she could argue, I turned and walked out of the movie room. I hadn't expected to walk straight into the guys, but that's exactly what happened.

"Trying to escape already?" Gav asked.

"I need some fresh air." I went to move around them, but he grabbed my arm, his eyes narrowed with concern.

"I'll come with you."

"Gav, you don't have to do that," I said.

"I know I don't, but I want to. Let me help."

"Fine, okay. But only if you promise to find me another drink."

I didn't want to witness the night in black and white, I wanted to see it in Technicolor. I wanted to be so overstimulated that it was impossible to dwell on what had happened.

"I'm not sure that's—"

"I swear to God, Gav, if you say that's not a good idea, I will lose my... Ever. Loving. Shit."

"Understood." He smirked, motioning for me to follow him out of the house and into the yard.

"How's it going then?"

"How's what going?" he asked.

"You know, the pussy hunt."

"Pussy hunt." He spluttered. "Wow, Leigh, how many of those have you had tonight?" His gaze dropped to the empty glass still in my hand.

I hadn't realized I'd brought it with me. But now I had, part of me never wanted to let it go.

"I'm fine. But I do need another drink."

"Lily will hang me by the balls if she finds out I plied you with alcohol and let you drown your sorrows with the likes of me."

"What's wrong with the likes of you?"

"Nothing. I'm... Forget it."

"You're not that bad, Gav."

"Nice, Leigh Leigh, real nice." He slung his arm around my shoulder and led me toward the kitchen, grabbing a bottle of something as we passed. I didn't really care what it was, I just needed to get out of here.

I needed air.

I needed to get out of my goddamn head.

A few people gawked at us but the alcohol coursing through my veins made everything fade into the background.

Mom and Dad would kill me if they knew I was drinking.

But I liked it. I liked being out of my own head, not overthinking, overanalyzing, obsessing over everything I'd lost.

Because that was exhausting.

"Here we go," Gav guided me to a chair and nudged me down. I fell with an *oomph*, giggling as my ass hit the seat.

"You're drunk," he said.

"So I am." I flashed him a toothy grin.

"Well, I might as well join you." He unscrewed the bottle of liquor and drank a generous amount, hissing through his teeth when he was done. "That's strong."

"Wimp." I chuckled, leaning back in the chair and kicking my legs out in front of me. A blanket of stars twinkled down on us. Inky black sky for miles. It was so beautiful. Vast and endless.

For that split second in time, it made me feel better, like things would all work out and be okay.

Until Gav opened his mouth and ruined it.

"Repeating senior year, that's gotta be rough."

"Yeah," I murmured, really not wanting to get into it.

"If it's any consolation, I'll still be around."

"What?" I glanced over at him. "I thought you were heading to Maryland."

"That was the plan. But I can't leave my mom and sister." He shrugged as if it was no big deal. I sensed it was though. "Can't do it."

"What will you do instead?"

"I spoke to Rixon Community College. I can take some classes there, look into getting a part-time job."

"Giving up college for your family." I let out a thin breath. "That's a big deal."

"Yeah, well, sometimes you gotta do what you can do. And they need me... more than I need freshman pussy."

"Oh my God, you're such a dork."

"A hot dork though, right?" Gav smirked but it didn't reach his eyes. He looked... lost.

Without thinking, I reached for his hand and grabbed it. His eyes widened a little. "You're a good guy, Gav," I said. "Don't ever forget that."

"You know what they say about good guys, Leigh Leigh?"

"What?"

"Good guys always finish last."

CHAPTER NINE

Ezra

"EZRA." Pen smiled, weaving her way toward me through the empty diner. "I wasn't expecting to see you tonight."

"Needed one of Manny's burgers."

It wasn't a total lie.

There wasn't much that one of his homemade patties couldn't fix, but I wasn't only here for the food. There was a party at Bryan Hughes's house. I'd heard Sofia and Aaron talking about it. It was a low-key thing. Football team players and their girls only.

And Ashleigh.

I'd wanted to rage at them—to tell them she wasn't ready to be at some party, getting drunk, and making all kinds of teenage mistakes. But it wasn't my right, so I'd done the next best thing. Gone for a run, showered, and then headed straight here.

Although from the way Penny was looking at me, I was thinking it was a mistake coming here.

"Usual table?" she said, breaking the thick tension. I

nodded, following her toward the back of the diner. "You need a menu, or do you want your usual?"

"Usual, please."

"Every time." She smiled again, her eyes glittering with something I didn't want to acknowledge.

Aaron was right, she was cute. Those dark, long lashes framing big brown eyes. Legs for days peeking out from under The Junction standard issue red and white striped outfit.

"What?"

Her voice snapped me from my thoughts.

"I... uh, shit, sorry."

"It's okay." That soft laughter of hers made the knot in my stomach unravel. "I'll ring your order through and get your drink."

"Thanks."

I pulled out my cell, unsurprised to find a string of text messages from Aaron.

Aaron: You should come party with us.

Aaron: E, man, come on. Everyone's here. Leigh is here...

DAMN HIM. Dangling her in front of me like temptation I wasn't strong enough to resist.

But I had to. Because me going after Ashleigh would only result in more pain and anguish.

Too many people were involved now.

I had to stay away.

Even if it fucking killed me.

I clenched my fist as I considered my reply.

Me: I'm out.

Aaron: On a hot date?

Me: You wish.

Aaron: Yeah, I do. Maybe if you got laid, you wouldn't be such a grumpy asshole.

I SMILED AT THAT.

"Something funny?" Penny arrived with my drink.

"Nah, just Aaron being a dick."

"Aaron? Is that the guy you came in with the other night?"

"Yeah, he's my... foster brother."

"He seemed nice."

"He's a pain in my ass." I snorted.

"Aren't brothers supposed to be?"

"You have a brother?"

She nodded. "Max. He's eleven and a total pain in my ass too." Her eyes lit up with affection. "But I love that kid, something fierce. He's the reason I kill myself with double shifts here."

My brows furrowed. "What do you mean?"

"I... our mom isn't on the scene. Hasn't been for a long time. We live with my gran but she's sick." Her expression faltered. "And you didn't come here to hear me offload all this. I'm sorry, I'll be back with your order soon."

Penny went to walk away, but I blurted out, "Wait."

"Yeah?" Hope shone in her eyes.

"Do you have a break coming up?"

"It's pretty dead, I'm sure Manny won't mind me taking ten."

I flicked my eyes to the empty seat opposite me.

"Oh. Oh, okay." She slid onto the bench. "This is... unexpected."

"I figured you could use the company as much as me." I shrugged.

I didn't want her to get the wrong impression, but there was something about her admission a minute ago that struck a chord with me.

"So you look after your brother?" I asked.

"Something like that. My gran raised us, did a fine job too. But she fell sick right before my senior year. She had to stop working but the bills didn't stop coming, you know? So I begged Manny for a job and I've been here ever since."

"You take classes at Rixon Community College too?"

"Yeah. Only part-time though because I need to work. I want to be a teacher one day. But until Max is old enough..." She trailed off.

"I had no idea."

"Well, we've never really talked." She gave me a shy smile. "What about you, Ezra Jackson? What's your story?"

"You know my story." I slouched back and ran a hand over my jaw.

"No, I only know what I've heard around town and from Manny."

"The accident..."

"People talk, Ezra."

And wasn't that the truth. But it had always been background noise before. When I'd moved to Rixon and become the Bennets' foster child. When I didn't fit in with the kids at school. When I wandered around town in my hoodies, keeping my head down and my mouth shut.

Rixon was a small town. Everyone knew everyone. They greeted each other in the street or at the store. They came out on game night to support their beloved Raiders. The football team were local celebrities, worshipped and adored.

And I was the outsider.

The strange boy from out of town plucked up by the Bennets and given a shot at a better life.

The boy who to everyone around him, was squandering that chance.

"Yeah, well people don't usually know what the fuck they're talking about."

"You're preaching to the choir, E." A dark shadow lingered in her eyes. "Just because they talk doesn't mean I listen to what they're saying."

"Is that right?"

Shit. It sounded like I was flirting.

I wasn't.

Was I?

Pen was cute, sure. Easy to talk to, and like me, she clearly had baggage of her own. But I wasn't about that. Not with her. Not with Ashleigh or anyone else.

Yet, it felt good to know that maybe someone got it.

Ashleigh had always tried to understand, to pick me apart and understand what made me tick. But I'd always felt like a science project; a puzzle she needed to solve. She had the perfect life. The perfect parents. A lovely home, and a bright future. I was nothing more than a square peg in a round hole. I didn't fit.

I couldn't *make* myself fit.

So no matter how much Ashleigh pushed, no matter how much she wanted me—and I knew she did, it was in her eyes every time she looked at me—I would never let myself trust her motivations because we were from different worlds. Two planets set on entirely different trajectories.

Pen gave me another smile. She didn't push or dig or try to get me to open up. She was content with the silence.

Just like me.

———

"YOU'RE HEADING OUT?" Pen asked me some time later.

She hadn't sat and talked for long. A group of people just passing through town had arrived, looking for something to eat before they got on the road again. But I'd stuck around, happy to watch the world go by. Trying my best not to think about Ashleigh at that fucking party.

Even after everything that had happened, she would bounce back. Ashleigh's friends and family would make sure she felt like one of them still. And it was a selfish fucking thing, a masochistic thing, but part of me wondered if it was better she didn't get those missing memories back. The ones of us together, her following me around, pushing herself into my space. Her unrelenting attempts at breaking down my steel reinforced walls... The occasional times she slipped through, and she had. Ashleigh had forced her way into my life and buried herself under my skin in a way I hadn't expected.

So yeah, maybe it was for the best she didn't remember.

Remember me. Us. And how epically I'd fucked things up.

"Yeah, it's late," I said. "I should get back. Someone is around to help you lock up, right?"

Manny had left earlier when they stopped taking food orders.

"Yeah, Jarod is out back somewhere. He gives me a ride home."

"Good, that's... good."

"So I was thinking." She scribbled something down on her notepad and tore off the page, holding it out for me. "If you ever want to meet outside of work hours..."

"Pen." I let out a heavy sigh.

"I know, I know. You're not into me like that." I could have sworn I saw a hint of disappointment in her eyes. "But I liked talking to you tonight, and I think you liked talking to me too. And well, we could all use another friend in the world. Just think about it."

Plucking the note from her fingers, I shoved it in my pocket. "Yeah, I'll think about it."

A soft chuckle escaped her lips. "You do that. Goodnight, Ezra."

"Night, Pen." I slipped out of the diner and shoved my hands in my pocket, my fingers grazing Pen's number.

Friends.

I could do friends.

And maybe she was right, maybe we could all do with another friend in the world.

THE HOUSE WAS quiet when I finally got back. I grabbed a bottle of water and headed straight for my room. It was only then I heard Sofia and Poppy's muted giggles.

Drunken giggles.

Rolling my eyes, I kept walking, until I caught a name.

Ashleigh.

"Did you see her with Gav? They make a cute couple."

Gav?

My body went rigid.

"I don't think they're into each other like that," Sofia said.

"Yeah, but they could be. I heard him tell Kaiden and Bryan he's not going away to Maryland. He's staying in Rixon. Something to do with his mom and sister."

"I always figured Ashleigh would wear Ezra down. The two of them would be so good together, but it's like he's..."

Their voices became muffled. Probably a good thing. I didn't want to hear whatever Sofia had to say about me.

Whatever it was, it wouldn't be good.

Heading for my room, I closed the door behind me and peeled out of my clothes and dropped onto the bed.

Ashleigh and Gav.

It shouldn't have bothered me half as much as it did. He was an okay guy. Seemed to care about her in his own way. They'd gone to prom together as friends. But I didn't know how to feel about the fact he would be staying in Rixon.

I guess it didn't really matter now. Ashleigh needed friends. She needed people in her corner and Gavin McKay was the perfect candidate.

I'd added Penny's number to my contacts, so I scrolled through and found it. She would be home now. Possibly even asleep.

Fuck. I wouldn't even know what to say anyway.

The vibration of my cell phone startled the shit out of me, and I pulled up the message from an unknown number.

Weird.

Until I read the words and my stomach dropped into my fucking toes.

Unknown: Everyone keeps telling me you're avoiding me because of what happened. Because you blame yourself. But I know you, Ezra… something else is going on. Just tell me, please… Please talk to me.

FUCK.

Fuck!

I clenched my teeth together until it hurt, needing the flash of pain to ground me. Ashleigh knew—of course she fucking knew—something was wrong.

My fingers hovered, but I couldn't do it. I couldn't text her back and explain.

Even if I wanted to.

So I did the only thing I could.

I deleted her message and texted Penny instead.

CHAPTER TEN

Ashleigh

"WHAT THE—" My eyelids fluttered open, my stomach lurching as I tried to get my bearings.

Strange room. Unfamiliar bed. Half-clothed boy beside me.

"Please tell me we didn't—"

"Stop. Talking," Gav grumbled from somewhere under his hair. He was face down on the bed, hair falling into his eyes.

"What the hell happened?"

"Vodka. Too much vodka." He finally rolled onto his side, meeting my horrified stare. "Good morning to you too."

"Why are we *in* bed together?"

"We're not in bed, we're on it. And it was either crash here or sleep outside. I figured you'd appreciate somewhere more comfortable than Bryan's loungers."

"I... damn, my head hurts." I fumbled for the nightstand, grabbing my cell phone. There was a couple of messages from my parents, telling me to enjoy the party and be careful.

Another saying they were happy for me to stay over so long as Lily was too.

I exited out of the message thread, but my eye caught on another thread.

Oh no.

Ezra.

I'd texted Ezra last night. But how had I—

The memory slammed into me. Stealing Aaron's cell phone to get Ezra's number while we were all soaking up the copious amounts of alcohol with cold pizza.

It was pretty astonishing for someone as drunk as I'd been. But it didn't matter because Ezra hadn't replied. I'd pretty much begged him to tell me what the matter was... and he'd completely ignored me.

If that wasn't a giant sign, I didn't know what was.

"Hey, you okay?"

I glanced over to find Gav watching me. "Yeah, fine."

"Wouldn't happen to be anything to do with that drunken text message you sent Ezra, would it?"

"I told you about that?" My eyes widened.

"I have vague memories of you making me check it for spelling accuracy."

"I did not."

"No." He chuckled around an amused smirk. "But you told me you were texting him."

"Oh." My stomach sank deeper.

"I'm guessing from the glum expression that he didn't text back."

I shook my head, my cheeks burning with dejection.

"His loss."

It didn't feel like it, but I swallowed the words.

"I need water... and a shower... and something to soak up this hangover. Maybe not in that order."

Gav sat up and kicked his legs over the side of the bed, the sheet sliding off his body, revealing his very bare, very muscular legs. He didn't seem fazed though, grabbing his cargo shorts and hiking them on. He glanced back at me and smiled. "I'll see what I can do."

"Oh, I didn't mean—"

"Relax. I can manage to hunt down a glass of water, some Advil, and a pancake or two." He headed for the door, but I called after him. "Yeah?"

"Thanks," I said. "For everything."

"Stick with me, Leigh Leigh, and you won't go wrong." He winked and slipped into the hall.

And I sat there wondering what the hell had just happened.

———

GAV DIDN'T RETURN, so after washing up as best I could, I went in search of him.

"Shit, sorry," he said when I found him in Bryan's huge, open plan kitchen. "I was just coming, I swear."

"It's okay. Can I?" I motioned to the bottle of water and pain pills in his hands.

"Sure, here."

"It was my fault," Bryan said. "I was trying to make him see sense about college."

"I already told you, man. It's a done deal. Mom won't admit it, but she needs me here."

"You shouldn't have to—"

"Dude," Gav snapped, letting out a sigh of frustration, "I said leave it."

"Fine." Bryan held up his hands in defeat. "But I think you're making the wrong call."

"It's only college. I can reapply next year."

"Hmm, something smells good." Carrie-Anne wandered into the kitchen, looking far too bright and breezy given how rough I felt.

"Morning, Kitty Cat." Bryan hooked his arm around her neck and pulled her in for a kiss.

Gav caught my eye and shook his head as if to say, 'told you,' but I'd seen enough of their PDA last night to know they couldn't keep their hands off each other.

"Where are Lily and Kaiden?" I asked. Poppy and Sofia had gone home with Aaron and Cole last night, but Lily had promised she wouldn't leave without me, so I assumed she was still here somewhere.

"Oh, don't expect them to rise until at least ten."

"Yeah, they were awake most of the night if the noises coming from—"

"Bry." Carrie-Anne nudged his ribs with her elbow.

"What? Lily is a—"

"Lily is a what?" Kaiden appeared in the doorway, brow cocked.

"Is a sweetheart, of course," Bryan stuttered and we all snickered.

"I'm glad you think so." Lily strolled into the kitchen so full of confidence and poise, it was almost like looking at a different girl to the one I'd known ten months ago.

How time changed things.

She came over to me. "How are you feeling?"

"Like I drank my body weight in vodka."

"You did a pretty good job."

I flipped Gav off and he chuckled.

"I was worried," she whispered.

"I'm fine. I think I just needed to let loose, ya know?"

Her pinched expression told me she didn't. But I couldn't

really explain it beyond that. Watching them all together, it was hard. Harder than I anticipated. Like being present but unable to reach them, a crystal-clear glass wall separating us. I could hear them, see them, and communicate with them. But I wasn't *with* them.

So I'd gone outside with Gav and we'd drank and talked and drank some more. It wasn't my brightest idea ever, but it was what I needed in that moment. And surprisingly, as the night went on, I could understand why Gav and I had become friends over the last few months. He was witty and smart and didn't take himself too seriously. But he also let me talk. And he wasn't afraid of the silence. The stilted moments when neither of us wanted to speak or knew what to say.

It wasn't like that with Ezra. Every conversation we'd ever had was hard work. Usually me fighting, clawing for every word and response from him. And in the rare moments he did open up to me, he never really let me past his defenses.

I was beginning to wonder why I'd bothered. He clearly didn't care—not the way I did.

He hadn't visited me in the hospital. He didn't text me back or speak to me at the store. In fact, he'd gone out of his way to ignore me.

It hurt, knowing that the boy I'd always rooted for, the boy my heart had long ago decided was hers, had written me off so easily.

Had something happened between us that I couldn't remember? Is that why things were so awkward between us? Why he didn't want anything to do with me?

We were obviously still talking for me to be in his car the night of graduation. But what had happened leading up to that, I had no idea because he wouldn't talk to me.

"Your mom and dad will kill me if they find out you were—"

"That's why we won't tell them." I flashed her the best smile I could muster.

The truth was, I felt like I could sleep for a week. And maybe I would now we were another day closer to Lily leaving and senior year commencing.

I had zero desire to be a senior again. Especially when everyone around me knew the truth. Maybe I could talk my parents out of it? I was nineteen in a couple of months. An adult. Surely, it was my decision to make?

Oh, who was I kidding? They were just doing what they thought was best for me. But I wasn't sure spending another year with Ezra was a good idea. We'd be forced to see one another, to take classes together, and play nice.

When all I wanted was to keep him in the past...

Where he clearly wanted to be.

I SPENT the day sleeping off the hangover from hell. Thankfully, when I got home, Mom and Dad were out, so I was able to sneak upstairs and crash.

When I woke up, my stomach growled. So I pulled on a hoodie and slipped out of my room to go in search of food, but paused when I heard Uncle Jason's voice.

"Don't like it."

"He failed senior year, Jase." That was Aunt Felicity. "He deserves a shot at—"

"She almost died."

The animosity in his voice startled me. Lily had said they blamed Ezra, but I hadn't expected to hear such venom in his words.

"She's okay, Jase," Dad said. "Ashleigh is a fighter; she's going to get through this. If he's on the team..."

Team?

Surely not?

The last thing Ezra would ever want to do was join the Rixon Raiders. He barely made it to gym class last year. Ezra Jackson and team sports were two phrases that had no business being put together.

Ezra wasn't a team player.

He was a lone wolf.

Someone who marched to the beat of his own drum.

Heart racing in my chest, I slowly maneuvered the stairs, heading for the kitchen before I could overhear anything else.

The adults all paused the second I stepped inside.

"Ashleigh, sweetheart." Mom smiled. "We didn't realize you were awake."

"Hey, Mom. I got hungry."

"I'm making spaghetti. It shouldn't be too long now."

"Cool," I said, heading for the breakfast counter.

"How was the party?" Dad asked, pulling out a stool for me. He helped me onto it, and I rested my chin on my fists, watching as Mom stirred the sauce.

"It was good."

"We heard it got a little crowded," Uncle Jase said with a hint of accusation.

"Yeah, a lot of people turned up uninvited, but there wasn't any trouble or anything."

"You should have called—"

"Relax, Dad. I was fine. The girls looked after me."

"Good." He nodded. "That's good. How did you get home?"

There was concern in my dad's every sentence. It was exhausting, but I couldn't tell him. Not when I understood why it was there. It would have been nice to just be able to join in like I remembered I would have pre-accident. Just be able to take a seat and join in whatever conversation was happening.

"Kaiden gave me a ride."

"I can't believe they leave for college soon." Uncle Jase whipped off his ball cap and ran a hand through his dark hair.

"Kaiden is a good kid, he'll look out for Lily." Dad patted my uncle's arm.

"It's not Kaiden I'm worried about," he grumbled. "You know what college kids can be like. Everything's different. New and.... more."

"Lily can handle it," I said. She seemed to have things under control.

"Yeah." Aunt Felicity smiled. "She's come a long way."

Mom came over and pulled me into a hug. "Your day will come, baby. You just have to take a little detour first."

Yeah, a detour right back to senior year.

"Sure, Mom," I murmured.

"Look at it this way." She held me at arm's length. "You get a second shot at it, sweetheart. Not many people can say that."

"Hmm, not really selling it to me, Mom."

"No, I guess not." Sympathy flooded her expression. "But I think it's for the best. At least until..." She didn't say the words, because with every new day that dawned where I didn't have a memory epiphany, the hope that they would ever return seemed further out of reach.

CHAPTER ELEVEN

Ashleigh

THE SUN BEAT down on me as I lay on one of the Bennets' loungers while my cousins and friends fooled around in the swimming pool.

I hadn't wanted to go in, still feeling a little delicate after my hangover yesterday. But I was content watching them, soaking up our last summer together before everything changed. Again.

Mya was with my mom at the gallery, helping her prepare for her upcoming installation. She'd always been creative, ever since high school. A passion I unfortunately did not share. She'd suggested painting might help with things, but I wasn't feeling it. Mya had a ton of suggestions, different therapies and exercises to try. But she hadn't pushed. If anything, she was still a little standoffish with me. But she was spending the day with Mom, so things couldn't be that strained between them.

"I made virgin margaritas," Sofia said, her and Lily

appearing with a tray of drinks in their hands. "They're so freaking good."

"They'd be even better with the tequila, Sofe," Aaron said.

"Like you didn't drink enough Saturday night."

"I wasn't that bad." He poked his tongue out at her.

"Bad enough that Dad threatened your ass with pool cleaning duty for the rest of the summer."

"He's all talk. I apologized for puking in the flower bed."

"Ugh, gross, you didn't." Poppy blanched.

"It had to come out, Pops." He grinned back at her.

"Here, Leigh." Sofia handed me a drink.

"Don't let party girl near the liquor."

"Haha." I narrowed my eyes at Cole.

"Leave her alone. She's allowed to have a blow out after everything."

"Never again," I murmured. "I still don't feel right."

"We've all been there." Aaron lazed back on his floatie, a huge green crocodile he'd nicknamed Nile.

He was such a goofball.

Poppy and Carrie-Anne shared a conspiratorial look and then in a coordinated attack, grabbed Nile's tail and flipped Aaron clean off into the water. He surfaced, spluttering and choking while we all laughed.

"Oh, it's like that, huh?" His eyes lasered in on Poppy.

"Aaron." She started backing away. "It was a joke. We were—"

He dived at her, pulling her under with him. When she surfaced, she was red in the face and seething.

"You ass. I didn't want to get my hair wet."

"Shouldn't play with fire, Pops, if you don't wanna get burned." He smirked and we all caught the moment between them.

RUINED HOPES

Poppy and Aaron shared something rare and precious. They'd always gravitated to one another, but neither of them were brave enough to act on it, always quick to point out they were just friends. But Aaron looked at her the way Kaiden looked at Lily, and Bryan looked at Carrie-Anne. Full of love and longing. The fact she chose to ignore it was impressive. But sometimes the truth scared people. I understood that better than anyone.

While I'd always been pretty upfront with Ezra about my intentions, I'd never wholly admitted how I felt about him.

I got up and excused myself to go use the bathroom. I didn't need it, but I did need a second to collect my emotions. When I returned, the guys were all in the pool playing water polo with Lily and Carrie-Anne. Sofia and Poppy were sitting on their loungers talking, but when they noticed me, their expressions dropped.

"What's wrong?" Dread snaked through me.

Poppy glanced at Sofia, and she let out a sigh. "Aaron thinks Ezra has a date."

The words echoed through me.

A date.

He had a date.

The ground felt shaky beneath my feet.

"With who?" The tremor in my voice matched the way my body vibrated.

Sofia gave me a sympathetic smile. "He thinks it's the girl from the diner, the waitress."

The waitress...

My heart sank. He'd moved on. I'd been in a coma and woken up with almost a year of my life missing and Ezra had walked away and gotten himself a date.

I guess life really had moved on.

"We're so sorry, Leigh. Maybe he's—"

"Don't," I clipped out.

My heart was already in tatters, I wasn't sure I could handle anything else.

"At least we've got Lily's going away party to look forward to, although I guess you might not want to come now—"

"Of course I'm coming," I replied, a little too harshly. But sometimes Poppy was so clueless to people's feelings.

"Sorry. I just didn't know if you'd want to, given the circumstances."

"Lily's family. Of course I'll be there." Even if saying goodbye to her, watching our friends and family bestow her with well wishes for college would be incredibly hard.

I lay back down, and Sofia and Poppy went back to their conversation, avoiding Ezra's name in my presence.

But I couldn't avoid thoughts of him on a date with some waitress. Ezra didn't date—at least, that's the vibe he'd always given off. So if he'd found a girl he wanted to willingly spend time with, she must have been really special.

Maybe they'd been dating a while? No one knew he'd been hanging out at The Junction did they? Fact was no one really knew Ezra at all. Is that why he had been avoiding me? Maybe he'd rejected me but hadn't rejected her.

All I knew was I couldn't face seeing them together.

―――

EVERYONE HEADED down to Riverside after soaking up the summer sun at the Bennets' pool. I made my excuses.

Maybe I was a coward, avoiding any scenario where I ran into Ezra and his date. But I couldn't wrap my head around the idea, not yet. Not while I was still stuck in a time where I was the girl who managed to sometimes bring Ezra out of his shell.

He might not have been very forthcoming, but the scraps of attention he'd given me made me feel special. Made me feel like I was the only girl who could get through to him.

Had that all been a lie? Something I made up in my head to make myself feel better? And what the hell had happened between then and now to make him not even be able to reply to a simple text message?

Even if he didn't feel the same, he could text me back and tell me. It was unfair to leave me hanging like this. He knew what had happened in that ten months I couldn't remember.

He was there that night, the night everything went to shit.

So why not fill in the blanks for me, even if he then left me the hell alone? He owed me that much at least.

Gav offered to give me a ride home since he had to get back to babysit his sister, Millie.

"Thanks," I said when we arrived at my house.

"You good? You were quiet this afternoon."

"I found out something about Ezra."

I didn't know why I could talk to him about this, but there was something about him that put me at ease.

"About his date."

"So you heard?" I focused on my hands, wringing them in my lap.

"Yeah. Aaron was pretty excited… Shit, I didn't mean—"

"It's okay. I get it." I sucked in a sharp breath. "I just want to know what happened. I mean, I know what people keep telling me… but Ezra wouldn't just quit on me like that. He wouldn't."

"Ten months is a long time, maybe something happened—"

My head whipped up. "Do you know something?"

"I swear, I don't." He held up his hands. "I'm just saying, a lot can happen in ten months. And you two weren't exactly open about your relationship."

Because we didn't have a relationship. We had a tenuous friendship at best. Ezra would never have pursued me, not the way I relentlessly went after him. But everyone deserved at least one friend in the world. And ever since the day he had arrived at the Bennets, I'd been dead set on being his.

"It's not... it wasn't like that between us."

He gave me a knowing look. "But you wanted it to be."

It wasn't a question, and I wondered if I'd confided in Gav like this before.

"You haven't," he said as if he knew exactly what I was thinking. "I mean, we've talked about him before. But not like this."

"So why now?"

"Because things are different now and I know what it's like to feel like your life is out of your control."

"Your mom—"

"Let's not make this about me. I'm fully aware of my decisions and the consequences they bear."

"You're doing what's right for your family."

"Yeah." He ran a hand down his face and blew out a steady breath. "If only it were that simple."

"I'm here. If you ever need to talk, I'm here." It seemed only fair to reciprocate his patience and understanding, even if I still didn't truly understand the depths of our friendships. After all, actions spoke louder than words, and Gav had been nothing but there for me since I got out of the hospital.

"Thanks, Leigh Leigh, but you don't have to worry about me." His expression hardened, and I knew that was the end of that particular conversation.

And it hit me how strange it was that I felt more

comfortable with Gav—a guy I couldn't even remember being friends with—than my own friends and family.

"I'll see you soon, okay?"

"Sure thing," he said, his expression giving little away.

I climbed out of his car and started for the door. But his voice gave me pause. "You've got this, Ashleigh. Even if it feels like right now you don't."

I gave him a small nod, too choked up to reply.

How did he know what I was thinking as I walked away? How did he know exactly the right thing to say to ease the knot in my stomach?

I didn't have all the answers, but I was grateful.

The second I went inside, Dad called, "Leigh, is that you?"

"Yeah. Be right in." I kicked off my sandals and put my purse on the stairs before going to find my dad.

"How was your day?" he asked.

"It was good. Everyone went on to Riverside, but I didn't feel like it."

"Headache?"

"No, I'm okay."

It came and went, but for the most part, it was manageable now.

"Just remember to take it easy, okay? The doctor said—"

"I know, Dad. You don't have to worry."

"Of course I do, you're my little girl. That's never going to change, Ashleigh."

"I love you, Dad." I went over and laid my head on his arm. He wrapped it around me and pulled me closer.

"I love you too, sweetheart. So much. And I want you to know, I'm so proud of how you're handling everything."

"Don't really have much choice." Strained laughter bubbled out of me.

"That's not true." He looked at me with those all-seeing eyes of his. "You could have locked yourself in your room and refused to face this head on. But you didn't. I can't pretend to know what it's like... to be missing so much... but I am in awe of your strength, sweetheart. Of how mature you've been about everything."

His nice words were too much. Didn't he see the cracks in my carefully constructed veneer? Didn't he see that I was barely holding on by a thread? Couldn't he smell the fear lingering on my skin?

Obviously not. The words clanged through my mind, splitting my chest wide open.

"I'm trying, Dad." I smiled. But it was fake and full of bitterness.

He looked at me with such pride. I wanted to roar at him and make him see how hard this was for me. To really see me.

But I didn't.

I wouldn't.

Because that's what you did for family, you protected them at all costs.

No matter the cost to your own heart.

CHAPTER TWELVE

Ezra

I STARED at the text message, clenching my fist over and over. Open and release. Open and release. It did little to ease the giant fucking pit in my stomach, but it stopped me from doing something stupid, like texting her back.

I read the words again, absorbing every letter.

Ashleigh: Is it true? Were you on a date? I keep thinking it's not possible. You don't date. But everything has changed, so why can't you change too, right? I want to be angry… maybe a small part of me is. But I also only want good things for you… always. Just wish I remembered…

EVEN NOW, in the aftermath of so much pain and ruin, Ashleigh managed to handle herself with grace. I didn't deserve her blessing just like I didn't deserve her understanding.

But it didn't stop me from wanting to beg for it.

"Everything okay?" Pen asked, glancing over at me. We'd met at the diner after she finished the lunch shift. She'd suggested going to Riverside, but I'd wanted to avoid anywhere I might cross paths with Ashleigh.

I was a cold-hearted bastard, but I didn't want to rub this —whatever *this* was—into her face.

Playing it safe, I'd suggested we head out of town to Halston. Pen didn't mind the short drive and she didn't question the location.

"Yeah, just my brother," I lied.

"You know, E, I'm glad you texted me. This has been nice."

"Yeah." I stared out of the window, watching the streets turn familiar as we entered Rixon.

It was my home and yet, the air became thinner with every passing minute. An invisible weight pressing down on my chest as Pen navigated the streets with ease.

"This is the nice end of town." She whistled through her teeth.

She wasn't wrong. Asher was a partner in his father's successful tech company, where they set up security systems for celebrity clients, affording him the best of everything. Best house in the neighborhood, with the best views and biggest yard. He wasn't flashy about it, but it didn't change the fact Asher came from money.

"Yeah, you could say that."

"I mean, I've heard of your dad... do you call him that?" She peeked over at me.

"Asher. I call him Asher."

"Asher Bennet. Best friends with Jason Ford, right?"

"Careful, Pen, or you might sound like you're stalking me." I smirked.

"You wish." She smirked back. "Everyone has heard of Jason Ford, he's Rixon royalty."

And damn if that weren't the truth.

Rixon royalty and also my new coach if he and Asher had anything to do with it.

"Don't tell me you're a Rixon Raider fan?"

"Football isn't really my thing." She shrugged.

Thank fuck for that.

Football wasn't my thing either.

I mean, it could have been. I had the speed, the throwing arm. But I didn't have what it took to play on a team, to fall in line and take orders from Coach Ford and his assistant coaches.

Making me practice with the team wasn't an opportunity, it was punishment. I knew it, they knew it, everyone would know it soon e-fucking-nough.

"But Max, he loves it. Makes me play with him whenever I'm home."

Pen talked about Max a lot. I didn't have blood siblings, so I didn't know what it was like to have someone depend on you, to look up to you and worship you. But I could tell they were close. She'd sacrificed so much for him, it was admirable. And he sounded like a cool kid. Funny, smart, and wise beyond his years.

Not that it was any surprise. Growing up without your parents did that to a kid. By the time I was ten, I'd seen and heard things no kid ever should. I'd learned to stay alert, keep my head down, and try not to draw attention to myself. Didn't always work, but even at that age, I had inbuilt survival instincts.

"Ezra?" Pen's soft voice grounded me from the memories, the fucking nightmares that haunted me.

"I'm okay." I gave her a small nod.

But I wasn't okay, I was itching for a smoke or a drink, something to take my mind off things.

"Here we are," she said, rolling to a stop before the turn for the Bennets' winding driveway.

"You can stop here, thanks."

The air turned thick with anticipation. I hadn't agreed to go out with her as a date, but I wasn't stupid enough to think that lines wouldn't blur the more time we spent together. The best thing I could have done, for both of us, was to keep my distance. But Penny was like me. She knew hardship. She knew what it was like to be alone, to have the weight of the past on your shoulders.

I'd never had that before.

"I had fun today," she said, peeking over at me through her thick lashes.

"Yeah, me too."

"Maybe we can do it again sometime?"

"Pen, I—"

"No pressure," she blurted out. "But it's nice to interact with someone my own age."

"You're two years older than me." I cocked a brow.

"You know what I mean." She rolled her eyes playfully, but then her gaze went to the clock on the dash and her expression fell. "I need to get home. But I'll see you at work soon?"

"Yeah." I gave her a small wave and climbed out.

"Who was that?" Aaron appeared out of nowhere, scaring the shit out of me.

"No one," I said, taking off up the driveway.

"Come on, E, that wasn't no one. It was a girl who looked suspiciously like that chick from the din—"

"Aaron?"

"Yeah?"

"Shut the fuck up."

His mouth curved with triumph. "So you were on a hot date. This is good news, E." He slung his arm over my shoulder. "Good fucking news."

But I barely heard his words, too stuck on the unfamiliar and unwelcomed weight of his arm around me. As if we were friends sharing a joke.

Noticing my expression, Aaron snatched his arm back. "Sorry, I—"

"It's all good." I shrugged. He meant well; I just didn't know how to meet him halfway. I didn't know how to interpret his physical affection without fear skittering down my spine.

We walked back to the house together in suffocating silence. The second we stepped inside, he asked me to go hang out with him, but I made my excuses and went to my room.

Like I always did.

"EZRA, COME DOWN HERE, SON."

I bristled at that word, every damn time. It was like the more he said it, the more he hoped it would imprint on me, become something meaningful.

To me, it was a loaded word.

To be a son meant to have parents. To belong. To be loved and cherished.

I'd never had that. Those early attachment bonds had been severed when Alyson Jackson left me at daycare and never returned to get me.

Asher and Mya had tried to fix it, to repair the damage done by a childhood of abandonment, fear, and confusion.

I had no memories of being held or hugged or comforted. Foster care was a jungle, a constant fight for survival. One that stripped your soul and turned your heart into a dead, black thing in your chest.

Until Mya and Asher plucked me out of my last foster group home, I had zero experiences of what it meant to be a proper family, full of love and laughter.

I wasn't made for that environment. I didn't know how to *be* in that environment.

Yet here I was playing happy family with one of the richest families in Rixon.

"Ezra, let's go," Asher yelled again.

Throwing my sleeveless hoodie over my head, I shoved my arms into it and headed downstairs. "What's up?" I said, eyeing them. All of them.

"We thought we'd spend the day together."

"I'm good thanks, but you guys enjoy—"

"All of us, Ezra." Asher gave me the look, the one that said I wasn't getting out of this.

"Ash took some leave," Mya said. "We thought it would be nice to do something together."

"So long as there's food, I'm there," Aaron said.

"Fucking pig," I murmured and Mya shot me a terse glare. "Language."

"Sorry."

"So where are we going?" Sofia asked. "Can I invite Poppy?"

"And Cole?"

"No, today is about the five of us. You'll need sneakers and sunscreen. I've packed us plenty of water."

"That sounds like hard work, Dad." Sofia went to him and laid her head on his arm. "We could go down to the lake instead? Get the jet skis out?"

"Nice try, missy. But we are doing this. It'll be good for us all to get out in the fresh air and bond."

Bond, right.

"Do what exactly?" Aaron asked, and Asher grinned, pulling Mya into his side.

"We're going to hike Bake Oven Knob."

Fuck my life.

"NOW ISN'T THAT SOMETHING," Asher said as we stood at the foot of the Appalachian trail.

"How high is it?" Sofia asked, hiking her backpack up her shoulders.

"About forty feet. It's less than a mile to the peak, but the trail can get pretty rocky. It shouldn't take us more than an hour."

"Let's do it." Mya smiled at the four of us, her eyes lingering on me a little longer than the rest of them.

She was always watching, quietly assessing. It was the student counselor in her. I'd hated it at first, the way she tried to figure me out. She'd stopped doing it pretty soon after she realized I wasn't going to crack.

It didn't stop her from trying to reach me now and again, but on the whole, she'd pulled back over the last couple of years or so, trying to give me space to come to them when I was ready.

"Last one to the peak has to carry all the bags back down." Aaron grinned, taking off toward the start of the trail.

"Asshole," I muttered, coming up behind the rest of them.

Asher dropped back though, walking beside me.

"What?" I said, sensing him watching me.

"Do you resent us?"

"Resent you? Why the hell would I resent you?"

"For backing you into the corner about the adoption. You were always so resistant, we thought—"

"It means something to you." I shrugged.

"And it doesn't mean anything to you?" Hurt coated Asher's words and I knew if I looked at him, disappointment would be etched into the lines of his face. But he wanted something I couldn't give them—something I didn't know how to give them.

"It doesn't matter. It's done now. You got what you wanted." I tried to speed up, but he grabbed my arm, slowing me again.

"Jeez, Ezra. Do you have to be so cold all of the time?"

His words barely penetrated me, my mind clouded with a potent mix of fear and anger as I glanced to where he was holding me. "You knew who I was when you stood in the courthouse and signed those papers," I spat. "I'll never be like Aaron or Sofia. I don't know how to do... this." I motioned between us.

"Nobody expects you to be like them, Son. We love you for you. Nothing more. Nothing less. But it kills me that you still don't feel like part of this family."

"Can we not do this?" I yanked out of his hold and took off after the others. If this was Asher's attempt at family bonding, he was way off the mark.

Because it was my idea of hell.

CHAPTER THIRTEEN

Ashleigh

ALMOST TWO WEEKS had passed since the party at Bryan's. Two weeks since I'd texted Ezra... and he'd ignored me again. But I'd refused to sit around and mope, making the most of my time with Lily.

We'd hung out with Carrie-Anne and the guys, until her and Bryan left for college. She was heading to Ohio State and Bryan was going to play football for the Michigan Wolverines. Sometimes Peyton joined us, but since she was working full-time, she couldn't get away a lot.

We hung out at the Bennets, swimming in the pool and goofing around in the lake. We played arcade games down at Riverside and spent lazy days on the embankment, stuffing our faces from the various food trucks. It was nice. Normal.

But it was also bittersweet.

Because occasionally, I caught a glimpse of Ezra. But he always took off or made sure to stay out of my way.

"Sweetheart, you okay?" Dad asked as I stared up at Lily's

house. Tonight was the night of her going away party. Her and Kaiden were leaving tomorrow.

I could no longer pretend it wasn't happening. And once they were gone, the countdown to senior year was on.

Two weeks.

Two more weeks until I went back to Rixon High.

"Leigh Leigh?" His voice pulled me back into the moment and I blinked over at him.

"I'm fine." I plastered on a smile. I'd gotten good over the last month at showing people what they wanted to see.

My lost memories had made no appearance, not even a flicker of recognition as I spent the summer in all my favorite places. Word had begun to travel that I'd emerged from the accident with more than just a few physical injuries, and I knew it wouldn't be long before everyone in Rixon learned the truth.

But I was happy to let it happen naturally. To buy myself as much time as possible before I became the freak show.

Dad climbed out of the car and came around and opened the door for me. I was walking unaided now, having got the green light from my physical therapist two days ago. My ribs still smarted on occasion, but they took longer to heal.

We walked up to the house together. Mom was already here, after spending the afternoon helping Aunt Felicity get things organized for the party. My heart raced in my chest as I went around the back. There was a big white tent set up, with a buffet table and a couple of round tables decorated in Penn State blue and white.

"Ashleigh." Lily bounded over to me, her smile infectious. She slung her arms around me and hugged me tight.

"I'll miss you too, Lil," I said, choking up.

"Gav is here somewhere." She gave me a strange look. "Sofia, Poppy, Aaron, and Cole too."

"Ezra?" I mouthed, and she shook her head.

Of course he wasn't here.

I expected nothing less.

And yet, part of me had hoped he might show.

Slipping her arm through mine, Lily led me away from the adults, toward the lake. "Everyone's out here," she said, motioning to our friends all sitting around the fire pit.

Gav patted the chair beside him, and I sat down. Lily slid onto Kaiden's lap, kissing the corner of his mouth.

"So are you guys all set?" Aaron asked.

"Yeah, I think so."

"Nervous?"

"Nah." Kaiden hugged Lily tighter, resting his chin on her shoulder. "I'm ready."

"*We're* ready." She nudged his ribs. "Don't think you get to forget about me, Mr. Hotshot Football Player."

He tickled her and she burst out laughing, the two of them lost in their own little world as the rest of us watched on.

"How's it going?" Gav asked me, sneaking me a bottle of beer.

"It's... going."

"That good, huh?" A smirk played on his lips. "Ready for senior year?"

"Ready for community college?" I threw back.

"Touché, Leigh Leigh. Tou-fucking-ché." He tipped his beer back, draining it.

"Are you sure you're okay?" I whispered, noting the shadows under his eyes.

"Rough night with Millie. She was up half the night and Mom was too tired from her shift at the hospital."

"Is she okay?"

"Yeah, she's cutting her back teeth. I gave her a frozen

binky and it seemed to do the trick, but she wouldn't go down in her own bed."

"I can't imagine you babysitting your little sister."

"I'll have you know, I'm the best babysitter around." Humor laced his words, but it didn't reach his eyes.

"I guess neither of us are where we hoped to be," I said, feeling the weight of each word on my shoulders.

"It could always be worse."

"It could." We shared a smile.

"At least we'll have each other," Gav added. "You can bitch to me about how awful senior year is and I can moan about playing nanny to a two-year-old".

"Deal." I held out my hand, chuckling when he pretended to spit on his palm. Gav slid his hand against mine and we shook on it.

And on the night before the day where I lost my best friend to college, I didn't feel as alone.

———

"HEY YOU." Lily joined me on the bench down by the lake. I'd wandered down here a while ago, after listening to Uncle Jason toast Lily and Kaiden on their new adventure, the big wide world theirs for the taking.

I was happy for them, so freaking happy. But his words were like tiny shards of glass against my skin. And then started the perpetual cycle of shame and guilt.

I was a mess, so I'd stepped away and came down here to get some fresh air.

"Hey," I said quietly.

"I missed you. You've been down here a while."

"I needed a breather."

"You're struggling."

RUINED HOPES

An observation, not a question.

"It's hard, I won't lie. But it doesn't mean I'm not happy for you. I am. So happy, Lil." I took her hand in mine, unable to meet her eyes. "You deserve this, so much."

"You deserved it too, you know. It kills me that you won't be off at UPenn living your best life. But it's just college, Leigh. You being here, in one piece, is far more important than that. College will still be there when you're ready."

People kept saying that to me. As if one day, I'd wake up and everything would be normal again. When deep down, I think everyone knew I wouldn't be.

"I don't want to talk about it." I stared out at the lake.

Lily nudged me gently with her shoulder. "We'll talk every day, Leigh. Well, text and call and we'll see each other at holidays. It'll be like I never left, you'll see."

Another lie.

Another lie we told to make ourselves feel better.

"I know," I said. Because what else was there to say?

She was leaving.

She would have new friends, new classes and pressures, a whole new life that wouldn't include me.

I was supposed to have all that too. It would have softened the blow of leaving each other, knowing the other was off chasing their dreams.

But the reality was, she was leaving me behind now. And like it or not, that would drive a wedge between us. It would be foolish to assume otherwise.

"Come here." Lily pulled me into a hug, and we sat there, two girls; family by marriage, friends by choice, as I cried for everything I'd lost and everything I was about to lose.

"I love you, Lil." I clung to her delicate frame, never wanting to let go. My heart stuttered in my chest, every breath like lead.

I don't know how long we sat there, with Lily holding me while my world fell apart around me. Until strong arms pulled me away from Lily and into a hard chest.

"It's fine," Gav said. "I've got her."

I was too lost in my grief to care.

"We've got to stop meeting like this," Gav said, chuckling. Clawing a small smile from deep inside me.

"There she is." He stared down at me as I wiped my eyes. "I'd offer you some vodka, but I figured the parentals will freak out if you end up drunk."

I hiccoughed, drying my eyes with the back of my hand. "You're turning into a bit of a knight-in-shining-armor, you know that, right?"

"I try my best." He held my gaze, his eyes glittering under the moonlight.

"Your eyes are the strangest shade of brown," I said.

"Gee, thanks."

Silence crept over us. Slow and suffocating. Gav slipped his arm around me, and I rested my head there, taking the comfort he offered.

Until I felt someone watching us.

Not someone.

Ezra.

I sucked in a sharp breath as I turned slowly and found him, in the tree line, watching. Our eyes collided and my heart jolted.

"Leigh Leigh, what is it?" Gav asked, glancing back at the shadows to see what had my attention.

Ezra had slipped away though, disappearing as quickly as he had arrived.

"I thought I heard something," I said. "But it was nothing."

Liar.

The way he'd looked at me, with such loathing. A shudder went through me.

"You're cold?" Gav asked, and I nodded. "Here."

He scooted closer, wrapping his arm around me again. There was no ulterior motive or crackle of expectation. It was just a friend doing a good deed for another friend. And in that moment, it was exactly what I needed.

But as we sat there in the shadows, talking about everything and nothing, I couldn't get Ezra's face out of my head. The way he'd stood there, deathly still, watching.

Because I was sure I'd seen something in his expression.

Something that looked a lot like jealousy.

———

THE PARTY WAS WINDING DOWN. The adults were in that strange place between not being fully drunk but not being sober either. My mom and dad kept asking me if I was okay, and like always, I kept telling them I was fine.

Gav had left earlier, since he was on 'Millie-duty' as he liked to call it, in the morning.

Mom was helping Aunt Felicity clean up, and I was sitting outside still, on my bench, avoiding more questions, more stares of pity.

This was Lily and Kaiden's night and I hadn't wanted to detract from that.

When a twig snapped behind me, I half-expected to see Mom or Dad sneaking up on me. Checking in. Suffocating me with their concern.

But it wasn't my parents at all.

"You," I said, my eyes locking on Ezra.

I'd assumed he'd left after seeing him earlier. But here he was, standing in front of me like a mirage.

"You're with him now?"

"With who?" My brows knitted.

"McKay."

Indignation burned through me as I clenched my fists at my sides. "Wow." It came out strangled. "The first words you say to me after everything... and that's what you choose? Fuck you, Ezra," I spat, anger coursing through me like wildfire. "Fuck. You."

"Well." He ran his tongue over his teeth, making a tsking sound. "Is it true?"

"Do you care?"

Something blazed in his eyes as he stepped forward, taking the air with him.

"E-Ezra?" We were almost nose to nose, him all up in my space, staring down at me with such intensity it made my heart gallop in my chest. Wild and unrelenting, a frenetic storm rose inside me.

He was so close I could see the ring of amber in his eyes, like flames licking the night sky. Threatening to burn me from the inside out.

"You should be with someone like him," he said quietly. A cold, quiet statement that made my stomach dip.

"W-what?" I breathed, so confused. He was too close... too everything.

The energy was a living, breathing thing between us, crackling and shifting, making it hard to breathe.

I was at a disadvantage. He could remember. He knew everything that had transpired between us over the last ten months.

I didn't.

"You should be with someone like him, someone like McKay."

"I heard you the first time," I rushed out. "But I don't

understand why you're saying that to me... not when..." *Not when it's you I want. Not when it's always been you.*

I trapped the words behind my lips, refusing to let them out. Because Ezra wasn't here to smooth things over, to get on his knees and apologize for shutting me out, to beg for forgiveness. He was here to put the final nail in the coffin of there ever being an *us*.

A sudden flood of emotion engulfed me, tears pricking the corners of my eyes. "I don't know what happened to us... to you, but you're right, I should be with someone like him. Someone who isn't incapable of owning their feelings, someone who doesn't push everyone away because they're scared. I deserve more, Ezra. I deserve so much more."

Something flickered in his eyes, but he shut it down, his cold mask sliding back into place. "You need to quit texting me."

"I—"

"Just stop, Ashleigh. Because I'm never going to text you back and you're starting to look desperate."

I gasped at his cruel words, silent tears streaming down my cheeks as the final tether between us snapped. For reasons I might never understand, Ezra had ruined us.

He'd ruined any hopes I ever had of him being mine.

CHAPTER FOURTEEN

Ashleigh

I WAS A COWARD.

The next morning, when Mom and Dad had shouted out for me to leave to go see Lily and Kaiden off, I'd feigned a headache and stayed behind.

Of course, they let me. Urging me to call if I needed them. I didn't.

I just needed to be alone. I didn't like the sticky fingers of jealousy that seemed to wrap a fist around my heart as I imagined everyone wishing them well.

I wanted that.

I wanted to be packing my life's things into my car and heading to college.

But Mom and Dad were right. I didn't want it like this. I couldn't imagine arriving on campus and trying to make friends, the awkward questions that would follow. The even more awkward answers.

Deferring for a year was the smart option, the only option, but it didn't make it any easier to accept.

As if the universe summoned her, my cell phone vibrated, and Lily's name appeared. I opened the message, regret snaking through me.

Lily: Your mom said you weren't feeling well. If that's true, I hope you feel better. But if it isn't, if you couldn't come because... Well, I just want you to know, I get it. And I love you. And you'll always be my best friend. No amount of time and distance will change that. I love you, Leigh Leigh, I'll call you when we get there xo

TEARS ROLLED down my cheeks as I breathed through the pain and regret and shame. I should have gone; I should have been the bigger person and gone to say goodbye. But after my run in with Ezra last night, the last shred of my shaky resolve had been ripped away.

You should be with someone like him.

As if he knew what was best for me. As if I could just switch off what I felt for him.

God, he made me so angry. And even now, it wasn't necessarily anger toward him, but rather, anger at the situation. Because even though he'd walked away from me without looking back, I'd seen the jealousy in his eyes.

I had.

But I knew Ezra well enough to know that once he dug his heels in about something, there would be no convincing him otherwise. And I had bigger things to worry about, like the looming school semester.

Grabbing a pillow, I hugged it to my chest and rolled onto my back, staring up at my ceiling. Why couldn't I just remember?

It had been almost six weeks since I woke up in the hospital... and nothing. Everyone kept telling me not to get disillusioned, but they weren't the ones with almost an eighteenth of their life missing. It didn't sound like much when you broke it down, but it was such a vital ten months. The year when you discovered who you were and where you wanted to go. It was the year big decisions were made and so many life changing moments occurred.

All lost.

How could I even trust what everyone told me about the last ten months? It would be easy for them to make an error or mistake when they recalled those memories. Something that, to them, could seem small and insignificant, but to me, it could be huge.

Ugh. This was a road I didn't want to go down. Obsessing over what might or might not have happened in my life over the missing months. I still had the supportive same friends, a family who loved me, a place at UPenn that the administration was willing to defer until next year. Things could be worse. I knew that. But I couldn't get past it—I couldn't just accept that I might never get those memories back. It was incredibly frustrating, but more than that, it was a deep sense of feeling incomplete. As if those missing memories had inexplicably changed me.

I was different now.

And I had to learn to live with that.

———

THE DAYS PASSED. Sofia and Poppy tried to include me in their last-ditch efforts to enjoy the rest of summer. But with Lily gone, it was hard keeping up pretenses. They were so excited about senior year, eager to soak up every experience and make the most of their final months at Rixon High... and I wasn't.

In fact, I was dreading it.

"What's with the frown?" Gav asked me as we watched Millie fist handfuls of sand and giggle as it fell through her chubby fingers.

"School starts next week."

"It'll be okay," he said, swooping in to steady her as she began to topple.

Hanging out with Gav and his baby sister was about the only thing that made me smile these days. She was such a cutie pie and watching him with her was enough to melt some of the ice around my heart.

"Will it? Everyone's going to find out... Mya has already met with the faculty staff to brief them on my *condition*." I air-quoted the words. "I'm not sure I can handle a whole year of pity stares."

"It won't be that bad. And the doctor said you'll probably be able to remember the actual work, right? So that'll help."

I made a dismissive noise in the back of my throat. The doctor had said it was common for procedural memory to remain intact. So there was every chance once I sat down in classes, I would recall at least some of the learning. Mom and Dad had tried to encourage me to pick up some textbooks from last year and see if anything sounded familiar, but so far, I hadn't been brave enough.

Denial was my preferred state of mind.

Denial that I was about to repeat my entire senior year.

Denial that I may or may not remember the learning,

because what a waste of my time if I did, and if I didn't... well, I didn't want to think about how that would feel.

But most of all, denial that I would have to see Ezra around school every day.

I'd overheard Mom and Dad talking about him and how he'd promised Asher and Mya to keep his head down and 'do what needed to be done,' whatever the hell that meant. I tried really hard not to think about it, about him, but I'd never been very smart where Ezra Jackson was concerned.

Clearly.

A kid on a scooter whizzed past us and we both glanced after him. "Dude's got a death wish." Gav chuckled but cussed under his breath as we watched the kid pull and fail to land a stunt. He wiped out with an *oomph*.

"Oh my God, Max," someone yelled, and a young woman ran toward him.

"Shit, he looks hurt." Gav clambered to his feet. "Watch Millie for me."

"Of course." I leaned over and plucked Millie up and bounced her in my lap, watching as Gav helped the kid to his feet. Blood poured out of his knee, trickling down his leg onto the sidewalk but the boy seemed unaffected. The young woman, however, was furious, yelling at him as Gav picked up the mangled scooter and tried to fix it.

"I think this is good for the scrap yard," he said, handing it to the woman.

"Third one this year," she muttered, glancing over toward me and Millie. There was something familiar about her, but I couldn't quite reach the memory.

Fear sluiced up my spine, but quickly turned to utter relief when the memory slammed into me. Picking Millie up, I walked over to them and said, "Penelope, right?"

The woman frowned at me. "Sorry, do I—" Her eyes

widened, and she smiled. "Oh my God, Riverside... I almost covered you in soda."

"That's me. Ashleigh." I returned her smile.

"Hi." She turned her attention on Gav and touched a finger to her lips. "And you're... Gaz?"

"Gav," he corrected with a bemused chuckle. "Sorry, I didn't recognize you."

"Too busy picking up my klutz of a brother up off the sidewalk. Clearly it's in our genes to be clumsy! Thanks for that by the way."

"Anytime. You good, little man?" Gav asked the kid who was gawking at the three of us.

"Who you calling little, asshole? I'm eleven." He puffed out his chest, and Penelope turned a bright shade of red.

"Max, don't be so rude. Now say thank you to Gav."

He dropped his head and muttered, "Thank you."

"And who is this little princess?" Penelope reached for Millie, and she grabbed onto one of the woman's fingers, giggling.

"This is my baby sister, Millie."

"She's adorable."

"She's something all right." He chuckled. "Are you going to be okay getting him back—"

"Oh, we'll be fine. Thanks again though. Max, let's go get you cleaned up." She grabbed him by the scruff of his neck and began leading him away.

"We met her already?" Gav asked perplexed as he watched them walk away.

"Yeah, at Riverside. She tripped and spilled her soda everywhere."

"Huh." He kept staring at their retreating form, until Millie let out a high-pitched squeal, demanding his attention.

"Hungry?" Gav asked her, and she clapped her hands

together with glee. "Want to come back to the house and have lunch with us?" He took her from me, but I didn't miss how he glanced back toward where Penelope and her brother had disappeared.

I had no right to feel jealous; it wasn't like that between us. But it didn't stop the irrational pang of envy that went through me. He liked her, or in the very least, was attracted to her. Not that I blamed him. She was gorgeous and older and knew what it was like to take care of a younger sibling.

I shook off the ridiculous thoughts. It was Ezra's fault. His blatant rejection had left me feeling like a wounded puppy. To the point where part of me wanted to make him think there was something between me and Gav. But then I remembered one vital thing: Ezra didn't care enough to let it affect him, and I'd only end up hurting myself more. Besides, Gav didn't deserve being used like that. Not when he'd been such a good friend to me.

"I... no, that's okay," I said. "I'll see you tomorrow though?" I'd agreed to go with him to check out the community college.

"I'll pick you up at ten."

"Sounds good." I ran a hand over Millie's head. "And I'll see you soon, princess."

WHEN I FINALLY RETURNED HOME, Aunt Felicity and Uncle Jason were over.

"Hi, sweetheart." She held out her arms and I went willingly. "How are you?"

"I'm okay."

"All set for school?"

I flinched, folding my arms around myself. "I guess."

"Sofia and Poppy will look out for you." She gave me a reassuring smile. "They're excited to have you with them this year."

"Fee's right, Ashleigh." Uncle Jason gave me a knowing look. "You've got this."

"Yeah, well, it's not like I have a choice." The refrigerator was a good distraction and I pulled it open, looking for something, anything to drink.

"Your dad said you've been hanging out with Gavin McKay?"

"We've been spending some time together, yeah."

"He also said Gav decided not to go to Maryland, after all."

I shrugged. "He didn't want to leave his mom and sister. He's going to take some classes at Rixon Community College."

"Good for him," Uncle Jase grumbled, and Aunt Felicity reprimanded him.

"He's doing what he thinks is best for his family."

"Yeah, I know. It's just such a waste of talent."

"Jason!"

"I didn't mean it like that... I... forget it," he conceded.

"Forget what?" Dad appeared.

"Jase is disappointed Gavin McKay isn't going off to college."

"It's a big sacrifice to make."

"Too big." Uncle Jase tsked under his breath.

I got it. He'd had his dream ripped away from him after being injured. Football had been everything to him. Well, everything until he met Aunt Felicity and realized there was more to life than the gridiron. But he was driven to the core, and he only wanted good things for his players.

"Have you heard from Lily?" Mom asked. "Have they settled in okay?"

"Yeah, they're fine. I still can't believe my baby girl is at college."

"I still can't believe we ever thought it was a good idea to send her off to college with her boyfriend," Uncle Jase mumbled.

"Kaiden is a good guy," I said, and all the adults looked at me.

"Of course, he is, sweetheart." Dad smiled. "But you'll understand one day when you have kids, and they grow up and fly the nest." He winked, but I barely smiled. Because I should have flown the nest too, but I was stuck here.

They didn't allow the silence to become awkward, filling it with chitchat about the upcoming season, and my uncle's plans to defend the championship. Aaron and Cole were seniors now, ready to lead the team all the way. But he was worried about losing his star quarterback in Kaiden and still hadn't decided who would replace him yet.

I excused myself, not really in the mood to talk football or school or any of the things I once loved. But as I left to go to my room, I couldn't help but overhear Mom say, "Are you sure it's a good idea making Ezra join the team?"

There was the unmistakable sound of one of Uncle Jason's derisive snorts. Then he said, "It's the least he deserves."

CHAPTER FIFTEEN

Ezra

"EZRA, LET'S GO," Asher called.

I dragged myself out of bed and stretched around a yawn. I was fucking tired, my muscles and limbs weary from a crap night's sleep. The nightmares had been bad. But then, they always were when I didn't have a smoke to settle the ghosts that haunted me.

And since Asher and Mya were riding me about staying clean, getting high in the house wasn't an option.

"Ez—"

"Yeah, I'm up," I yelled, padding into my small bathroom. It was one of the definite upsides of the Bennets' money. My own bathroom meant privacy. Something I'd grown up without.

After washing up, I pulled on some clean sweatpants and a hoodie. It was the first day of school, but I wasn't looking to impress anyone. The bag Asher had given me yesterday taunted me from its place beside the door. He and Coach

Ford were dead set on my joining the team. I'd reluctantly attended one of their training camps a few days ago and it had been a fucking disaster. I didn't want to play football. I didn't want to be part of any team. Aaron, Cole, and their friends knew it. Coach knew it. And my stubborn ass couldn't get past it.

Asher and Jason said I had to show up; they didn't say I had to play. So I'd refused to participate until Coach lost his cool and ripped me out of the practice drills to sit on the bench and watch.

It was fine by me. I had no intentions of becoming a Raider, even if I had to endure a season of football practice. It was better than the alternative.

For a second, I contemplated leaving the kit behind. But knowing Coach Ford he would make me wear something from lost and found to train in and enjoy every damn second.

Leaving my room, I almost walked straight into Aaron as he flew down the hall.

"Shit, sorry, I overslept." I let him go ahead of me. "All set for today?"

"What do you think?" I said.

"I think you need to lighten the hell up. It's senior year, E, and we get to do it together. It's going to be epic."

"Doesn't it ever get boring being so... upbeat?"

Hurt flashed over his face but he quickly replaced it with a smile. "We can't all be grumpy assholes like you." He smirked, and dammit, I found myself fighting a smirk of my own.

"Morning," he said as we entered the kitchen. Mya had already left for the day, eager to get back to her emotionally damaged kids no doubt.

"About time," Asher grumbled. "Sofia has been up for almost an hour."

She shot us a smug look before going back to her cereal.

"You'll all ride together?" he asked no one in particular.

"I can walk."

"Like hell you can." He pinned me with a dark look. "Aaron will drive you and Sofia."

"Actually," she said. "I'm giving Ashleigh and Poppy a ride. But I guess I could give the guys a ride too."

"No, that's okay. She's probably feeling overwhelmed." Asher cast me a sideways glance, but I didn't acknowledge it, making a beeline for the refrigerator.

After Lily and Kaiden's farewell party, I would be the last person on Earth Ashleigh wanted to see. Not that I wanted to ride with her anyway.

I didn't want to be anywhere near her.

If I was going to survive this year, me and her needed to stay out of each other's way.

Period.

Because Ashleigh had always been my one weakness. But the thing about weaknesses...

In the end they ruined you.

RIXON HIGH WAS EXACTLY the same.

I don't know what I'd expected but I guessed I thought something would feel different. Aside from the neatly mowed lawns and polished windows, everything looked the same.

Same blue and white 'Go Raiders' banner hung above the doors, welcoming the students into the building. Same locker banks lining the hall. Same rumble of chatter as kids fell into their cliques. The jocks migrated around Aaron and Cole. They were seniors now, at the top of the social hierarchy. He beckoned me over, but I kept walking. Enduring practices with them was one thing, but I had no intentions of socializing with them.

My eyes snagged on the cheerleaders beyond them, in their standard issue blue and white skirts and cropped tanks. A couple of them met my eyes, letting their gazes rake down my body. Any regular guy would have appreciated being checked out by the cute cheerleaders, but I wasn't any guy. I had nothing in common with girls like that, girls who cared too much about their appearance and status. Girls who had the entire world at their feet simply because of their good looks and daddies trust funds.

I kept my head down and moved down the hall. I felt her before I saw her. It was always the same whenever Ashleigh was in the vicinity. Even before I'd really known who she was, I'd noticed her.

Noticed her in a way that knocked me on my ass even at the tender age of eleven.

Ashleigh wasn't conceited. She wasn't vapid or vain or a mean girl, she was good. Pure. Devoted to her friends and family...

And she'd taken one look at me and decided that she was going to be my friend.

Of course, our story wasn't that simple because nothing in my life was simple. I was broken. Damaged. My heart was made up of jagged shards that no longer fit quite right.

I had nothing to offer a girl like Ashleigh Chase, but it didn't stop her from trying to get to know me.

"E, hold up," Aaron called after me and I sped up, hoping to escape him. But he was too quick, rounding me before I had a chance to disappear around the corner.

"If you meet me after first period, we can head to the gym together."

"I think I can find it."

"Yeah, but it might go more smoothly if we arrive together." His brow lifted.

"I don't need a babysitter, Aaron."

"No, but maybe a friend wouldn't hurt."

"I don't need—Forget it. I'll see you at practice."

"Atta boy." He clapped me on the shoulder, and I flinched, stepping away. His brows pinched, but his confusion quickly passed. He knew I didn't like people being all up in my space.

He spun around and walked backward. "We're going to have a lot of fun this year."

Fun. Yeah. Wasn't the word I'd use for it.

Living nightmare is more like it.

"OKAY, OKAY, GATHER ROUND," Coach Ford called us in, and everyone stopped running drills to join him.

I hovered at the back of the huddle, the way I had for most of practice. I wasn't here to make the team or earn my spot. I was here because Asher and Jason held my future in their hands. It was the only reason I'd bothered to show up.

"We lost a lot of good players last year. That means there are some big shoes to fill and a lot of pressure on your shoulders. But I'm confident that we have a strong team this year, a team who can go all the way again.

"Over the course of the next couple of weeks, your job is to show me why you're indispensable to this team. There are forty-two of you and only twenty-two spots on my starting lineup. Game time goes to those who work for it. Now get back out there and show me you've got what it takes to wear a Raiders jersey."

A chorus of, "Yes, Coach," rang out across the field as the

huddle broke formation to continue working through the conditioning activities. I could handle the basic stuff, sprint ladders and tempo runs. That didn't require working in a team. But running drills did.

I was a new face, and it didn't take much for the rest of the guys to put two and two together—I didn't want to be here, and Coach Ford didn't give a shit what I wanted.

No one asked why I was here, but their curiosity brushed up against me all the same.

Nobody trained with the team unless they were dead set on wearing a Raiders jersey one day. And I'd never made a single suggestion that I wanted it. It was bound to rub some of the guys the wrong way. But if Coach noticed, he didn't say anything, treating me no differently to any other newcomer.

"Ezra, let's go," he boomed, and I internally flinched.

I wasn't used to following orders. Especially not from someone like Jason Ford. But like an obedient dog, I joined the line and got ready to run sprint intervals.

A couple of guys ahead of me tried to make conversation, but I immediately looked away, and they took the hint.

I wasn't here to make friends.

I was here to be punished.

―――

AFTER A GRUELING SIXTY MINUTES, Coach finally gave the order for us to head to the locker room. But he beckoned me to stay behind.

"What's up?" I said with a defensive tone.

"How did you find it?"

"Anyone can run a few sprints," I said, ignoring the burning in my thighs and calves.

"An attitude like that won't get you far." Disapproval coated his words.

"Just speaking the truth."

"I guess we'll see how you fair when I put a ball in your hands."

"I already told you, I'm not—"

"Playing." He stepped closer, his words meant only for my ears. "Yeah, I got the memo. But this can go one of two ways, Ezra. You can grab the opportunity by both hands, or you can fight me every step of the way. But mark my words, you will learn to respect me and respect this team."

My eyes narrowed as anger heated my blood. The urge to argue, to resist, and lash out rose inside me like a tidal wave. I'd promised myself a long time ago, I was done taking orders from men with too much power over me. But this wasn't just any man. It was Jason Ford. Coach of the Rixon Raiders, one of Asher and Mya's best friends, and Ashleigh's uncle. I could fight him all I wanted, but it didn't change the fact that he owned my ass for the next four months.

"Is that the plan, Coach?" The words spewed out before I could stop them. "To wear me down until I break? Ain't nothing you can do to me that hasn't been done ten times over."

"Ezra?" Coach's expression guttered and I realized I'd gone too far.

Fuck.

"What are—"

"I'd better go shower," I said, hauling ass toward the locker room before he had a chance to ask me again.

I hadn't meant for those words to spew out, but I hadn't been cornered like that for a long fucking time. Hopefully he wouldn't read too much into it or else I could expect Mya to call me into her office at some point.

And being in there... well, it was almost as bad as being out here.

The locker room was a hive of activity, everyone excited about the looming season. Coach wasn't lying when he said they had big shoes to fill, more specifically, a championship to defend. Kaiden Thatcher was one of the best quarterbacks in the state. Finding his replacement was going to be a problem. I only knew because I'd heard Aaron and his dad talking about it enough. There was a junior named Deacon Faris, Aaron thought could do it, but he lacked the presence required by the quarterback. Even I knew that a weak quarterback usually led to a weak team. They were the heartbeat of any team, the playmaker, the leader, the driving force behind the players grit and determination.

Just because I didn't enjoy playing football, didn't mean I didn't enjoy watching it on ESPN. But it wasn't my life the same way it was for so many young men in Rixon.

Football was canon here. If you didn't play it, you watched it. Worshipped and adored it. And if you didn't live, eat, and breathe it, at the very least, you supported those that did.

The very foundations of Rixon were built on Friday night football.

"Hey, E," Aaron said the second he saw me across the locker room. "What did Coach want?"

"Probably to blow him," someone snickered, and Aaron went deathly still.

"What the fuck did you just say, Carrick?" He moved toward a couple of guys—juniors, I think—in the corner of the room.

"Clearly, he's getting special treatment. He flunked out of high school like a loser, yet, here he is, training with the team as if—"

"I'd think very carefully about the next words out of your mouth," Aaron seethed, his eyes two deadly orbs as he glared at Nathan Carrick.

I'd noticed him out on the field. Cocky little thing with too much smack talk.

"Relax, Aaron," I said, ignoring the fact he looked ready to go to war over some asshole making an unoriginal insult. I'd heard worse over the years.

Far worse.

"I can fight my own battles." I pinned the guy in question with a hard look. He held my stare, even going so far as to lift his chin in defiance. Bringing my hands out in front of me, I cracked my knuckles loudly, keeping my eyes locked on his.

It didn't take long for him to relent.

Predictable and a total pussy.

But Aaron wasn't done. He scanned the sea of faces as he stepped forward. "Ezra is a part of this team whether you like it or not. Anyone else who has a problem with that can take it up with me."

"You're not the captain," another junior said.

"No, I'm not. But I am a senior which means I outrank all of you."

"That's some bul—"

"You should listen to him," I said with cold indifference.

"Or what, Jackson? What the fuck are you going to do about it?"

Aaron slammed into the guy, pushing him up against the locker. "He's a Bennet now, and you need to drop this shit. We're Raiders. Quit complaining and focus on the task at hand, winning the championship."

Aaron caught himself and stepped back, letting out a long sigh. He raked a hand through his hair and glanced in my direction. "You good?"

"Never better," I grumbled, and grabbed my towel, heading for the showers.

Before I did something stupid...

Like prove all those guys right.

CHAPTER SIXTEEN

Ashleigh

"THERE YOU ARE." Sofia and Poppy found me standing outside the cafeteria, too overwhelmed to go inside.

"Oh no," Poppy said, gently touching my elbow. "What's wrong?"

"I... nothing." If I ignored all the curious stares and constant hum of whispers that seemed to follow me wherever I went, and the fact that neither Lily nor Peyton were here, it was like nothing had really changed. I felt seventeen all over again, starting out senior year.

But that was precisely the problem.

"Come on, the guys are waiting," Sofia said around an encouraging smile.

She went first, with Poppy lacing her arm through mine. "It won't be that bad, I promise."

The second I stepped inside, the noise hit me. Loud, rambunctious chatter that made my heart race in my chest. Class was different, it was safe. My teachers knew the deal and tried to accommodate the fact I was here because of things beyond my control. But the cafeteria was a jungle where kids were left to fend for themselves. It hadn't bothered me before. I'd sat and laughed and talked with the best of them.

Today, I wanted the ground to open up and swallow me whole.

"Come on, I see them." There was a lilt in Poppy's voice that told me she'd spotted Aaron.

He and Cole were seated at the table next to the football players, reserving seats for the girls no doubt. We made our way over to them, but Sofia drew up short when Zara Willis appeared at Aaron's side. She draped her manicured fingers over his shoulder and leaned down to whisper something in his ear.

Poppy went still beside me.

"Pop?" I asked, watching the blood drain from her face. "Relax, Aaron isn't into—"

Zara turned to her friends and beckoned them over. They all sat down, Zara taking the seat right beside Aaron.

"I guess we'll have to find somewhere else to sit," Sofia said, quietly seething.

"Yeah." The defeat in Poppy's voice made my stomach knot.

We passed them to get to an empty table in the corner, but the guys were too interested in whatever Zara and her friends were saying to notice us.

"They're seniors now," Sofia murmured as we sat down. "The power and status is going to their heads." She didn't take her eyes off her brother and Cole.

"Rumor has it Zara is going to be head cheerleader; makes sense she's staking an early claim on Aaron."

Poppy looked away, suddenly finding her lunch more interesting. "He can do what he wants," she mumbled.

I kept watching though. Surprised at how oblivious Aaron was sometimes. Poppy was desperately in love with him, and we were all pretty sure he felt the same. But something stopped them from ever crossing that line.

Zara glanced up as if she felt me staring. Her lips curved into a wicked smile as she pressed closer to Aaron, sliding her hand up his bicep.

"Fake bitch," I hissed under my breath. When I turned back around, Sofia and Poppy were both staring at me. "What?"

"Nothing." Sofia smirked. "Nothing at all. Have you seen Ezra yet? I heard there was a confrontation in the locker room after practice."

"Confrontation?" My stomach dipped, and I wondered if I would ever stop feeling so protective over him.

"Some juniors aren't happy that he's training with the team and getting special treatment from Coach."

"It's the first day of the semester. How the hell can he be getting special treatment?"

I didn't want to talk about Ezra. I didn't. But my heart had a mind of its own where he was concerned. I'd always made it my business to look out for him, to try and be there if he needed me. Since the accident, I was questioning a lot of things though. Looking at things through a different lens. One where I realized that perhaps Ezra only tolerated me. Let me come around like a stray puppy who couldn't stay away.

Losing so many memories had tainted every moment I'd ever spent with him: talking, sitting in complete silence, watching the moon ripple over the lake. When I thought about it, really thought about it, I had perhaps skewed things between us. Let my feelings for him cloud my judgment about *his* intentions.

It didn't matter now though, because he'd made his feelings perfectly clear.

My appetite vanished and I pushed my plate away.

"You need to eat something," Poppy argued.

"Not hungry."

"Sorry, I didn't mean to upset you."

"You didn't, I'm fine." I got up, suddenly needing to be away from here. Away from them. "I'm going to grab some books from the library. I'll see you both later, okay?"

I didn't give them a chance to talk me into staying. I had to get out of here.

With every step, the walls began to close in around me, the laughter and chatter rising above me until I was drowning under the noise. My heart beat so hard it made it hard to breathe. Rushing out of the doors, I stumbled into the nearest locker bank and pressed my forehead against the cool metal, willing myself to calm down.

This was happening more and more. Irrational moments of sheer panic where everything felt out of control. I hadn't mentioned it to anyone because I didn't want them to worry.

But something wasn't right.

I wasn't right anymore.

"ASHLEIGH." Zara approached my desk, slowing her steps as if she wanted to talk.

God, I hoped she didn't.

"Can I help you?"

She jerked back as if the sneer in my words had physically slapped her. "There's no need to be so rude. I just wanted to see how you're doing... you know." She leaned down, giving me a conspiratorial glance. "After everything."

"I'm fine, thanks for asking."

"That's good to hear. It can't be easy being back at Rixon High when all your friends have moved on."

I bristled at the venom in her words. Zara Willis was everything wrong with the world. A true Regina George, she was only happy when she was basking in the misery of others.

Bitch.

I was almost about to tell her to go fuck herself when the teacher breezed into the classroom.

"Seats please people," she said. "Let's go."

Zara sauntered to the back of the room and joined her friends.

I remembered this routine from last year. Mrs. Hanks would take the register, introduce this semester's topic, and then force us to play an awkward round of get to know your partner. Last year, I'd been sitting next to Peyton, so it was easy. This year, I was sitting beside some freckle-faced guy who had overdone it on the cologne.

"Hi, I'm Harrison," he said.

"Ashleigh."

"Oh, I know who you are." A wide grin split his face.

"Okay," Mrs. Hanks said. "I'll call the—Mr. Bennet, how lovely of you to join us."

I sank further into my chair as Ezra scanned the room. I had hoped to avoid him as much as possible. But there he was, staring at the empty chair on my other side.

"Take a seat, Mr. Bennet. I don't have all day."

My fingers curled around the edge of the table, bracing myself. But he didn't sit next to me. Instead, he went straight to the empty desk at the back of the room, next to Zara and her crew.

I wasn't sure what to think, given that he would rather sit with her than next to me. But I shook those pointless thoughts out of my head, and I forced myself to focus my attention on the teacher. Looking back at Ezra would only hurt.

"Okay, for those of you familiar with my class, you know the drill by now." Mrs. Hanks perched on the edge of her desk. "Turn to the person on your right and spend the next couple of minutes getting to know each other."

A chorus of groans filled the room.

"Five minutes, go."

With a heavy sigh, I twisted around to give my partner my full attention. But before I could get a word out, he said, "Is it true what they're saying?"

"What who are saying?"

"Well, people... kids around school."

"And what are they saying?" The pit gnawed deep in my stomach.

"That you're repeating senior year because you banged your head so hard you can't even remember how to tie your shoelaces anymore."

I gawked at him, red-hot indignation burning through me. "They're... they're saying that?" My cheeks burned.

He shrugged. "There's a few versions."

"A few versions... right." I inhaled a deep breath, forcing myself to stay put. If I left; if I grabbed my bag and walked the hell out of there it would only fuel the rumors.

"So, is it?"

"Is it what?" I frowned.

"True." His tongue practically wagged out of his mouth as he awaited my answer.

"Oh yeah, that. What do you think, Harry, was it?"

"Harrison." He cracked a toothy grin. "I mean, you seem pretty coherent."

I bent down to my feet and faked tying a shoelace and

then gave Harrison a fake smile. If this was a sign of things to come, this year was going to be a hard slog.

"Okay, time." The teacher clapped her hands. "Let's share what we've learned. Any volunteers?"

A couple of eager hands went up, but mine stayed firmly in my lap.

"Ah, Miss Willis, let's start with you."

I barely suppressed an eye roll. Of course she had volunteered.

"My partner was Ezra." My spine stiffened. "He's eighteen, but as most of you know, he's repeating senior year. He's hoping to make the football team. Enjoys hiking with his family and hanging out by the pool. Oh, and his favorite food is pizza."

Bitter laughter bubbled inside me, and I clapped a hand over my mouth to stop it from escaping. Ezra had fed her a bunch of lies, although I was surprised he'd talked to her at all.

I didn't let myself dwell on that thought too long because Mrs. Hanks asked Ezra to inform the class what he'd learned about Zara.

"She's a cheerleader."

A couple of people snickered.

"Anything else, Ezra?"

"She wants to be Homecoming Queen and take the cheer squad to nationals."

Stupidly, I glanced back at him, thinking we might share a moment of solidarity at our disdain for girls like Zara. But he didn't even meet my gaze.

"Yes, well, very good. Let's move on."

I shut off after that. I didn't care who liked football or wanted to play in the school band. These kids weren't my friends. They were people I had to spend the next year with under duress.

Maybe I could talk to my parents again, try to persuade them that spending the year doing some work experience would be a better use of my time. By then, maybe my memories would return.

Or maybe they won't.

Frustration snaked through me. There was no quick fix here, no magic solution. There was only time and a bucket load of disappointment every day my memory didn't return.

"You should come to the party Friday."

I homed in on Zara's saccharine voice.

"I don't party," Ezra replied, flatly.

"No, but you're practically a Raider now, so you should come. Meet my girls, hang out with the guys. It's at Cole's house. He's best friends with your brother, practically family."

I risked peeking over my shoulder again. Ezra was slouched low in his chair, his hood pulled up over his head, one hand draped over the desk in that easy, don't-give-a-shit way. But Ezra did care—sometimes I thought he cared too much. He just didn't know how to show it.

His eyes snagged mine this time, tension crackling between us, as Zara kept talking. Kept trying to get his attention. She was so wrapped up in herself and her story, she failed to see that his attention was elsewhere. And just for a second, I wanted to catch her attention and rub it in her face.

But I didn't.

I forced myself to break the connection first. Because that's what it had always felt like when Ezra looked at me. A connection. A living, breathing thing between us. He set those deep amber eyes on me, and it was like I became grounded. Pulled into his orbit. He was the sun, and I was willing to burn for one second longer with him.

God, I was pathetic.

Why couldn't I let him go when he'd clearly decided I wasn't worth his time anymore?

"Miss Chase?" Mrs. Hanks frowned at me. "Are you with us?"

"Yes, sorry, I... uh... what did you say?"

Snickers rang out around me, but she quickly silenced them. "Mrs. Bennet would like to see you in her office."

Mya.

Right.

She'd said she wanted to touch base today. I just hadn't expected to be pulled out of class in the middle of the day.

"I'll have Harrison take notes for you."

"Great." Sarcasm dripped from my one word reply. I stuffed my things in my bag and headed for the door.

And I could have sworn, Ezra's icy cold stare followed me the whole way.

CHAPTER SEVENTEEN

Ashleigh

THE REST of the week didn't get much better. I resented every second I was inside the walls of Rixon High. I resented the teachers every time they offered me another sympathetic smile or tried to break something down for me as if I was incapable of understanding. I resented the stares and whispers and Zara's attempts at getting under my skin, even if nine times out of ten it worked. I resented that I was slapped in the face with school spirit everywhere I turned. But most of all, I resented my peers and the way they soaked it all up. The best year of their lives.

They had it all to look forward to. Homecoming. Prom. Graduation. They would get to live every milestone, while I watched on from the sidelines trying desperately to uncover my memories.

When Mrs. Bennet had called me out of class the first day of the semester, she'd told me not to be too hard on myself, to give myself time to adjust. Her door was always open if I wanted to talk.

I didn't want to talk. I wanted to wake up and remember.

"Hey, you okay?" Sofia asked.

We rode together every day. I still hadn't plucked up the courage to drive my car. Just the thought of it made my heart race and palms sweat, which was odd because I had no problem getting into Sofia's car.

"Yeah," I murmured. "Just tired."

I wasn't sleeping well. My parents wanted me to talk to the doctor about it, but I didn't. A pill wasn't going to cure me. It would mask the problem, sure, maybe give me a few nights of good sleep, but it wouldn't chase away the nightmares.

"You're going to come tonight, right?" Poppy asked from the back seat.

"No," I said, flatly.

"Leigh, you said you'd try."

"Yeah, and I changed my mind." My cell phone vibrated, and my lips twitched at the incoming photo from Gav. It was an action shot of Millie crawling toward the camera with her pudgy little hand outstretched. Getting Millie updates was one of my favorite parts of the day.

"Gav?"

"Yeah." I texted him back.

"You know, he's hoping to be there. The two of you could hang out..."

"Don't, Pops."

"What? I'm just saying the two of you spend a lot of time together. You can spend time together at the party."

We didn't spend that much time together, but he had picked me up from school a couple of times. We'd hung out with Millie and gone to the park.

There was zero pressure being around Gav and his sister. He didn't ask questions or push for answers I didn't have.

Even though Ezra's words played over in my head whenever I was with him, Gav was easy to be around.

My cell phone pinged again.

Gav: Maybe I should have repeated senior year. College classes are hard.

Me: Trust me, it's not half as fun the second time around.

Gav: Yeah, I guess. Aaron texted me about the party tonight. Are you going?

"YES, TELL HIM YES."

"Poppy." I pushed her away and she flopped back against the seat.

"Sorry, I'm just trying to help. You and Gav would be good together."

"It isn't like that."

"But it could be."

"I don't want to talk about it."

Because talking about another guy felt like a betrayal to Ezra. Even though my head knew things between us were over—not that they'd ever really begun—my stupid heart couldn't comprehend it.

Before I could reply to Gav, another text came through.

Gav: You should come. We can keep each other company and people watch.

Me: People watch? Who are you and what have you done to Gavin McKay?

Gav: Think about it. I'll even stay sober and drive you home.

Me: Fine, I'll think about it.

I SHOVED my cell in my bag and got ready to climb out of Sofia's car, but paused when I saw Aaron, Cole, and Ezra.

The sight was so unexpected, the way they moved together as a unit, a team. Guys stopped to high-five Aaron and girls flocked around them.

Ezra hovered on the periphery, but he didn't walk away.

Interesting.

If not a little strange.

"He's been at practice every day," Sofia said before climbing out. I followed, unable to take my eyes off Ezra and the guys.

"He's like a different person." Poppy looped her arm through mine.

"Who, Ezra?"

"No, Aaron, silly. Senior year has gone to his head. Look at him." She clucked her tongue. "That isn't the Aaron I know."

"You're still one of his favorite friends, Pops."

She shot me a pensive look. One that said, 'Maybe I don't want to be his friend anymore.'

But I had no words of encouragement for her, not when my own love life was in tatters.

"Come on, we should get to class."

We walked away from Aaron and Ezra, and I noticed her footsteps were almost as reluctant as mine.

THE SURPRISES DIDN'T STOP COMING. At lunch in the cafeteria, the entire room almost fell quiet when Ezra entered, joined the line for his lunch and then joined the football players at their usual table. He did sit at the end, eating in relative silence, but he was still sitting with them.

"I feel like I stepped into an alternate universe," I murmured, picking at my salad.

"I heard my dad telling Mom that he's determined to break him."

"What the hell?" My head whipped up.

"Relax." She rolled her eyes. "Obviously he means in some kind of metaphorical way."

"Yeah." But something about the whole thing still didn't add up. I was missing too many pieces to uncover why though.

"Aaron made him promise he'll go tonight, but I don't think he's got it in him."

"Wait, Ezra's going to the party?"

She shrugged. "You know E. He doesn't party."

He didn't eat lunch with his foster brother and the football team either, but there he was.

"I don't get it," I murmured.

"Maybe he's just trying to make the most of this year," Poppy suggested. "I mean, it's long overdue."

"Maybe."

I wasn't buying it though.

But an unwelcome thought went through me. What if Poppy was right? What if she was right and this was a new and improved Ezra?

An Ezra who didn't want or need me in his life?

I glanced over in his direction again, my lips parting on a harsh breath when Zara strolled up to him and slid her hands around Ezra and Aaron's shoulders, leaning down and laughing.

What the hell was happening right now?

Ezra immediately moved away, but it didn't ease the knot in my stomach.

"I swear she's just trying to piss me off," Poppy muttered.

"She's never gotten over the fact that she didn't make the gymnastic team."

"She tried out for gymnastics?" I asked them, and Poppy nodded.

"In ninth grade. There was one spot left. I got picked. She went to the cheer squad instead."

"I didn't know that."

"Because it wasn't a big deal. Or at least, I didn't think it was. She's never been so... blatant before."

"Maybe she's just settling into her role as cheer captain," Sofia said. But from the look she and Poppy shared, I knew neither of them believed that.

"Aaron knows she's a bitch though. He would never—"

"Team politics. The team needs the cheer squad, just like the cheer squad needs the team. After last season, all the coaching staff are trying to smooth things over."

"What happened last season?" I had vague memories of Zara's sister Candice and her bestie Lindsey Filmer being Grade A bitches, but couldn't remember anything to warrant the coaching staff going out of their way to make sure the teams played nice together.

Poppy and Sofia shared a look, and Poppy let out a long sigh. "Lily didn't tell you?"

"Tell me what?"

God, I hated this.

"Lindsey was jealous of Lily and Kaiden, so she went after her at Homecoming. It was a shitshow. Dad was fuming."

"What did she do?"

Poppy launched into a detailed account of how Lindsey had blackmailed Kaiden to attend Homecoming with her and then embarrassed Lily in front of the entire dance.

After she finished, I sat there dumbfounded. In all our conversations about what had happened over the last ten months, Lily hadn't breathed a single word about Homecoming.

"Ashleigh?" one of them said. I didn't know which because I couldn't think, blood roaring between my ears.

"Leigh?"

"I'm fine."

They both watched me with concern. "She probably didn't want to relive it or upset you," Poppy offered, and I murmured some half-hearted reply.

"I need to go." I stood up.

"Go? But you haven't finished your lunch."

"I'm not hungry. Help yourself."

"Leigh, come on. You can't keep doing this." Poppy gave me a thin smile.

"Do what?" My eyes narrowed.

"We know it's hard, but you can't run every time you get overwhelmed."

Swallowing harshly, I inhaled a deep breath and said, "I'll see you guys later."

GAV WAS WAITING in the parking lot by the time I finally left the girls' bathroom.

Poppy's words had a struck a chord with me. I didn't want to run, of course I didn't. But they didn't understand what it was like to be a clueless bystander to almost a year of your life.

I felt so stupid.

"Rough day?" he said when I slid into the passenger seat.

"You could say that." I clutched my bag in my lap like a life raft, as if it would somehow keep me afloat in these uncharted waters.

"Want to talk about it?"

"Nope. Where's Millie?"

"Mom has a rare afternoon off, so they're spending some quality time together."

"You didn't want to join them?"

He pinned me with an intent look. "You needed me; I came." Gav shrugged as if it was nothing.

It wasn't.

"What do you want to do? We could head to Riverside and—"

My cell phone started vibrating and Dad's name flashed across the screen.

"That was quick," Gav said.

I rejected the call and quickly texted him that I was fine but needed some space.

Dad: I don't like it, sweetheart. You can't just

RUINED HOPES

take off whenever things get to be too much. Mya's door is always open, use her.

Me: I know, Dad. But I just... I can't stay there this afternoon. I'll be home later. I promise.

"IS HE ANGRY?"

I shrugged. "Probably. But I'm almost nineteen. What are they going to do?"

"So what happened back there?"

"I found out some things that Lily didn't tell me." I pressed my head against the cool glass. "It isn't even the fact she didn't tell me, it's that I didn't remember. My friends had all this life changing stuff going on and I can't remember any of it."

"Yeah, that must suck."

"It does." Looking over at him, he cracked a smile.

"What?"

"You're going to be okay, Leigh Leigh. You know that right?"

I didn't want to talk about this, so I asked, "Why do you call me Leigh Leigh?"

A strange expression washed over him. "We're friends, aren't we?"

"Yeah, I guess we are." The air turned heavy. Thick and suffocating.

Gav must have noticed my discomfort because he said, "So I'm thinking milkshakes from Cindy's Grill and a trip down to the river."

"I don't feel like being around people." And Riverside would be crowded.

"Not Riverside," he added, following my train of thought. "I know a place."

"You... know a place." I fought a smile. "Sounds interesting."

"Oh, it is. And since we're friends, I don't mind sharing it with you."

He grinned and I grinned back.

"Milkshakes and the river then."

CHAPTER EIGHTEEN

Ezra

I'D LOST my fucking mind.

That was the only possible explanation for why I was standing in Cole Kandon's yard, swarmed by football players and cheerleaders, watching Aaron neck a yard of ale like he was born to do it.

"Raiders," he yelled. "Let's get fucked up."

Everyone went wild... everyone except me.

I watched carefully. The wide easy smile, the twinkle in his eye, the way he laughed and high-fived his teammates.

This wasn't the Aaron Bennet I knew. The boy I'd grown up with.

"What?" He came bounding over, saluting a couple of half-naked girls over by Kandon's pool.

"What's up with you?"

"Up with me...? I don't follow."

"This isn't you," I said. "You're acting like an asshole jock."

He grabbed my shoulders and shook me gently, but I

immediately batted him away, still not used to his touch. A frown crossed his expression, but then his easy smile slid back into place. "Nice to see you finally care, E."

"This isn't about me."

"I'm fine." He gave me a grin, but I didn't buy it, not for a second.

"Fine, right."

"Relax, man. It's a party." He tapped my cheek. "Everything's going to be fine."

I swatted him away again. "You're—"

"Yo, Bennet. Get the hell over here, dude. It's your turn."

"Duty calls." Aaron waggled his brows at me and took off toward his little fan club.

I almost went after him but decided against it. It was his business, and I had no desire to get tangled up in it.

The familiar scent of weed hit my senses and I drifted over to a group of guys sitting around the fire pit.

"Ezra Jackson, that you?" one of them said.

"Yeah, what of it?" The defensive edge to my voice cut through the air. I didn't know these kids, but they knew me.

It was hardly any surprise when you were one of the few mixed-race kids in town.

"You want a smoke?" another one said, holding out his blunt.

"What, just like that?" My brows knitted.

"Yeah, why not?" He shrugged. "You look like you could use it."

Asher and Mya would lose their shit if I came back high, but damn if it didn't call to me.

"Go on, man," the guy smirked. "You know you want to."

Against my better judgment, I sat down and accepted the blunt from him, bringing it to my lips and inhaling deeply. Acrid smoke filled my lungs, burning deep. But it felt so fucking good, slowly uncoiling the huge, messy knot in my stomach. I blew out a streak of rings and offered it to the guy beside me.

"Go again, something tells me you need it more than me."

So I did. Sucking on the end until my lungs expanded and smoke worked its way deeper into my bloodstream. I fucking loved this feeling, the calm that washed over me. The quiet. The chemicals chasing away my demons until they couldn't touch me. I was safe here.

I was free.

"Whoa, man. Take it easy, that's some strong shit. Got it from a guy over in Halston. He said it's his best product."

With one last toke, I handed the blunt off to him. "Appreciate it, thanks."

"Anytime. I'm Jude. And this is Mikey and Travis."

"Ezra," I said, and they all laughed.

"So you're like what, one of them now?" He flicked his head toward where most of the football team were still drinking and goofing around.

"It's a long story. I take it you're not on the team?"

"Yeah, right. Do I look like a football player to you?"

Long dark hair, a line of piercings in his ear, a nose ring, and an arm lined with black leather bands, he looked like something straight out of a punk band.

"Guess not."

"We're Cole's bandmates."

"Were, we were Cole's bandmates," one of them muttered.

I lifted a brow and Jude said, "It's complicated."

"So Kandon has an alter ego?"

"Something like that."

Interesting. I glanced over at him laughing with Aaron. Cole was around a lot. He and Aaron had been best friends since I came to Rixon. But I didn't know much about him, which was hardly a surprise given how I avoided them as much as I could.

But not tonight. Tonight, I'd let Aaron and Asher railroad me into coming to the party. Even Coach Ford had suggested I show my face and 'get to know the team outside of practice.' Whatever the fuck that meant.

I didn't have the energy to argue and since Ashleigh had skipped her afternoon classes—I only knew because I'd overheard Aaron and Sofia talking about it—it was unlikely she was going to be here.

"Do you think you'll get a spot on the team?" Jude asked.

I leaned back in the chair, running a hand down my face. "Coach would have to be fucking desperate to give me a spot."

Besides, I didn't want one. I was there because he and Asher demanded it. Not because I had any intentions of actually playing for the Raiders this season.

"A little birdie told me you've got a strong throwing arm. And with Coach one quarterback short..."

"Yeah," I snorted. "Never going to fucking happen."

The three of them launched into a discussion about possible candidates for the quarterback position. Whoever it was, they needed to be able to lead the team with an iron fist and handle the pressure of Coach Ford breathing down their neck. The guy was borderline psychotic about his team, and everyone knew defending a championship was harder than trying to win one because you had everything to lose.

"Holy shit, is that Ashleigh Chase?"

My head whipped around, and my eyes immediately found her, moving toward Aaron and Cole. Her hair was curled down her back in thick, silky waves, and her dress clung to her body like a second skin. Dark smokey makeup lined her eyes, making them stand out more. She looked good enough to eat and a bolt of lust went through me.

Fuck.

"She looks wasted," Jude said.

He wasn't wrong.

Ashleigh swayed slightly on her feet. Thank fuck she had sandals on and not heels, because if she fell over, everyone would get an eyeful of her ass.

What the fuck was she wearing?

I went to move, to go tell Aaron to take her home and save her from herself. But McKay appeared at her side, wrapping his arm around Ashleigh's waist to steady her. She gazed up at him through hooded eyes. That look... she might as well have stabbed a knife through my fucking heart. It was the way she used to look at me. Such honesty and unyielding loyalty.

Motherfucker.

I clenched my fist, inhaling a shaky breath. She wasn't supposed to be here. If I'd have known she would be, I wouldn't have come.

But there she was, standing half-dressed, looking like all my dreams come true... and yet, so far out of my fucking reach it actually hurt to look at her.

I needed to get out of here, before I did something really fucking stupid.

"You're leaving?" Jude asked as I stood.

"Yeah, I can't stay here." I fought the urge to look over at Ashleigh again.

"Well, it was good hanging with you. We should do it again some time."

"Maybe." I eyed the fresh blunt in his hand. Jude and his guys knew Cole. Cole was best friends with Aaron. And Aaron knew his parents would lose their shit if they found out I was high.

But something told me they weren't the gossiping type.

I DIDN'T LEAVE the party. Instead, I sat against the wall in the shadows, watching Ashleigh dance and drink and act like one of them.

The cool kids.

The kids who valued popularity over integrity. The ones who would sell their souls if it meant having more followers on social media or being higher up the social ladder at school.

Ashleigh wasn't that girl. I knew it. She knew it. And last year, everyone else would have known it too.

But this Ashleigh... well, no one knew her. Not really. And from the looks of it, she didn't know herself anymore either.

McKay hovered close to her and the girls. Poppy and Sofia had found Ashleigh almost straight away, sticking to her side like glue. But even they had looked a little concerned at the state she was in.

My cell phone vibrated, distracting me, and I dug it out of my pocket, scanning Aaron's text.

Aaron: Where the hell did you go? You're supposed to be partying with us.

HE WAS WORSE than a dog with a bone. I shoved it back in my pocket and tried to pick out Ashleigh again. Poppy and Sofia were right there, but there was no sign of her.

RUINED HOPES

I climbed to my feet, careful to stay hidden in the shadows, searching for her.

She'd wandered down the edge of Kandon's yard, propping herself up with a hand to a thick tree trunk. A radiant angel in the darkness of the shadows. As if she felt me watching, her head snapped over to me and she narrowed her eyes.

I couldn't resist stepping into her line of sight. The second she saw me, her breath caught, her eyes widening, glazed with all the beer I'd watched her drink.

"What are you doing, buttercup?" I whispered, holding her gaze. A rainbow of emotion passed over her. Surprise. Longing... Anger.

Oh yeah, she was pissed.

And she was marching right toward me.

I ducked back into the cover of darkness, realizing my epic mistake. I didn't want to do this with her, not tonight.

Not ever.

We'd said everything we needed to say to each other. Ashleigh needed to move past whatever had once existed between us and get on with her life. And for as much as I didn't like to admit it, I needed to follow through on my word to Asher and graduate senior year. If I didn't, I had no hopes of ever getting out of Rixon.

I slipped between the tree line and around the side of Kandon's house, but delicate fingers snagged my arm. "You're spying on me, why?" Her voice was steady. Too fucking steady.

Hostile anger radiated from Ashleigh like a forcefield, but I made myself turn around and meet her accusatory gaze. "You're a mess." The words spewed out before I could stop them.

"Excuse me?"

"You heard me. Someone needed to stick around and make sure you didn't do anything stupid since you clearly can't rely on Aaron or the girls."

Hurt flashed in her eyes but quickly morphed into rage. "How dare you."

"You should go back to the party." I dismissed her.

"And you should stay out of my life. After all, that's what you want isn't it?"

"You have no idea what I want."

That gave her pause and her eyes fluttered closed as she drew in a deep breath.

When she opened them again, she pinned me with an intense look. "Why don't you enlighten me then, Ezra. What do you want?"

Ashleigh stepped closer. I was aware of every inch of her. The curve of her neck as she lifted her chin in defiance, staring me down with smug victory. The way her dress dipped low in the front, the curve of her tits taunting me. The blood-red lipstick painted on her mouth, both an invitation and a warning.

Ashleigh had pulled out all the big guns tonight... but for who?

"Where's McKay," I sneered. "Shouldn't he be keeping you company?"

"You'd like that, wouldn't you? If I went back to him and absolved you of whatever... this is." She motioned between us. "But something tells me you wouldn't like it if he kissed me. You wouldn't like it if he stripped me out of this dress and—"

"Watch it," I said, pushing back into her space until we were pressed in close. Jealousy burned through me like wildfire. It was a mistake to be so near and unable to touch her. I'd always been careful in the past to maintain control. But she was seriously pushing my restraint tonight.

"Or what?" she snarled, right up in my face, her hot, liquor-scented breath dusting my skin. "What the hell are you going to do about it?"

The air crackled between us, the stream of moonlight illuminating her face, making her furious eyes glitter.

Her lips curved into a wicked smile. "Yeah, just what I thought. You're a coward, Ezra. You've always been a coward. And we're done here. We are so fucking done." She whirled around and went to storm off, but I grabbed her arm, yanking her back to me.

"Ezra, what the hell?" If looks could have killed, Ashleigh would have cut me wide open with that glare, spilling my insides out all over the ground.

"What happened to you?"

"M-me?" She staggered back, shucking out of my hold.

"This isn't you. You're not... one of them."

"You mean I'm not like Zara?"

"Zara? What the fuck does she have to do with this?"

Ashleigh's expression guttered but she quickly shook it off. "I'm leaving. I don't know what happened between us. But I'm sick of trying to figure it out."

She went to leave again, but I couldn't do it.

I couldn't let her walk away.

Grabbing her, I pulled her to me, but this time Ashleigh lashed out. Her palm cracked against my cheek, the sting startling me.

She'd hit me. She'd fucking hit me.

Anger flooded me, making me tremble as I glared at her.

"Crap, Ezra," the blood drained from her face, "I didn't..."

"Shut up," I spat, my fingers tightening around her arm.

"I'm sorry. You just make me so mad."

The defeat in her voice should have calmed the lava

coursing through my veins, but I was lost to another time. Another crack of an unwelcome hand on my skin.

"E-Ezra?" Ashleigh closed the distance between us, reaching out for me.

"Don't." I jerked back but she didn't stop, laying her hand against my cheek. "Don't touch me."

"I'm sorry."

I was paralyzed, rooted to the spot as she leaned up on her tiptoes and brushed her lips over her fingers, right over the spot where she'd hit me. "I don't know what came over me."

Gently, she eased her fingers away, letting her mouth linger. My body was rigid, my breathing ragged. She was too close.

Too fucking close.

I could almost taste her liquor-scented breath, feel her soft curves pushed up against me. Taunting me. Daring me to take what she'd always wanted me to.

"This can't happen," I forced the words past my lips. "This can't ever fucking happen."

Her expression turned murderous. "Fine." She started to pull away, leaving me cold. "I guess I'll go find Gav, after all."

CHAPTER NINETEEN

Ashleigh

EZRA GLOWERED at me as I slowly started backing away. He was the most infuriating, stubborn creature I'd ever met.

He wanted me. It was in his eyes every time he looked at me. But something was holding him back.

Something always held him back.

"Remember this," I said, with liquor-induced confidence. "Remember that you let me walk away. You—"

His arm shot out and grabbed me round the waist. Ezra yanked me forward and we stumbled back, further into the shadows. My hands went to his chest to steady myself, and I noticed the glint of a silver chain hanging around his neck. I'd never seen it before—or at least, I couldn't remember—but there was something about it... My fingers drifted toward it but he ground out, "Don't."

"Don't what?" My arms hovered in midair, adrenaline rushing through me.

"Don't touch me."

Brows furrowed, my hands fell away to my sides. "But—"

"Shh." He dipped his head, moving in dangerously close to my face. "Just give me a second." His amber eyes darted to my mouth sending my heart into a free fall.

He wanted to kiss me.

Ezra Jackson wanted to kiss me.

And I wanted it.

I wanted it more than I'd ever wanted anything in my life.

"Do it," I breathed, clenching my fists to stop myself from reaching out to touch him. "Kiss me."

"I can't."

"You can. Kiss me, Ezra. Please." *Don't make me beg.*

"Fuck... *fuck.*" His eyes searched mine, pleading with me to walk away. I wanted to scream at him, to demand to know what the hell his problem was. But I didn't want to move and break whatever spell we'd both fallen under.

"What is it?" I went to cup his face again, but he jerked back again as if my touch burned.

It cooled down the fire inside me and I stepped back. "I should—"

Ezra's mouth came down on mine, hard and unyielding, an unexpected storm I couldn't shelter myself from.

I reached for him again, needing something to ground me, to steady myself from the emotions battering my insides. But Ezra grabbed my wrists, lifting my hands above my head. He spun us and pushed me back against the tree, pinning my hands. His eyes glittered with hunger as he heaved a ragged breath, rubbing his thumb over my bottom lip. "I've wondered for so long... wondered what you would taste like."

"And what do I taste like?"

He leaned in, rubbing his nose along my jaw and nipping my lip. "You taste like sunshine, buttercup."

My stomach clenched at the yearning in his voice.

"Ezra..."

"Shh." His tongue darted out, licking the seam of my mouth. Exploring. Teasing. He touched his head to mine, pressing up against me, trapping me between his body and the tree.

I gasped when I felt him hard at my stomach, whimpering when he rolled his hips against me, letting me feel exactly just how much he didn't want this.

Liar.

"Fuck," he hissed, letting a hand slide down my spine to grab my ass and pull my body closer until I was grinding on him.

"More." My voice cracked with lust, a flash of desire shooting through me. "It feels—"

He cussed again under his breath and immediately put some distance between us. Not much, but enough that I almost groaned at the loss of his warm body.

"What's—"

One of his hands slid down to my neck, his fingers closing around my throat. Not enough to hurt, but enough that a trickle of fear raced down my spine.

"You're angry," I said, sensing his warring emotions. He wanted me, but he hated himself for it.

"What do you think?" His eyes narrowed. "You're drunk at a party, dressed like... *that*."

"What's wrong with the way I'm dressed?" I huffed indignantly.

So maybe I'd gone a little overboard with my outfit choice. But after Gav had persuaded me to come to the party, I'd gone home, dug out the sexiest thing I could find and stolen a bottle of Dad's vodka.

I didn't want to be Ashleigh Chase, the girl repeating senior year because of her unfortunate accident. So I'd put on a tight dress, smoothed over the cracks on my face with makeup, and curled my hair within an inch of its life. And I'd felt good, sexy even. But it had all been a lie. A liquor-induced mirage.

Until I saw him.

The second my eyes had found Ezra across Cole's yard, everything else melted away. And maybe part of me had dressed up for him in hopes that he'd see me, instead of looking straight through me.

Now his attention almost felt like too much though. It was hard to breathe with him stroking my pulse point, my wrists still pinned in his other hand.

I was completely and utterly at his mercy.

"What happened to us?" I whispered, desperate for the answers only he could give me. "And why won't you let me touch you?"

Surprise registered on his face, but his expression quickly darkened. "You should go back to the party."

Bitter laughter spilled off my lips. "You're joking, right?" My head swam with the effects of all the alcohol. "You can't kiss me like that and then act like nothing happened."

"Ashleigh..." There was a dark warning in his voice, laced with pain.

But this didn't have to hurt. I wanted Ezra and he wanted me. Kissing him was like coming home. He anchored me. He made me feel like me again. The rest would all fall into place.

I leaned in, trying to kiss him again, but he hovered out of reach.

"We can't."

"*Bullshit*. I'm telling you we can." Irritation coated my words.

He let out a long breath. "It isn't that simple." His eyes darted away from me, and it was enough to cool the heat between us.

I'd lost him again.

Ezra's stone walls slammed back into place, ripping open barely healed wounds inside me.

"You kissed me," I said, unable to keep the disbelief out of my voice. "You... want me."

I'd felt it in every stroke of his tongue, every press of his lips.

Ezra ran his thumb over my jaw, studying me intently, as if he was imprinting this moment to memory.

"It doesn't matter, buttercup," he said quietly, releasing me. "This... us," his voice turned cold again. "It can never happen."

"THERE YOU ARE, I've been looking everywhere." Gav found me over by the tree line. He took one look at my tear-stained cheeks and said, "What happened?"

"Nothing. Can we go?"

"Sure. Let me say bye to the guys."

I nodded, folding my arms around myself. Ezra was long gone. He'd slipped away into the shadows as if he'd never been there at all. Except, I could still taste him on my lips, feel the dull ache deep inside me.

It had been real.

But it still wasn't enough.

Or I wasn't enough.

It hurt my head trying to analyze Ezra's actions. The things he said and did.

It didn't take long for Gav to find me again. "Ready?" he asked, and I nodded.

"Come on." He slung his arm over my shoulder and guided me around the front of the house to where his car was parked. He'd offered to be the designated driver tonight and for that, I was grateful.

"Ready to talk about it?" he asked the second we were settled in his car.

"Not really." I shrugged, the heavy pounding in my head making me reach for the bottle of water in the cup holder.

"I saw him, Leigh Leigh." Gav pinned me with a knowing look. "You were with Ezra, right?"

"I... it's complicated."

"Complicated how? Explain it to me."

There was no judgment in his eyes. No consternation in his voice. Only mild curiosity.

I didn't answer so Gav started the car and backed out of Cole's driveway.

"I saw Penelope today," Gav said, breaking the awful silence.

"The woman from the park?"

"Yeah. Turns out she's taking some classes at the community college too."

"You didn't say anything... before, I mean."

"There wasn't really much to say." He shrugged.

"Did you talk to her?"

"We said hello in passing."

"You like her," I said, that strange feeling taking root again.

"Like her?" His eyes flicked to mine in question, humor sparkling there. "I don't even know her."

"You know what I mean. When we saw her at the park you were checking her out."

"I wasn't... okay, you got me. Maybe I was just a little. This isn't weird for you?"

"Is it supposed to be?"

"I don't know." He let out a heavy sigh. "I don't know what the rules are here."

"We're friends, aren't we?"

"Friends, right." There was something in his voice that made my stomach curl.

Gav hadn't given me those vibes. But he seemed a little annoyed at me.

"Do we... need to talk about this?" I glanced over at him, and he met my gaze.

"Friends. I can live with that."

"But you wanted to be more than friends?"

"I... I don't know, okay?" He sighed. "I don't fucking know."

Pressing back into the seat, I wanted it to swallow me whole. Navigating this was hard. Especially with ten months of memories that I couldn't remember between us. But I needed to know.

"Gav," I whispered. "Did we ever...?"

"No. *No*! I've always known you were hung up on him, so I never... Listen, I'm not asking you for anything, Ashleigh. I just... I don't want to see you get hurt."

"I wish I could remember." My fingers curled into the seat. "I feel like I'm missing something important. He wasn't like this before. I mean, he's never been easy, but it's like he hates me now."

"He doesn't hate you."

"How can you know that?"

"Because I've seen the way he looks at you. As if you're forbidden fruit."

"He doesn't... that's not..."

But it was.

What had he said to me earlier?

This... us, it can never happen.

He'd tried so hard to hold himself back. To *not* kiss me.

"He says he doesn't deserve me," I confessed.

"Maybe he doesn't. But sometimes the thing we shouldn't want, the thing we think we don't deserve, the thing that is off-limits, is exactly the thing that we need."

"You almost sound like you're rooting for us." I chuckled, but it died on my lips when he shot me a weak, defeated smile.

"You deserve nothing but good things, Ashleigh. And hey, you can't help who you fall for, right?"

"Gav, I—"

"Don't. You don't need to do that with me. I'm okay."

I didn't ever want to hurt Gav, but I didn't feel that way about him. He knew that. Yet he was prepared to put his feelings aside to be a friend to me.

"You're a good friend," I said, folding my hands into my lap.

"I'm the best fucking friend you'll ever have." His playful lilt made my shoulders relax.

"Did you enjoy the party?" I asked.

"It was okay. Although I think I'm kind of over high school parties."

"So why did you come?"

Gav glanced over, lifted a brow, and said, "Because that's what friends do."

BY THE TIME I got home, I was sober. Which was a good thing considering Dad opened the front door before I'd even made it there.

"Gavin gave you a ride home?"

"I told you he would."

Dad nodded. "How was the party?"

"It was good." *Ezra kissed me and then stalked off into the shadows like it meant nothing.* "I'm tired, so I think I'll go straight up to bed." I moved around him and disappeared into the house.

"You were drinking?"

His words gave me pause and I glanced back at him. "I had a few beers."

"And the missing bottle of vodka?"

Crap.

"I... I didn't want to turn up empty-handed."

"Do I need to be worried?"

"No, Dad. I'm fine. It's just hard sometimes, you know."

"I know, sweetheart, but cutting class and getting drunk at parties isn't going to fix anything."

"But it might make me feel normal."

"Oh, Ashleigh." He closed the distance between us, pulling me into his arms. "You're still you, sweetheart. I know it doesn't feel like that, but ten months don't define you."

"Don't they?" Pain laced my words. "There's so much I don't remember, Dad. Things are different now." I dropped my gaze, trying desperately to blink away the tears.

"What things, Leigh Leigh?" He gently cupped my jaw and lifted my face to meet his.

"It doesn't matter," I said.

"I'm here, sweetheart. Talk to me..."

"What happened with Ezra, Dad? He's being... weird. I know something happened."

"Ezra... this is about Ezra?" He frowned, his eyes clouded with confusion.

"He's barely talked to me since I got out of the hospital."

"I didn't realize the two of you were friends."

"What do you mean?" I jerked back. "Of course we were

friends; why else would I have been in the car with him that night?"

"He said you were feeling sick, so he offered you a ride home."

"He said that?"

"Well, yes. Why? Do you remember it differently?"

"I don't remember it at all." Frustration coated my words.

"But you were friends?" He rubbed his jaw. "I didn't know that."

"We hung out sometimes. At least, I know we did before senior year."

"Huh."

My brows furrowed. "What aren't you telling me?" I demanded.

"Nothing, sweetheart. It's late. You should probably get some sleep."

He was lying but I didn't push. Because too many things didn't add up. Like why Ezra had lied to my dad and why he was avoiding me like the plague.

But he'd kissed me. Tonight, he'd let his walls come down and he'd kissed me.

Only, he hadn't let me touch him.

And it wasn't until I left my dad standing in the hall and went up to my room, that I realized that meant something.

CHAPTER TWENTY

Ashleigh

I STAYED in my room for most of the weekend. I was confused. Trying to wade through muddy waters and make sense of everything.

Ezra wanted me, of that I was sure. The way he'd kissed me... it had left me breathless and wanting.

But underneath all the lust and wanting and hunger, I'd felt his anger. His hatred. And I kept coming back to the fact he hadn't wanted—hadn't allowed—me to touch him.

In all the interactions I could remember between us, I'd never been brave enough to reach out and touch him. The closest I'd ever got was a light brush of our hands.

Had something happened between then and now to make him hate the thought of me touching him?

Or was it something else... something that stemmed from his past. Because when I considered his inability to let people in, the way he kept to himself, and how I'd never seen him with a girl before, it all pointed to intimacy avoidance. But he'd had no problem kissing me, pinning me against that tree and—

I forced those thoughts into their little box. Going there only made the dull ache deep inside me roar.

Kissing Ezra wasn't enough. I wanted more. I wanted to discover his deepest secrets and lie with him in the dark. But he refused to meet me halfway. And I wasn't stupid enough to think that when I saw him in school today, anything would be different.

I got my answer when I spotted him heading around the building toward the football field.

"Ezra." I went after him, weaving against the stream of kids all heading inside.

This morning on the ride in with Sofia and Poppy, I'd told myself to let it go. But I couldn't. I needed to know. I needed him to look me in the eye and tell me what his problem was.

"Ezra, wait."

But he kept walking, almost jogging toward the gym. I picked up my pace, breaking into a run. It wasn't until I got close enough that I realized he had his earbuds in. Reaching for his arm, I hesitated. He must have felt me because he ground to a halt and turned to face me.

"What?" It came out as icy as his cold expression.

"I... can we talk?"

My heart crashed violently against my chest as he glowered at me.

"I need to get to practice," he said, flatly. Devoid of any emotion.

"Why are you doing this? You hate team sports."

"It doesn't matter."

"I think it does. Are you... punishing yourself?" My voice grew weak. "Because of the accident?"

He made a tsking sound. "Not everything is about you,

Ashleigh. We can't all rely on daddy to swoop in and fix our problems."

"What… I didn't…" My cheeks burned, his words making little sense but hitting me like a punch to the gut all the same. "Why are you being so mean? I only came to make sure you're okay."

"Newsflash, *Leigh Leigh*," he sneered. "I don't need you to check in on me anymore. We're not friends."

Anger flashed through me. "You weren't saying that Friday night when you had your tongue down my throat."

"I was high and horny." His eyes narrowed to dangerous slits.

"Bullshit," I said, stepping closer to him. Unable to fight the pull I felt. "You were watching me. You were jealous."

"You should go." He went to leave but I grabbed his wrist, frowning when he visibly flinched. "Ashleigh," he warned, his nostrils flaring as I held his arm.

"Why is this an issue for you? It's just me… I would never hurt you."

"You're right." He pinned me with a cold, dead stare. "You couldn't ever hurt me because I won't give you the power to."

"Why are you being like this?" My voice was thick with emotion as I fought to withhold the tears building behind my eyes.

He stepped into me, stealing the air from my lungs. Gone was the lust and the hunger from Saturday night, replaced with nothing but hatred.

Hatred, I felt all the way down to the tips of my toes.

"Stay away from me, Ashleigh. Or you won't like the consequences." He took off toward the football field.

Leaving me more confused than ever.

BY LUNCH TIME, I was ready to cut class again. Thankfully, I hadn't had a class with Ezra, but it didn't stop me from obsessing over our conversation earlier and at the party.

I was more frustrated than ever—not understanding his cryptic words and my growing sense that I was missing something important. Gav swore he didn't know any more than what he'd been told by Lily. And she was busy settling in at college. I didn't want to keep bothering her with this.

Spotting Poppy leaving her class, I hurried after her, gently grasping her arm.

"Oh hey." She smiled. "I didn't see you there."

"Are you okay?" I frowned at her sullen expression.

"It looks like Aaron is going to be made captain."

"Is he? That's... it's not great?"

She shook her head, pulling me out of the stream of bodies. "If Zara makes cheer captain it means they'll be spending more time together."

"I feel like I'm missing something here. I thought you and Aaron weren't—"

"We're not," she said a little too defensively. "But it doesn't mean I want to see Zara freaking Willis get her claws into him. You know what Lindsey and Candice did to Lily last year."

"She'd be stupid to come after you," I said.

"I don't think she'll come after me directly..." She pinned me with a wide look.

"You think she'll go through Aaron to get to you."

"Maybe." Poppy shrugged, toying with the collar on her tank top. "She's never liked me."

"Because everyone loves you and she has to manipulate people into being her friend."

Poppy grinned. "You make a good point. I just... I don't want Aaron to lose himself this year."

"Have you talked to him about it?"

"And say what? I don't think you should hang out with Zara because she's a desperate skank who only wants to use you to climb the social ladder?"

"It's a start."

"Hmm, I don't know. I don't want him to think I'm interfering. Anyway, what's happening with you and Gav? You two seemed pretty close at the party."

"I..." Guilt coiled through me. "It's not like that between us."

"Because you're still hung up on a certain brooding bad boy?"

"Ezra isn't bad, Poppy." I rolled my eyes.

"No, but he isn't exactly good either. You know Sofia said his birth mom is still contacting them, pushing to meet him."

"She is?"

Poppy nodded. "She reached out at the end of last year. But Ezra doesn't want to see her. Won't even talk to them about it."

"I had no idea..."

Because no one had told me. Yet, why would they? My own dad was surprised to find out me and Ezra were even friends.

If that's what you could ever define our relationship as.

It wasn't any surprise. That's how withdrawn and detached Ezra had always been from everyone. No one noticed me following him around because he was practically invisible.

Regardless of what I didn't know, it was glaringly obvious

we hadn't progressed past our occasional chats and stolen moments together.

"Poppy, can I ask you something?"

"Sure..." She eyed me warily.

"Do you know why Asher and Coach Ford made Ezra join the team?"

"They don't want him to mess up again. And have you seen him run sprints? He's too good not to play."

"But he doesn't like sports."

"You're worried about him."

"I'm worried he's punishing himself or they're punishing him. I can't figure it out. But I feel like I'm missing something."

She took my hand. "Ezra is a complicated guy, Leigh. He's always been a complicated guy. What happened... it's changed him. This year is a chance to find yourself, for both of you. But maybe you're not supposed to do it together."

Her words cut deep. Raw and brutal lashes over my heart. I didn't want to give up on Ezra, not until I understood what had happened.

"I... I can't."

"Then prepare to get your heart broken." She gave me a sad smile. "Ezra isn't boyfriend material, Ashleigh. He never was."

―――

"ASHLEIGH, IS THAT YOU?" Lily sounded a million miles away.

"Yes, is this a bad time?"

"N-no, it's fine." Her voice was drowned out by a rumble of laughter. She laughed, a sound that made my heart constrict. "Give me a second." The line went quiet all of a sudden and then I heard a door click. "That's better."

"What's going on?"

"Another dorm thing. I think today is Fiesta Day. The girls made these silly hats and... and you didn't call to talk about this. What's up?"

"I just wanted to see how you're doing."

"Good. Things are good. I miss you though."

"I miss you too. How's Kaiden?"

"He's fine. Training hard with the team. He says it's a whole other level compared to high school football, but he seems settled."

"That's good."

Awkward silence filled the line, but it was all me. Lily had her new life now. New friends and experiences and classes.

"Babe." She let out a soft sigh. "Talk to me."

"I don't know what I'm doing, Lil. School is horrible. Everyone looks at me like I'm a freak. The rumors are out of control. Sofia and Poppy are thriving; they don't get it. I can't talk to them." *Not the way I used to talk to you.*

"It's only high school, Leigh. You survived it once, you can survive it again."

"That's the thing though, maybe I don't want to survive it." Tears pricked the corner of my eyes, my chest tightening enough to make me lightheaded. "I just want to remember, Lily."

"Breathe, you need to breathe."

I sucked in a greedy lungful of air, letting it calm my racing heart.

"Have you talked to Mya about this? Your parents?"

"They don't get it."

"But have you talked to them? People aren't mind readers,

Leigh, and you can't carry all this alone. Trust me, I know that better than anyone. Nobody expects you to be okay with this."

"I went to a party," I blurted out, needing to talk about something else. "At Cole's house."

"See, that's progress."

"It was a mess..."

"What happened?"

"I went with Gav and ended up kissing Ezra."

"*What?*"

"Yeah, I know."

"But I... I don't understand. How did that even happen? He's—" She stopped herself.

"He's what, Lil?"

"Nothing. I'm just shocked is all. It's Ezra we're talking about."

"He wasn't there with friends or anything... I think he was there to watch me."

"What do you mean?"

"He was in the shadows watching me. I confronted him, and one thing led to another..."

"What happened afterward?"

"We had a big fight, we both said some things, and he left."

He always leaves.

"I know you've always felt protective of him, Leigh, but I don't like it. Ezra is... he's not in a good place since the accident. You should stay away from him."

"How can you say that? He doesn't have anyone else, Lily. Even if he... doesn't want me like that, I can be there for him as a friend. Poppy said his birth mom wants to see him. I can't even imagine what must be going through his head."

"Ashleigh, don't do this to yourself."

"What do you mean?"

"How long has it been?"

"I don't follow."

"Have long have you had this obsession with fixing Ezra?"

"W-what? That's not... I don't..." The words got stuck over the lump in my throat.

"You're a good person, Leigh. The best. But Ezra isn't like us. He isn't going to get therapy and change. He isn't going to suddenly open his eyes and realize what's standing in front of him. He has issues, babe. Real issues. Issues he needs to work on before he'll ever be ready to let someone in."

"I just want to help." My voice cracked as I finally heard what I'd been unwilling to accept.

"I know you do." Her voice grew quiet, and I knew I wasn't going to like whatever came next.

"But has it ever occurred to you that maybe he doesn't want your help?"

CHAPTER TWENTY-ONE

Ezra

OOMPH.

The defensive player careened into me, sending me flying. The ball tumbled out of my hands as I went down, hitting the ground hard.

Somewhere across the field, a whistle blew, and Coach started yelling something. But the wind had been sucked clean from my lungs and I lay there trying to remember how to breathe.

"Carrick, what the hell was that?" Coach Ford was looming over me now, guys gathering round us. "You good?" he asked, and I nodded.

Unclipping my helmet, I tore it off, needing to get some fucking air into my lungs.

Aaron bounded over, breathless and sweating. "Everything okay?"

"Yeah, I'm fine." I sat up, running a hand down my face.

He held out his hand and pulled me to my feet. My glare cut straight to Carrick. "Low fucking blow, asshole."

"What? It was a good tackle." He shrugged. "I didn't—"

"Take a walk, now," Coach bellowed.

"But Coach, I—"

"Now, Carrick. Unless you want to spend the rest of practice running suicides."

He skulked off, but not before shooting me a dark look.

"He's a liability," Aaron said. "He's had it out for Ezra all practice."

"Let me handle Carrick." Coach's eyes narrowed. "You two get back out there. I want to run it again, but this time I want to switch out Deacon with Ezra."

"No," I said.

At the same time Aaron said, "For real?"

"Just humor me." Coach gave me a pointed look, but there was no way on Earth I was stepping into the quarterback's position.

"Ezra." He let out a heavy sigh. "You have one of the strongest throwing arms on the field right now."

"It's not gonna happen," I said.

It was a miracle I was out here playing at all. But I didn't mind catching the ball and running down the wing. Ninety percent of the time the defensive line couldn't catch me because throwing wasn't my only strong suit. I was fast. Really fucking fast. Until Carrick homed in on my style of play and came at me like a bull out of a gate.

I shook off the lingering pulse of anger surging through me and met Coach's stern gaze. "I'm not doing it."

"Ezra, just hear me out…"

"I'm here. I'm playing your fucking game, but I am not going to play that position."

Everyone was looking now, waiting for Coach to lose his shit. Much to everyone's surprise, he let it go.

"We'll talk about this later."

"Whatever."

"Cole, swap out with Deacon and let's see what you've got."

"I don't play QB—" Coach glowered at Kandon, and he swallowed. "I'll do it."

"Good. Now let's run it again, just like we went over earlier." He followed Cole toward the centerfield, but Aaron lingered.

"On a scale of one to ten, how much do you want to KO Carrick right now?"

"Eleven. He's a fucking idiot."

"He's just jealous you can outrun him."

I shrugged, pulling on my helmet.

"You should have done it, you know."

He wasn't talking about punching Carrick.

"I don't want it."

"I know," Aaron scoffed. "But maybe it's what you need. And fuck only knows we could use it. Kaiden has left a big hole."

"Deacon isn't bad."

"No, but he's too green. We can't afford to spend a season getting him to the level he needs to be at; not if we want to keep hold of the championship."

"Maybe Kandon will step up."

"He doesn't want it either. He's a wide receiver, not a QB."

"Well, someone's got to step up."

And it sure as fuck wasn't going to be me.

―――

"OKAY, OKAY, SETTLE DOWN," Coach yelled over the locker room chaos. We all settled onto the benches and waited.

"That was... better. But I'm not going to sugarcoat it, we need a lot of work before we're ready to defend the title. Deacon, good effort, son. You've got control of the field, and your arm is strong. But I won't deny I'm worried. Cole, you surprised me out there today. Your passes were clean and precise, and you commanded the team with confidence. We might be looking at our new first string QB."

A chorus of cheers went up, but Cole didn't look pleased about it. In fact, he looked downright sick.

"I... I'm not sure, Coach. I'm a wide receiver."

"And a good one at that. But this team needs a quarterback with experience. I want you and Deacon to work with the offense coach over the next couple of weeks and see how things go." He settled his gaze on Deacon. "You're still young, coming into your strengths. But I anticipate with some hard work you'll make a fine quarterback."

He nodded eagerly. "Thanks, Coach."

"The season doesn't start for another two weeks, so we don't have long but we can do this. With Aaron and Cole leading us, I'm confident we can defend our championship and show every team across the state why the Rixon Raiders are the best. Now gather in."

Everyone got up and huddled together but I held back. I wasn't one of them. No matter how much Coach demanded I play, I would *never* be one of them.

"Hands in, Raiders on three."

I still held back, hovering on the periphery. I was used to this space, straddling the line between being close enough to something to appear part of it but far away enough to keep my distance.

Their battle cry filled the air, sending a strange sensation down my spine. I'd never had this before, and even though I didn't want it—resented every fucking second I was forced to be out on the field—I couldn't deny it did affect me.

For a second, it did make me think 'what if.'

What if I hadn't been abandoned by the one person who was supposed to love and protect me.

What if I hadn't been shipped from foster home to foster home.

What if I'd have found a family like the Bennets sooner. Before the damage was done. Before I was broken and changed into this version of myself.

What if.

But what ifs didn't change the here and now and I had no interest in dwelling on the past. It was why I'd refused to talk to Asher or Mya about Alyson after she tried to get in touch with me earlier this year. I didn't want to meet the woman who abandoned me, who gave me up like I was nothing more than an unwanted store purchase, condemning me to a childhood of nightmares.

The huddle dispersed, and everyone started gathering up their things, but Coach locked eyes with mine and mouthed, "My office."

I grabbed my bag and weaved through the crush, but someone stepped into me, making me falter.

"Shit, sorry. Didn't you see you there, Jackson." Carrick smirked.

"Move," I said.

"Why don't you make me, asshole?" he whispered the words, so they didn't carry over the noise.

A couple of guys noticed us but didn't say anything.

Bunch of pussies. Coach had already disappeared into his office and the assistant coaches were nowhere to be seen; not that I needed anyone to fight my battles. But I also couldn't afford to land myself a visit with Principal Kiln, not if I wanted to stay under the radar.

"Hey, what's going on?" A heavy hand landed on my shoulder, and I flinched. Carrick narrowed his eyes, obviously noticing my reaction.

"Nothing," I said, shirking his arm off me. "Carrick was just apologizing for his dumb move earlier."

"Good to see the two of you working things out. We're a team," Aaron said. "We need to act like one."

"A team, right." Carrick's brow went up as he sized me up.

Something told me the two of us would never play well on a team together. But I could be the bigger man and walk away —this time.

Shoving past him, I ignored Aaron calling after me and made my way to Coach's office.

"Take a seat," he said the second I stepped inside.

I closed the door and sat down.

"You did well today."

I shrugged.

I hadn't played to impress him or anyone else. I hadn't even played to prove to myself that I could. But after Carrick's constant taunts, I couldn't deny part of me had played to shut him the fuck up.

"But I've got to ask why you're so against trying out for quarterback."

"I don't want it."

"But why? Most guys can only dream of being good enough to earn that spot."

"I'm not most guys. If you think that just because you've given me a second chance that I'm somehow going to turn into Aaron or Cole or the next Kaiden Thatcher, then you're going to be sorely disappointed."

He sat back, quietly assessing me. I didn't like it, the way he watched me. As if he was trying to get inside my head and figure me out.

I wasn't a puzzle he or anyone else could fix.

"What?" I said, unable to stand the silence any longer.

"You could be so much more than... this. All this anger and indifference and resentment, it isn't going to get you anywhere except a one-way ticket to jail, son."

"What the fuck do you know about my life?"

"I know you're hurting. I know you're trying to outrun something from your past. Trying to numb the pain."

"You don't know anything." I shot up, my body trembling. "Has it ever occurred to you that maybe I just don't wanna be here? In this town, at this school? I know who I am and where I fit in the world. It's the rest of you that can't seem to get the message."

I grabbed my bag and hauled ass out of there before he had a chance to say another word.

I didn't need him.

And I sure as fuck didn't need his team.

Like a whirlwind, I blew through the locker room, shouldering the door to the hall leading to the main exit. A trash can went flying as I kicked it, letting out a roar of anger.

"E-Ezra?" Ashleigh stood at the end of the hall, like a deer caught in headlights. Her big blue eyes were wide with surprise and something I didn't want to acknowledge. "What happened?" She stepped forward.

"Are you following me?" I spat, taking long strides toward her. She retreated until her back hit the wall, leaving her with nowhere to run.

Her breath hitched. "I came to see my uncle."

I tsked between my gritted teeth. She was the last person I

wanted to see. But I was hardly surprised. Ashleigh had a track record of finding me at the worst times.

"You're upset," she said.

The air grew impossibly thin, and I knew without a doubt it was her. It had been like this before the accident. Her always in my space. Pushing and pushing. Demanding my time and attention. Checking on me. Forcing her way into my life.

We stared at one another, the silence eating up what little space was left between us.

"I'm not doing this with you." I went to move around her, but she stepped into my way.

"You don't want me. I get it. Loud and clear. But we were friends once, weren't we?" Her eyes pleaded with me. "I just want to help."

"You keep saying that," I sneered, getting right in her face. "But you seem to forget one thing... the only way you can help, is by staying the fuck away from me."

A door slammed somewhere in the locker room, startling us both enough to put some distance between us. Her eyes were narrowed, full of fire and frustration. It shouldn't have affected me nearly as much as it did.

"Is this what you really want? To make me hate you?" Her bottom lip quivered and all I could remember was kissing her. Tasting her as I pinned her up against the tree. Soft and eager underneath my touch.

I blinked, forcing the memory out of my head, and she seethed, "Because you're doing a pretty good job at it."

"That's exactly what I want, buttercup. We're not friends. I'm not some charity case you can fix. I. Don't. Need. You."

"Fine," she snapped, her body trembling as she clenched her fists by her sides.

"Fine," I hissed.

Another door slammed, this time footsteps sounding somewhere behind us. I glared at her for another second before shouldering past her and walking out of the building like she didn't get under my skin in the worst kind of way.

CHAPTER TWENTY-TWO

Ashleigh

ANGER BOILED in my blood as I watched Ezra storm out of the building. He was so angry, tormented, and too freaking stubborn for his own good. Although he said one thing, his actions and the way he looked at me said another thing entirely.

But he was determined to make me hate him and was doing a pretty good job at it.

"Ashleigh?" Uncle Jason appeared at the end of the hall. "Is something wrong? I thought I heard voices."

"Nope." I pasted on the best smile I could muster. "I was just coming by to tell you Dad has been trying to get hold of you, but he says your cell phone is off."

"It isn't." He dug it out of his pocket and frowned. "So it is. Must have run out of battery earlier. Damn thing. I'll call him from my office."

I nodded. "I should probably go."

"Wait," he said. "Are you sure everything is okay? Cam mentioned you've been finding it hard... at school, I mean."

"It is what it is."

"You know you can always talk to me or Mya, right?" He ran a hand over his jaw. "You're not alone in this."

"I know but there are some things I have to handle myself."

"Your classmates..."

"There are some rumors going around. Stupid stuff..."

His expression darkened, and I knew he was probably thinking of what happened with Lily and Lindsey Filmer last year.

"I can talk to Principal Kiln."

"No, you don't need to do that. I can handle it."

He studied me, his ice-blue eyes pinning me to the spot.

Uncle Jason was intense. Fiercely protective of his friends and family. It should have comforted me knowing he was always around. But there was a niggling voice in the back of my mind. He blamed Ezra for what happened, and now Ezra was training with the football team.

"Are you punishing him?" The words tumbled out before I could stop them.

"What?"

"Ezra... is making him play on the team your way of punishing him?"

"Ezra needs to learn discipline, Ashleigh." He didn't miss a beat. "And he needs to take responsibility for his future. He failed senior year. After everything Asher and Mya have done for him, he just gave up. That is unacceptable."

"He's been through a lot."

Defending him was as easy as breathing. Maybe Lily was right. Maybe I did want to fix him. To save him. But I never once saw him as a charity case or a project. I cared about him.

Was that so awful?

"He has." Uncle Jason's expression softened a fraction.

"But he refuses to let anyone help him and he's an angry young man with nowhere to channel that energy. Football will be good for him."

"So, it's not about the accident?"

His brows pinched. "Is that what you think? That I'm forcing him to play for the team to punish him?"

"Aren't you?"

His brows crinkled. "I'm trying to help."

"If you say so."

"Ashleigh—"

"I should go. I have to get to last period."

"Will you be at the pep rally Friday? It would be good to see you there."

"I'll think about it."

THERE WAS no escaping the pep rally. It was all anyone talked about. In class, at lunch, in the halls as kids moved between periods. Everyone was eager to see who Coach would name for his starting lineup.

Football season was upon Rixon High, and everyone was swept up in football fever. This was familiar territory, the flashes of Raider blue and white everywhere I turned, the constant cheers for the senior players everyone knew were a sure thing, not to mention the daily bulletin announcements counting down for Friday night.

What wasn't familiar, was hearing Ezra's name banded around as one of the possible picks for Coach's first-string team.

"Ugh, could she be any more obvious." Poppy groaned as we entered school the next day. Zara and her cheer friends hovered around Aaron and Cole and a few players I didn't recognize. Juniors, I assumed.

"Have you talked to him about her yet?" I asked.

"No, he's too consumed with the team. I was over at their house last night and we hung out, but all he talked about was the team this, the team that. He didn't even ask me how tryouts went."

"I'm sorry."

Poppy shrugged. "I'm not going to beg him to notice me. I'm still the same girl I've always been. It's him who's changing. Besides." She gave me a conspiratorial glance. "Eli Hannigan asked Sofia if I was going to be at the pep rally."

"Eli Hannigan?"

"Yeah, he's a boy from one of my classes. He's on the swim team. Super cute and genuine."

"And you like him?"

"I don't dislike him." She grinned.

"As long as you're not going to use him to get to Aaron... then go for it."

Poppy pulled up short, glaring at me. "You mean like you're not using Gav to make Ezra jealous?"

My breath caught and her expression immediately dropped. "Crap, I'm sorry. That was a mean thing to say. I know you and Gav are friends... I just meant—"

"Forget it," I said, coolly. "I need to get to class. I'll see you later." I took off down the hall.

"Leigh, wait, I..."

Her words were drowned out by the morning chatter as I hurried down the hall.

I don't know what bothered me more—that Poppy thought I was using Gav to make Ezra jealous, or that I wasn't sure she was wrong.

After all, I had baited Ezra about Gav, but only because he hurt me first.

Two wrongs didn't make a right though.

I didn't head for class. Instead, I marched right out of the back entrance and into the warm, fall sun. From here I could see the gym, and beyond it, the football field. Rixon High was lucky enough to have an athletic field where the team practiced and then Dawson Stadium, reserved for football games once the season started.

Hiking my bag up my shoulder, I took off toward the bleachers. But the second I reached the entrance, I heard Ezra's voice. He was already sitting in the stands, staring out at the field. At first, I thought he was talking to himself, but then I realized he was on the phone.

Before I could stop myself, I'd moved closer, slipping under the stands like some stalker.

"I don't want to play. I've never wanted to play," he said to whoever was on the end of the call. "Yeah... but it feels like selling out."

He laughed.

Ezra laughed, and the sound was so glorious, so full of life, I was stunned. He'd never laughed like that around me, not that I could remember anyway.

My heart withered in my chest.

"Yeah, I like talking to you too."

Oh God.

It was her. He was talking to the waitress, the girl Aaron thought he'd taken on a date.

My stomach fell away, freefalling into my toes. But I couldn't make myself leave.

"Oh really." He chuckled again. "Well, I'd like to see that some time."

Was he... flirting?

He sounded like he was flirting.

"Yeah maybe, it was fun." He started talking to her about his week. The way some of the team shut him out at practice, how my uncle was always riding him to play.

This was torture.

The boy I'd wanted since I was too young to understand what wanting a boy meant, was sitting here, flirting with another girl. Laughing with her and talking to her.

That hurt the most.

That he was opening up to her, when all I'd ever wanted was for Ezra to let *me* in.

You need to leave, right now. Just walk away and don't let him break your heart any more than he already has.

I forced myself to move, to put one foot in front of the other and leave. I didn't need to hear this, and I shouldn't have been eavesdropping.

But his next words gave me pause.

"Girls here..." He made a derisive noise in the back of his throat. "You've got to be kidding me. They're all vain, stuck-up bitches who think they're something special. They make me fucking sick."

The ground trembled beneath my feet, my heart splintering in my chest.

He thought I was like them. Like the Zara Willises of the world. He was attracted to me, yes. But he would never let himself be with someone like me because I represented everything he hated.

Silent tears rolled down my cheeks as I ducked out of the stands and hurried back toward the school building.

Leaving a trail of pieces of my broken, bloody heart behind.

RUINED HOPES

WHEN I GOT HOME, Mom informed me Uncle Xander and Peyton were stopping by for dinner. With the day I'd had, the last thing I wanted was to spend a night pretending I was okay. But I couldn't keep making excuses that I had a headache or they would haul me back to the hospital.

After overhearing Ezra, I'd gone back to class only to spend two hours listening to Zara drone on about the pep rally and her big plans for the party after at Bell's, a local bar and favorite hangout of the team. She'd even gone out of her way to ask if I was attending, only to quickly add that it probably wasn't the best environment for me, given *my condition*.

Fucking bitch.

I wasn't a particularly violent person, that had always been Peyton's penchant in our small group of friends. But Zara Willis made me want to punch something. Preferably her perfectly made-up face.

The fact Ezra thought I was like her only made it ten times worse.

I was nothing like her. I didn't tread on others to get a foot up the social ladder. I didn't even care about the social freaking ladder. I cared about my friends and school and my future. At least, I had before the accident.

Now I was indifferent.

Numb.

But I wasn't like the Zara Willises of the world. Not at all.

"Sweetheart, are you coming down?" Dad called and I reluctantly got off my bed, and traipsed downstairs.

"There you are." Peyton almost tackled me to the floor, hugging me so tight I couldn't breathe.

"Uh, need air," I breathed, and she chuckled.

"Drama queen. I wasn't squeezing you that tightly. I've missed you."

"I've missed you too."

"I'm sorry I haven't been around much. Life is—"

"Don't worry about it."

"Hey, Leigh Leigh." Uncle Xander gave me a small nod. "It's good to see you."

"You too." I managed a small smile.

"Let's go into the kitchen." Dad motioned for us to follow him, but Peyton held me back.

"Lily called me. She said Ezra kissed you."

"Pey!" I glanced down the hall, relieved to see my dad and Uncle Xander had already disappeared into the kitchen.

"So... what happened?"

"Nothing, it doesn't matter." I shucked out of her hold and took off down the hall.

"Leigh, don't do that." She hurried after me, keeping her voice low. "Don't shut me out."

Letting out a heavy sigh, I stopped. "I don't want to talk about it."

"Okay." Peyton gave me a sympathetic smile. "But I'm only at the end of a call or text. I hope you know that."

"Thanks."

There was a time I'd once turned to Peyton and Lily with everything, but it was different now. They both had these new exciting lives with grown-up responsibilities and relationships to manage. Maybe it was irrational but moaning to them about high school and Ezra and mean girls felt stupid.

"Come on. Let's go eat your mom's ribs and laugh at Xander and Cam trying to one up each other."

She was radiant. Happy and in love. And like Lily, she deserved it. She deserved it so damn much.

But it made me wonder if I'd ever find that, if I'd find the person I was destined to be with.

Especially when I thought I'd already found him...

And he wanted nothing to do with me.

CHAPTER TWENTY-THREE

Ashleigh

"WAS pep rally day always this annoying?" I mumbled as we weaved our way through the morning crush.

The cheer squad already had their faces painted with the Raiders shield; and Vinnie the Viking, the team mascot, was lurking around every corner, ready to work everyone into a frenzy.

It was a lot.

"Oh, I don't know," Poppy said. "There's always something kind of special about it."

"Spoken like a true coach's daughter." Sofia chuckled. "You've been coming to these things since you were old enough to walk."

It was true. Even before we started high school, Uncle Jason used to let Lily, Poppy, and me tag along to the pep rally at Dawson Stadium. Lily never wanted to go; she didn't like the crowds, the noise, and fuss. But I'd always enjoyed being a part of it.

"How was he this morning?"

"Stressed. He's worried there aren't enough senior players to carry the team."

"Aaron seems confident they can go all the way," Sofia added. "He was like a hyper child this morning, bouncing around the kitchen."

"Anyway, we're all going, right?" Poppy looked at me.

"I hadn't planned on it."

"Leigh, you have to come." She pouted. "It's like a senior year rite of passage."

"Been there, done that, got no memory of it."

"Please." They both turned on the puppy dog eyes. "I bet Gav would come if you asked him."

"I'm not asking Gav."

"Why not?"

"Because..."

"That isn't an answer, and you know it." Poppy rolled her eyes. "Look, I know it sucks you're repeating senior year and I know it hasn't been easy coming back here. But you are here. For the foreseeable future. You might as well try to embrace it. Who knows, you might actually end up enjoying yourself."

"Besides, you'll get to see if Ezra made the team or not," Sofia added.

"I don't care."

"Of course you don't. Just like Poppy doesn't care if Aaron hooks up with Zara Willis at the party." She smirked.

"I'll have you know, I don't. I told Eli I'd meet him at Bell's."

"Good for you. Maybe that'll kick my brother up the ass and make him realize that—"

"Realize what?" Aaron appeared out of nowhere, dropping his arms over Poppy and Sofia's shoulder and pulling them close.

"Nothing," Poppy grumbled. "Where's Zara?"

"How the fuck should I know?"

"You mean she isn't permanently attached to your arm? My mistake." She ducked out of his hold and came to stand by me.

Aaron glanced between us. "Why do I feel like I've done something wrong?"

"You haven't done anything wrong," Poppy said. "If you like Zara that's... Do you know what, good for you. I'm sure the two of you will be very happy with each other." She tossed her hair off her shoulder and stormed off down the hall.

"Okay, that was just weird." Aaron ran a hand down his face. "Tell me that was weird."

"God, you really are a clueless idiot at times." Sofia rolled her eyes. "I'll see you later, Leigh."

"Yeah, bye." I gave her a small wave, and she took off down the hall after Poppy.

"Care to enlighten me as to what the hell that was all about?"

"If you have to ask, you don't deserve to know." I tapped him on the cheek. "I have class, see you around."

"Hey, Leigh," he called after me as I started down the hall. "You'll be there tonight?"

My shoulders lifted in a half-hearted shrug as I glanced back. "We'll see."

"You know you want to."

No, I really didn't. But it wasn't like I could tell anyone why.

I waved him off and turned around to head for class, but I slammed straight into Zara.

"Watch where you're going, you dumb bitch."

Lifting a brow, I took a deep breath, forcing myself to count to three before I engaged her. "Zara, always a pleasure."

"Yeah, whatever." She glared at me with the intensity of a thousand burning suns.

"Oh, Aaron, wait up." Barging past me, she hurried after him.

I didn't want to get involved with his business, but if he decided to hook up with her, I would seriously question his sanity.

The vibration of my cell phone startled me, and I dug it out of my pocket.

Gav: I've been ordered by Aaron to intervene. Pep rally tonight, be there or be…

Me: If you say square, I'm not sure we can be friends anymore.

Gav: Millie begs to differ.

A PHOTO MESSAGE followed of her holding up a handwritten sign that said, 'Go Raiders.'

Another text came through.

Gav: We're going. I'll swing by and pick you up at six.

Me: Fine.

Gav: Fine.

Me: I'm cutting you off now.

Gav: Good. I was already bored of talking to you.

SOFT LAUGHTER BUBBLED out of me. Why was this so easy between us? The banter and constant texts back and forth.

Why couldn't it ever be this easy between me and Ezra?

But love wasn't supposed to be easy, was it? It was supposed to be hard and messy and hurt sometimes. Because any love worth having, was a love worth fighting for. I'd always believed that. It's one of the reasons I never gave up on Ezra.

Lily and Kaiden hadn't had it easy in the beginning; neither had Peyton and Xander. They didn't give up though. They followed their hearts and in the end everything turned out good.

But their feelings had been reciprocated. They'd fought for it *together*.

I couldn't keep fighting for someone who didn't want me back.

―――

THE PEP RALLY was everything I remembered Rixon High pep rallies to be. Loud and chaotic, the bleachers drenched in a swathe of blue and white, everyone paying homage to their favorite football team. I stuck close to Poppy and Sofia as they tried to find us decent seats, but we ended up crammed in on a row in the back because we were late getting there.

I scanned the field, stifling a groan when I spotted Zara

making a show of stretching with the cheer squad. She freaking loved herself and didn't care who knew it.

"Okay?" Poppy squeezed my hand and I nodded. Part of me wished Gav was here, he would have some lame joke to tell that would immediately ease the tension inside me. But he'd got pulled into last minute Millie-duty.

"Gah, I'm so excited for him." Poppy bounced on the balls of her feet. She meant Aaron, of course. Despite the strangeness between them, she was still his number one fan, and she knew what it meant to him to be named captain for his final season.

"Oh, here they come." The Raiders fight song filled the stadium as the players poured out of the tunnel, smashing through the banner. Aaron and Cole were up front, jogging and waving, helmets dangling at their sides. But my gaze went straight past them to find Ezra. He was near the back, looking out at the rowdy crowd like he didn't understand. Even from my spot all the way in the back, I could see his lost expression.

Ezra had never shown even an ounce of interest in joining the football team before. He was a solitary person, living in the shadows, preferring his own company. But there he was in Raider blue and white, surrounded by his teammates.

And I didn't know whether I wanted to go down there and hug him and tell him everything was going to be okay, or clap and cheer his name like his biggest fan.

The players arrived at the stage and my uncle and the assistant coaches high-fived them all as they fell into two lines behind them.

"You're looking good tonight, Rixon High," Uncle Jason's voice filled the stadium.

Another loud boom of cheers went up, making my heart splutter in my chest. I tucked closer to Poppy, overwhelmed.

"Last year, the Raiders went all the way and showed

everyone why they're the best. This year, they have a big task ahead of them.

"Winning a championship is no easy feat, but defending a championship is going to take grit and determination and a fight to the bitter end. But I'm confident we can do it. I'm confident that when playoffs roll around, we'll be right there with the best of them, ready to prove to everyone that we're still the team to beat."

"Your dad gives the best speeches," Sofia whispered, and Poppy grinned.

"So without further ado, this year's starting lineup. Number nine and this year's captain, Aaron Bennet."

"Go Aaron." Poppy cupped her hands around her mouth and screamed his name.

He held up his hand, waving at the crowd and the place roared back at him.

"Number four, and this year's quarterback, Cole Kandon."

"Holy shit," Sofia breathed. "He's... quarterback?"

"No wonder my dad was keeping the starting line-up a secret. This is huge."

"Can he do it?" I asked them. Cole played wide receiver, he didn't play QB.

"I guess we'll find out."

A rumble of chatter filled the air. Cole wasn't the obvious choice, but then everyone knew the Raiders were missing a strong quarterback going into the season.

I didn't hear the rest of the announcements, too busy watching Ezra. He stood at the end of the line, rigid like a statue.

But then Coach was calling his name. "Number sixteen, wide receiver, Ezra Bennet."

"Oh. My. God. He did it. He actually gave him a starting position," Poppy breathed the words.

The crowd fell silent, a ripple of disbelief going through the air. We'd all heard the rumors, but hearing it and seeing it were two very different things.

"He's a... Raider." The words made my chest tighten because nothing made sense anymore.

Since I'd woken up in the hospital my world had been tipped on its axis. The boy I'd spent so long pining after hated me, and he was slowly becoming a different person, right in front of my eyes.

It didn't make any sense.

"Go, Ezra," someone yelled. "Number sixteen."

Zara.

The crowd followed her, breaking into a round of cheers for him. But Ezra looked unaffected by it, his expression flat and devoid of any emotion. Until a faceless player behind him leaned over and whispered something in his ear that made Ezra rear up. He spun around and got all up in the guy's face, smashing his forehead violently against his.

"Oh God." I gripped Poppy's arm, fear racing down my spine.

One of the assistant coaches immediately waded in to split them up, shoving them both away from each other, hard. My uncle gave someone a nod and the stadium plunged into darkness, music booming through the sound system.

"Oh goodie, now we get to watch Zara shake her ass like the slutty whorebag she is.'"

"Poppy Ford," I gasped. "Who are you and what have you done with my cousin?"

"Well, it's true."

"Yeah." I laid my head on her shoulder and tried to find Ezra again as the stage lights flickered to life. But I couldn't spot him among the huddle of football players all watching the cheer squad with their tongues hanging out of their mouths.

"Remind me later when I'm comparing Eli to Aaron, that Aaron has become a shallow jock with no standards."

"You don't mean that," Sofia said.

"Yes, I do. Look at him... he's practically panting."

She wasn't wrong. Aaron was high-fiving a couple of the guys as Zara did a high kick and threw him a suggestive look over her shoulder.

"If he sleeps with her, I'm done." Poppy sighed. "So done."

"He won't..." I said.

But it lacked conviction. Because guys couldn't be trusted not to break your heart. Even if they were supposed to be different.

I knew that better than anyone.

CHAPTER TWENTY-FOUR

Ezra

NATHAN CARRICK WAS A FUCKING ASSHOLE.

When he'd leaned over my shoulder during Coach's speech and asked me how many times I'd gotten on my knees for Coach to land my place on the team, I'd almost lost it. Probably would have left him in a bloody mess if Assistant Coach Macintosh hadn't jumped in and told me to go cool off.

Guys like Carrick were a dime a dozen. An entitled piece of shit that looked down on anyone who didn't fit into his idealistic view of the world. Rixon was a postcard town with its quaint high street and small-town appeal, sure, but prejudices still lurked, especially toward a guy like me.

A biracial kid who had grown up in the system.

I knew Mya had faced the same prejudices when she'd first moved to Rixon back in the day. She'd tried to talk to me about it once, probably hoping our shared experience would bridge the gap between us.

It didn't.

I didn't care what people thought. I'd seen what kinds of

monsters lurked behind some of the most upstanding members of society, witnessed the damage they could do. Men and women who were supposed to care about making a difference to young boys like me.

"Yo, E, let's go." Aaron motioned for me to join them.

I didn't want to head to the thing at Bell's, the Raiders official bar downtown. But after returning to the locker room when the rally had finished, Coach Ford had said he expected me to show up.

"You good?" Cole asked me, and I nodded.

"Just keep Carrick away from me."

"He's a fucking idiot. If he carries on, I'm going to speak to Coach."

"I don't need you to fight my—"

"Battles, yeah. I got the memo before." Aaron let out a steady breath. "But this affects the team. We need to be united, not fighting among ourselves."

"You're letting this power go to your head, man." Cole shot him a bemused look.

"I want to win. Is that so bad?"

"I'm just saying, there's more to life than football."

We reached Aaron's car, and all climbed inside.

"Like that two-bit band that want you back?" Aaron snarked.

"Nice, asshole." Cole spat. "Real nice."

"Dude, you just got named as starting quarterback. Do you know how many guys would kill for a shot at that?"

"I can have more than one hobby, jackass."

"Hobby," Aaron muttered, starting the car. "Being a Raider isn't a hobby. It's a fucking privilege."

"Who the fuck are you right now?" Cole murmured, shaking his head.

"It's senior year, Kandon. Time to look to the future and

get serious about life. You can't be a football player *and* a rock star."

"I never said... forget it." Cole stared out of the passenger window, tension swirling in the car.

"Cole has a point," I said, and Aaron's eyes snapped to mine in the rearview mirror. "It's just a game."

"Just a game... of course you would say that. You don't get it." Aaron let out a frustrated sigh. "Football is my chance to make something of myself. To be someone people take notice of. I'm not giving that up for anything."

BELL'S WAS CROWDED. Aaron immediately left me and Cole and made a beeline for the other football players who grabbed him and started chanting his name like he was the second coming.

"I'm so over this shit," Cole murmured. "You want to get a drink? I need to get fucked up."

With a small shrug, I followed him to the bar, hardly surprised when the bartender slid two beers in our direction. Being a Raider meant something in Rixon. It meant overlooking the rules once in a while because football was religion here, and everyone wanted to uphold their faith.

"So what's up with you and Aaron?" I asked. Better to keep conversation on him than on me.

"He doesn't like the fact that my old band wants me back."

"I met them at the party you had. Jude, Travis, and Mikey, right?"

He nodded. "We played together, seventh through ninth grade. But then football got more serious, and I didn't have the time to do both."

"So you chose football."

"Something like that. I like playing, I like being on the team. But it's not my whole life, you know?"

"I guess you either bleed white and blue or you don't." I glanced over at the football players. "Aaron must have gotten a blood transfusion this year."

Cole snorted. "You could say that. What about you? What's your story?"

"You mean, you don't listen to all the locker room gossip?" My brow lifted.

"What do you think?" he shot back.

"I think you're okay, Kandon."

"Likewise."

We clinked our beers together as we sat and watched Aaron hold court. But my attention snagged on the door when Carrick and his friends walked in.

"I really fucking hate that guy."

"He's just trying to make his mark on the team. His father is alumni, makes a hefty donation to the booster fund every year."

That made sense given the way Carrick threw his weight about.

"Do you think he's going to be a problem?" I asked.

"I think you should try and stay out of his way if you want an easy year, yeah."

I scrubbed my jaw. Just what I didn't need. Carrick and his father making it their mission to single me out.

"Relax, man. Let Coach handle them."

"Yeah." My jaw clenched as I took another pull on my beer.

It wasn't enough to quiet the noise in my head, but it would have to do for now, because right as I glanced at the door, Asher walked into the bar with Ashleigh's dad, Cameron.

"Fuck," I hissed, dropping the beer onto the bar like it was a grenade.

"Trouble in paradise?" Cole asked.

"Something like that."

Asher spotted us and made his way over. "Tell me I didn't just see what I thought I saw."

"Hi, Mr. B," Cole said with an easy smile.

"Cole. Did you just see Ezra drinking a beer?"

I cast him a sideways warning.

"Not me, sir."

"I see you're a loyal guy, Cole. Loyal but stupid. Let me talk to Ezra for a second, will you, please?"

"Sure." Cole turned to me, and said, "I'll catch you later."

Asher perched on one of the stools and studied me. "How was the pep rally?"

"Let me guess, you spoke to Coach Ford."

"He may have called me. Is Nathan Carrick going to be a problem?"

"I don't know, you tell me. Cole said his dad is an important booster."

"John is a big fan of the team, yes. But if this little punk is singling you out, I can go to—"

"Relax, you don't need to go all protector on me. I can handle a guy like Carrick."

"Without beating his ass six ways to Sunday?"

I lifted a shoulder. "I haven't decided yet."

Asher smirked. "Atta boy. You know, I'm proud of how you've handled the last few weeks. Things haven't been easy, but I already feel like you're turning it around."

My lips thinned. "You didn't really give me a choice."

"No, we didn't. But this was for the best, Ezra. Surely, you can see that?"

I didn't answer because what did he want me to say?

"This could be exactly what you need to find yourself, Son. There's a certain kind of strength and discipline and pride that comes with being a Raider. And I really hope you'll embrace all that it offers you."

"I don't want this," I said, defiance burning in my soul.

"I know." Asher got up, giving me a sad smile. "But sometimes it isn't about what we want, it's about what we need. Don't forget that. Enjoy the party," he said, quickly adding, "But don't let me catch you with another beer in your hand."

He disappeared into the crowd, leaving me alone. Until Cole reappeared.

"Everything okay?"

"Yeah." The lie rolled off my tongue.

I wasn't sure what was happening anymore.

Asher was trying to pull some Jedi-mind shit on me with all his philosophical speeches, Coach Ford had named me as part of the starting lineup for the team he wanted to defend the championship title, Cole was talking to me like we were old friends, and I was sitting in a busy bar surrounded by people who all knew my name for more reasons than the fact I was Asher Bennet's newly-adopted kid.

It was as weird as fuck, and a little unnerving.

And I couldn't help but think it was all Ashleigh's fault. Because if it wasn't for her...

I wouldn't be in this situation.

I WAS DRUNK.

I didn't know how it had happened, but one drink with Cole turned into two, and two turned into four. We'd hidden in the back of Bell's, surrounded by cheerleaders and a bunch of guys all wanting to rub shoulders with the team, and gotten wasted. Although Cole didn't seem friendly with a lot of them, when someone had suggested moving on to a party at Deacon's house, he talked me into going.

It seemed like a better alternative than going back to the Bennets'.

"Do you even like these people?" I asked Cole. We'd taken up two seats in the yard, overlooking Deacon's kidney-shaped pool. Next to it was a sheltered area where someone had set up a music system and a group of girls had turned it into a makeshift dance floor.

"Oh shit," Cole muttered, shifting in his chair.

"What?" I glanced in the direction he was looking, to find Poppy with some guy I vaguely recognized from school.

"Aaron is going to lose his shit."

"Aaron is probably balls deep in Zara by now." She'd been over him like a rash all night.

"Nah, she's not his type." Cole tsked. "He knows it's good optics is all."

"Good optics?"

"Yeah, for the football team and cheer squad to be a united front. After last year, all that shit with Lily and Lindsey Filmer... everyone's eager for things to be more cooperative."

I dropped my head back, the world spinning around me. "Fuck, I think I drank too much."

"You need something to take the edge off," a voice said, and I found Jude looming down over us. "Thought I'd find you here."

"Jude," Cole clipped out.

"Don't look so worried, Kandon. I come in peace." He held up his hands with a smirk.

"Whatever."

"So." Jude turned his attention on me. "You in?" He pulled out a fresh blunt and waved it in front of me.

It was the worst kind of torture, trying to resist. Especially when I knew the high would dull the noise.

"Go on, bro. You know you want to."

My gaze cut to Cole, and he shrugged. "Don't look at me, I'm not your keeper."

"Light it up," I said, motioning to the empty chair across from us.

"Right choice, my friend." Jude dropped down and put the blunt between his lips, igniting the tip. The paper burned, the cherry red end calling to me like a siren in dark, murky seas.

"Fuck, this is good shit." He took another hit and blew out a string of smoke rings before handing me the blunt.

I should have passed. I should have told him to walk on by and take his weed with him. But I'd stood on a football field tonight and sold my soul to the devil because I'd fucked up and given Asher and Jason leverage over me. If I didn't fall in line and do what they asked, it could land me in some serious shit.

I had no control over that aspect of my life now. Or at least, that's how it felt. So taking the blunt from Jude and putting it between my lips and inhaling a deep hit felt like a small 'fuck you' to them, and everyone else who had ever tried to fix me.

One I'd probably regret tomorrow, but for now, I was too wasted to give a shit.

CHAPTER TWENTY-FIVE

Ashleigh

"YOU LOOK like you could use this." A guy came up beside me and offered me a drink. I frowned at it, and he chuckled. "Relax, it's just beer. Got it straight out of the keg. I'm Nathan, Eli's cousin."

"Ashleigh."

"I know who you are." He smirked. "You're the hot name on everyone's lips."

"I really don't know what to say to that."

He laughed again, pushing the cup at me.

"I'm okay thanks."

His brows pinched, as if he couldn't quite believe I was turning down his offer of a drink. "Fine. Suit yourself." He downed it in one and wiped his mouth with the back of his hand. "Shame for it to go to waste."

"So, you're Eli's cousin?" Because they didn't seem anything alike.

"Yeah. I'm a junior. I'm also a Raider." He puffed out his

chest. "My dad is one of the biggest donors to the booster fund."

"That's... nice." I scanned the party for any sign of Poppy and Eli. They were supposed to be getting us drinks and then coming back. Sofia had been waiting with me, but she'd gone to find Aaron, so I'd stayed here, where it was quieter and less crowded.

"Fuck yeah, it is. I can't wait for the opening game. We're going to kick some Millington ass. Do you like football, babe?"

"Ashleigh."

"What?"

"You called me babe, but my name is Ashleigh."

"But babe suits you." He smirked, moving in closer. "You know, your friend is probably busy with Eli. We could find somewhere quiet to go and—"

"I don't think so." I stepped back, putting some space between us.

"What?" His lips twisted. "You think you're too good for me or something?"

"Oh, I know I am." Indignation burned inside me. "Now if you'll excuse me." I barged past and went in search of Poppy.

"What's wrong?" she said, as I almost walked straight into her and Eli returning with our drinks.

"Nothing," I lied. "Everything is fine."

"IS HE LOOKING?" Poppy asked for the third time since we'd spotted Aaron up close and personal with Zara. I'd noticed she touched him more than he touched her, but he didn't push her away or try to escape her flirtations.

And the worst part was, the two of them looked good

together—the football player and the cheerleader. It didn't get more cliché and perfect than that.

"Sorry, Pops," I whispered, as she continued hanging off Eli's arm.

She was right. Eli was cute, and a real gentleman. Unlike his asshole cousin.

"Let's dance." She grabbed my hand. "Come on, Sofe. We're dancing."

Sofia threw me a questioning glance and I shrugged. I didn't want to dance, not really, but I also didn't want to deal with a Poppy tantrum either.

We followed her over to the makeshift dance floor, a small patio area next to the pool, and started dancing. Poppy managed to look the perfect mix of graceful and sexy, her gymnast's body moving and swaying to the beat with ease. But I felt self-conscious on display in front of everyone. No one was really paying us any attention, but I was still uncomfortable. But for Poppy—and her quest to get Aaron's attention—I sucked it up and forced myself to move to the beat.

After a couple of songs, my skin was damp with sweat, and I was in desperate need of a drink.

"I'm going to get some water," I called over the music. "Do you two want anything?"

"A beer," Poppy said, grinning.

"Nothing for me," Sofia added. "Will you be okay going alone?"

"I'll be fine." I weaved back through the crowd and slipped into the house. It was a big open plan kitchen, and I had no problem locating the refrigerator.

Bottle of water in hand, I decided to use the bathroom before heading back outside but had to ask someone for directions. They pointed to a dark hall toward the back of the kitchen.

"Thanks," I said, making my way toward it. There were a couple of people coming and going but it was much quieter out here. I hurried, the hairs prickling along the back of my neck.

Thankfully, no one was in the bathroom, so I got in and out quickly and headed straight back outside. But the second I stepped into the yard, someone blocked my way.

"Well, well, we have got to stop meeting like this," Nathan said, his eyes glassy, a wicked slash across his mouth.

"Please move," I said, holding myself tall. The party was crowded, people everywhere, but everyone was too busy with their friends and partners for the night to notice us standing in the shadows.

"Come on, babe." He moved in closer, his hand snapping out to brush the fine hairs off my neck. A violent shudder went through me.

"Don't touch me." I shoved his hand away and ducked around him. But he was blocking my route to Poppy and Eli, so I took off in the other direction.

"Whoa, there." He snagged my arm and yanked me backward, pushing me against the side of the house. "What's your problem?" It was a devious sneer.

"I'll scream."

"The only thing you'll be screaming is my name." He chuckled darkly, leaning in to run his nose along my jaw. "Fuck, you smell good."

I thrashed against him, but he'd used his body to plaster me against the shiplap.

"What part of no, don't you understand?" I gritted out, my body trembling with equal amounts of fear and anger.

"Don't be shy, beautiful. I'm—"

He was ripped away from me. "What the fuck?" he shrieked as Ezra shoved him hard.

"Did he touch you?" His eyes slid to mine, pure rage and fire burning there.

"N-no." My voice shook with the weight of what could have happened.

"Look at you," Nathan clambered to his feet. "Swooping in like a real fucking hero."

"You need to walk away," Ezra said, his fists clenched at his sides as he stood like an immovable wall between me and Nathan.

A handful of people noticed, moving closer to watch the drama unfold.

"Or what, Jackson?" Nathan advanced on Ezra. "What the fuck are you going to do about it?"

"Ezra," I said, reaching for him, but he shirked me off, meeting Nathan toe-to-toe.

"I've been waiting for an excuse to beat your ass."

"Whoa, whoa, what's going on?" Aaron jogged over to us, casting me a nervous look. "E, man, what's happening?"

"He... uh, Nathan tried to..." The words got stuck in my throat.

"Carrick, talk to me?" Aaron said.

"We were just talking. She misread the situation."

"The situation?" Ezra hissed. "You had her pinned to the fucking wall." There was a slight slur to his speech that made me wonder if he was drunk... or high. Maybe even both. Either way, Aaron needed to diffuse the situation before it got royally out of hand.

"Leigh, is that true?" Aaron glanced at me, and I nodded, emotion welling in my throat.

"He... uh, I told him I wasn't interested and he... he followed me—"

"Fuck," Nathan grunted as Ezra drove his fist right into his face.

"Shit." Aaron grabbed hold of Ezra and wrenched him backward. "Calm the fuck down."

Poppy and Sofia rushed over with Eli and Cole in tow.

"What happened?" Eli asked.

"Your cousin is a fucking asshole, get him out of here," Aaron barked.

"Don't speak to him like that." Poppy wedged herself in-between them.

"Poppy." Aaron glowered.

"Uh, somebody should probably deal with that." Cole flicked his head over to where Nathan was groaning in agony, clutching his face. I couldn't see any blood, but he already had a nasty bruise forming.

"Come on, I'll give you a ride home." Eli helped his cousin, but he dug in his feet, jabbing a finger in Ezra's direction.

"You're fucked, Jackson. When my dad hears—"

"Hears what?" Aaron seethed. "That you almost assaulted Ashleigh because you're an entitled little prick who can't take no for an answer?"

"It's her word against mine."

"No, asshole, it's your word against all ours. Poppy and Sofia saw the whole thing, didn't you?"

They both nodded.

"That's bullshit and you know it."

"No, what I know is you don't deserve to call yourself a Raider. You're a fucking disgrace. And if you so much as look at Leigh wrong again, it won't just be Ezra you're dealing with. Got it?"

He mumbled something under his breath and barged past Aaron, toward the gate leading around the front of the house.

"I'm... shit, I'm really sorry about all this," Eli said. "I'll call you, okay?" He gave Poppy an apologetic smile.

"Okay." She smiled back.

Aaron went rigid, but if Poppy noticed, she didn't acknowledge it.

"You good?" He turned his attention onto Ezra who was swaying slightly on the spot.

"We need to take him home," Sofia said.

"The night is still young. We can go hang out at the man cave," Aaron suggested.

"Text your mom and dad and tell them you're staying at mine?" Sofia asked Poppy. Her eyes flicked to Aaron but quickly darted away.

"Yeah." She sighed. "Okay."

"Let's get out of here then." Aaron put a hand on Ezra's shoulder and guided him toward the gate.

"Are you coming?" Poppy asked when I made no effort to follow.

"I... yeah, okay."

Because no matter how much I wanted to ignore the fact Ezra had saved me from Nathan tonight, I couldn't.

―――

ASHER AND MYA were still out when we got back to the Bennets' house. My dad, Uncle Jason, and Asher had apparently gone to meet their wives for drinks after showing their faces at the party at Bell's.

Aaron and Sofia got into an argument on the ride back about whether to tell their parents about what happened with Ezra and Nathan. They were still arguing when we reached the front door.

"Carrick won't do anything. Not if he knows what's good for him," Aaron said.

"Still, I think we should tell them. In case it comes back to bite E in the ass." She glanced over her shoulder and frowned. "Speaking of E, where the hell is he?"

I turned around and searched the shadows. Sure enough, he was gone.

"Great. Freaking great. He's gone. He could be anywhere..."

"I might know where he is," I blurted out.

Aaron stared at me expectantly. "So... are you going to tell us?"

"I'll go look for him."

"Leigh, I'm not sure that's a good—"

"It's fine, Pops. I know where he'll be." I'd followed him out to his place down by the lake enough over the years.

I took off before they could stop me. A shiver worked its way down my spine as the shadows shifted around me, swallowing me whole as I slipped between the trees following the trail down to the lake.

It didn't take me long to find Ezra. Sitting by the water's edge, his arm was resting on his bent knees, his head lowered.

"You shouldn't be here," he said quietly.

"Yeah, well, we can't always get what we want." I sat down, folding my hands underneath my thighs. "What was that back there tonight?"

"Nathan Carrick is an asshole."

"I agree, he really is."

That got Ezra's attention, and he lifted his face to mine. "If you came to thank me, you might as well save your breath." His eyes were hooded, his expression lax. I knew this version of Ezra. He was high. There would be no talking to him or reasoning with him while he was like this.

RUINED HOPES

With a heavy sigh, I went to get up.

"You ruined everything, you know?"

"E-excuse me?"

"It's true." He picked up a stone and ran his fingers over it before skimming it across the water. "I'm only here, pretending to be one of them, because of you."

"Ezra, I don't understand. You're not making any sense."

"They don't know... but it's true. It's true and I hate you. I fucking hate you for it."

His words reverberated inside me, and I sank down into the grass, the air *whooshing* from my lungs.

"I'm sorry." Tears pricked the corners of my eyes, but I desperately fought to contain them. I didn't want to keep crying over him, no matter how much his words cut me up inside.

Ezra lay down, staring up at the sky. I didn't want to leave him out here alone, but I also couldn't take any more of his criticism.

So I sat there, silent and still, watching over him. For a moment, I thought he'd fallen asleep. But then he finally broke the suffocating silence.

"Buttercup?" he whispered.

"Yeah, Ezra?"

"Does it make you feel good about yourself acting like my friend? Is that why you do it?"

What?

"I've always considered myself your friend, E."

"Liar."

"Okay, if you say so."

"I do. I do say so. And I know shit. I know a lot of shit about a lot of stuff." He chuckled, a deep gravelly sound that made my stomach clench.

"You're high."

"Soooo fucking high. Jude had some good shit. I can't feel my face. Here." He grabbed my hand and pressed my fingers to his cheeks. "Can't feel a thing." Ezra smoothed my fingers up and down his cheeks. "You can touch me, and I can't feel a thing. It's the only way..." His eyes stared right into mine, two amber pools bewitching me.

His fingers curled around my pointer finger and dragged it over his mouth, along the seam of his lips. He bared his teeth, nipping the pad gently, sending a thousand tiny shivers through me. I smothered a whimper, not wanting to break whatever spell he'd cast. Because I knew this wouldn't be happening if he wasn't high and Carrick hadn't tried to force himself on me.

"You're touching me," he said, a strange reverence in his voice. As if he couldn't quite believe it. "You're touching me and I don't feel a thing." A soft sigh slipped from his lips, making my stomach curl. In that moment, he sounded so content, so at peace, it put a lump in my throat.

"What happened to you, Ezra?" I whispered even though he'd closed his eyes.

"Bad things, buttercup. Bad, bad things."

CHAPTER TWENTY-SIX

Ashleigh

"LEIGH, wake up. Ashleigh, you have to—"

"Huh?" My eyes fluttered open, and my teeth chattered. "Aaron?"

"We need to get you inside before my parents get back."

"W-what..." I sat up, scanning my surroundings. I was outside, at Ezra's spot down by the lake, behind the tree line.

"Ezra—"

Aaron shook his head, and I had my answer. He'd gone inside and left me out here.

I really didn't know what to say to that.

"He asked me to come and wake you."

"Of course he did," I murmured, accepting Aaron's hand. He pulled me to my feet, and I worked out the kink in my neck.

"What time is it?"

"Almost two."

"How long were we down here?"

"Almost two hours. You must have fallen asleep."

"I didn't want to leave him."

"He doesn't deserve you, Leigh. You know that, right?"

"I..." I trapped the words behind my lips.

Aaron was right, Ezra didn't deserve me. He didn't even want me. But I couldn't just switch off my feelings for him, or the innate sense of protectiveness I felt.

It would have been easier if I didn't feel it. But fighting it felt like fighting the universe.

And everyone knew you couldn't fight fate.

Aaron led me around the back of the house and into the kitchen. "Here, I made you this." He offered me a mug of hot cocoa, but I declined.

I couldn't stomach anything.

"So what happened out there?"

"What do you know about Ezra's life before he came here?" I asked.

"What do you mean?"

"Well, have you ever noticed how he won't let anyone touch him?"

Aaron paled. "I did wonder... But it's Ezra, he's always been weird about that stuff. You... you think..."

I nodded.

"He's been with us for years. How would we not know?"

"Because he doesn't want you to know."

"But Mom and Dad—"

"Probably suspect something. Your mom has no doubt tried to broach it with him many times. But Ezra is a closed book. Even more so since the accident."

"Shit." Aaron looked like he'd had the wind knocked from his sails. "It makes a lot of sense."

"I don't know anything for sure, but he said some things tonight..."

"What things?"

"It's not my story to tell, Aaron. And he was high. He probably didn't know what he was saying."

Silence settled over us as we both considered what this meant. If my suspicions were true and Ezra had been hurt in foster care, it explained a lot.

"Are you okay?" Aaron finally broke the silence. "After what happened tonight with Carrick, I mean."

"I'm fine."

"You don't always have to do that, you know. It's okay to be not fine too."

"Is it?" I gave him a sad smile. "It's late. I need to get some sleep. Thank you for coming to get me."

"Leigh, come on. I'm still me."

"Yeah, I guess you are." My smile grew. "Night, Aaron."

"Night, Leigh."

I made my way up to one of the Bennets' guest rooms, pausing before I went inside. Ezra's room was right down the hall. He was in there, all alone.

You're touching me and I don't feel a thing.

There had been something so vulnerable in that moment, as he ghosted my fingers over his lips and stared up at me like I was all his prayers and nightmares come true.

I wanted to be there for him, more than anything, but he'd already made it perfectly clear he didn't want me as his person.

Which truly sucked when I still wanted him as mine.

―――

EZRA WAS NOWHERE to be seen the next morning when we all descended to the kitchen.

"Whoa, just how many of you are up there?" Mya smiled, plating up another stack of pancakes.

"Don't worry, Mom," Sofia said. "We're not hiding anyone."

"Speak for yourself." Aaron chuckled.

"Ew gross, and please tell me it's not Zara Willis."

"The cheerleader?" Mya frowned. "Are you and she—"

"Nice try, Mom, but a guy never kisses and tells." He kissed her cheek and moved around her to the refrigerator.

"Ashleigh, are you going to eat something?"

"Sorry, what?"

"Breakfast... the pancakes."

"Oh yes, thank you, Mrs. B."

"Sweetheart, how many times do I have to tell you to call me Mya." She went back to the pan and my shoulders sagged a little.

She seemed okay with me this morning. Warm and friendly. The way she always had been... before. It had still been a little frosty when I went to see her at school, but then, I guess it was a strange time for everyone.

I was a constant reminder of what had happened. Of how lucky Ezra was to walk away unharmed, and how close he'd come to being hurt.

It was bound to cause some friction between everyone.

"Where's Ezra?" she asked a moment later, and awkward tension fell over us.

"He's... uh, he's probably still sleeping. You know, E." Aaron shrugged.

Sofia glowered at him, but he glowered right back. They obviously still disagreed on what to tell Asher and Mya about last night.

I decided not to get involved. He was their brother. They knew best how their parents might respond to what had happened. Besides, I didn't want to give him any more reason to hate me.

"How was the party?"

"Good, Mom. It was good."

"I hoped you all behaved." She gave Aaron a suspicious look.

"Come on, Mom. You know you can trust us." He grinned.

"Hmm, don't think I don't remember what I got up to back in senior year."

"Oh, I have a story or two about your mother in our senior year." Asher breezed into the kitchen and went straight to his wife, sliding his arms around her waist and nuzzling her neck. "But I'm not sure you'd want to hear all our crazy sex stories."

"Dad!" Sofia balked. "Oh my God, I think I'm going to puke."

"That is... wow, Dad. That's a new low, even for you."

"What?" He smirked. "You're seniors now. Ashleigh is almost nineteen. I hope to God you all know what sex is or we have a serious problem on our hands."

"Ash." Mya nudged his ribs.

"Come on, babe. We're not raising little saints. They're going to experiment."

"Yes, well... so long as they do it safely and with birth control. Lots and lots of birth control."

"Jesus," Aaron breathed, and Cole snorted. He threw him a scathing look and Cole shrugged.

"What? They're not my parents."

"Heard that, Kandon," Asher said.

Just then, Ezra appeared in the doorway.

"Well, you look like shit." Aaron snickered.

"Morning to you too," he grumbled, going to the refrigerator and grabbing a bottle of water.

"Do we need to be concerned?" Asher's expression turned serious.

"It's my fault, Mr. and Mrs. B. I was in a bad place last night and Ezra kept me company. I may have persuaded him to have a few more drinks with me." Cole ran a hand through his hair.

"Is that true?" Asher asked, and Ezra shrugged. "We'll talk about this later."

"Well, I'm just glad you all got home in one piece."

"Says the woman who was still out drinking in the middle of the night," Aaron quipped.

"Watch it, kiddo. You might be captain of the football team now, but I am still your mother, and I can still ground you."

"How do you know we were out drinking anyway?" Asher said. "How do you know we weren't down at the lake—"

"Okay, mister. That is enough from you." Mya clapped her hand over Asher's mouth. "Let the kids eat in peace."

She plated up the bacon and placed it down on the breakfast counter. "Enjoy. Me and your dad are going for a run."

"A run?" Aaron spluttered. "You and Dad never go for a run."

"Well, this morning we are. Try not to kill each other while we're gone." She laid her hand on Ezra's shoulder and leaned in to whisper, "It's nice to see you down here this morning. I'm proud of you, E."

I didn't miss the way he visibly tensed or how his jaw clenched as if he was fighting the urge to recoil from her touch.

Asher and Mya left, and Ezra's gaze snapped to mine. He narrowed his eyes, and I glanced away, overwhelmed at the contempt there. Clearly, he couldn't remember what happened down by the lake... Or he could, and it was just another thing he was going to hold against me.

"I need to go home," I said, standing abruptly.

"Are you okay?" Cole asked.

"Yeah, just tired. I need my own bed."

"I can give you a ride," he offered. "I should probably get home too."

"Thanks."

"Want to hang out later?" Sofia asked. "We could head down to Riverside or watch a movie."

"I... yeah, maybe."

Cole finished his pancake and stood up. "Ready when you are. I'll catch you later," he said to Aaron.

"Okay. And listen, last night, I was an asshole."

"Yeah, you were. But I get it."

He nodded.

"Let's go." Cole led the way, passing Ezra first. His hand shot out, stopping Cole from leaving.

"Thanks, for covering for me."

"Anytime, man." Cole went to clap him on the shoulder but caught himself at the last second. "If I don't see you before, I guess I'll see you at practice Monday."

I glanced at Aaron, but he was too busy watching his best friend and brother with a strange look on his face.

Cole disappeared into the hall, and I lingered, unable to fight the urge to look at Ezra. His brows crinkled as if he didn't understand why I'd stopped in front of him.

"What?" It was a low growl.

"Nothing." I shook my head, my chest caving in on itself as I walked away from him.

Wondering how many more times I could put myself through this.

"MORNING, SWEETHEART," Dad called the second I entered the house.

"Hey, Dad." I found him in the kitchen, washing the breakfast dishes.

"Good night?"

"It was okay," I said, trying to ignore the sense of dread I felt. And not just at Nathan's slimy hands all over me.

But there was no point in upsetting my parents any more than they already were. Knowing them, they would probably do something stupid like insist on homeschooling me for the year. Or making me take online classes.

No, they had enough to worry about. Besides, nothing had really happened. Ezra had made sure of that.

"Sweetheart?" Dad's concerned voice pulled me from my thoughts. "I asked if you wanted some coffee?"

"No, I'm good, thanks. I think I'm going to lie down and catch up on some sleep."

"I think your mom is still sleeping. It's been a long time since we stayed out so late."

"Did you have a nice time?"

"We did, thank you. When you have kids, you forget sometimes that you're still people with needs."

"Oh God, Dad. Please no talk about needs... Asher scarred us for life enough this morning with all the sex talk."

He sprayed his mouthful of coffee everywhere. "Asher was talking to you about... *sex*?"

"The whole conversation was weird and unnecessary."

"Hmm, I think I'll be having a stern word with him later."

Soft laughter spilled out of me. "I'll see you later, okay, Dad."

"Yeah, go get some rest, sweetheart."

RUINED HOPES

I made for the door, but he wasn't done.
"And Ashleigh?"
"Yeah, Dad?"
"You're okay, right? You're going to be okay?"
"I'm getting there," I said.
One day at a time.

CHAPTER TWENTY-SEVEN

Ezra

"SO, what happened last night with you and Ashleigh?"

I glanced over at Aaron and frowned. "What do you mean?"

"Well, you were out there for at least two hours... I thought maybe—"

"Nothing happened. She followed me down there. I passed out, woke up, and she was asleep. I hauled ass out of there and told you to go get her."

Dick move, maybe. But when I'd woken up with the moon shining down on me and Ashleigh's glossy blonde hair plastered over my chest, I'd panicked. And gotten the fuck out of there as quickly as I could.

She hadn't even stirred when I'd gently lifted her arm off my stomach and laid it down on the grass.

"So, nothing happened..."

"Like I told you already, I was out of it."

"You need to decide, E."

"Decide what?"

"Whether to let her in or let her go. I saw you, you know. I saw you go after Carrick the second you spotted him with her."

"I don't know what the fuck you're talking about. I would have done the same for Poppy or Sofia." But as I said the words, something inside me twisted. Because I wasn't being entirely honest with myself and from the look on Aaron's face, he knew it.

"I like to think you would... but I don't know, man. You've never cared before. Not like this. And I'm trying to figure out what's going on with you two."

"Nothing's going on," I bit out.

"Yeah, keep telling yourself that." He snorted but I saw the flash of concern in his eyes. "Ashleigh has been through a lot. She's confused and hurting... and you two have always been... intense."

"We haven't—"

"Dude," he hissed. "She is the only girl you've ever allowed to get close. And then this shit with the accident happened and it's like... it's like you blame her or blame yourself... maybe both. But it's got to stop. Ashleigh needs people around her who've got her back. She needs..."

"Someone like McKay?" His name tasted bitter on my tongue.

"Jesus, Ezra, this isn't about Gav. Don't you get it? She doesn't see anyone but you."

He might as well have punched me in the stomach.

"I know you've been spending time with the waitress," he went on. "But I've gotta ask why... why now?"

"Don't," I snapped, feeling a lick of anger up my spine. "She's got nothing to do with this."

"Doesn't she? She likes you; Ashleigh is pretty much in

love with you... and you're... I don't even know what the fuck you're doing.

"She doesn't love me."

She couldn't.

Because I wasn't... I wasn't loveable.

I was cold and indifferent, and I was pretty sure I didn't have the capacity to feel those emotions.

Aaron was right about Carrick. When I'd spotted him all up in Ashleigh's space, the way she had tried to shove him away, I'd seen red. And nothing had mattered except getting to them and tearing him the fuck away from her.

But that wasn't love. It was... residual anger from my childhood. From all the times I'd witnessed other foster kids get cornered by some asshole. Bigger and meaner and too fucking strong.

All the times it had been *me* cowering against a wall.

No one deserved to feel powerless like that, least of all Ashleigh.

But it wasn't love. It wasn't even close.

It was survival.

The need to fight back and not be taken advantage of, ever again.

"Why can't you let anyone in, E?"

"I'm not doing this with you." I got up and went to leave.

"You need to talk to someone about it. Me, Mom, Ashleigh... your friend at the diner. Just talk to someone, I'm begging you."

"Why do you care?" The words were like sandpaper against my throat.

"Are you serious? You're my brother, of course I care."

"I can't do this." I raked a hand down my face as he stared at me, silently willing me to reciprocate whatever the fuck this was.

"E, come on—"

"I'm out."

I walked out of there.

And didn't look back.

"HEY, STRANGER," Pen greeted me the second I entered The Junction. She took one look at my expression and her smile dropped. "What happened?"

"Any chance you have a break coming up?"

"I actually get off soon, if you don't mind waiting around?"

"Yeah, okay." I didn't want to stay here. I wanted her to drive me as far away from Rixon as she could. Away from Aaron and his dad with all their unwanted advice, away from the team and school and everyone's opinions on me.

Away from Ashleigh.

Fuck, I wanted to get as far away from her as possible and never look back.

Because what Aaron had said earlier... it fucking haunted me.

I grabbed a seat at my usual table and Pen brought me over a milkshake on the house. "I'll be as quick as I can," she said.

I watched her deal with a couple of tables, smiling and laughing with the customers. She was a ray of pure light, lighting up the entire place. But I saw the signs of exhaustion, the dark circles hidden behind layers of makeup, and the shadows in her eyes. She was working herself to the bone trying to make things work for her, Max, and her gran. Splitting her time between taking care of them, night classes, and her job here.

It made my life, where I didn't have to want for anything—except a new car that I knew Asher and Mya were in no great hurry to buy me—look like a walk in the park.

Twenty minutes later, Pen came over. "I'm all set. Max is having a playdate over at our neighbors so I'm all yours."

Any other guy would have had a visceral reaction to those words, but they only made me clam up.

What the fuck was wrong with me?

She was a nice girl. A girl who knew hardship and not to take anything in life for granted. A girl who took responsibility, and made things happen with her own two hands.

Pen was pretty fucking awesome, and she liked me, and I really didn't know how to feel about that.

"How are classes?" I asked her as we walked to her car.

"Good. I picked up an extra class with the day students."

"Yeah?"

She nodded. "It was nice to be around people my own age instead of all the mature students."

"Make any new friends?"

"One or two." Her lips curved into a shy smile. "So what did you want to do?"

"Fancy taking a ride out of town?"

Her eyes twinkled with curiosity. "Where will we go?"

"Anywhere."

Anywhere away from here.

———

PEN DROVE US TO HALSTON, and we sat down by the river eating corn dogs and drinking some weird, funky looking shit she reassured me tasted better than it looked.

"So, what do you think?"

"It's not bad, I guess."

"You guess?" She nudged my shoulder, laughing. "It's basically liquid sugar. I love it."

"The corn dog is good."

"Right? I used to bring Max here sometimes when he was younger. He liked getting out of Rixon too." She gave me a knowing look. "Want to talk about it?"

Swallowing the final mouthful of corn dog, I lay back, resting on my elbows. "How do you do it?"

"Do what?" Pen laid on her side, watching me.

"Hold everything together. Some days I feel like just saying to hell with it and packing a bag and never looking back."

"You'd leave Rixon?"

"Wouldn't you, if you didn't have Max or your gran to think about?"

"I don't know. Rixon is my home. It hasn't always been easy, but it's still home."

But it wasn't my home. It was just the place where I'd ended up. Sure, it was a whole lot nicer than some of my homes over the years, but with it came so much expectation that sometimes I felt like I was drowning.

"Running is the easy way out, sticking around is a lot harder."

"So you like making things difficult for yourself?" I asked, and she rolled her eyes.

"No, idiot, I like doing the right thing. I like knowing that when my gran finally leaves us, and Max grows up that I'll look back and know I did everything I could to make life easier for them."

"You're a good person, Penny."

"You say that like you're not. But you're wrong, you know."

"You don't know anything about me."

"I know that you care enough to not burden your family and friends with whatever haunts you. I know that you always tip me twice the amount required. I know that you stick around because deep down you don't want to disappoint the family who took you in and gave you a home."

"Someone's been watching me very closely." I said it to tease her, for fun, but Pen wasn't laughing. She was staring at my mouth, desire simmering in her eyes.

And for a second, I wondered; I wondered what it would be like to kiss her. Wondered if maybe she could settle the storm constantly raging inside me.

I shuffled closer, until our shoulders were almost touching and threaded my fingers into her hair.

"Ezra, what are—"

"Shh," I breathed, pulling her face down to mine and running my nose along her jaw.

Penny was the kind of girl I should want. Smart. Resilient. A survivor. The kind of girl who took whatever life handed her and made it into something good. She was nothing like Ashleigh who had the world at her fingertips. She would never want for anything. But Pen... she would fight and claw for the things she wanted, the things she needed for herself and those she loved.

Penny, not Ashleigh, was the right choice for a guy like me. A guy who the world had chewed up and spit out more times than I could count.

My fingers brushed her throat as I hovered my lips over the corner of her mouth, willing myself to feel something. Anything. Like the fire under my skin, burning me up that I'd felt when I kissed Ashleigh or the violent thud of my heart as it had tried to claw its way out of my chest.

Nothing came though.

Her lips were soft, sweet and willing. But they felt all wrong.

She felt all wrong.

"Fuck," I murmured, pulling away a fraction.

Pen dropped her head to mine and inhaled deeply. "That was a mistake, wasn't it?"

"Yeah, I fucked up. I'm sorry. I just wanted to see—" I stopped myself, not wanting to be a bigger asshole than I was already.

"Wanted to see if you felt it." Her soft sigh made me flinch with shame. "I guess from the fact we're not still kissing, you don't."

"I want to... feel it, I mean. At least, I think I do. Shit." I sank back into the grass and threw my arm over my face. "I'm a mess."

"Is there someone else?"

"There's not... it's complicated."

"Ah, two little words that no girl ever wants to hear a guy she's crushing on say about another girl." She chuckled but it was strained.

"I'm an asshole."

"No," she sighed. "You're human. And we mess up and make mistakes. It's how we handle those mistakes that defines us."

I glanced up at her. "I wanted it to be you."

"Because I'm the safe option?"

"Because you get it. You know how hard life can be. And you get me." *And you don't make me feel unworthy.*

"And she doesn't?"

"She says she wants to... but like I said, it's complicated."

"Obviously, if you're kissing me to try to get her out of your system."

"Told you," I jabbed a finger at my chest. "Asshole."

"So what's the deal... talk to me."

"It doesn't matter." I ran a hand down my face, exhaling a long breath. "We can't be together."

"Well now I am intrigued."

My eyes flicked to Pen, and I frowned. "Why are you being so cool about this?"

"Because like I told you once already, we could all use one more friend in the world, Ezra. And regardless of... this, you're stuck with me."

Fuck. Why couldn't it have been her?

She wouldn't push and scratch at wounds I didn't want to reopen. She wouldn't try to change me into someone I wasn't. To try to push me to achieve my potential.

Ashleigh wanted all those things.

And the worst of it was, she deserved them. She deserved to meet someone who could give her the world, someone who would fight her demons and lift her up whenever she fell down.

She deserved all of it so fucking much.

Which is why it could never happen. Because we were too different. Her with her perfect life and me with my damaged past and closet full of skeletons I had no desire to unbury.

Her uncle and Asher had done her a favor keeping me away from her this semester. Because they knew what everyone else around us knew: if I got too close to Ashleigh, I'd ruin her.

More than I already had.

"What—Ashleigh?"

I shot upright, twisting around to where Penny was staring... right at Ashleigh.

She stood halfway up the embankment, a small child in her arms, tears rolling down her cheeks.

"Ashleigh?" Her name sounded foreign on my lips as I clambered to my feet. Probably because I couldn't hear over the roaring in my ears. "What are you—"

"Leigh, what's—" Peyton appeared, glancing between the two of us. "*Ezra?*"

"I feel like I'm missing something." Pen stood up beside me. "You know Ashleigh?"

"Something like that," I murmured, my head spinning.

What was she doing here?

How long had she been standing there?

From the tears streaming down her face, she'd obviously seen me kiss Penny.

Fuck.

Fuck!

"It's not what you think," the words spewed out of me.

"Oh my God, she's the girl," Pen breathed.

As if the universe hadn't fucked me over enough, McKay came bounding over the top of the embankment, grinding to a halt when his eyes fell on me and—

"Penelope?"

"Hold up, you two know each other?" I said.

"Gavin?"

"Well, this is..."

Fucked up.

It was totally and utterly fucked up.

CHAPTER TWENTY-EIGHT

Ashleigh

"YOUR WAITRESS IS PENELOPE?" I stepped forward, still holding Millie. She fussed in my arms, pulling on strands of my hair, but I barely felt it, reeling from seeing Ezra kiss her.

At first, I'd thought I was dreaming. It wasn't Ezra—*my Ezra*—lying on the riverside with his hand tangled in another girl's hair as his lips met hers.

It had lasted all but a few seconds, but I couldn't drag my eyes away from them, even as they talked.

It was as if I needed to see it all play out, to know that I was chasing a dream.

A fantasy.

Ezra didn't want me for many reasons.

And she was one of them.

Of course it was some kind of cruel joke that I knew her. That she was the woman Gav had checked out that day in the park.

They were both into her.

What were the odds?

God, I'd never felt more stupid, more insignificant, than I did in that moment.

"Please take her," I said to no one in particular as I held out Millie. She cooed softly, thinking we were playing. Thankfully, Gav scooped her out of my arms.

"So does someone want to clue me in as to how you two know each other?" he asked Penelope.

She moved ever so slightly away from Ezra. Anyone else might have missed it, but I couldn't stop staring at them together. The waitress and the misfit.

Except, Ezra had never been a misfit in my eyes. He'd only ever been a lost boy in need of an anchor, and I'd been all too willing to keep him grounded.

But he hadn't wanted me back then, and he didn't want me now.

"Ezra is a regular customer at the diner where I work," she said, her gaze fixed firmly on me. "Ashleigh, we should talk—"

"No, we really shouldn't. I-I need to go." I turned and started running, my lungs smarting as my chest constricted. I couldn't breathe over the big, fat, ugly sobs that racked my body as my feet pounded on the ground.

"Leigh, wait up," Peyton called after me, but I didn't stop, I couldn't. I needed to get away, far, far away from Ezra. Away from the memory of his lips on another woman.

Time and time again my friends had warned me he would only hurt me, and time and time again I didn't listen. Because I didn't want to give up on him. Not now, not ever.

But there were some things you couldn't deny... and seeing them together, seeing the way he'd kissed her, was one of them.

He'd kissed me out of hate.

But he'd kissed her out of desire.

"Ashleigh, what's wrong?" Uncle Xander strode toward me, catching me as I stumbled into his arms.

"I need to go, now. Please, please, you have to take me home."

"What's—"

"Thank God." Peyton arrived breathless and panting behind me.

"What the fuck happened?"

"I'm not entirely sure," she said. "But Ezra is down there with someone, and Ashleigh freaked out."

"Ezra?"

"Can we just go, please?"

"Sure, come on, let's get you back to the apartment."

I didn't want to go to their apartment, I wanted to go home. I wanted to lock my door and bury myself in my pillows and nurse my broken heart.

"I told Gav he's welcome to come back to the apartment."

"Oh God, Gav."

"Relax, he's okay. He's going to head over to us."

I nodded. It had been Peyton's idea for us all to hang out. There was a great park near their apartment block for Millie and then we'd driven down to the river to feed the ducks.

It had been lovely, until I'd spotted Ezra.

Peyton and Uncle Xander ushered me into the back of his car.

"Tell me now, do I need to go kick his ass?" He gripped the steering wheel, the blood draining from his knuckles.

"First, we need to know what the hell happened, but she's in no state to talk yet." Peyton cradled my head in her lap. "Let's get you home, babe, and then you can tell me what happened."

"GAV IS GOING to hang around at the park with Millie. He thought we might need the space." I pocketed my cell phone and accepted the mug of coffee off Peyton. "Thanks."

"Feeling a bit better? You scared me back there."

"I scared myself," I admitted. To lose control like that, it wasn't me. But ever since the accident, I'd been feeling less and less stable.

"What happened with Ezra, Leigh?"

I glanced to Uncle Xander, and he rubbed his jaw. "I'm Switzerland." He circled a finger around himself. "Anything you say shall remain in this room."

"Anything?" My brow lifted.

"Well, not everything. There are some things that supersede Switzerland neutrality rules. But I know you're not going to tell me Ezra physically hurt you, because—"

"Okay, babe, we get the point." Peyton clapped a hand over his mouth. "Give us some space, please?"

Uncle Xander held up his hands. "I'll go."

"Thank you."

The second the door closed, Peyton reached for my hand, squeezing gently. "What happened?"

"I... he... I saw them kissing. Ezra was kissing her, Peyton." Fresh tears cascaded down my cheeks. "I thought he just needed time or something... that he was blaming himself because of the accident. But it's not... he really doesn't want *me*."

"Oh, babe, come here." She pulled me into her arms, stroking my back. "He's an idiot. A stupid, foolish, stubborn idiot."

I wished it were that simple. But if he was the idiot, why did I feel like the idiot?

He'd made it clear he didn't want me, but I'd persisted. I'd refused to give up on him when the signs were all right there.

"Who is she?"

"Penelope?" How was it possible to hate a name so much? "She's a waitress at the diner he hangs out at. She's older, I think. And pretty. She's like really pretty, Peyton."

"Oh no, don't do this. Don't make this into something it's not." She cupped my face. "Do you have any idea how beautiful you are? Inside and out? You have spent years trying to reach Ezra. Most people would have long given up on him."

Exactly. I wanted to roar.

I'd spent years... and look where it had got me.

On the receiving end of a broken bruised heart.

All this time I thought...

Foolish girl.

"It hurts," I whispered, pain fisting my heart. "It hurts so damn much."

"I know, babe. I know." Peyton hugged me again, reassuring me that my guy was out there somewhere. Waiting to swoop into my life when I least expected it. But even thinking about another guy felt like betraying Ezra. Because my heart belonged to him.

It always had.

Whether he wanted it or not.

WHEN SCHOOL ROLLED around Monday morning, a ball of dread sat heavy in my stomach.

I didn't want to see Ezra. Because I knew what I had to do.

I had to let him go.

Ezra deserved to be happy. I'd always hoped I would be the girl to do that for him, but I wasn't. I had to accept that.

So last night, while lying in bed nursing my broken heart, I decided that today I would do it. I would set him free.

Of course, I didn't expect him to care. He'd made it more than obvious that he didn't. But I needed closure. I needed him to know that I would be okay and that all I'd ever wanted for him was for him to be happy and feel like he had someone to turn to.

I would never truly understand what happened after the accident. But maybe it was better this way. Near death experiences changed people. I was living proof of that. Changed in a way I still hadn't come to terms with.

"Morning, sweetheart," Dad said as I entered the kitchen. "How was it seeing your Uncle Xan and Peyton yesterday? You didn't say much when you got home."

"It was good, Dad." I kissed him on the cheek and went to the refrigerator, grabbing some juice. Needing a second to fix my expression.

"Sofia is here, so I need to go."

"Already? I was hoping we could have breakfast together and talk."

"Maybe tomorrow?" I forced a smile.

"Yeah, okay. Have a good day at school." Something passed over his face and he added, "You know, Ashleigh, me and your mom only want the best for you, sweetheart."

"I know, Dad. See you later." I grabbed a banana from the fruit bowl and headed out.

Sofia's car was already waiting.

"Hey," she said, as I slid into the back seat.

"You good?"

"Yeah, I'm fine." My stomach twisted but I ignored it.

Poppy turned around and grinned. "How was yesterday? With Gav and Millie?"

"It was fine."

"Only fine?" Her brows knitted. "You two could be so good together, I don't get it."

"Pops," Sofia warned.

"Gav doesn't like me, Poppy. He likes someone else."

"Someone else? I'm confused."

"It doesn't matter." I waved her off, pretending to play on my cell phone. Part of me had wondered if Ezra would text me last night to try to explain. He hadn't. I didn't know whether to be bitterly disappointed or mildly relieved.

But it didn't matter.

After today, that chapter of my life would be behind me. I could focus on the future. On surviving the next year of high school and dealing with the likelihood that my memories might never return.

Part of me wondered if, after everything, it would be easier if they didn't. I didn't need to suddenly remember ten extra months of chasing Ezra around. But I knew something inside me would always feel like it was missing if they never came back.

Our memories made us who we were, and I wasn't truly Ashleigh Chase without them.

By the time we pulled up to school, my stomach was a tight ball of nerves. But I realized it was silly to feel nervous about doing something that wouldn't affect the other person.

"Are the guys practicing this morning?" I asked Sofia.

She found a parking spot and cut the engine. "Yep. Aaron was moaning about how hard Coach is going to push them this week in the run up to their first game."

"Why?" They both twisted around to look at me.

"Because I need to talk to Ezra."

"You do?" Poppy frowned.

"Yeah," I said.

"Are you sure that's a good idea, babe? I don't want you to—"

"It's fine. I'm doing what I should have done a long time ago."

They shared a concerned glance.

"I'm setting him free."

I WAITED in the bleachers for football practice to end. Poppy and Lily had wanted to come with me, but I told them this was something I needed to do alone.

Only, the second I sat down, Uncle Jason spotted me.

He jogged straight over. "Everything okay?"

"Everything's fine, Uncle Jase. I'm just waiting for Ezra to get done."

"Ezra?" His brows went up.

"Yeah, I need to talk to him."

He yanked off his Raiders ball cap and ran a hand through his dark hair. "Is everything okay?"

"It will be." I smiled. That tight unfamiliar smile I'd grown so accustomed to wearing over the last few weeks.

"Well, okay. I'll send him your way once we get done."

"Thanks."

Despite looking like he wanted to say more, Uncle Jase jogged back over to his team and had them run a couple more plays.

I couldn't help but search out number sixteen. He moved up and down the sideline like a rocket, zipping back and forth as Cole threw the ball to him. And although I didn't understand the sudden change of heart where football was concerned, I couldn't deny Ezra looked good out there.

He looked like he belonged.

In that moment, it occurred to me that maybe the accident hadn't only changed me.

We weren't the same people anymore.

Maybe it really was time to put the past behind us.

CHAPTER TWENTY-NINE

Ashleigh

WHEN THE TEAM STARTED DISPERSING, Coach called Ezra over. He walked closely beside him, guiding Ezra around to face the bleachers and pointed at me, saying something. I couldn't make out what. But whatever it was, it had Ezra jogging in my direction. I didn't get up to meet him, instead waiting for him to join me on the bench. He kept a reasonable distance between us, the space filled with soul-aching tension.

"Coach said you wanted to talk."

"I thought we should clear the air... about yesterday—"

"Ashleigh, listen, I—"

"No, let me. I need to do this, okay." I peeked up at him, hit with a wave of anguish so intense that I struggled to find my next words.

But I had to do this. I had to let him go. Because he wasn't mine.

He never had been.

And I needed to move on. I needed to move on and let myself heal.

His jaw ticked as he nodded.

"It was unfair of me to act like that yesterday." I took a deep breath, trying to calm my racing pulse. "All I've ever wanted was to be your friend, Ezra. When you first arrived in Rixon, I saw a lost, angry boy and I wanted to help. I can't really explain it, but it was like I knew that was my job. To be your friend.

"It wasn't easy. Constantly pushing you to let me in. To open up. But I was determined to break down your walls, Ezra. Because you deserve a friend. You deserve so many good things. I just wanted you to know that."

"Leigh, look, you don't have to—"

"Yes, I do." I nodded, sucking in a shaky breath. "I realize now that I let things between us grow into something in my mind that was never there to begin with. I thought I'd wear you down and you'd finally realize how I felt. That you just needed time to realize you felt the same. I thought... well, it doesn't matter anymore." My cheeks burned with shame. I'd been so blinded by my need to fix him, to bring him into our world, that I'd failed to realize one thing.

He didn't want it.

"Why are you telling me all this?" His voice was a low, broken rasp, but I knew not to mistake it for something it wasn't.

"Because I'm letting you go." Silent tears slipped down my cheeks. "I can't keep fighting for something that's never going to happen." My heart slammed against my chest, over and over like a beating drum, as I considered my next words.

I could keep them to myself and never tell him, but he deserved to know, didn't he?

Ezra deserved to know that someone loved him. Even if

he didn't feel the same, I wanted him to know. I needed to say the words just this once.

"I love you, Ezra. I think a part of me has loved you since the first time I saw you and I didn't understand the gravity of my feelings toward the new boy in town." A wistful smile tugged at my lips.

His fingers curled around the edge of the bench. "You don't mean that." He sounded angry but I couldn't find it in me to take them back.

"Yes, I do. And I know you don't feel the same, and that's okay. I have to be okay with that. When I saw you kissing Penelope, I knew. I knew you were never mine the way I've always been yours."

The tears came thick and fast, my chest cracking wide open as I severed the tether that had snapped in place that day when Asher and Mya had brought over their new foster kid to meet us.

"You probably think this is stupid and unnecessary, but I needed to do it. I needed to look you in the eye and tell you it's okay. I'll be okay, Ezra. Because knowing you're happy and that you've found someone you want to open your heart to, is more important than me getting my feelings hurt."

He ran a hand down his face, his expression indifferent. Even now, he felt... nothing.

God, it hurt.

It hurt so freaking much. But I had come this far, I could survive the next minute or so.

"I watched you play earlier, and you're good, E. You're so freaking good. It's okay to want it, you know. To go after it. You deserve it." My smile grew because it was true. He did deserve it. "I don't know everything that happened last year, between us, with you failing senior year. But none of that matters. All that matters is what happens next, the choices we make going forward.

"I want good things for you. I want you to be happy. I want you to finally let someone in." *Even if it's not me.*

Silence echoed around us. Ezra stared at me as if he didn't even recognize me, and that hurt the most. That even now, he couldn't give me a sign that it had all meant something.

"Well, that's all I wanted to say." I stood up on shaky legs and ran my hands down my jeans. My stomach churned violently, and there was every chance I would run off the field and throw up in a trashcan. But I'd done it.

"Good luck on Friday with your first game. I'll be cheering you on from the bleachers."

I'll always be cheering you on.

"Buttercup—"

I couldn't stand to hear that name on his lips, so I cut him off. "I don't want things to be awkward between us, so let's just... put this behind us, okay?" I held out my hand to him. I hadn't planned on doing it, but it seemed like an appropriate way to end the very one-sided conversation.

But Ezra just kept staring.

"Yeah, okay, it was a stupid idea." Dejection swarmed inside of me. "I guess I'll see you around then."

I waited, even now, even after I'd let him go, I waited for him to give me something. Anything.

But it never came.

IT WAS STRANGE, actively trying *not* to search out Ezra wherever I went. The class we shared was the hardest. I was so aware of him, to the point my mind even played tricks on me, imagining his intense stare burning into my back.

Of course, every time I risked peeking over my shoulder at him, he was paying me no attention.

Nobody asked me about him. Not Poppy or Sofia or the guys. Gav tried to talk to me once in the aftermath, but the second he said Ezra's name, I changed the subject and asked him about Millie instead.

If I was going to move on, truly put him out of my head, I needed to stop obsessing over him.

By Thursday, it was getting a little easier. The school was psyched for the first football game of the season, especially since it was at Dawson Stadium. Everyone was going, including our families. And Kaiden and Lily were going to try to get down there if they could.

It was impossible not to get swept up in the excitement. Until I heard the whispers around school.

Ezra Jackson and Nathan Carrick were fighting at practice today.

I heard Coach lost his shit.

It looks like they could both be suspended for the opening game.

It took everything inside me not to ask Sofia about it. If she noticed, she didn't say anything, and she was careful not to bring it up around me.

"I'll see you tomorrow," I said as she pulled up outside my house.

"You don't want to hang later?"

"I have a ton of homework so I'm going to stay in. But have fun," I said, climbing out.

"Leigh, wait... Are you sure you're okay?"

"I'm fine." Offering her one of my picture-perfect smiles, I headed up to the house and slipped inside.

It was easier to believe the lie if I kept telling it.

I'm fine.

No, I don't want to talk about it.
I want to focus on the future.

Kicking off my sneakers, I dropped my bag next to the stairs and made my way to the kitchen, but my parents' voices gave me pause.

"Worried we did the wrong thing."

"Cam, you didn't. This was best, for both of them. Can you imagine what would have happened to him if Jase hadn't stepped in?"

Ezra. They had to be talking about Ezra.

But it didn't make any sense. What did my dad have to do with anything?

I crept closer to the door, torn between revealing myself and listening a little longer.

I was supposed to be avoiding situations like this, situations where my natural instinct was to want to go to him and make sure he was okay.

"Jase is worried—"

Be the bigger person.

"Mom, Dad, I'm home," I called, alerting them to my presence as I entered the kitchen.

"Hi, sweetheart. We didn't hear you come in."

I noted my dad sitting at the breakfast counter. Mom standing between his legs with her arms looped around his neck as if she was comforting him.

"Is everything okay?"

"Everything's fine, baby. How was your day?"

"Same old." I gave a noncommittal shrug and made a beeline for the tray of cookies. When I looked up, they were both watching me. "What?" I asked.

"I don't know, Leigh, you seem... different."

I guess that's what giving up another intrinsic part of you

did. But it wasn't like I could tell them that. They wouldn't understand.

So I shoved down those thoughts and locked them away in the little box deep inside my soul.

"Everyone is going wild over the game tomorrow." I changed the subject to safer shores.

"I remember opening night well," Dad said. "The lights, the noise, the smell of freshly mowed grass. There's nothing quite like Friday night football."

"Do you miss it?"

Dad had given up football in college when Grandma got sick. He'd left Mom in Michigan and come home to help Grandad Clark look after Xander. He'd given up his dreams for his family.

"Miss it?" he said. "How could I miss it when I gained the best family a man could ever wish for." He held out his hand and I took it, letting him pull me into his and Mom's arms. They hugged me tight, just like they used to when I was a kid.

"We're proud of you, Ashleigh. So freaking proud. Don't ever forget that."

"I won't, Dad." Emotion balled in my throat. No matter what, I would always have this, the unconditional love of my family. Swallowing back the tears, I whispered, "I promise."

WHEN I CAME out of third period on Friday, Nathan Carrick was waiting for me.

"You're in my way," I said, moving around him. But his arm shot out. I stepped back, trying to keep some distance between us.

"I heard something interesting about you and lover boy."

"Excuse me?"

"That's right, babe, I found out something real interesting."

Ice cold dread skated down my spine. "I don't know what you're talking about."

"Oh, but you will," he sneered, leaning in until his warm breath fanned my face. A shudder went through me as I tried to catch the attention of the passing students. But everyone was too busy going about their business, and besides, it was Nathan Carrick, a Rixon Raider. Nobody would bat an eyelid at us.

"What do you want, Nathan?"

He ran a finger down my cheek. "Don't worry your pretty little head about it, babe. It'll all come out soon enough and then Jackson will be back where he belongs."

My brows creased. What the hell was he talking about?

"Carrick," Aaron boomed down the hall and he jerked away from me, plastering a smile on his evil face.

"Everything good, Leigh?" Aaron's questioning gaze slid to mine.

"Yeah, everything's fine. Nathan was just leaving."

"See you around, *Leigh Leigh*."

A shudder went through me at the dark notes in his voice. I was still frowning as he walked off down the hall.

"What the fuck was that about?" Aaron glared after him.

"Nothing, forget it." I went to walk off, but he grabbed my wrist.

"You sure you're okay?"

I let out a heavy sigh. "I really wish people would stop asking me that."

CHAPTER THIRTY

Ezra

"WHAT?" I snapped at Carrick as he smirked at me from across the table.

Fucker had watched me all week. I'd managed to keep out of his way, but he seemed to be everywhere I fucking turned. Right there, goading me. A wicked glint in his eye as if he was plotting... or waiting for something to happen.

I didn't know how I kept it together because after watching Ashleigh walk away from me Monday morning, I was a fucking mess.

"You'll get what's coming," he mumbled, and my ears pricked up.

"What the fuck did you say?"

"I said, you'll get—"

"Carrick, shut the fuck up," Aaron pinned him with a dark look. "Have you forgotten we have a game tonight?"

"I'm out," I said, standing abruptly. "I'll see you later."

Before anyone could talk me out of it, I stalked out of the cafeteria and headed for the doors. I needed some air.

"E, wait up," Aaron called, jogging after me. "You good?" he asked me, falling into step beside me.

I pressed my lips together and kept walking. I didn't want to talk. Not about Carrick, not about Ashleigh, not about the game tonight.

I broke away from Aaron, cutting across the path to the football field.

"E, come on. Don't shut me out." Aaron had been on me all week, wanting to know what was wrong.

Ashleigh obviously hadn't told him what had happened last weekend. From the way Sofia and Poppy gave me the cold shoulder all week, I suspected they knew something, but it wasn't like I could fix anything.

I'd fucked up.

When I'd kissed Penny, I hadn't done it to hurt Ashleigh. I'd done it because I wanted to feel something. Something besides the gnawing darkness that lived inside me.

But when I saw Ashleigh standing there, I knew I'd fucked up. The devastation in her eyes would haunt me forever.

I'd broken her.

Obliterated her heart and made her question everything that had once existed between us.

I'd never wanted that. I'd just wanted her to stay away and stop making things so fucking hard for both of us.

I didn't think...

I love you, Ezra.

Four little words that had ruined me.

Four little words I didn't deserve to hear.

Four little words that had played on repeat in my head for the entire week as Ashleigh avoided me.

"Seriously, man. What the fuck is your problem? We have a game tonight. It's important—"

I whirled around, glaring at him. "To you. It's important to *you*," I spat through clenched teeth.

"It could be important to you too, if you'd let it." He let out a steady breath. "Why are you so against making something of yourself, huh? You're good at football, E. Coach gave you a chance—"

"I didn't fucking ask for it." My chest heaved with the weight of the words. "Do you think I'd really be here, on the team, if it was my choice?"

"Is it really that bad?"

I glanced away, running a hand down my face. When I looked back at him, his expression guttered. "You don't get it," I said quietly. "You have everything, Aaron. You can do anything, be anything. The world is literally at your feet."

"What happened to you?"

The words pierced the air like a gunshot.

"W-what?"

"In foster care. What happened to you?"

"I don't know what the fuck you're talking about." The invisible walls around me went into defense mode.

"You think I haven't noticed the way you clam up whenever somebody touches you? You don't get close, E, to anyone." He stared at me, waiting.

But what was there to say? I was never going to tell him about my childhood. About the endless days of darkness.

That shit needed to stay locked up inside me, where it couldn't bleed into the life I had here.

"You can talk to me," he pleaded. "I'm your brother, your friend..."

"There's nothing to talk about," I said, flatly. "Besides, didn't you just tell Carrick we have a game to focus on?"

"E, come on, that isn't—"

"Go back to lunch, Aaron. I'm not talking about this with you." I took off toward the bleachers, but he couldn't let it go.

"Will you talk to me about Ashleigh then?"

Her name crashed into me, and I ground to a halt, letting out a muted groan.

"I know something happened between you two. She won't tell me anything, but it's obvious she's upset. And you're walking around like someone stole your favorite toy. She wants you, E. She's always wanted you... I don't understand why you keep pushing her away."

Glancing back over my shoulder, I met his confused stare and said, "Leave Ashleigh out of this."

———

I LOVE YOU, *Ezra*.

I love you, Ezra.

I love you, Ezra.

I couldn't fucking escape those four little words. They played on repeat over and over in my head.

She loved me. Aaron was right all along; Ashleigh was in love with me.

I hadn't wanted to believe it then. I hadn't wanted to believe it when she'd sat next to me in the bleachers and told me. Even after she'd walked away from me, I still hadn't wanted to fucking believe it.

Because how could she love me?

People didn't love me, they left me. They hurt me... they fucking ruined me.

Not the Bennets. I couldn't ignore the little voice reminding me how good they had been to me. How hard they had tried to make me feel like one of them.

But that broken part inside of me still couldn't trust it.

And now, I had to spend an hour in class with her.

It was fifth period and all anyone was talking about was the game against Millington later. I couldn't think straight, let alone think about the game. A game I shouldn't even be a part of.

My eyes burned into the back of Ashleigh's head. I couldn't help it. But I didn't know if I was silently willing her to look at me or remain with her eyes glued up front.

She didn't turn around. Not that I was surprised, she had barely looked at me all week. But I was unnerved about how much it got under my skin. I was used to her being there, her eyes following me wherever I went.

Looking back, before the accident, maybe I'd taken her presence for granted. I'd known how she felt about me, known she'd wanted more than I could ever give her, and I'd taken advantage of that. I'd played into it.

Because Ashleigh was the one person—the only person until Penny—to see me.

But I'd gone and blown it all to hell the night of graduation.

I could still remember everything. Every single moment.

SHE STORMED *over to the car and ripped the door open.* "What are you doing here?"

"*Good to see you too, buttercup.*"

"*Don't call me that,*" *Ashleigh seethed but she looked too fucking adorable pissed at me.* "*You're too late, the party's over.*"

"*I didn't come for the party.*" *I didn't give a fuck about graduation. Not since I'd flunked senior year. But Ashleigh wouldn't let it go. She'd been texting me all night, begging me to show up and party with them.*

Begging me to come see her.

"I'm not doing this, not tonight."

She went to slam the door, but I said, "Come on, Leigh. Don't be like that." *A beat passed and I released a long breath.* "You know why I didn't come."

"No, I don't."

Fucking liar. She knew—she knew me in ways nobody else did.

"Take a ride with me," *I said quietly.*

"A ride? Now? It's almost two in the morning."

"Please?" *A faint smile traced my mouth and I saw the second she relented. Her expression softened, her big blue eyes giving in to me. My smile grew but her eyes narrowed.*

"You're high."

Busted.

"I had a smoke earlier," *I said.* "But I'm fine. Stop worrying." *She hesitated, glancing back at the house so I added,* "Take a ride with me, come on." *I pouted, dragging my bottom lip between my teeth, letting it slowly pop out.* "Come on, buttercup, you know you want to."

"Fine, but just for a little while." *Ashleigh slid into the car, sending someone—Lily, no doubt—a quick text.*

Chilled music pumped out of the speaker as I backed out of the Hughes' driveway, and neither of us spoke until the house grew small in the rearview mirror.

"Where are we going?" *Ashleigh asked.*

Ashleigh was always so willing to trust me. I didn't deserve it.

I didn't deserve her. And I tried, I tried so fucking hard to keep her at arm's length, but she was like an addiction. A bad habit I couldn't shake.

"Wanna see how fast she can go?" *I grinned over at her, feeling wild and reckless.*

"Ezra, I don't think that's—" I floored the gas and the car shot off like a rocket. "Ezra, what the hell?" Her hands curled around the edge of the seat, fear glittering in her eyes.

But didn't she know she didn't need to fear me... that she was the one who held all the power here?

"Relax, buttercup," I drawled, trying to shake off the strange hold she had over me. "It's just a little fun. Something to get the heart pumping."

"EZRA?" Someone touched me and I almost bolted out of my chair.

"What the fuck?" I glowered at Zara.

"Relax, I was just trying to... are you okay?" Her expression softened. "I didn't mean to startle you. But you were totally spaced out and the bell rang like two minutes ago."

Shit, it had?

Sure enough, the class was emptying. Ashleigh was already at the door. I almost got up and went after her. I couldn't leave things the way they were between us. Not after everything she'd said on Monday.

I love you, Ezra.

She at least deserved to know that the last few weeks weren't about her—they were about me. About my fuck ups. That being around her was just a permanent reminder of how much I'd screwed up.

But I didn't go after her.

Because Ashleigh had finally let me go.

And it was the best thing.

For both of us.

THE ROAR of the crowd was like nothing I'd ever experienced. Adrenaline pumped through me, making my heart crash against my chest.

It looked like the entire town had turned up to watch the opening game of the season. A sea of Raider colors filled the bleachers, with a small section reserved for Millington fans.

"It's something, huh?" Aaron came up beside me, but he didn't touch me. I'd noticed he tried not to at practice too. It was inevitable that guys slammed into me, jostled, and nudged me. But that was different. I usually saw it coming and could manage my reaction accordingly.

It was the times I didn't know to expect it that caught me off guard.

Aaron hadn't asked me about it again and I'd offered no further explanation. I meant what I'd said, I didn't want to talk about it. Not now. Not ever.

"It's... I didn't know it would be like this."

"Soak it up, man. Because this is just the beginning. We've got a whole season ahead of us." He grinned, snapping on his helmet, and jogging off at the sound of Coach's voice.

I'd never once imagined this moment because it wasn't something I'd ever wanted. But hearing the roar of the crowd, the ripple of anticipation in the air, the bright glare of the Friday night lights, something shifted inside me. I wasn't foolish enough to think football was my salvation or even a light at the end of the tunnel, but it was a distraction, and I was good at it, that had to count for something. I could spend the next two months fighting Coach every step of the way, or I could embrace this opportunity and show everyone that there was more to Ezra Jackson.

Inhaling a deep breath, I ran a hand down my face and shook out all the reservations, the thoughts, and memories. Everyone was expecting me to go out there tonight and play like I wanted it. I needed to get out of my head and into the game.

"Raiders, let's go," Coach yelled again, and I turned to jog over to the huddle. Carrick collared me, falling into step beside me. I went on high alert.

"Big night, Jackson. Try not to fumble the ball." He smirked.

"Fucking idiot," I muttered to myself, reaching the edge of the huddle. Aaron caught my eye, silently asking me if everything was okay. I nodded.

I could handle Carrick. Even if there was something disconcerting about the way he watched me.

"This is it," Coach Ford said. "Our first game will determine how we go forward this season. Play hard… win hard. Cole, son, you hanging in there?"

"Yes, Coach."

"Glad to hear it, son. Millington has a big defense. Raiders, keep your heads up and follow the ball." He scanned the team and locked eyes on me in the back. "Ezra, feeling ready?"

"As I'll ever be."

Coach nodded, nothing but determination and hunger for the win shining in his eyes. "Okay, Raiders on three."

Hands went in as everyone stood shoulder to shoulder.

"One, two, three… Raiders."

The team dispersed to the rumble of cheers and clapping. The atmosphere was electric, and not even I could deny the shiver of anticipation that ran down my spine.

"Ezra, a word." Coach beckoned me over.

"Yes, Coach?"

"Where's your head at right now?"

"My head?"

"You've been distracted this week, and I haven't wanted to push you too hard, but if something's—"

"Nothing's wrong, Coach. I'm ready." The words poured out of their own volition.

"Good. I want you to give it your all tonight, son. Make everyone proud." He glanced over to the friends and family section where Asher, Mya, Sofia, Coach's wife, Poppy, Ashleigh and her mom all sat. I quickly looked away.

Coach gave me a strange look. "You sure you're—"

"I'm ready," I said again.

"Okay, then get out there and show them what you've got."

CHAPTER THIRTY-ONE

Ashleigh

THE GAME WAS INTENSE. Millington came out hungry for it. They had a big defense and a strong offense. But Cole wielded his team with impressive command.

"He's good," Dad said for the third time already. "Really good."

"He's... I can't believe he's playing quarterback." Sofia had her arm looped through mine as we watched the guys try to gain much needed yards.

"They need a touchdown," I murmured. "Come on."

Being here, among the crowd, the noise, and frenetic energy was so familiar. Like a warm blanket wrapped around me. Football was a part of me, the way it was for everyone in Rixon, and despite the constant ache in my chest, part of me was excited to cheer the team on.

Even Ezra.

He looked so freaking good in his jersey and shoulder pads. But it wasn't just the uniform... it was him. He still held back a little, operating on the periphery of the team. But he was focused, whipping up and down the sideline like he was born to do it.

The change in him was a little disarming. But I couldn't help but feel proud that the lost, angry boy who had arrived in Rixon all those years ago had finally found his place.

I'd wanted to be the one to save him, to fix him. But standing there, watching Ezra track the ball across the field, and cheer for his teammates when a Raider hit the end zone and slammed the ball down, was enough.

It had to be.

"Touchdoooown," the announcer boomed over the PA system and the crowd. Went. Wild.

It was electrifying, as every single Raider in the bleachers got on their feet to celebrate the first touchdown of the season.

"Holy crap, that never gets old," Sofia breathed, grinning up at me.

"They're looking in good shape," Dad said to no one in particular. "Maybe Jase will be able to make champs out of them yet."

Everyone was too busy to notice Nathan Carrick shoulder check Ezra as the team jogged into position for the field goal. But I saw it. Ezra pulled up short, glaring at his teammate. I clutched Sofia's arm, unable to tear my eyes from them.

What the hell was his problem?

"You okay, sweetheart?" Dad asked me and I slid my eyes to his, nodding. "How does it feel, being here?"

"Familiar." Hope glittered in his eyes and my stomach sank. "I don't mean... it isn't sparking anything, Dad. Sorry."

"Ashleigh." He wrapped an arm around me and hugged me into his side. "You don't ever have to be sorry. I wish..." His voice cracked.

"It's okay, Dad."

Part of me had accepted my memories were never coming back. It was easier to move forward if I wasn't waiting for it to happen.

"It's a shame Kaiden and Lily couldn't make it," he added.

Kaiden had gotten pulled into a team thing and couldn't get out of it.

"They have their own lives now, Dad." Sadness snaked through me. But I no longer felt the pang of bitterness I'd had earlier in the summer. I would survive this. I would survive losing UPenn and repeating senior year... and letting Ezra go. Because I didn't have a choice. I had too much life left ahead of me to quit now.

But God, it hurt to look at him. To know that he wasn't mine...

And never would be.

THE RAIDERS WON, 20 - 13. By the time the final whistle blew, Cole had won over every single person in the stadium. And if the chants were anything to go by, Ezra had a few new fans too.

"Where is the party again?" Dad asked as we waited around the back of the stadium for the team to come out.

"Deacon's house."

"And his parents are—"

"Probably out of town, Dad. Relax. We'll be fine," I said.

"Give the kids a break, Cam." Asher chuckled. "We spent most of our senior year partying."

Dad glowered. "Do we need to talk about the rules of parenting again?"

Asher smirked. "Just because you're jealous I'm the cool dad."

"Hey, I'm cool. Isn't that right, sweetheart."

"Sure, Dad." I grimaced. "Really cool."

"Oh, here they are." Poppy rushed over to greet Aaron.

"She's so obvious," Sofia whispered around an amused expression. "Loves him even when she hates him."

"They'll figure it out," I said, a pang of regret echoing inside me.

I'd wanted nothing more than to figure things out with Ezra, but in the end, it wasn't meant to be.

I wasn't what he needed.

I swallowed down the ball of emotion as the rest of the players poured out of the doors, heading straight for their family and friends.

Aaron scooped Poppy up, swinging her around like a rag doll. Their laughter filled the air as we all advanced on them.

"Good game, Son." Asher clapped him on the back.

"Thanks, Dad." He glanced at Poppy, her cheeks bright red as she stepped away to give Aaron some time with his family.

"Where's Ezra?" Sofia asked.

"He'll be out soon. He's just in with Coach and Carrick."

Dad stiffened beside me, shooting Asher a silent look.

"What happened?" I asked Aaron.

"They got into it in the locker room again. Coach is pissed."

"Maybe I should—"

"Leave it, Ash," Dad shook his head. "Jase can handle his players."

I glanced back at the doors. Nathan Carrick had a vendetta against Ezra, that much was obvious. Although I was trying my hardest to stand back and let Ezra live his own life, I couldn't curb the pit of dread sitting heavy in my stomach that I was still missing something.

After what seemed like a lifetime, Ezra and Uncle Jason finally emerged out of the heavy doors. Poppy and Aunt Felicity made a beeline for him while Ezra wandered over to us.

"Well done, Son. I'm proud of you. Real fucking proud." Asher went to hook his arm around Ezra's neck, but hesitated at the last second.

"You did so well, sweetheart," Mya said, and I stepped away, suddenly feeling like a bystander to their intimate moment.

Mom and Dad had migrated over to Uncle Jason, leaving me standing in the middle of them all celebrating the team's success.

Alone.

It wasn't intentional, I knew that, but I couldn't help but feel like I'd become the elephant in the room. No one ever acknowledged the accident or what happened when we were all together. It had caused tensions between the adults, but they all seemed okay now, happier to pretend everything was fine.

But it felt disingenuous somehow. Like maybe we should have sat down and talked about what had happened. That maybe as our parents, they should have encouraged me and Ezra to talk about it, together.

The more I pondered it, the stranger it was, and the more awkward I felt.

Until Ezra looked up and caught my eye. His amber gaze burned with intensity. Apologies I didn't want to hear. Because an 'I'm sorry' wouldn't change anything.

It wouldn't make him mine.

Still, despite my efforts to avoid him, I found myself mouthing, "Congratulations."

I half-expected him to duck his head and ignore me. But to my surprise, his lips curved a fraction. It wasn't a smile, not like the one I'd seen him give Penelope, but it was something.

A warm sensation spread through me, and I scolded myself for letting something so small cause such a visceral reaction in me. But it was going to take time. Although my head knew things between us were over, my heart needed to catch up in her own time.

I broke the connection.

If I was going to maintain any dignity tonight, I had to.

THE PARTY WAS ALREADY in full swing by the time we got there. I'd tried to get out of it, but Poppy and Sofia were insistent that I come. Besides, Gav was meeting us here. He couldn't make the game due to Millie-duty, but he was going to stop by later.

Things had been a little weird between us since last weekend when we found Ezra and Penelope down by the river, and then he'd been busy with classes and Millie. But I wanted us to be okay. I needed us to be. Gav had been nothing but a good friend to me, and I didn't want to lose him.

"Come on, let's find the guys," Poppy said, grabbing my hand. They'd ridden ahead in Aaron's car, happy to attend in their Raider jerseys. But not Poppy and Sofia. We'd gone back to Poppy's house to get changed first. I'd stuck to jeans and a cropped sweater with the word 'Varsity' printed across the chest. I looked cute. Not that I had anyone to impress.

"You don't think he'll bring her, right?" I whispered to Poppy as we made our way through Deacon's house.

"Who?" She frowned.

"Penelope."

"I thought you and Ezra weren't—"

"We're not," I rushed out. "But Jesus, Poppy. I don't want to see him with her." It would crush me. "Maybe this was a bad idea." I hesitated and Poppy stopped. Grabbing my arm gently, she pulled me over to a quiet spot and gave me a soft smile.

"Sorry. I'm doing it again, aren't I?"

"Doing what?"

"Being insensitive. I don't mean to be. I'm just... I'm nervous."

"N-nervous? But why?"

"Because I like Aaron, Leigh. I really freaking like him and I'm tired of pretending I don't. And when he picked me up outside the stadium and spun me around, I felt it."

"You know he feels the same, Poppy," I said. "You have nothing to worry about."

"Don't I? He's so determined to make it this year. To do right by the team and Coach and the entire town. I'm not sure I fit into his plans."

I reached for her hair and lifted it off her shoulder, tucking it behind her ear. "Well, you'll never know if you don't ask him."

"You're right. Oh my God, you're right. Come on." She grabbed my hand. "Let's go and party like it's senior year."

But the second we walked out of the patio doors and into Deacon's yard, she froze. "N-no."

At first, I couldn't see what she saw. Then I saw them. Aaron sitting in a garden chair with Zara straddling his lap, her arms draped around his shoulders, and her mouth pressed on his.

"I think I'm going to puke." Poppy turned and ran back toward the house.

"Pop—"

"What happened?" Sofia came rushing up beside me, gasping when she spotted her brother and Zara. "I'll kill him. I'll fucking kill him."

"He's a guy, Sofe," I whispered. "They mess up. And he doesn't know... he doesn't know how she feels."

Sofia gawked at me with disbelief. "Of course he knows. Everyone knows. Just like you and—" She stopped herself, realization dawning in her eyes.

Knowing hadn't changed anything for Ezra. He still didn't want me, so for me to defend Aaron seemed like a betrayal to Poppy. But the words had just poured out because deep down, I accepted it.

"We should go after her," I said, barely able to meet Sofia's gaze.

"I'll go. You get a drink and find Gav. I think I just saw him arrive."

"You're sure?"

"You know, Leigh. What happened with you and Ezra isn't the same as what's happening with Poppy and Aaron."

Her words were like a punch to the stomach.

"Aaron is acting up. Embracing his newfound celebrity status. He wants Poppy, but he also wants to be young and single." She gave me a sad smile. "But Ezra... it's different. He doesn't let himself feel anything... I'm not even sure he knows how to."

That wasn't true though. I'd seen him kiss Penelope. Saw the way he'd held her face and laughed with her. The way he'd looked at her. I'd thought I'd felt the same thing the night when he'd kissed me. But I couldn't trust myself anymore, not when I'd built things up between us to be something they weren't.

I'd done that.

Me.

Sofia was wrong though. Ezra had the capacity to feel. It just took a special person to bring it out in him.

A person who *wasn't* me.

CHAPTER THIRTY-TWO

Ashleigh

"ARE we going to hide out here all night?" Gav asked me. After I'd found him, we'd grabbed some drinks and made our way out to Deacon's yard. But I hadn't wanted to join the crowd, so we'd gone down to the edge of the Faris's property and found an old bench to sit on.

"We're not hiding... we're reflecting." I gave him a shy smile.

"Reflecting? And what exactly are we reflecting on...?" His brow arched playfully.

"Have you spoken to Penelope?" I hadn't been brave enough to ask yet.

Because what was there to say?

"I have," he said. "And I think you should talk to Ezra."

"I already told you, things between me and Ezra are done." Over.

"Still, you really should—"

"Gav, please," I snapped, curving my hand around the

edge of the bench. Letting the bite of the rough wood against my palm ground me. "I don't want to talk about it."

It wasn't fair to act so petulant, especially not when I knew he liked Penelope too. But I couldn't do it, I couldn't keep rehashing everything.

Draining my beer, I reached for another.

"Is that a good idea?" Gav asked.

"Really, you're going to be that guy now?"

"Leigh Leigh, come on. I'm trying to help."

"Yeah, I know." I let out a weary sigh. "I thought I was doing okay, you know. All week, I thought I was being strong and putting the past behind me and focusing on the future, then tonight, at the game..."

"What happened?"

"That's just it, nothing happened. We went to the game, and it was just like old times. My friends and family were all there, all cheering on the team like we've done so many times before... then at the end, when we greeted the team, it just felt like... I don't know. I'm talking nonsense."

"Hey, don't say that." He shuffled closer, wrapping his arm around me. "You're entitled to your feelings, Ashleigh."

"We were both right there and nobody said anything. That's weird, right? That our families have never tried to sit down and talk to us about it together?"

"I don't know. It's not like you and Ezra were close before... in their eyes, I mean."

"Yeah, but we were both there that night. The more I think about it, the more I don't get it."

"Want to know what I think?" I shrugged, and he went on, "They're protecting you. You were hurt, Leigh. Really hurt, and something life changing happened to you."

"Yeah, I know, but..." Something still didn't add up. "Ezra told them I was feeling sick that night and that's why he was giving me a ride home. He didn't want them to know the truth..."

"To protect you."

"But..."

"Honestly, I don't think there's a right or wrong answer here. But they're your family, Leigh Leigh, everything they do is because they want to protect you."

"I need to speak to Ezra." I shot up.

"W-what? I thought—"

"Something doesn't add up. I need to talk to him." I couldn't explain it, but the threads of every conversation, every time I'd overheard my parents or Uncle Jase talking about it, were unravelling in my head. They still didn't make sense... but I couldn't let it go.

"Ashleigh, I don't think..."

"I need answers, Gav."

He gave me a sympathetic smile. "Yeah, okay. You should talk to him. Get everything out in the air."

We got up and made our way back over to the fire pit where most of the team were gathered. I wasn't surprised to see Poppy and Sofia talking to some guys not on the team. That seemed to be Poppy's go-to response to Aaron's actions. But I got it. It hurt to see the boy you wanted flirt with other girls.

I spotted Ezra sitting with Cole, the two of them completely disinterested in the swarm of girls vying for their attention. Before I could reach them though, a figure stepped into my path.

"Well, well, look who it is." Nathan smirked, rubbing his thumb over his bottom lip as he let his eyes slide down my body.

"Move," I hissed.

"Whoa, babe, you don't need to be so—"

"She said move," Gav said, stepping up beside me.

"The fuck are—McKay. Didn't see you there." Nathan pulled to his full height, taking the air with him. The chatter around us died down until everyone's attention was right on us.

"Ashleigh said move."

Nathan held up his hands. "So how does this work then? Do you get her on game nights and Jackson gets her—"

"Watch it," Gav warned, inching forward.

I grabbed his arm and pleaded with him. "He isn't worth it. Come on."

"What's going on?" Ezra appeared with Cole at his side.

"This asshole seems to have a problem with Ashleigh," Gav said.

"You just don't know when to quit, do you?" Ezra flicked his eyes to Gav and seemed to silently say something.

Gav placed his hand on the small of my back and started guiding me away, but I shoved him off, refusing to budge.

Ezra was not going to fight Nathan, not over me.

"Ezra," I said, urging him to look at me.

"You should really listen to her, Jackson," Nathan sneered. "Although do you think she would want anything to do with you if she knew the truth..."

Ezra stepped forward and Cole threw out his arm. "Don't let him bait you, man. It's a party, let's go get a drink."

"Come on," Gav said.

Ezra's hard gaze went to where Gav's hand touched my arm and his jaw clenched.

But that wasn't—

"She's better off with McKay than a lowlife stoner like you anyway," Nathan spat. "When you're done with her, McKay, let me know. I wouldn't mind taking her for a ride."

A low growl rumbled in Ezra's chest as he hurled himself at Nathan and the two of them went crashing to the ground.

"Ezra!" I yelled, rushing toward them, but Gav hooked me around the waist, hauling me backward.

"Oh no you don't."

"Help him," I screamed, watching with horror as Nathan clambered to his feet first and caught Ezra with a fist to his face as he tried to get upright.

"You're a fucking joke, Jackson. You think you're one of us, that you deserve to wear a Raiders jersey. You—"

Ezra swung for him, but Nathan leaped out of the way, his taunting laughter filling the air.

"You need to back off, Carrick," Cole said.

"Or what, Kandon? I don't see you wading in to protect him."

"I don't need anyone to fight my battles, asshole. You want me." Ezra spat a mouthful of blood at his feet. "I'm right here."

Nathan's eyes grew to thin slits as he threw himself at Ezra again. They collided in a blur of fists and grunts until Cole and a couple of other players finally pulled them apart.

"Oh my God, Ezra." I ran over to him, my hand flying to my mouth as I took in his bloody face.

"Shit, man." Gav came over. "You look like you could use a drink. Let's go inside."

I inhaled a shaky breath, some of the tension working out of my shoulders at Gav's solid presence. Ezra glanced between us, uncertainty glittering in his eyes. But I said, "Let us help, please."

He gave me a small nod, motioning for me to go ahead. I looked back to see Aaron and Cole trying to reason with Nathan and his friends.

He was a liability and clearly wasn't a team player. I

didn't understand why Uncle Jason kept someone like that on the team.

But I didn't understand a lot of things lately.

Gav made the group of kids in the kitchen give us some space and made Ezra a strong drink. "Here," he said, offering it to him.

Ezra leaned back against the counter and accepted it.

"I'll see if I can find a first aid kit." I started checking the obvious places, finding one stowed away in the bottom drawer. "You're a mess," I said. "I'm going to need to clean you up."

A couple of kids wandered through, stopping to stare.

"Come on," Gav said. "Let's move this to the bathroom."

My brows furrowed, but Ezra followed him out of the kitchen and down the hall. I grabbed the supplies and went after them.

"In here," Gav said, motioning to the open door. I squeezed in past him, and he whispered. "Go easy on him."

"W-what?"

"If you need me, just text, okay?"

"You're not—"

"He needs you, Leigh Leigh. Even if he doesn't realize it yet."

Gav closed the door behind me, leaving me alone with Ezra and my racing heart. The main light was off, the room illuminated by the dim lights above the mirror. I turned slowly, taking in his bruised, bloody face.

"Sit down." I motioned to the toilet, and Ezra slumped down on the seat.

"This might sting." I tore open an antiseptic wipe and went to him. "I'll need to touch you. Will that be okay?"

Ezra stared up at me, swallowing hard as he nodded.

"I'll try and be careful." Gently taking his chin, I angled

his face so I could clean the cut in his eyebrow. "You're lucky he didn't rip your piercing clean out," I said, ignoring the way my fingers trembled as I wiped the blood away.

Ezra hissed when I moved to work on his bloody nose.

"Sorry," I said. "I'm almost done."

He didn't speak. He just sat there, watching me. His eyes tracking my movements like a predator stalking its prey. Silently. Deadly.

Disarming.

When I was done, I disposed of all the bloody wipes and went back to check his face, but Ezra snagged his hand around my waist, pulling me between his legs. His other hand went to my hip, and he dropped his head, resting it against my stomach.

"E-Ezra?" I couldn't breathe with him holding me like that.

"Just give me a minute." He inhaled a deep breath, his lips precariously close to the slither of my bare stomach on display. When he exhaled, I smothered a whimper at the kick of hot breath skittering across my skin.

What was happening right now?

"What happened with Nath—"

"Don't. Don't ever fucking say his name."

"Ezra, we should talk…" I tried to cup his cheek, but he snagged my wrist.

Slowly, he lifted his face to mine. "Talk?" A small, uncertain smile traced his lips. "You think I want to… talk?"

"Y-you don't?"

A shiver went down my spine at the intensity in his words.

"I want to do a lot of things, buttercup. Talking isn't at the top of my list." His hands slid up my waist as he stood up.

Now I was the one staring up at him. "Does it hurt?"

"Not as much as thinking I'd lost you."

"What?" The ground moved beneath my feet. "I... I don't—"

One of his hands kept moving up my body until it brushed over my collarbone and curved around the back of my neck. "I can't stop thinking about what you said."

"You can't?"

"No one has ever said those words to me... not the way you said them. And it means something, Ashleigh. It means too much to..." He stopped himself.

"Too much to what? What are you talking about?"

He lowered his head to mine, our bodies aligned like two pieces of a puzzle. "I'm done fighting this..."

"What about Penelope?" I whispered, hating how insecure I sounded. But nothing made sense. Ezra was holding me like he never wanted to let go, talking like he wanted... *me*.

"Penelope?" He reared back to look at me. "McKay didn't tell you?"

"Tell me what?"

"Fuck..." His expression dropped. "All this time, you thought..."

"Ezra, what is going on?"

"I'm not with Pen."

"You're... not?"

"No." Quiet laughter spilled out of him. But I wasn't laughing, not even a little bit. I was strung tight, barely breathing as he clung to me like I was all his prayers come true.

"But you kissed her. I saw the two of you... together." I screwed my eyes shut as I tried to make sense of everything.

"Ashleigh." His hands drifted to my face. "Open your eyes." They flickered open and he smiled. Ezra smiled at me. "It's you, buttercup. It's always been you. I just couldn't—"

"Shh." I pressed my finger to his mouth, my head spinning at his revelation. "We need to talk... I know that. But first, I really need you to kiss me."

"Thank fuck," he breathed.

Ezra leaned down, running his thumb along my jaw as he kissed the corner of my mouth.

"Can I... touch you?" I asked.

He went still, staring at me with uncertainty as his body trembled.

"It's okay," I said. "I won't hurt you. You can show me, E. Give me a map."

The air crackled in the space between us. Ezra sucked in a harsh breath before taking one of my hands in his and lifting it to his collarbone.

"Here?" I asked, and he nodded.

"I-I can't..." His eyes shuttered.

"Ezra, look at me." He opened them again, fixing that fiery amber stare right on me. "One day, we are going to talk about this. You're going to tell me what happened to... to make you this way. But I will never push or demand anything from you you're not ready to give. Do you understand?"

Another small nod.

"Is this okay?" I asked, gently curving my hand around the back of his neck. His skin was on fire, burning up... for me.

I still couldn't believe it.

I had so many questions, but I didn't want to jeopardize this moment.

I didn't want the spell to break.

"It's okay." I could hear the pain in his voice, the anguish. But he was already closing the gap between us, already sliding his mouth against mine.

"Ezra," I whispered, shivers running through me as his tongue peeked out and demanded entrance.

"It's you, buttercup. It's fucking you." Ezra shoved me gently, backing me into the wall. His hands curled into my hips as he kissed me harder.

With every stroke of his tongue and press of his lips, the thoughts and the questions gnawing at me, melted away. Until there was nothing but us and this moment.

And a kiss I knew would ruin me for all other kisses.

"You taste so fucking good," he rasped, lifting one of his hands to thread it in my hair and hold the nape of my neck. "Why do you taste so good?"

I smiled at him. "Is this really happening?"

Something flashed in his eyes, but he crashed his mouth down on mine, pushing up against me and pinning me to the wall.

And every doubt I had, ceased to exist.

CHAPTER THIRTY-THREE

Ezra

I'D LOST my fucking mind.

But I couldn't stop myself.

All week, I'd tried to fight it. The growing restlessness inside of me every time Ashleigh didn't look at me or turned around and walked in another direction. I wasn't used to her avoiding me. I was used to being the center of her world.

Even after the accident, when things turned sour between us, she was still around. Still getting all up in my space and trying to make me see her.

I'd always fucking seen her. How could I not? She was gorgeous. All that long, dark-blonde hair and those piercing blue eyes.

I hadn't realized how much comfort I found in her gaze until it was no longer cast in my direction.

"Is this really happening?" she asked, flushed and breathless, her eyes glittering with lust and love and so many things I didn't fucking deserve.

It was a mistake, going after her without telling her everything first. But I needed her.

I needed her before I went back out there and did something really fucking stupid like beat Carrick's ass into next week.

He'd sneered at me the entire game, looking down on me like I didn't deserve to breathe the same air as him. But it was what he'd said tonight about Ashleigh that snapped something inside me.

She gazed up at me, waiting. But I didn't want to talk. I didn't want to fucking explain... so I slammed my mouth down on hers and kissed her.

Her fingers stroked the hair at the back of my neck, sending my body into a frenzy. Her touch was... it was fucking electric. And I couldn't believe how long I'd gone without letting her touch me, always trying to keep her at arm's length.

But I hadn't understood the gravity of her feelings for me back then, hadn't wanted to understand them. Because it was easier to push her away than let her in. Easier to shut her out than have to explain just how fucked up I really was.

"Say it," I murmured against her lips. "I need you to say it."

She blinked at me, eyes hooded with desire. "Say what...? *Oh.*" Her expression softened. "I... I love you, Ezra."

Fuck.

Relief slammed into me. Sweet, unexpected relief.

I touched my head to hers, breathing her in. "I'm sorry. I'm so fucking sorry..."

Her fingers flexed around my neck, dragging me closer until we were breathing each other's air.

"Don't shut me out again, promise me."

"I... I promise. But we should talk."

She nodded. "Later." Her lips found mine again and she whispered, "I'm not ready to let go yet."

Neither was I. Because the second I did, everything would turn to shit again. And maybe it made me an asshole, but I didn't want to waste a single second with Ashleigh before the world came crashing down around us.

Because it would. Too many people were involved in our lives for it not to.

So I kissed her. I learned the ways to make her whimper, how to stroke my tongue into her mouth and make her moan. My hand on her hip slipped under her cropped sweater, brushing her ribs and the curve of her waist.

"That feels nice," she said, gazing at me with lust-filled eyes, silent permission shining there.

I grazed my hand up, up over the curve of her tits. Her skin was silky soft, smooth and warm. Ashleigh arched into my touch, spurring me on. "I've dreamed about this," she said.

"Yeah, buttercup. You've dreamed about me touching you?"

She nodded, pupils blown and shining with desire, and fuck, if the sight of her like that, the feel of her under my hand, didn't do things to me.

Strange, unfamiliar things.

"I want you," she breathed, scratching her nails down my neck.

"Fuck, Ashleigh. We can't... I..."

"Shh, it's okay." She kissed me, cutting off whatever it was I'd been about to say. And there was a lot—too fucking much that needed to be said.

But words ruined everything. So for now, they could stay beyond the door, and for once in my life, I would be selfish where Ashleigh was concerned.

We kissed, my hands mapping her curves, the soft dips

and planes of her body. I couldn't get enough, kissing her jaw, down the column of her neck, nipping the skin there. She shuddered, whimpering my name.

It hit me then. I wanted her.

I wanted her to touch me and make me feel things. I wanted her to erase the past, the pain and fear and all of the monsters that haunted me in my sleep.

Ashleigh was the girl who held my heart in the palm of her hands. I'd just been too stubborn to admit it.

But things were different now. We were different. There were secrets between us—things that would ruin this. But still, I couldn't stop myself from stealing this moment.

"I lost you again," she said.

"Huh?" I stared at her, confused.

"Just now. You weren't with me... Where did you go?"

I couldn't tell her. Not yet. Not here. Not like this.

"Ashleigh—"

"No. Don't look at me like that, like you're going to ruin everything. I need this, Ezra. We need it. *Please*." Her other hand reached for me, but she hesitated.

I lifted my hand to hers, threading our fingers together and pressed our joined hands to the wall beside her head. "Do you want me to touch you, buttercup?" The words were rough against my throat.

"More than anything."

My other hand drifted down the flat of her stomach, hovering at the waistband of her jeans. Ashleigh squirmed beneath my teasing touch. I flicked the button open and dipped my hand inside and she gasped.

"Ezra, I want to touch you too."

"No," I said harsher than I intended. "This is about you. I want to watch you fall apart, buttercup."

She pressed her lips together, smothering another whimper as I rubbed her over her damp panties.

"You're wet for me," I said in awe.

I'd never touched anyone like this before. The first and only time I'd tried to have sex had been a fucking disaster. A chemical and alcohol induced blur of clumsy, unnatural touches, and in the end, the faceless girl had given up and I'd decided it wasn't worth the effort.

But I wanted Ashleigh. I wanted to try—for her.

"Show me what you like," I said, blood roaring in my ears and other places as I continued touching her.

"You've never...?" Ashleigh let the words hang between us as understanding dawned on her.

"I tried once." Shame rolled over me and I went still.

"Let me show you." She covered her hand with mine and pressed harder, grinding the heel of my hand against her clit.

"Yeah?" I asked, and she nodded

"Use your fingers too." Ashleigh hooked her underwear to the side, encouraging me to touch her bare pussy.

My dick jolted, straining painfully against my jeans. A low groan rumbled in my chest as Ashleigh began to ride my hand. It was supposed to be about her, about making her come undone. But watching her, heavy-lidded, mouth parted as tiny, breathy moans fell from her lips, was enough to make me come in my jeans. She was the most beautiful thing I'd ever seen.

"Fuck, that feels..."

"Good, yeah," she breathed as I sunk two fingers inside her. My thumb circled her clit trying to make it good for her.

"More..."

I kissed her, swallowing her little cries of pleasure as I worked her with my fingers, following her body's lead.

"God, Ezra... it's... ah..." Her legs quivered, her hand wrapping around my shoulder as she clung to me.

I didn't flinch or recoil from her touch. Instead, I moved into it.

"Is this okay?" she asked, gazing up at me.

"Yeah, buttercup." I kissed her again. Slow, deep licks as I curled my fingers deep inside her and rubbed.

Ashleigh clenched around me, murmuring my name as she fell quietly over the edge. It was intense, being with her like this.

"Oh God." She buried her face in my neck, her nervous laughter brushing my skin. "That was..."

"Yeah." I swallowed hard.

"Would you like me to..." She peeked up at me. "You know, return the favor?"

"We should probably get back to the party."

Dejection washed over her, and I cussed under my breath. "I didn't mean... I want you, Ashleigh." *I want you so fucking much.* "But there's some stuff we need to talk about."

"Like the fact you're a virgin?" She flashed me a playful smile.

"You're never going to let me live that down, are you?"

"Oh, I don't know." Ashleigh wrapped her arms around my neck and leaned in, sliding her mouth over mine. "I quite like the idea that I'm the only girl you've ever been with."

"I haven't been with you..." I arched a brow.

"Yet." She smirked.

"I'm not sure I'll be able to..."

Her expression dropped. "I would never force you to do anything you didn't want."

"I know that. I just... the first and only time I tried... it was a disaster."

"We can go at your pace, E. Always. I'm just glad you're

here." Her fingers toyed with the hair at the back of my neck again. Such a simple touch that felt so fucking good.

I inhaled a shaky breath. "We should really get back to the party."

No fucking way was our first time going to be in Deacon Faris's bathroom with McKay standing guard outside.

Fuck. McKay.

"Maybe I don't want to go back to the party." Ashleigh kissed the corner of my mouth, teasing the seam of my lips with her tongue. I sucked the end between my teeth and bit down gently. "We can go somewhere and—"

"Leigh," McKay's voice came through the door. "You should probably get out here."

She shot me a concerned look before slipping out from between me and the wall and going over to the door.

"What's wrong?" she asked, cracking it open a fraction.

"Poppy and Zara got into it. She's hurt."

"What?"

I moved up beside her and slid my hand around her waist. McKay caught the move, his eyes locking on mine.

It was a dick move, but I couldn't help myself.

"Where is she?" Ashleigh demanded.

"Cole is going to give her and Sofia a ride home."

She glanced back at me. "I need to go and check if she's okay."

I nodded, reluctantly releasing her.

"But we can talk tomorrow?"

"Yeah." Dread slid down my spine.

"Okay, I'll text you. Both of you." She moved around McKay and took off down the hall.

Heavy silence lingered between us.

"You didn't tell her what really happened with me and Pen. Why?"

"Because she deserved to hear it from you."

"What's your deal?"

"My deal?" He let out a bitter laugh. "I just want her to be happy. And I'm guessing you weren't in here all that time talking about the weather?"

I pressed my lips together. Ashleigh vouched for him. Penny too. But was it possible McKay was just a good guy?

"Do I need to be worried?"

"I don't know, do you?" His brow lifted but I saw no threat there. "Listen, Ashleigh is my friend. But I've always known where her heart lies. Do I wish it was different? Maybe. But I'm not some douchebag out to play games. Why the fuck do you think I left her alone in there with you."

"So you were doing me a favor?"

"Look, Ezra, I'm not suggesting we be friends, but I am not the enemy here. It's you she wants; it's always been you."

His words hit me dead in the chest.

"Just promise me one thing?" he added.

"What?"

"Don't hurt her again."

CHAPTER THIRTY-FOUR

Ashleigh

I FOUND Poppy and Sofia outside the front of Deacon's house waiting for Cole.

"What happened?"

"That fucking bitch almost pulled out my hair."

Sofia smothered a chuckle. "You got her back good though, babe."

"Yeah." Poppy flipped her hair off her shoulder and let out a long breath. "Tonight has been the worst."

"What do you need?" I asked, because I saw how brave she was being, playing off her heartache from finding Aaron and Zara kissing.

"Ice cream. A pint of cookie dough ice cream and maybe a grilled cheese."

"Sorry." Cole came jogging out of the house.

"My idiot of a brother?" Sofia asked and his lips flattened into a grim line.

"Let's just go, please," Poppy said, hugging herself tightly.

"Yeah, okay." I glanced back at the house. I didn't want to

leave Ezra. Not after everything that had happened. But Poppy needed me, and I never wanted to be the kind of person who bailed on her friends for a guy.

Pulling out my phone, I texted him.

Me: Taking Poppy home, she's upset. See you tomorrow?

THEN I TEXTED GAV.

Me: I have a favor to ask. Please make sure Ezra gets home okay.

HE TEXTED BACK FIRST.

Gav: Yeah, I'll give him a ride. I think we need to have a chat about some things anyway.

OH GOD.

Me: Please go easy on him.

Gav: Pinky promise.

Ezra: McKay just offered me a ride home, should I be worried?

Me: He's been a good friend to me, Ezra. It would mean the world to me if you two could find a way to get along.

Ezra: I can't promise anything… but I'll try.

MY LIPS CURVED into a smile as I clutched my cell to my chest.

"What are you smiling at?" Poppy asked me.

"N-nothing."

She eyed me with suspicion. "You're hiding something."

"It's nothing."

I wasn't going to tell her—or anyone—about Ezra and me until the two of us had talked about everything.

I'd had so many questions but had gotten distracted with all the fighting and kissing and touching. Warmth spread through me as I remembered how good it felt to finally have Ezra's hands on me.

And he'd let me touch him.

It hadn't been nearly enough, but it meant everything to me that he trusted me.

I sank against Cole's back seat and watched the town roll by.

"I can't believe he kissed her," Poppy whispered, resting her head on my shoulder.

"He's an idiot."

"She doesn't even like him, Leigh. She likes what he represents."

"So what exactly happened with you two anyway?"

Poppy made a derisive sound in the back of her throat. "She came at me, taunting me about what a good kisser Aaron was. Said it was too bad she got there first. My drink may have accidentally slipped out of my hand and landed all over her."

"Poppy!"

"What?" She shrugged. "She deserved it. She's a bitch, Leigh. And it wasn't like I could go throw my drink at Aaron, so she was the next best choice."

"Then what happened?"

"She completely freaked out and tried to rip Poppy's hair out," Sofia said with a hint of amusement. Even Cole snorted.

"Thanks for the support, assholes. It hurt."

"Not nearly as much as you tearing her shirt open like that."

"That was pretty epic."

"I can't believe you were fighting with Zara... over Aaron."

"It wasn't my best moment," Poppy said. "But she had it coming, and now maybe she'll think twice about messing with me."

"And Aaron?"

"We are not talking about him right now," she hissed.

"Got it." I glanced up, finding Cole's eyes in the rearview mirror and he pursed his lips.

He wasn't impressed with his best friend either.

By the time we pulled up outside Uncle Jason's house, I was exhausted.

"Mom and Dad aren't back," Poppy said. "You guys are going to come in with me, right?"

"Hell yeah, you promised me a pint of ice cream, and

grilled cheese." Sofia climbed out, but ducked her head back in. "Thanks for the ride, Cole."

"Anytime," he mumbled, letting his eyes linger a little too long on her retreating form as she headed for the house.

"Yeah, thanks," Poppy said. "I owe you. And you can tell Aaron if he sleeps with her, I hope his dick rots and falls off."

Laughter pealed out of me as Cole gawked at her.

"You can tell him that yourself."

"Fine," she huffed, sliding out. "I will."

"He's a fucking idiot," Cole muttered as I grabbed the door handle.

"They'll figure it out eventually."

"How can you be so sure?"

"Call it a lucky guess. Night, Cole."

"Night, Leigh."

I got out of the car and followed my cousin and Sofia into the house. I would rather have stayed at the party with Ezra. But maybe some space would be a good thing so I could figure out everything I wanted to ask him. Everything I wanted to say.

Still, it didn't stop me from texting him again.

Me: Are you still at the party?"

Ezra: No, McKay is giving me a ride home.

Me: Thank you for going with him.

Ezra: Well, it wasn't like I had a reason to stay there.

"WHO'S THAT?" Sofia asked as we perched at the breakfast counter while Poppy went in search of the ice cream.

"No one." My cheeks burned as I hit send on my reply and pocketed my cell phone.

"I know it's Ezra, Leigh."

I shrugged, really not wanting to do this now. Not when I was still wearing his kisses.

"Fine. But if you're really going to try with him, then you can't hide it from us forever."

I didn't like the way she said try. As if the outcome of our relationship was already a foregone conclusion. She hadn't been there earlier; she hadn't witnessed what had happened between us.

But part of me got it.

I'd already been hurt so much, and she was my friend. She felt it was her job to look out for me.

Her concerns were misplaced this time though.

Ezra had finally met me halfway, and he wouldn't hurt me again.

I knew he wouldn't.

RAISED VOICES STARTLED ME. I cracked an eye open and sat up, trying to get my bearings. Sofia and Poppy were asleep on the bed, both snoring slightly, an empty tub of cookie dough ice cream on the nightstand. I'd curled up on the love seat and must have fallen asleep while we watched a movie.

My uncle's voice filtered through the house again, and then a door banged somewhere downstairs.

Strange.

Kicking off the blanket, I sat up, pulled on one of Poppy's Rixon hoodies and grabbed my cell phone. There was a message from Ezra saying good morning. It sent butterflies fluttering through me.

I quickly texted him back and then slipped out of the room, going in search of coffee.

But when I got downstairs, the kitchen was empty.

Huh.

I could hear my uncle yelling down the hall. He was a hot head, sure, but I'd never heard him speak to my aunt that way before. Tiptoeing down the hall, I reached his office at the back of the house and braced myself to knock. But another male voice made me freeze.

"John, calm down."

"That boy is dangerous. He is a danger to himself, and the other players and I think—"

"I don't know what you think you know, but I can assure you—"

"Honestly," he cut Uncle Jason off, seething, "I find it abhorrent that you covered up his actions to protect him."

"Don't test me, Carrick."

John Carrick? Nathan's father was here?

I shook my head, barely making sense of what was happening.

"Test you?" John spat. "What do you think the board will say when they discover their beloved coach covered up a crime to protect—"

No.

No, no.

It wasn't possible.

Blood roared in my ears, making it hard to hear.

"What do you want me to do, John? Don't you think they've both suffered enough?"

"He was driving, Jason, and if my suspicions are correct, he was driving under the influence of drugs and alcohol. He almost killed her. I would think, as her uncle, you would care a little more about that, than reforming him into one of your star players."

I staggered back, bumping into the sideboard. Something slipped off and crashed to the floor, and Uncle Jason rushed out of his office.

"A-Ashleigh?"

"I... I..." Oh God. I couldn't breathe.

I couldn't get air into my lungs.

The accident was Ezra's fault, and Uncle Jason had covered it up somehow, and then lied to me.

They had all lied to me. Because I didn't doubt that my dad and Asher were in on it too.

"Is it true?" I asked at the same time as John Carrick came out. "What on Earth is going on out here?"

He narrowed his eyes at me, a deep frown crinkling his eyes. Uncle Jason immediately stepped between us, shielding me from the man's scrutiny. "Go back upstairs, Ashleigh. We'll talk in a minute, okay."

"But I..." I inhaled in a shuddering breath as tears rolled down my cheeks.

They'd all lied.

Including Ezra.

"Ashleigh," he said. "Go upstairs, please."

Something in his icy gaze jolted me into action. Uncle Jason was worried. But he wasn't worried for me—he was worried for Ezra.

"O-okay." I stumbled forward and hurried back upstairs.

"Ashleigh, what is it?" Poppy burst out of her room, her

expression sleepy and confused. "We heard a crash and—are you okay? What happened?"

I slipped into the room and started pacing. "Did you know?" I snapped, the second she closed the door.

"Know? Know what?" Her eyes clouded. "What are you talking about?"

"The accident... Ezra... all of it." I raked my fingers through my hair and pulled the ends in frustration. "I feel like I'm losing my goddamn mind. I knew something was going on... I knew it and everyone made me feel like I was overreacting."

"Ashleigh, babe, stop." Poppy gently shoved my hands down. "Take a deep breath and tell me what happened."

"I-I don't even know... I can't..."

"Oh my God, Leigh." Sofia appeared in the doorway separating Poppy's bedroom from her small bathroom. "What happened?"

"Did you know?" I blurted out, pain bubbling up inside me like lava. "He's your brother," I shrieked. "Did you know?"

"I..." She glanced at Poppy.

"Don't look at me. I have no idea what she's talking about."

"Did something happen... with Ezra?"

"I... Uncle Jason said—"

A loud knock at the door stole my words.

"Girls, can I come in?"

"Sure, Dad."

He peered inside. "Ashleigh, sweetheart. Can we talk?"

I nodded, feeling the adrenaline crash from my body. I was numb. A hollow pit carving through me and sucking out every ounce of joy and relief I'd felt since last night.

Ezra had said we needed to talk, he'd said that, and I'd been too desperate to kiss him, to just be with him, that I hadn't stopped and taken a second to consider that what he might tell me would change everything.

"What's going on, Dad?" Poppy asked.

"Nothing, sweetheart. Me and Ashleigh just need to talk about some things. You girls don't worry, okay?"

She frowned and then turned her attention on me. "You'll be okay?"

"I... yeah." I didn't look at my uncle as I left the room and made my way downstairs. There was no sign of John Carrick, thank God. The way he'd looked at me... with pity and anger.

Now Nathan Carrick's vendetta against Ezra made sense. He knew—he knew what Uncle Jason had done to protect him.

It was like I'd woken up in the middle of a nightmare, except it was my life. But this felt far worse than losing my memories, because my family—the people I was supposed to be able to trust with my life—had taken away my right to know the truth.

And I didn't know what the hell to do with that.

CHAPTER THIRTY-FIVE

Ashleigh

UNCLE JASON WATCHED me across his desk. His eyes were haunted, a huge dark shadow over him. "How much did you hear?"

"Enough." The word soured on my tongue. "But I still don't understand... I don't—"

He let out a weary sigh and leaned back in his chair, dragging a hand over his five o'clock shadow. "The night of graduation, your dad, Asher, and I went out for drinks. It was a celebration and commiseration of sorts. Me and your dad were so proud of you and Lily. But Asher was... upset. He'd known for a while Ezra wasn't going to graduate, but I think it really hit him that day, watching the rest of you go up on stage and get your diplomas.

"Ezra was MIA. Off doing whatever it is Ezra does when he disappears. It wasn't until Asher got a call from him that we knew something was wrong."

A shudder went through me. I couldn't remember any of it. The graduation ceremony, the party... the accident. But hearing him tell the story, it resonated with me. Maybe it was lost memories trying to fight their way back to the surface, or maybe it was pure muscle memory. I didn't know. But this felt different.

"He was incoherent... said there had been an accident. I thought it was just shock. I didn't think he would have driven in that state." The blood drained from his face. "Asher and I headed straight to the accident, your dad had gone home by that point. But when we got there... Jesus, I was terrified."

I clapped a hand over my mouth and smothered the big fat sob caught in my throat.

"The car was totaled. How Ezra walked away with only a few scratches is still beyond me. The driver of the truck you collided with was fine though a little shocked. He'd been about to call 9-1-1 when we got there, but then Asher pulled me to one side and said Ezra was high and had been drinking..."

"What did you do, Uncle Jason?" My voice shook as my fingers curled into the edge of the seat.

"I knew where Asher's head was at. Exactly where my head would have been at if it had been Lily or Poppy. Ezra had already failed high school. If the police turned up and drug tested him... I spoke to the driver, got him on side—"

"You mean you paid him off?" Disbelief coated my words.

"I asked him to let us handle it; as a family."

"And he agreed?"

"He was happy to not have to deal with the police and just go home. But he left and then Ezra stumbled over to the car, wailing something about... about you." He heaved a ragged breath. "We hadn't known, Ashleigh. We didn't know how badly you were hurt. We didn't know if... Asher was in pieces. Ezra was shell-shocked, and you were..." He couldn't say the words, and I was relieved. I was relieved he didn't sit there and tell me what we all knew.

I could have died.

And it would have been Ezra's fault. Because he was lost and angry and couldn't deal with whatever it was that haunted him.

What a mess.

"Who else knows the truth?" I asked.

"We kept it need to know only. Me and your aunt, your parents, and Asher and Mya."

"And Ezra and the truck driver... And John Carrick."

"He's a complication, yes. But you don't need to worry about John, I'll handle him."

"What does that even mean, you'll handle him?" I shot up out of my seat. "Don't you think there's been enough 'handling?'"

"We only wanted to protect him, Ashleigh. I don't know if we'd have done the same if we had known you were in the car too, but we didn't. We didn't let you know the truth to protect you. To prevent you from carrying that burden."

"By lying to me?" I laughed bitterly. "Look where that got us. I have spent weeks questioning myself, questioning every little thing. I knew something didn't add up... I knew, but I never imagined it would be this."

"Ezra didn't—"

"Ezra? You think this is about Ezra?" I was yelling now. "I asked you. I looked you in the eye and asked you if you were punishing him by making him join the team and you told me no. You lied to my face."

"Now, Ashleigh, that's not—"

"STOP. LYING." I inhaled a ragged breath, tears dripping off my cheeks and onto Poppy's hoodie. "You covered up the truth, but demanded Ezra repeat senior year and join the team, didn't you?"

His silence was answer enough.

"And did you tell him to stay away from me?"

"That's not—"

"Did you tell Ezra to stay away from me?"

"We told him not to tell you the truth, yes. We thought that given the circumstances, it would be better if you didn't learn the truth. Not until your memories—"

"If. *If* my memories ever return." I stared at him, my uncle, a man who would go to any lengths to protect his family and the people he cared about.

I wasn't mad that they had tried to protect Ezra. How could I be when I'd spent so long trying to do the same. But the whole thing felt like a betrayal. We were pawns in a cruel game; only unlike Ezra, I didn't know the rules.

"Could you get into trouble? If John goes public?"

"You don't need to worry about John Carrick, Ashleigh. He doesn't know anything concrete." His jaw clenched.

"Whatever." I glanced away, needing a minute.

Everything had been so perfect last night with Ezra. I'd known we still had a lot to talk about, but I'd never once imagined...

I dropped into the chair, the air whooshing from my lungs.

"Ashleigh?" Uncle Jason asked.

"I love him," I blurted out. "I'm in love with Ezra... and all this time I thought he hated me. I thought he..." The words caught on the lump in my throat.

"Y-you love him? But how... I don't... Fuck," he breathed. "And since the accident, all this time, you thought..."

"I thought he blamed me for the accident, and the fact you were punishing him and made him join the team... I thought..."

"We just wanted to protect you, both of you. We knew your recovery was going to be hard. We didn't want you to have to deal with this as well."

"Yet here we are."

"For what it's worth, Ashleigh, I am sorry."

"Yeah." My shoulders sagged. "Me too."

AFTER THE REVELATIONS of the morning, I'd wanted to go and see Ezra, but Uncle Jason called my dad, and he came to get me before I could escape to the Bennets' house.

The mood was tense to say the least as I sat in the kitchen with Mom and Dad.

"Do we need to talk about this?" he asked.

"Talk about what, Dad? The fact Uncle Jason and Asher covered up the details of the accident or the fact you all lied to me?"

"Sweetheart." Mom covered my hand with hers, but I wrenched it away.

"No, Mom. Don't do that... you don't get to do that." I shoved my hand under the table.

Hurt flashed across her face, but I couldn't find it in myself to care. The more I thought about it, the angrier I became.

I'd been desperate to know the events of that night... and they'd kept it from me.

Worse than that, they'd *lied* to me.

"I was talking about the fact you told Jase you're in love with Ezra. Jesus, Ashleigh. I know you told me you were friends, but how... *when* did this even happen?"

"Cam," Mom warned.

"No, Hailee. We are talking about this. Did you know... did you know he was high and had been drinking?"

"Nice, Dad, real freaking nice," I seethed. "I can't remember, remember?"

"Ashleigh, shit, I—"

"What your father is trying to say, sweetheart, is that we're worried. You've never once mentioned having feelings for Ezra before now."

I scoffed. "And I suppose you told your parents everything when you were growing up?"

"But, sweetheart, it's Ezra..."

"Why does everyone keep saying that? Is it so hard to believe I could care about him?"

"No, baby. It's just... he's so quiet and withdrawn and you're so bubbly and confident." Her expression fell the second she realized her mistake.

Because I wasn't that girl anymore. Not since the accident.

"Regardless of what you do or don't feel about him, Ashleigh, he drove recklessly under the influence of drugs and alcohol with you in the car. That's not exactly a glowing endorsement."

"Newsflash, Dad, he's a teenager, we make mistakes. I don't know what happened that night, I can't remember. But Sofia told me his birth mom has been contacting Asher and Mya. Maybe he was upset. Maybe he—"

"He almost killed you." Dad slammed his hand down on the table, stunning me into silence.

My blood ran cold at his gutted expression.

"Dad, it's okay..." I leaned over and touched his arm. "I'm okay. I got into the car with him, Dad. I did that."

"Cam," Mom said in that soothing tone of hers. "You promised not to do this. Ashleigh's right, he's just a kid. It was a mistake he'll have to live with for the rest of his life." She gave me a sympathetic smile.

"I can't even imagine what Ezra must be feeling if cares about you even half as much as you seem to care about him."

"I do, Mom. I care about him so much. And I'm sorry I never told you, but honestly, it's always scared me how intensely I feel about him. And you're right, it's Ezra... he doesn't exactly make things easy. But I'm not going to give up on him just because... because..."

It's all his fault.

The thought hit me out of left field with such clarity it knocked the air clean from my lungs. That's what he truly believed.

That's what everyone who knew believed.

Ezra's reckless actions had almost killed me that night, left me with a gaping hole in my memory, left me changed... forever.

Oh God.

My stomach lurched and I bolted out of my seat.

"Ashleigh?" Mom called as I ran out of the kitchen and down the hall, straight into the bathroom. I dropped to the tiles just in time, clutching the bowl as I retched.

"Oh, sweetheart." She kneeled beside me, pulling my hair off my face, rubbing my back. "It'll be okay, Ashleigh. I was so angry at Jase and Asher at first, it caused a lot of tension between all of us. But then I realized there is nothing I wouldn't do to protect you and your brother. To keep you safe."

I heaved again, leaning up to press the flush. I slumped back into her, letting her wrap me up in her arms the way she had so many times before.

"I love him, Mom. I love him, but where do we go from here?" Tears flowed freely down my cheeks as she hugged me.

"Shh, baby. Shh. It'll be okay, it'll all be okay."

I wanted to believe her, I did.

But I was tired.

I was so fucking tired of the lies and heartache and disappointment. And to make matters worse, there was every chance I would never regain my memories and remember exactly what happened that night.

But after what I'd found out today.

Maybe that was a good thing.

CHAPTER THIRTY-SIX

Ezra

I TEXTED ASHLEIGH AGAIN. It was the third or fourth time this morning, but she still hadn't replied.

I'd told myself it was nothing, that maybe she was asleep or having breakfast with her family. But it hadn't taken long for the seeds of doubt to creep in.

Did she regret what happened last night?

Did it freak her out when she found out I was a virgin?

Did she decide that she wanted McKay instead of me, after all?

Fuck.

I didn't like feeling like this. Obsessing over every little thing. The way she moaned my name, her fingers toying with the ends of my hair. How soft her skin felt underneath my fingers. She was so fucking perfect. It was hard to believe I'd resisted her for so long.

But she deserved more than a guy like me.

I love you, Ezra.

Those words had ruined me. Smashed straight through every defense I'd ever wielded against her.

I wanted her.

I wanted to *try* for her.

But first, I needed to come clean and tell her the truth. She deserved to know what really happened that night. Even if she never wanted another thing to do with me, Ashleigh deserved to know.

I was about to text her again when Asher called my name.

"Ezra, come down here."

Sliding off my bed, I padded downstairs and into the kitchen. "What's—Coach? What are you doing here?"

"We've got a problem."

"I'm listening."

"Take a seat, Son." Asher motioned to a stool.

Obeying, I sat down, my pulse ratcheting. "Let me guess, this is something to do with Carrick?"

Jase looked to Asher, and he rubbed his jaw. "They got into it at the party."

"I take it he's to blame for that." He motioned to my face.

"He got in a lucky hit or two."

"I thought I told you two to stay away from each other."

"He said some things..." I shrugged. "About Ashleigh."

"What things?" Anger swirled in Coach Ford's eyes.

"He's been giving her shit. I don't know if it's a way to get to me or he's just taken an interest in her, but it's happened a couple of times now."

"He's been harassing her?" His expression turned murderous. "And no one thought to tell me?"

"I figured if she wanted you to know, she would have told you."

"Ezra!" Asher groaned. "It is never acceptable for a guy to—"

"Why do you think I beat his ass, twice?" Okay, so that wasn't entirely true, but I'd stood up for Ashleigh. Even when things between us were sour, I'd stepped in.

"You should have come to us."

"Well, I'm telling you now." I looked him in the eye, refusing to back down.

"Because the two of you are..." He gave me a pointed look and Asher stuttered, "Excuse me?"

"Something happened this morning."

"Seriously, Jase, you need to stop being cryptic and tell me what the hell is going on." Asher glowered.

"John Carrick stopped by for a chat. I didn't realize Ashleigh was over at ours; she heard some stuff."

My spine stiffened. "What stuff?"

"He knows, and she... she overheard our conversation." For the first time since the accident, I saw something like regret flash over Coach's face. "I don't know how the fuck he found out. But John knows."

"Fuck," Asher's expression dropped. "What does he want?"

"Ezra off the team. Nathan to become the Rixon Raider's star player. Usual rich man bullshit."

"I'll quit." I shot up. "I never wanted to play on the team anyway." But as I said the words, a strange feeling took root inside me.

For the first time in my life, I was a part of something. I hadn't wanted it, had fought at first, but I couldn't deny that, with the exception of Carrick and his douchebag friends, the rest of the team had become something to me.

"Now, just a second," Coach said, holding out his hand, "I've dealt with plenty of men like John Carrick before. And I'm not about to let him swoop in and tell me how to run my team."

"Jase, maybe we need to be smart about this. If he goes to the police—"

"I said I'll handle it, and I will. I just thought you should both know." He got up and made for the door. "As far as I'm concerned this changes nothing. You're a Raider now, Ezra. I expect you to act like one. Stay away from Carrick though, and if he goes near Ashleigh again, you come straight to me. Do you understand?"

I nodded because what else was there to say?

Asher followed him out, mumbling under his breath. "Are you sure about this?"

"I'll handle it."

"Jase, if anything happens to him—"

"Nothing is going to happen. It was a mistake," Coach said quietly. "One he'll pay for every day of his life if this thing between him and Ashleigh is real."

"Fuck," Asher breathed. "I had no idea..."

"Maybe we weren't looking hard enough."

"I don't know what I'm supposed to do here."

"You go back in there and be a father to him. That's all he needs, to know you're there for him whenever he's ready to talk."

"Thank you. For everything. If I'd have known what a mess—"

"Stop. You're as good as family, Ash. You'd do the same for me."

Asher said goodbye and the front door slammed shut. When he reappeared, his expression was grim. "I think we need to talk."

"Yeah," I said. "I guess we do."

Surprise registered on his face. "You're not going to fight me on this?"

"I guess I'm not."

He sat down and said, "Talk to me, Son."

"She told me she loved me."

"Ashleigh?"

I nodded.

"That's... intense. You look surprised."

"Well, yeah. I didn't think..." Fuck, this was awkward. I didn't talk about this stuff to anyone.

"You didn't think what?"

"That I was... you know?"

He frowned and then his eyes widened with realization. "Loveable? Ezra, Son, you know Mya and I love you, right?"

"Yeah, but that's different. You're my... family. You have to say that." He stared at me with a strange expression, and I balked. "What?"

"Y-you called us your family. You've never said that before."

"Oh, I didn't—"

"Don't take it back. It was... nice. It's all we've wanted for a very long time."

"Okay, you need to stop looking at me like that."

"Too much?" He smirked.

"A little."

"So, Ashleigh, huh? You couldn't have picked someone who isn't my best friend's daughter?" His mouth kicked up.

"It wasn't supposed to happen."

"It never is. Do you... feel the same about her?"

"She's under my skin, yeah."

"That's not what I asked. Do you love her, Son?"

"I'm not... I can't..."

"It's not supposed to be a difficult question, Ezra."

"I thought I could fight it. After the accident, I thought I could forget about everything..."

"But she didn't go away?"

"No, she didn't. And it made me angry. She made me so fucking angry. Every time I saw McKay near her, I wanted to kill something."

"Sounds like you have a little issue with sharing your toys." Asher chuckled but I wasn't laughing.

"She's not—"

"I know. It was a lame analogy. Ashleigh is a good girl. Her heart is in the right place, but I won't deny, I'm a little worried about this. The accident is always going to be an obstacle you might not be able to overcome. Especially if she doesn't regain her memories."

"You think I don't know that?"

She knew.

Ashleigh knew the truth now.

Which meant she knew I'd been lying to her.

But more than that, she knew it was all my fault.

I wouldn't blame her if she never wanted to talk to me again.

"I need to talk to her," I said. I couldn't lose her, not now, not after I finally got her back.

"Ezra." Asher blew out a heavy breath. "You need to give her time, Son. She's hurting right now. It's going to take time for her to come to terms with everything. It might be better to wait, let her come to you on her terms."

Wait.

He thought I should wait.

"There's something else I'd like to talk about," he said. "When you're ready."

"What?"

"This aversion to anyone touching you..."

"Did Aaron say something—"

"He's worried, we all are. We've been patient, Ezra, hoping you'd come to us."

Every cell in my body urged me to get up and get the hell out of there. I didn't want to have this conversation. But I forced myself to stay put.

Asher didn't push. He didn't try to get me to open up. He just sat there patiently, waiting. Giving me the space to come to him when I was ready.

But I couldn't do it.

I couldn't force the words past my lips.

I'd kept them inside for so long. I didn't want to give them life. Because if I gave them life, they became true, and if they became true... I couldn't go there.

"I... I can't."

Asher's expression dropped. "Okay, Son. I respect that. But I want you to know that whenever you're ready, I'm here. Mya too."

"Thanks."

"We love you, Ezra. And you are a part of this family. I need you to know that. Now get out of here before I do something to embarrass myself like cry."

He smiled at me.

And this time, I found myself smiling back.

I WENT DOWN to my spot at the lake. I couldn't sit up in my room, waiting for Ashleigh to text me.

Maybe she wouldn't.

Maybe this would be the thing that pushed her too far over the edge.

I had regrets—a fucking ton of them. But there was no point in dwelling on them. I couldn't change the past. I couldn't give Ashleigh her memories back or undo the events of that night. All I could do was hope she would at least give me a chance to explain my side of the story.

Because for the first time in my life, I wanted to open up to somebody.

I wanted to open up to her.

Ashleigh was it for me. I'd just been too stubborn and damaged to see it. But things had changed since the accident.

I'd changed.

I'd almost lost her. Then I'd been forced to walk away from her, and it had made me realize how much I needed her.

I couldn't stand the thought of McKay or Carrick or anyone else touching her. Loving or hurting her. She was mine.

And deep down, although I hadn't wanted to admit it, I was hers.

So I refused to believe that this was it. That I'd lost her before we ever got a chance to begin. I could fix this, if she only gave me a chance. I would spend every single day trying to fix it.

But the hours ticked by as I sat down there, watching the water ripple, and she didn't come.

Leaves crunched underfoot and I whipped my head around hoping to find her, only for my stomach to drop when I found Aaron instead.

"Hey, Dad said you were still down here."

"Hey."

"I brought you some leftovers." He offered me the bowl of pasta, but I declined.

"Not hungry."

"You're waiting for her," he said.

"I... I don't know what the fuck I'm doing."

"Is it true?"

"Asher told you?"

"I overheard some stuff, he filled me in on the rest."

"Yeah, it's true."

"Shit, E, I'm sorry."

"It's on me. All of it. The accident... Ashleigh getting hurt... pushing her away. It's fucked up. I fucked up."

"Yeah, you did, but we all make mistakes."

"She could have died, Aaron."

I could have killed her.

And I would have deserved to rot in jail for the rest of my life.

"But she didn't. Ashleigh is okay, she'll be okay. And yeah, it is fucked up. And Mom and Dad should probably make you ride a bike for the next ten years, but you can't punish yourself forever. All you can do is figure out how to make the most of the second chance you've been given and make sure you don't screw it up."

"You sound like him, you know?"

"Who?" Aaron frowned.

"Asher."

"Yeah, well, he can be a pretty cool dad sometimes."

"Yeah, he can."

Aaron's eyes almost bugged out at that. "Coach Ford and Dad did what they did because you don't deserve to have your entire life ruined over one mistake."

Silence echoed between us.

"Thank you, Aaron. For everything. You've been a real friend to me over the last few weeks and I've been—"

"A stubborn ass most of the time." He chuckled. "You don't need to thank me. We're family, E. I want you to figure this shit out. Get your head on straight and ace senior year."

"Yeah."

I owed it to them.

I owed it to myself to do this thing.

But there was one person I owed the world to, if she would ever forgive me.

I closed my eyes and let the fall breeze drift over my face.

"Hey," Ashleigh's voice filled my head and I thought I must be dreaming because she wasn't down here. "Can we talk?"

My lips curved. If only she really was here...

"Dude," Aaron nudged me.

"What, asshole?" I blinked over at him, pissed he'd ruined my fantasy.

"You've got company." His eyes flicked to where Ashleigh stood looking like all my dreams come true.

"You're here." I stood up, rubbing the back of my neck.

"I'm here." She gave me a weak smile. "We should talk."

A shudder ran through me. She didn't exactly sound pleased to see me.

But then, what did I expect?

I'd ruined her.

I'd ruined us.

I'd ruined the best thing ever to happen to me.

CHAPTER THIRTY-SEVEN

Ashleigh

"I'LL, uh... leave you guys to it." Aaron took off and Ezra motioned to the bench.

I sat down, running my hands over my knees. I'd had so much to say on the walk over here, but now I felt out of my depth.

So much had happened.

He'd lied, kept things from me. He'd made me think he hated me rather than telling me the truth.

What was I supposed to do with that?

"How are you?" he asked, breaking the thick silence.

"I... I had all this stuff I wanted to say..." I inhaled a shuddering breath. "But now I can't remember any of it."

"I'm sorry, Leigh. I'm so fucking sorry."

"I... this is harder than I thought it would be."

Ezra stood up, pacing in front of me. "Just do it, just rip the Band-Aid off and do it."

My brows furrowed. "Do what?"

"Tell me you hate me. Tell me you never want anything to

do with me again. Just do it, buttercup. Put me out of my misery."

"Ezra." I stood up, reaching for his hands and hesitating.

His eyes dropped to my outstretched fingers, and he nodded. Slow and uncertain, Ezra gave me permission to touch him.

I threaded our fingers together, stepping closer to him. "I'm not here to put you out of your misery." My lips curved into a tentative smile.

"You're... you're not?" He dropped his head to mine, inhaling a harsh breath.

"No, I'm here to talk." I pressed a palm to his cheek, my eyes fluttering closed. The connection between us burned brighter than ever, but I forced myself to take a backward step, putting some space between us.

"Let's sit," I suggested, my heart pounding in my chest.

Ezra kept a safe distance, lowering himself onto the end of the bench. "I wanted to tell you," he said. "Every time I saw you, every time you called me out on my bullshit, I wanted to tell you."

"So why didn't you? I mean, I know Uncle Jason and Asher told you not to, but it's me, Ezra... I thought..."

He ran a hand down his face, his expression falling. "It was my fault... my fucking fault that you were in the hospital. I didn't deserve you before, Ashleigh, and I sure as fuck didn't deserve you after." He glanced away and let out a strained breath.

"It's a mess," I said. Because no matter how I tried to rationalize everything, that's the only conclusion I arrived at.

"Yeah, it is... and if I could take it all back; if I could go back in time and ignore your text messages that night, I would. Because then none of this would have happened and you wouldn't be looking at me like that."

"How am I looking at you?"

"Like you don't know me anymore."

"Ezra..." The pain in his voice gutted me, but I couldn't lie to him and pretend I wasn't hurt and confused and angry. Because I was all of those things.

"What happened that night? What really happened?"

"You sure you want to know?" he said, and I nodded.

"The whole day was a shit show. I fought with Asher and Mya over not wanting to attend the graduation ceremony. Then Alyson texted them again—"

"Alyson?"

"My birth mom."

"Of course, Sofia told me she'd tried to make contact."

"It wasn't a secret. I just didn't—"

"It's okay," I said. "You were upset."

"I was pissed. She gave me up, Leigh. She abandoned me like some fucking disused toy. Who does that?"

"I'm sorry."

"I want nothing to do with her. Nothing. She lost that right a long time ago. But her sudden reappearance threw me for a loop. Brought up a lot of anger and pain I've never dealt with.

"I went and scored some weed and spent the day smoking down by the river. I knew there was a party, and that you wanted me to go. But I wasn't in a good headspace."

"But you did come in the end."

"Yeah, turns out I have a hard time saying no to you." His lips curved into an uncertain smile.

I smiled. "So then what?"

"It was late. The buzz was wearing off and you were so pissed at me for missing the party. I didn't want you all angry with me, so I talked you into coming for a ride."

"In the middle of the night?" My brow went up.

"Stranger things have happened, buttercup."

"Then what happened?"

"I was being hit with all these emotions and I couldn't think straight. I just needed out of my head, so I hit the gas. You were so fucking angry at me. I'd never seen you like that before. But by the time I regained control... it was too late."

A tiny breath caught in my throat. He remembered everything. Ezra had carried the weight of that night with him for weeks and weeks. It was too much for anyone to deal with alone, and yet, that's exactly what he did.

Silent tears rolled down my cheeks as I stared at him. The boy who had stolen my heart all those years ago. We weren't the same people now. Too much had happened. But whether he realized it or not, Ezra still held my heart in his hands. Nothing about the accident changed that.

Was I mad he was driving under the influence that night? Of course I was. And when—*if*—he ever got a new car, I would probably demand a drug test every time he drove the freaking thing, but teenagers made mistakes. It was how we learned to do better, to *be* better.

I survived that night, and here we were with the chance at a do over. Senior year. Graduation... Our relationship.

We got to do it all again. Only this time, we could do it together. For real.

"You're smiling," he said, awe coating his words.

"I am."

"Is this where you tell me you've finally realized that McKay is the better choice?"

"Ezra." I frowned, letting out a weary sigh.

"Sorry, that was a shitty thing to say. He's a good guy. The kind of guy you should be with."

"Don't. Don't do that. It's you I want. It's always been

you." I shuffled across the bench and took his face in my hands. "I love you, Ezra Bennet. I. Love. You."

"You love me, buttercup?" he whispered with so much uncertainty and disbelief in his voice.

"I do."

He swallowed hard and said, "I want to try, Ashleigh. I want to try for you."

―――

"DO we need to go over the rules?" Asher said while Mya smothered her amusement.

"Seriously?" Ezra rolled his eyes.

When we'd walked back to the house hand in hand, I'd assumed he would release his hold on me the second we went inside, but he hadn't. Instead, Ezra pulled me closer, looping his arm around my waist.

"Door stays open. At all times. No groping, humping, and definitely no sex."

"Oh my God," I breathed, barely keeping it together as my cheeks turned fire-truck red.

"Sorry, Ashleigh, but it needs to be said. You're Ezra's first... Are we labelling this?" He raised a brow, wagging a finger between us.

"We... we haven't gotten that far," I said, right as Ezra said, "Girlfriend, she's my girlfriend."

Mya hid a grin as I fought to stay upright.

Girlfriend.

He'd called me his girlfriend.

"O-okay," I squeaked.

"Girlfriend, good." Asher nodded his approval. "Now, where was I? Oh yes, no groping, no humping, and definitely—"

"Okay, mister." Mya grabbed her husband's arm. "I think they got the memo. I'm sure Ashleigh is more than capable of following the rules." Her eyes twinkled with silent laughter. "We're actually going out—"

"Out?" Asher grumbled. "We don't have plans. I thought we'd stay here and—"

"We have that thing, remember?"

"Thing?" His brows pinched.

"Yes, the thing. I'll tell you all about it on the way. Have fun and be safe," she said over her shoulder, ushering Asher out of the kitchen.

"That was—" Laughter bubbled in my chest, but when I glanced up at Ezra he wasn't smiling. "What's wrong?"

"N-nothing." He ran a hand over his hair and down the back of his neck. "I... uh, drink, do you want a drink?"

"Ezra," I said softly, tugging his hand.

"Yeah?"

"You don't need to be nervous, not with me. I don't expect anything more than you're willing to give me."

He released a steady breath, but still looked like he was ready to bolt.

"Why don't we go sit in the living room and watch a movie?" I suggested; anything to try to get him out of his head.

We'd talked down by the lake. About the accident, about his mom, about us. But we still hadn't talked about him, not really.

Ezra took a deep breath and grabbed my hand. "Come on." He led me upstairs to his room, pushing the door open and letting me go inside first.

It was exactly as I expected his room to be. A vast cold space. Gray and moody-blue walls matched the comforter. There was a dark-gray, hi-gloss desk and dresser. Dark-blue curtains blocking out most of the moonlight.

It was like being in the eye of a storm, and yet, there was something sad about it too. He didn't have any posters pinned on the walls or personal effects littered on the shelves above his desk, nothing but a few books and a wireless speaker.

It was almost as if he'd refused to make the space his, to put his own stamp on it, in case he didn't get to stay.

Oh, Ezra.

Strong arms slid around my waist and Ezra dropped his chin onto my shoulder. "Boring, I know."

"It's not boring," I said. "It's... you."

"You know, no one's ever been in here except for Mya and Asher and I can count on one hand how many times Asher has been in here."

I twisted my head to look at him. "Will you tell me why?"

A dark shadow passed over his face. "You really want to know?"

"I want to know everything about you, Ezra."

"Okay. But it's not a pretty story, buttercup."

"Life isn't supposed to be pretty, E. But that doesn't mean we can't find beauty in it." I leaned up, brushing my lips over his.

A low groan rumbled in his chest, and he deepened the kiss, sliding his fingers into my hair and anchoring us together.

"I love you," I whispered.

"Fuck, buttercup." His gravelly voice sent shivers through me. "We're already breaking the rules."

"We've done it now, maybe we should break them a little more." I smiled. I couldn't help it. Being with Ezra—kissing Ezra—was my new favorite thing. But it was even better without any secrets between us.

"Later." He pecked my nose. "I want to get this over with before I lose my nerves." He moved around me, but I snagged his wrist.

"You don't have to tell me anything—"

"Yes, I do. If we're going to do this, I don't want anything between us."

He pulled me down on the bed and we lay on our sides, facing each other.

"You're smiling again," he said.

"Because I like knowing I'm the first girl to lie here with you."

"The only girl." Ezra kissed me softly, tucking a stray hair behind my ear.

"I like that even better."

His expression darkened. "There's a reason I don't... can't let people touch me, Ashleigh." He looked away from me, but I slid my fingers under his jaw, coaxing his eyes back to me.

"Nothing you say will change how I feel about you. It isn't even about me knowing your past, E, it's about you knowing you can always talk to me. About anything."

Torment flickered in his amber gaze. "I don't fucking deserve—"

"Shh." I pressed a finger to his lips. "I thought we were past all that. I'm here, aren't I?"

He nodded, inhaling a shuddering breath.

"The first time it happened, I was six."

Six?

Bile washed in my stomach, but I steeled my expression. This wasn't about me; it was about Ezra. About learning he could trust people not to hurt and take advantage of him.

"It was a group home. I hated it. It was loud and scary and some of the kids were mean. But George the manager was the worst. He caught me stealing an extra cookie once after dinner and hit me so hard I blacked out."

"Oh my God," I breathed.

"He was just one of many." The light dimmed from his

eyes. "It wasn't always the foster parents. Sometimes, it was the other kids."

"Did... did anyone ever...?" I couldn't say it.

"Touch me?" Shame washed over him, so I moved closer, until our knees nudged together.

"I was never... raped." He took a shuddering breath I felt all the way down to my soul. "But stuff happened a few times. Stuff I can't... I can't talk about it, Leigh. Not yet."

"I'm so sorry."

Ezra lifted his hand to my face, willing away my tears with the pad of his thumb. "I wasn't always the victim. Sometimes, I gave as good as I got. But I quickly learned to shut myself off from everyone and keep my head down. It was easier to be invisible."

God, I couldn't imagine him, all alone and living in those vile, unsafe places. It wasn't fair.

"You deserved more," I whispered. "So much more."

"The Bennets' is the first home I've lived in where everyone actually likes each other." He laughed, but it didn't reach his eyes.

"But..."

"But it wasn't easy, being dropped in the middle of a town like Rixon. With parents like Asher and Mya. They're everything I ever wanted, but it was too late, buttercup. I'm broken... I don't know how to do this."

CHAPTER THIRTY-EIGHT

Ashleigh

"YOU'RE SCARED."

"It's stupid, I know. They adopted me for fuck's sake. They... kept me."

Oh, Ezra.

My heart splintered down the middle. He was a product of his past. Of a mother who didn't want him and foster home after foster home that broke a little more of his spirit.

But that wasn't all he was.

The past didn't define him.

Just like my missing memories didn't define me.

"What do you want, Ezra?" He looked at me confused, so I added, "If you could have anything in the whole world, what would it be?"

"To be with you without wanting to puke my guts out."

"We can work on that." A small smirk traced my lips.

"Oh yeah?" He leaned in and stole a kiss.

"Yeah, hot stuff." I pressed a hand to his chest and shoved a little. "But not today, not like this."

He pouted. Ezra pouted and it was one of the sexiest things I'd ever seen.

"What else?"

"I want to graduate. Not for them or anyone else, but for me."

"What about the team?"

"What about them?" He shrugged, his walls rising a little.

"I watched you out there, you were good, really good."

"Carrick doesn't want me there."

"Nathan Carrick is one player, E. Don't let him or his father make you feel less than you are. Because you're mine, Ezra Bennet." I looped my arm around his neck. "And I happen to think you're pretty damn special."

"Your faith in me is a little unnerving."

"Well, until you believe in yourself, I'll believe in you enough for the both of us. Now what else?"

"I want to make it up to you."

My heart fluttered. "You do?"

He nodded. "You stuck by me when no one else did, Leigh. You pushed and pushed and refused to give up. And sometimes, I hated you for it. Sometimes, you drove me in-fucking-sane. But the second you let me go, the second you walked away from me on the football field, I felt like I'd lost my anchor.

"You ground me, buttercup. You tether me to this place, this life, in ways I can't even explain. So yeah, I might be broken and damaged and ruined... but you make me want to fix myself. You make me want to be more."

"Don't just want it, Ezra. Do it."

His brows furrowed, panic washing over him. "What if I can't?"

"You can. I know you can."

Because I'd be with him every step of the way.

RUINED HOPES

"SO THIS ISN'T weird at all." Aaron grinned as we all sat in his man cave on Sunday. Well, all except Poppy. She'd refused to come, not that I blamed her.

"Make yourself useful, Brother, and get us all something to drink." Sofia snickered.

"Beer?" he asked Ezra and Cole, and they both nodded. "Leigh?"

"Just soda please."

"Don't give me that look," he said, handing out the drinks.

"What look?"

"Like you think I'm the dirt on your shoe."

"I don't... I'm still mad at you."

"Yeah, get in line." He dived over the back of the couch and cracked open his beer. "It was one kiss. A drunken, unmemorable kiss."

"With Zara Willis, Poppy's archenemy," Sofia added.

"Jesus, will you back off. I don't know what the big deal is. It's not like..." He stopped himself, letting out a big sigh. "So I fucked up. I'm a guy, we do that. Ask Ezra."

"Whoa, asshole. Leave me out of this."

I leaned down and pecked his cheek. Ezra twisted around from his position on the floor between my legs and kissed me back.

"Okay, too weird. Too fucking weird." Aaron covered his eyes.

"How do you think it felt watching you make out with Zara?" My brow lifted.

"Okay, you've made your point. I'll work on my grovel."

"You'd better because it doesn't feel right without Poppy being here."

"Yeah." He raked a hand through his hair, regret etched

into his expression. Aaron wasn't a bad guy; he was just too wrapped up in senior year spirit.

"So what are you guys doing tonight?" Cole asked. "We're going to catch a movie if you want to tag along."

"Actually, we have plans," I said.

"We do?" Ezra frowned.

"Yep."

"Not sex plans, right? Because—" Cole threw a cushion at Aaron, drowning out his words.

"Thank you," I mouthed, grateful for his intervention.

"Anytime." Cole smiled.

"Well, I should probably go. But I'll see you later."

"You're leaving, already?" Ezra grumbled as I shuffled out from behind him.

"I need to get ready for our date."

"Date?" He frowned up at me, and Sofia and the guys snickered.

"You'll see." I winked.

"Are you heading out?" Aaron asked him.

"Actually," Ezra said. "I was going to stay a while, if that's okay?"

"Hell yeah." His whole expression lit up. "You want to play pool? I always beat Cole's ass, it's no fun anymore."

"Hey, I'm sitting right here."

"Yeah, and you're still shit at pool."

"I'm going to walk Ashleigh out and then go tackle my English assignment," Sofia said. "I'll leave you guys to it."

But they were too busy arguing to notice us leave.

"What the hell was that?" She grabbed my arm the second we were outside.

"That." I grinned, glancing back at the door. "Was Ezra trying."

RUINED HOPES

"YOU'RE SURE ABOUT THIS, SWEETHEART?" Dad frowned as I packed the rest of the picnic basket.

"I'll be fine, Dad. I have to drive my car again eventually, right?"

"I know, Ashleigh, I know. I just don't understand why it has to be today."

"Cam," Mom said. "This is Ashleigh's decision, and you already did a test run with her. She was fine."

"And where are you going again? Just in case—"

"Dad, please don't do this. I'm happy. Me and Ezra talked about everything. No more secrets, okay? Now, if it's okay with the two of you, I want to go on a date with my boyfriend."

"Jesus." He made a sharp intake of breath. "I don't think I'll ever get used to that."

"Well, you're going to have to, Dad. Because he's it for me. The one. My future baby daddy."

"Hailee," he croaked. "Make her stop."

I smothered my laughter, and Mom scowled. "Okay, sweetheart, you should probably go before you give your father a heart attack. Drive safe and remember to text us later, okay?"

"I will. And Dad?"

"Yes?"

"I'm still mad at you, but I get it, Dad, and I love you."

His expression softened as he tucked Mom into his side. "You might be Ezra's girl now, but you tell him you were my little girl first, and I won't hesitate to pay him a visit if he so much as thinks about breaking your heart."

"Got it, Dad." I grabbed my keys and the picnic basket and headed for my car.

It still felt a little strange getting behind the wheel, but I needed to do this. Besides, I had big plans for me and Ezra tonight.

I threw the basket into the back seat and climbed into the driver's seat, inhaling a steady breath. The drive to the Bennets' house was only a few minutes, but by the time I pulled up outside, my heart was galloping in my chest like a stampede of wild horses.

I was so nervous.

Nervous, he wouldn't like our date.

Nervous about being with him again, with no secrets or lies between us. Just the two of us and our feelings for one another.

Before I got out of the car, the front door swung open, and Ezra appeared.

He looked so good in grey sweatpants; a black, long-sleeved t-shirt, and his sneakers. Butterflies soared in my stomach.

"You drove," he said, slipping into the passenger seat.

"I did."

"How was it?"

"I took a test drive with my dad first. But I feel okay. I remember driver's ed, so that's a bonus." It was a joke, but it only made the air in the car turn thin.

"You're nervous," he said, studying me.

"I..."

Ezra leaned over, sliding his hand along my jaw and burying it in my hair. "You look beautiful, buttercup."

"Thank you," I whispered, my breath caught in my throat as he ghosted his lips over mine. Teasing me.

"I could just eat you up."

"Oh God." Heat coursed through me at his words. Ezra

licked his lips before kissing me. A slow, lazy kiss that made my head spin.

"Hi," he breathed.

"Hi." I smiled, my cheeks on fire. "That was... nice."

"Nice? Sounds like I need to work on my game if it was only *nice*."

He was flirting with me, and it was the best feeling in the whole world.

Ezra placed his hand on my thigh while I backed out of the driveway. "So where are we going?" he asked.

"You'll see."

I took the road through town toward the bridge dividing Rixon with Rixon East where Bryan and Gav lived.

"Do I need to be worried?"

"Actually, you should probably thank Gav. He helped me out with this."

"He did, huh?"

"Yeah." I smiled.

"What are you up to, buttercup?"

"You'll see."

WHEN WE FINALLY PULLED UP TO the small cabin, Ezra's face was a picture. "What is this place?"

"Gav knows someone who knows someone. They said it's ours for the night. Well, not all night because try explaining that to my dad. But it's ours for the next few hours."

"McKay did this for us?"

"He's a good guy, Ezra." Gav hadn't hesitated to help me out when I said I wanted somewhere off the grid for our first date.

It was perfect: deep in the woods, surrounded by nothing but the wilderness.

"Come on, let's go check it out." I climbed out of the car and went around to Ezra's door. He still looked a little shell-shocked when he got out.

"Don't you like it?" I asked, dread snaking through me. "I just thought it might be nice to be alone. It doesn't mean I expect anything to happen. I just want to be with you away from everyone else."

He still didn't say anything, and I began to feel like the world's biggest fool.

"Maybe this was a bad idea. We can go back and catch a movie or something." I turned around but Ezra caught me.

"Sorry, you just caught me off guard. I thought we'd be going for dinner or something."

"It's too much."

"It's not. I'm just not used to this."

My gaze dropped as I willed my heart to calm down.

"Ashleigh." He gently grasped my chin. "Look at me." I met his eyes and gave him a weak smile. "You're going to have to be patient with me, okay? Sometimes I don't do or say the right thing because I don't know—"

"I get it. I'm pushing too hard. I just wanted tonight to be perfect."

"Do you have a key?"

"It's a keypad." I smiled. "I have the code."

"Come on then, let's go take a look around."

CHAPTER THIRTY-NINE

Ezra

THE CABIN WASN'T anything special, not really. But the fact she'd organized this, for me, it meant the fucking world.

"So I know it doesn't look like much, but Gav said the deck out back makes up for it."

"Let's go find out."

After a couple of attempts, I managed to get the back door to slide open and sure enough, it opened out onto a wide deck overlooking a small lake.

"Wow, it's beautiful." Ashleigh went to the railing and looked out over the view. I moved behind her, pressing in close and brushing the hair off her neck.

"You're beautiful." I kissed the skin there, sucking gently.

"Ezra," she moaned, and my body stirred to life.

It was like being around Ashleigh had flipped a switch inside me, and I was finally able to sort my feelings and responses to physical touch from 'get the fuck off me' and into 'more please.'

And I wanted so much more with her.

But I still didn't know if I could do it; if I could be with her the way she so obviously wanted. Not without making a giant ass of myself.

"How long did you say we had this place for?"

"A while." She turned into my arms, gazing up at me. "But I didn't bring you here to try to seduce you."

"You didn't?"

"No. I brought you here to relax and get away from it all. Oh, and I brought snacks."

"Snacks, you say? There's always room for snacks." A smirk played on my lips, and she chuckled.

"I'll be right back."

Ashleigh kissed my cheek and left me on the deck. It really was something. Dusk falling over the lake in pink and orange streaks.

I was so engrossed in the quiet I didn't even hear Ashleigh approach.

"I come bearing blankets and food."

"Here, let me." I took the basket from her, watching with nervous anticipation as she lay down two thick blankets and kicked off her sneakers before sitting down.

"I packed sandwiches, crackers, cheese, chips, some cookies, and grapes."

My eyes almost bugged out and she let out a strained laugh. "I may have gone a little overboard."

"No, it's great." I didn't have the heart to tell her I wasn't sure I could stomach food. Not when all I could think about was laying her down and eating her.

We sat side by side, picking at the various containers and talking about everything and nothing.

"Have you ever thought about college?" she asked out of left field.

"Honestly, no. It was never part of the plan."

"And what is the plan, Ezra Bennet?"

The more she called me that, the more I liked how it sounded rolling off her tongue.

I still thought of myself as Ezra Jackson, unable to accept everything that came with being Asher and Mya's son, but when Ashleigh said it, it felt... right.

"I guess I always thought I'd get a job and one day leave Rixon."

"You'd... leave?"

"I run, buttercup. That's my M.O. because if I stand still for too long I feel like I can't breathe."

"And now?" She leaned over, palming my cheek. "Do you still want to run now?"

"I... I don't think it's something I can just get over, Leigh. But I think I'd like to try to stand still with you."

She went up onto her knees and moved closer, kissing me. "Is this okay?" she asked and I nodded, grabbing hold of her hips and helping her straddle my thighs.

"Ezra, we don't have—"

"Shh, it's okay. I want to feel you." My hands ran over her ass and up her spine, drawing Ashleigh onto me. I cupped the back of her neck, pulling her down until I could kiss her, plunging my tongue deep into her mouth.

We kissed like we were running out of air. Greedy and frantic. Deep, desperate licks. She tasted like fucking sunshine, lighting me up inside and burning away the darkness.

I couldn't get enough.

"Okay," she murmured, dropping her eyes. "Maybe we should slow down."

I wound her hair around my fist and tugged gently, lifting her face to mine. "I don't want to slow down, buttercup."

"Y-you don't?"

"What do you think?" I lifted my hips slightly, pulling her down over my rock hard dick. Her soft moan made my heart stutter in my chest.

"But I thought..."

"I want you, Ashleigh. More than I have ever wanted anything."

"You're sure?"

I nodded.

"Lie back. I want to try something." She pushed my chest gently and I dropped onto my elbows. Her hand slipped to the hem of my t-shirt, her eyes silently asking me permission.

"It's okay," I said.

Pushing the material up my torso, Ashleigh leaned down and placed a soft kiss on my hip bone. My body jolted at the strange, unfamiliar feel of her mouth on my skin.

"Shit, sorry, was it—"

"No, no, don't stop."

"Yeah?"

"Yeah." My head dropped back as she kissed me again, trailing her tongue along the deep grooves on either side of my pelvis.

"Fuck, that feels..."

Her hand ran up my thigh, palming my dick and I swear I almost came from that single touch.

"Jesus, buttercup. You're killing me."

"In a good way, I hope." Her laughter filled the cool air, but despite the falling temperatures, I felt like I was burning up. Her hand rubbed me through my sweats, testing my limits. Even though my heart was going wild in my chest and the innate instinct to push her away lingered in my consciousness, it felt good. So fucking good.

"I want to taste you," she said, gazing up at me through hooded eyes. "But only if—"

"I want." I ran my hand through her hair. "I really fucking want."

Untying my sweats, Ashleigh worked them down my hips and grasped my length, stroking me... Once. Twice.

"Fuuuck, Leigh..."

She flicked her tongue along the tip, tasting me before taking me in her mouth.

My body trembled, fear and pleasure licking up my spine. Her touch was like fire, but I didn't mind the burn.

She withdrew her mouth. "You're shaking," she said, glancing up my body.

"It's... intense."

A mischievous glint twinkled in her eyes as she sat up and pulled off her sweater and tank top.

"Is this real life?"

Because she couldn't be real.

Ashleigh was a living, breathing angel. She could have any guy she wanted, and she was here with me.

She wanted *me*.

"Ezra?"

"If I'm ever going to fall in love with someone, it's going to be you, buttercup."

Her lips parted on a soft sigh as she blinked back a tear. No more words were spoken between us as she lowered her head and took me in her mouth again, licking and sucking me so good I couldn't think straight.

"Shit, I'm going to... fuck... *fuck*." I buried my hand in her hair, holding her over me while she swallowed me down.

"Hmm, I liked that." Ashleigh licked her lips, tossing her hair over one shoulder as she sat up. "Was it... okay?" She gave me a shy smile.

"You..." I sat up, curving my arm around her waist. "Are amazing."

"I'm honored that you trust me to touch you."

Tightening my hold on Ashleigh, I flipped us over, so I was hovering over her.

"Smooth." She chuckled.

"I have some moves."

"Maybe you should show me the rest of them."

"Maybe I will." I dipped my head, brushing my lips over her collarbone, sucking and nipping her silky soft skin while my hands roamed all over her body. "I think these need to come off." I tugged at her jeans and Ashleigh lifted her ass off the blanket.

"Yeah?" She nodded, and I leaned back to peel them down her legs.

"I think it's only fair for you to be naked too though." Challenge shone in her eyes.

"Oh, it's like that, huh?"

Ashleigh bit down on her lip. "Lose 'em, Bennet."

I shoved my pants and boxers off my hips and kicked them off, before lowering myself back down over her.

"Is this okay?" she asked. Always checking I was good.

"You don't need to keep asking me that." I pushed the hair from her eyes.

"Yes, I do. It's important to me that you know I will never force you to do anything you don't want to. If you want stop, all you have to—"

"I don't want to stop." Stopping was the furthest thing from my mind. "I want to try... everything."

"Everything? I'm listening." A shy smile tugged at the corners of her mouth.

"Like I want to kiss you right here." I placed a soft kiss over the curve of her chest. "And here." I moved down, sucking right over the lace covering her nipple. "And here."

Lower and lower, I licked down to her navel, swirling my tongue there.

"Ezra…" Her fingers dug into my shoulder.

"And here, I really want to kiss you here." I moved further down her body until my mouth was right over her pussy.

Her body bowed into my touch as I blew a stream of hot air onto her.

"I wonder if here tastes like sunshine too." Her legs trembled as I hooked my fingers into her panties and pulled them to the side so I could taste her.

"Oh my God," she breathed.

"You're so fucking wet for me." I pushed a finger inside her, sucking on her clit until she writhed and moaned beneath me.

"Come for me, buttercup." Working another finger inside her, I curled them deep and watched as she came apart, moaning my name like a whispered prayer.

"That was… wow."

I crawled up her body, kissing her. Ashleigh kissed me back just as fiercely, running her hands over my shoulders, the back of my neck. Her touch didn't scare me anymore; it made me feel strong. Alive.

For the first time in my life, I felt whole.

"I love you, Ezra."

I kissed her, trying to show her what she meant to me. Trying to show her everything I couldn't yet say but felt in my soul.

Ashleigh hitched her legs around my hips, grinding against me, seeking more. I rocked into her, growing hard all over again.

"I want you," I whispered. "All of you."

"I'm yours."

I saw it then. The promise of forever in her eyes. Ashleigh

loved me with everything that she was. Even at my worst, she'd still decided to stand by me.

I didn't deserve her, but one way or another, I'd earn her love.

I couldn't stop trembling as I removed the final barrier between us and settled back over her body. Grasping myself, I slid one hand under her thigh and stilled, forcing myself to take a breath.

"It's okay. I'm on birth control," she said. "I want this. I want you."

"There's only ever been you, buttercup," I rasped, the fear I felt melting away at her gentle touch, the way her fingers danced across my skin, healing the invisible scars.

I pushed forward, groaning at how good she felt. How tight and warm and so fucking perfect. My mouth crashed down on hers, swallowing Ashleigh's moans as I pulled out and rocked back in, going deeper.

"Don't stop," she cried. "Don't ever stop."

She didn't demand anything of me. She didn't try to take control or set the pace. Ashleigh was content with handing me the reins and letting me lead.

"You're fucking perfect." I touched my head to hers, hissing through my teeth as I picked up the pace, going faster, harder, deeper.

Sweat rolled down my back, my muscles burning as I tried to make it last for her. But it was too much.

She was too much. Her sweet kisses and soft touches, her tight pussy gripping me like it never wanted to let go.

"Fuck, Ashleigh... *fuck*..." Another tingle started at the base of my spine, and I dipped my hand between us and found her clit, desperate to get her there before I came.

"Ezra," she cried, panting my name over and over.

"Together," I whispered, kissing her.

She nodded, breathless moans spilling off her lips as I pushed her toward the edge.

And when she fell, I went right alongside her. But I didn't feel fear or trepidation or anxiety about it… because Ashleigh would catch me.

Just like she always had.

CHAPTER FORTY

Ashleigh

"WHAT ARE YOU THINKING ABOUT?" I snuggled under the blanket, trailing my fingers up and down Ezra's chest.

He didn't seem to mind me touching him now, not after he'd touched and kissed and licked every inch of my body.

It was late, we'd been out here hours, but neither of us was in any hurry to get back to reality.

"That maybe it was a blessing in disguise that you found out the truth when you did."

I lifted my head to look at him. "You think that?"

"I mean, I'm not proud of the fact you found out like that. I wanted to tell you. I would have told you... eventually. But if it hadn't gone down like it did, maybe we wouldn't be here now."

"If it wasn't here, it would be somewhere else. I was in, Ezra. I was all-in the minute you kissed me at Deacon's party."

"So we're really doing this, huh? *Girlfriend*," he teased,

brushing my collarbone with his finger and sending a delicious shiver through me. It didn't matter that we'd already had sex twice. I already wanted him again. And again.

Being with him like this was incredible.

I never wanted it to end.

"You're stuck with me now." I stuck out my tongue at him, and he laughed.

"I can think of worse things." He let out a steady breath. "Are you worried about what John Carrick will do?"

"No, Uncle Jason said he'll handle it, and I believe him. In case you haven't noticed, he's pretty badass."

"Yeah, I know. But I don't want you caught in the crossfire if things go sour with—"

"Stop worrying." I leaned down, kissing him. "Nothing is more important to my uncle than family. He'll do whatever he needs to, to protect you."

"I'm going to owe him so badly, aren't I?"

"Ezra, you don't owe anyone anything. You're family, even if you don't feel like it yet."

"I did," he whispered. "Earlier in Aaron's man cave, I felt it." A sheepish expression crossed his face.

"Don't look so worried. It's a good thing. It's okay to let people in."

"Yeah, I'm starting to get that. Although I am a little worried about meeting your dad, officially."

"He'll go easy on you."

"Don't be so sure about that. I'm responsible—"

"No." I pressed my finger against his lips. "We're not doing this anymore. What happened, happened. Playing the blame game will only make you sad and angry. And I like happy, turned-on Ezra."

"Is that right, huh?" He grabbed my leg and pulled me across his body until I was lying on top of him.

"I was comfortable." I pouted.

"And I was lonely." His hand stroked down my spine. "I meant what I said earlier, Ashleigh. If I'm going to fall in love with anyone, it's going to be you."

"I know," I said, softly.

"You know?" He balked, laughter twinkling in his eyes.

"You're letting me use your body as a bed, that means something."

"Yeah, it does. And for as much as I could stay out here forever with you, it's late and I don't want to piss off your dad on our first date."

"Guess I'd better not tell him you made me come three times then."

"Three?" His brow arched with smug amusement. "It was at least four, wasn't it?"

"I'm pretty sure it was only three."

"Is that right?" Ezra worked his hand between our bodies and found my center, sliding his finger inside me. My breath caught in my throat as he stretched me. "Better make sure it's four then."

―――

"GOOD MORNING, SWEETHEART," Mom said as I entered the kitchen. "How was your hot date?"

"Mom!" My cheeks burned.

"What? It was just a question." She hid her grin behind a gallery brochure.

"It was really nice, Mom."

"I'm happy for you, baby. But remember to take things slow. You've both been through so much…"

"You don't need to worry," I said, bending to kiss her cheek. "We're going at our own pace."

"Good. You should invite Ezra for dinner tonight, your dad will love that."

"Mom, can I ask you something?"

"Sure, sweetheart, anything."

"Dad is okay with this, right?"

Her expression softened. "All he wants is for you to be happy, Ashleigh. It's hard, letting your kids go and find their own way. But you're not a child anymore. We trust you to make your own decisions." She sipped her coffee.

"Ezra is different now, Mom. The accident changed him... for the better, I think."

He'd opened up to me, talked about his past, and although there were still things he couldn't talk about, it was a start.

"Sometimes it takes almost losing somebody to realize what you've got."

"Uncle Jason will fix things with John Carrick, won't he?" I hated the thought that anything could jeopardize Ezra's senior year and place on the team. Especially someone who couldn't care less about anyone but himself and his son.

"You don't need to worry, I promise."

"Was Uncle Jase as ruthless as is he now, back when you were in high school?"

"Worse." Mom smiled. "He definitely mellowed out when he met your Aunt Felicity, and the girls were born. Love changes you."

"It does." My chest swelled as I replayed last night over in my head.

It had been perfect.

"My two favorite girls." Dad breezed into the kitchen. "How are we doing this morning?"

"Good, Dad."

"Ashleigh was just telling me about her date with Ezra."

Dad paused at the refrigerator, grumbling something under his breath.

"Ahh, don't be like that, Dad. Mom invited him over for dinner tonight."

"She did, did she?" He threw her a hard look.

"Play nice, Cam. Something tells me he's a keeper." She flashed me a conspiratorial glance and I chuckled.

"I need to go. Aaron and Ezra are giving me a ride to school."

"Of course they are," he groaned. "Tell Aaron and Ezra they'd better stick to the speed limit."

"Yes, Dad." I waved him off, heading out of the house.

They were already waiting. Ezra leaned up against Aaron's car looking so good, my heart fluttered wildly in my chest.

He pushed off the car and stalked toward me. "Hey."

"Hey."

His arm went around my waist, pulling me in close. "I missed you."

"It's only been a few hours."

"A few too many." He smirked, dipping his head to brush his lips over mine. My fingers curled into his hoodie, yanking him closer.

"Your dad is watching," he mumbled.

"Better put on a good show then."

Ezra smiled against my mouth. "You're a bad influence, buttercup."

"Only for you." I grinned up at him. "Ready for this?"

He took my hand and led me to the car. "As I'll ever be."

Ezra

"You two make me sick," Aaron said over his shoulder as he cut the engine.

"Sorry." Ashleigh buried her face into my shoulder.

"You're just jealous, bro."

"Yes, yes I am. Well, class calls. Let's go, lovebirds." He climbed out, giving us a moment of privacy.

"Maybe we should skip," I said. "We could go to McKay's cabin again and—

"Tease." She grabbed my face and kissed me. "I promised I'd meet the girls before class. So I'll see you later?"

"Yeah."

"It's going to be okay, E, you'll see." She stole another kiss before shouldering the door open and climbing out. I followed her, grabbing her arm and yanking her back to me.

"You forgot something." I turned her in my arms.

"I did?"

My mouth crashed down on hers, not caring that we had an audience. Ashleigh was mine and I wanted everyone to know it.

"Now you can go."

She looked at me with a dreamy expression. "I'll see you later. Bye, Aaron."

"Dude," he said the second she was out of earshot. "You've got it so bad."

"Yep."

"She looks good on you. I'm happy for you."

"Thanks. She's good for me."

"Glad to hear it. Ready to kill it in practice this morning?" I hesitated, and he added, "You know Coach has it handled, right? He wouldn't let you walk into the lion's den without warning."

"Yeah, maybe."

"Well, whatever happens, I've got your back, man."

"Thanks, appreciate it."

Aaron shot me a sly grin. "I have a good feeling about this year, E. A gooood feeling."

We walked to the gym in silence, but it wasn't awkward or uncomfortable. Slowly, brick by brick, Aaron was wearing down my defenses and it felt... good.

A lot of things I'd always avoided were starting to feel good.

The locker room was quiet when we got there. Aaron started getting changed for practice, but I hesitated, glancing at Coach's office door. It was closed, which wasn't unusual, but I had a strange feeling.

A second later, the door swung open, and John Carrick and his son stepped out. John shook Coach's hand, the two of them wearing grim expressions. Carrick's glare cut to me, narrowing with contempt.

"Looks like that went well," Aaron whispered.

Coach saw them both out and made his way over. "Ezra, I'm glad you're here."

"What was all that about?"

"You don't need to worry about Nathan or his father anymore."

"What did you do?" My brow arched.

"Everyone has secrets they would rather keep buried, son. You just have to know where to look. I gave Nathan the choice as to whether or not he remains a Raider. But if he does, he understands that this is my team and you're a part of that." He gave me a small nod. "Get changed and I'll see you both out on the field."

"Hey, Coach," I called after him.

"Yeah?"

"Why'd you do it? Why go to all this trouble for me?"

"Because you're family, Ezra. And I protect my family—always."

Jase walked back to his office.

"Now do you believe me?" Aaron said with a knowing smirk.

"I... you know you'd better tread carefully with Poppy, right?"

Aaron grimaced. "Tell me something I don't know."

―――

WHEN PRACTICE WAS OVER, I didn't expect to see Ashleigh sitting in the bleachers. I was about to make my way over when Coach collared me.

"You worked hard this morning, son," he said, as I drained my water bottle. "Keep it up and we might need to talk about college scholarships."

"Oh, I don't know about that, Coach."

College wasn't in the plan. I still didn't really have a plan, but things felt good. Like for the first time in my life, I wasn't craving the silence.

"Just think about it." His gaze went to where Ashleigh was sitting. "Something tells me your priorities are about to change. Go on, get out of here. Tell my niece I said hi."

"Will do, Coach." I jogged over to the bleachers and Ashleigh met me halfway, leaping into my arms. "You're supposed to be in class."

"I had an unexpected free period, so I thought I'd come and watch my boyfriend play football."

"Good thing I didn't notice you earlier or I would have struggled to focus."

"Are you saying I distract you?" She leaned up on her

tiptoes, nudging her nose against mine. "I noticed Nathan was missing. Do I need to be worried?"

"Your uncle handled it, just like you said he would."

"So Nathan is off the team?"

"No, he can choose to play so long as he falls in line."

She grinned. "How does it feel?"

"How does what feel?"

"Knowing that you're one of us now?"

"It's okay, I guess." I shrugged.

"Ezra!" She swatted my chest. "But seriously, you're okay with everything?"

"I'm okay." I looped my arms around her waist and pulled her closer. "For the first time in my life I feel like I can breathe and it's all down to you, buttercup."

"E, I—"

"No, hear me out." I dipped my head, looking right into her hypnotic eyes. "I spent all these years pushing you away because you scared me. You made me want things I didn't dare to ever want. You're my anchor, buttercup, you always have been. And now I have you, I don't plan on ever letting go."

"Well, that works out pretty well for me, because I don't ever plan on letting you go either. I love you, Ezra."

Ashleigh kissed me and although I wasn't ready to say the words yet, for the first time in my life, I felt the words clang through me.

I love you too, Ashleigh.

EPILOGUE

ASHLEIGH

"WHERE ARE WE GOING?" I asked Ezra as we walked hand in hand downtown.

"It's a surprise."

"A surprise?" Peering up at him, I pursed my lips. "You know I hate surprises."

"I think you'll like this one." He leaned down, brushing his lips over mine, and my heart fluttered wildly in my chest, the way it always did when he kissed me.

It had been a week since we spent the night at the cabin. At first, people had been curious about seeing us together, pointing and whispering. But it soon wore off when Aaron and Zara had a very public argument about their *relationship*. Turned out, she'd read a lot into their kiss at the party, and he wasn't looking to go steady with her, or anyone else apparently.

The whole school was talking about it. Everyone except Poppy who was still refusing to talk to Aaron.

"Come on, we're late." Ezra stopped outside Cindy's Grill and pulled me inside.

"Something smells—Gav?" I spotted him almost immediately, sitting in one of the booths. He lifted a hand in a small wave, and I frowned at Ezra. "Uh, why is Gav here?"

"I know you've been feeling guilty over everything... so I texted him."

"*You* texted Gav?"

"Stranger things have happened, buttercup." His lips twisted into a knowing smirk. "Come on, he's waiting."

Okay then.

When Ezra had said he wanted to take me out, this was the last thing I'd expected. But he was right, I had been feeling guilty over how things had gone down between the four of us. I didn't know Penelope enough to try to smooth things over with her, but Gav was important to me.

"Hey," he said, as we reached the booth.

"Hey." I smiled. "How are you?"

"I'm good, Leigh Leigh." He glanced at Ezra. "Does she know?"

"Know? Know what?"

Ezra shrugged, nudging me into the seat. "Thought you should tell her."

Gav nodded and I grumbled, "Will someone please tell me what's going on?"

"I'm not here to crash your date."

"You're not?"

"No, I'm here... with somebody."

"You are?" My brows went up. "Is this a joke? Because you're sitting here all—"

"Ashleigh?"

Gav snickered as I turned to find Penelope standing there. "You," I said.

"Hey, I hope this is okay. The guys thought it might—"

"Hold on a second, *you're* Gav's date?"

"Surprise." He grinned, but I wasn't grinning. I was frowning.

"I'm confused." I sank back into the leather seat, and Ezra took my hand in his.

"You knew I liked her," Gav said with complete honesty.

"Yeah, but isn't this... weird?" I looked at all of them. Penelope gave me a shy smile.

"It's only weird if we make it weird. I'm happy for you, Ashleigh. Ezra deserves to have someone like you in his life."

"I... thank you. And you," I jabbed my finger at Gav. "You didn't think to tell me this earlier?"

"And miss your reaction?" Amusement glittered in his eyes, but then his expression softened. "Honestly, I didn't think you would agree to come."

He was right, I would never have agreed.

"This is a good thing, Leigh Leigh. Me and Penelope have been spending time together at college and we hit it off." He smiled at her, and I saw it then, the spark between them.

"So, this is a double date?" I asked.

"Unless you're too freaked out," Penelope said. "I told Gavin it wasn't a good idea, but the guys outvoted me."

Gavin.

She'd called him Gavin, and if it wasn't the cutest thing.

"No, it's okay," I said. "I just want you both to be happy."

And I meant it.

Gav had been there for me. A true friend. I only wanted good things for him, and he and Penelope had a lot in common.

Ezra nuzzled my neck and whispered, "You're a good person, buttercup."

I blushed from my head to my toes. If I'd learned one

thing about the quiet, lost boy beside me, it was that he had absolutely no problem with PDA. In fact, he couldn't keep his hands off me.

"Okay, Bennet, put the girl down and let's eat." Penelope snorted and Gav groaned. "Food. Let's eat food, babe. Good to know where your heads at though." He smirked, and it was Penelope's turn to blush.

"We thought we could eat and then catch a movie?" Ezra said, keeping his arm wrapped around me.

I gazed up at him and smiled. "Sounds good to me."

"GOD, E, don't stop... don't..." Waves of pleasure crashed over me. Ezra trailed soft kisses over my hip bone and stomach as he crawled up my body and captured my mouth in a bruising kiss. I could taste myself on his tongue as he licked my mouth.

"Told you I'd eat you for dessert."

Laughter spilled out of me. Pure unfiltered laughter. "You're such a dork."

"A sexy dork though, right?" His eyes twinkled as he gazed down at me. There was something in his stare, like he was looking at me soul deep.

"What?" I asked, wondering what he was thinking.

"I love you, Ashleigh." The words came out so strong and firm, there was no mistaking his declaration.

The world went quiet around me, my heart crashing in my chest. But I still needed to hear him say it again. Because it was such a big deal.

"Y-you love me?"

"Yeah... I do."

I threw my arms around him, hugging him tight. It was

soon, really soon, and I knew what a big deal it was to him to say those words.

"I love you, too. So much."

Ezra eased back to look at me. "Don't cry, buttercup."

"They're happy tears, I promise."

He brushed them away with his fingers, letting his thumb linger on my mouth. The chain he always wore around his neck brushed against my chest and I plucked the silver anchor pendant between my fingers.

"Ashleigh?" His brows drew tight.

"I have the strangest sense of déjà vu," I said.

"You know, you gave me this last Christmas."

"I-I did?" I gawked at him.

"Yeah."

"You never said anything."

"Because I knew you couldn't remember... and I didn't want to make things any harder than they already were."

"But you wore it... you've been wearing it..."

"All this time."

I couldn't remember, not really. But I felt *something*. A connection to it.

I'd made my peace with losing my memories. The past didn't define me. What I chose to do now and every day after today did.

Even if they never returned, I chose this. Hope and love and Ezra.

"Yeah, buttercup. I told you once you're my anchor. I meant it."

"Ezra..." Emotion swelled inside me, overflowing as he kissed me, sliding his tongue against mine and pressing his body down on me. My arms slid over his shoulders and down his back, locking us together.

He shifted slightly, kissing me deeper as he rocked into

me with one smooth stroke. My breath caught at the sudden feeling of him buried deep inside me. "God, that feels…"

"Everything, Leigh. It's everything. I love you."

Ezra pulled back and slid back in, making me moan. He trailed hot, wet kisses down my jaw and my throat, grazing the skin along my collarbone with his teeth.

"I'll never get enough of this," he breathed the words against my neck, sliding his hands around my thighs and lifting my legs around his waist.

It was always intense between us, as if we couldn't quite believe we'd made it to this point.

I liked to think that if the accident had never happened, we would have found our way here one day, but we would never know that.

Sometimes you needed to go through the storm to get to the rainbow.

And no matter what the future held…

We'd face it together.

Ezra

"Fuck," I grunted as the ball rebounded off my shoulder.

"Seriously, bro, get your head in the game," Aaron said.

"Sorry, I was…"

"Daydreaming about a certain girl, no doubt," he scoffed.

"It's her birthday soon. I need to get her something."

"Hell yeah, you do. And it needs to be epic since she decided to forgive your sorry ass."

I scowled at him, and he grinned. "Relax, I'm just busting your balls. I can help you shop for her if you want. I'm good at stuff like that."

"That's just… weird."

He shrugged. "Fine, I won't help. But don't blame me when she kicks your ass for getting her some lame gift."

Coach yelled time and we both jogged over to the water station. "Have you talked to Poppy yet?"

"Nah," he said. "I'm letting her cool off."

"You know Zara is telling anyone who will listen that you screwed her over."

A dark shadow passed over him as he let out a weary sigh. "She's a bitch. I never should have gone there."

"You need to fix it with Poppy, and soon."

"Since when do you care?"

"Since it affects my girl. She hates that Poppy won't hang out with us."

"I'm not asking her to choose, E."

"Just... talk to her."

"Yeah, maybe." He stared over at the bleachers as if he was looking for her, but Poppy hadn't been around to watch practice in a while.

"You two," Coach stabbed his finger toward us. "Explain, now."

"Sorry, Coach," Aaron said. "But E has a bad case of the feels, sir."

The guys all snickered.

"Asshole." I nudged his ribs with my elbow.

"Ezra, it would be a damn shame if I have to bench you now. Get your head out of the clouds and into the game."

"Yes, sir."

"Carrick, you looked good out there today."

"Thanks, Coach," he murmured.

Fucker had decided to stay on the team, but so far, he had stayed out of my way. Coach assured me he knew the score, so I was letting it go, for now.

"We have our first away game Friday, and I expect a win. Okay," he said. "Get out of here. Ezra, a word."

Aaron and Cole smirked at me, before taking off toward the locker rooms.

"Do I need to be worried?" He studied me. "I know new relationships can be... intense—"

"Whoa, Coach. I appreciate the concern, but I'm not doing this with you. Ashleigh is—"

"I'm well aware Ashleigh is my niece, Ezra. And I won't deny it's as weird as fuck that the two of you are..." He gave me a pointed look. "But you're on this team and I need to know you're with us."

"I'm in, Coach. I'm all-in. It's just Ashleigh's birthday..."

"Ah, I see." A rare flash of understanding passed over his expression. "Word of advice, Ezra. Guys think girls want grand gestures, when usually they'll be happy with a cupcake from Sprinkles and a night watching one of their favorite chick flicks."

"Uh, thanks, I think."

He chuckled. "Just don't overthink it. And for the love of my sanity, try to keep your relationship off my field."

Yes, sir."

I watched him stalk off, leaving me gawking after him.

Coach giving me dating advice...

When had life gotten so fucking weird?

"THERE YOU ARE." I hooked my arm around Ashleigh and nuzzled her neck.

"Hey, you." Her laughter was like music to my fucking ears. Someone shouted, "Get a room," and I stuck up my arm, flipping off the busy hall.

I didn't give a shit what people thought about me kissing my girl up against her locker. I'd waited too damn long trying to keep her at arm's length. I wasn't going to waste a single second with her from here on out.

"How was practice?"

"A fucking disaster." Aaron popped up next to us.

"It was?" Her brows furrowed. "What happened?"

"Nothing," I said, right as Aaron said,

"Ezra was distracted."

"Distracted, you say?" A faint smile traced her lips.

"Asshole," I grumbled, and Aaron clapped me on the back. "Just sharing the love, bro. Have you seen Poppy?" he asked Ashleigh.

"She's around here somewhere."

"Nice, Leigh, real nice. I was hoping to talk to her."

"About time," she said under her breath.

"Yeah, yeah. I'm a shit friend. I deserve her wrath. But I'm ready to pull my head out of my ass and make amends. That's got to count for something, right?"

"I don't know, she's been... acting weird."

"Well, hopefully my major grovelling will improve her mood. Wish me luck."

"Good luck. Something tells me you'll need it," I teased.

He flipped me off and disappeared down the hall.

"I'd love to be a fly on that wall," Ashleigh said.

"They'll figure it out."

"Hopefully. Anyway," she ran her hands up my hoodie. "I don't want to talk about them."

"No?" My mouth kicked up as I crowded her against her locker again. "What do you want to talk about?"

"Did you agree to the therapy thing yet?"

"Actually, I did."

"You did?" A smile broke over her face. "Oh my God, E,

I'm so proud of you." She threw her arms around me. "This is a good thing, such a good thing."

"Yeah. I figured it's time." When Mya had suggested it again over the weekend, I'd immediately told her no. But Ashleigh was right, maybe it was time to deal with my past.

"But I told them if I did it, I wanted them to get rid of Alyson." Ashleigh's eyes almost bugged out, and I snorted. "Not like that. Fuck, buttercup, what do you take me for?"

"Have you met my uncle?"

"You're right, Coach Ford is badass. But I was thinking more that they can threaten her with an injunction or something. She's dead to me, Leigh. And I don't mean that in a mommy issue kind of way... I..."

"I get it," she said, eyes soft with understanding. "And I think it's a good idea. To ask them to handle it, I mean. But if you ever change your mind or feel in a place where you're ready to talk to her, just know that I'll always be there, right by your side."

Fuck. This girl. Just when I thought she couldn't blow my mind any more than she already had, she went and said something so perfect, it slayed me.

"What?" she smiled shyly at me.

"You, buttercup. Just you."

My best friend.

My anchor.

The girl who saved me.

Aaron

"Yo, Bennet, what's—"

"Not now, I have something I need to do." I gave the guys from the team a two fingered salute as I went in search of Poppy.

RUINED HOPES

Things had been all wrong between us since the semester started.

She was my best friend but somewhere along the way, the lines had become blurred. I needed to fix it, I needed to explain to her that I was feeling the pressure.

It was senior year, and my last season as a Rixon Raider. Coach Ford was relying on me. He'd named me as captain for fuck's sake. It didn't get much more serious than that.

There was nothing more I wanted than to do a good job, lead the team right, and make sure we defended the championship.

I wasn't the brightest kid in my class. I had to work for my grades. But football... football, I was good at. It was my ticket to a future that meant something.

Scanning the long hall, I looked for Poppy.

"Aaron?" My sister Sofia frowned when she saw me. "What are you doing?"

"Have you seen Poppy?"

"I think she went to the library, why? What did you do?"

"Nice, sis, real nice."

"Aaron, I didn't—"

"I want to apologize, okay?" I ran a hand down my face. "I've been an asshole."

She rolled her eyes. "You can say that again."

Guilt clanged through me. So maybe things had gotten a little out of control. But it was Poppy. We'd never talked about... us. About the connection that burned between us. We were friends—best friends—and honestly, I wasn't sure we should ever cross that line for a whole heap of reasons.

Number one, her father was my football coach and my dad's best friend. That shit had potential disaster written all over it. Two, if things went sour between us, I'd lose her.

And that wasn't an option. Ever.

Finally, it was senior year. Another few months and we'd all be going off to college, starting the next chapter of our lives. Did we really want to start something knowing that it was limited on time?

Fuck, what was I saying?

We couldn't go there... that's not what this was about.

I just wanted things to be okay between us.

I wanted my best friend back.

"Maybe you should just give her some space," Sofia suggested.

"Nah, I gotta do this. See you later." I took off down the hall and headed to the library.

It was quiet when I slipped inside, immediately searching for her. It wasn't long before I spotted Poppy disappearing between the stacks and smiled to myself.

Gotcha.

But when I reached the stairs leading up to the rows and rows of books, I heard voices.

Slipping down the next row, I peered through a gap in the books and frowned.

Eli Hannigan. What the hell was she doing in the library with him?

"This feels kind of bad. Mrs. Greggers is—"

"Shh." Poppy chuckled, pressing her finger against his lips. "We don't have much time."

Jealousy surged through me, my heart crashing against my chest as I watched them. Eli was a guy she'd hung out with at a party a few weeks ago. I'd stupidly thought she'd called it off after his cousin and my brother Ezra had gotten into it.

"Better make the most of it then." Eli cupped the back of her neck and started to lean in.

What. The. Fuck?

I stared in horror as they started to make out. Poppy

whimpered against his mouth, anchoring her arms around his shoulders.

It hit me then, this is what it had felt like when she'd seen me kissing Zara.

Fuck.

Fuck!

Eli broke off the kiss, touched his forehead to hers and smiled. "You know, my friends told me you were a lost cause. Said that you and Aaron Bennet were—"

"We're not," she rushed out, gazing up at him like he hung the moon. "It's not like that between us, we're just friends. At least, we used to be."

Pain lashed my insides as I stared slack-jawed at them like some fucking creeper.

I'd wanted to come and apologize, to fix things.

But as I watched Poppy palm his cheek, and lean up and brush her lips over his, I realized my error.

Poppy wasn't only my best friend.

She was more than that.

So much more.

And I was too fucking late.

PLAYLIST

Idfc – blackbear
Say Something – Boyce Avenue, Carly Rose
Fragile – KYGO, Labrinth
Feel Something – Jaymes Young
Colors – Halsey
Broken Roots – Michl
Lost – Dermot Kennedy
Atlantis – Seafret
All I Want – Kodaline
Medicine – Daughter
Never Let Me Go – Florence and the Machines

AUTHOR'S NOTE

I hope you enjoyed Ashleigh and Ezra's story. If you're familiar with my books, you'll know that I always let the characters lead the story, and Ruined Hopes was no exception. These two have to work hard for their HEA but I think it makes it all the more worth it.

The Rixon High series is slowly drawing to an end, and I can't wait to bring you the final two stories from Rixon High! Poppy and Aaron are up next (ANGST alert) and then we'll end the series with Sofia and Cole's story. Are you ready? I'm not sure I am!

As always, a huge thank you to everyone who helped polish this story into all its finished glory. Andrea, you went above and beyond for me this time. I owe you ALL the Toblerone. Annissia, thank you for beta reading for me at last minute. Darlene and Athena, thank you for your eagle-eyed proofreading. Candi at Candi Kane PR, thank you for keeping me on the straight and narrow with this release (it's been chaos to say the least). And to every book blogger who took the time to read an advance copy of Ruined Hopes your support, reviews, and messages, are everything. Never stop doing what you're doing because the book world needs you!

Until next time,

L A xo

ABOUT THE AUTHOR

Angsty. Edgy. Addictive Romance

Author of mature young adult and new adult novels, L. A. is happiest writing the kind of books she loves to read: addictive stories full of teenage angst, tension, twists and turns.

Home is a small town in the middle of England where she currently juggles being a full-time writer with being a mother/referee to two little people. In her spare time (and when she's not camped out in front of the laptop) you'll most likely find L. A. immersed in a book, escaping the chaos that is life.

L. A. loves connecting with readers.
The best places to find her are:
www.lacotton.com

Printed in Great Britain
by Amazon